FINAL HEIR

A Jane Yellowrock Novel

Faith Hunter

ACE
New York

ACE

Published by Berkley

An imprint of Penguin Random House LLC

penguinrandomhouse.com

Copyright © 2022 by Faith Hunter

Penguin Random House supports copyright. Copyright fuels creativity, encourages
diverse voices, promotes free speech, and creates a vibrant culture. Thank you for buying
an authorized edition of this book and for complying with copyright laws by not
reproducing, scanning, or distributing any part of it in any form without permission.
You are supporting writers and allowing Penguin Random House to continue to
publish books for every reader.

ACE is a registered trademark and the A colophon is a trademark of
Penguin Random House LLC.

ISBN: 9780593335819

First Edition: September 2022

Printed in the United States of America
3 5 7 9 10 8 6 4 2

To the Hubs:

You have been through this series as much as I,

and all the many books before.

You have supported my dreams and my hopes,

and held me when I cried or raged.

You have been my all and always will be.

You are the light in my darkness.

FINAL HEIR

CHAPTER 1

Like a Stray Animal Haunting Aggie's Home

Eyes closed, I felt the movement of unexpected cool air as the sweathouse door opened and shut. Last week, I had learned that Aggie One Feather, the Cherokee elder leading me into understanding my personal and tribal history, sometimes left and reentered when I was sweating through a haze of her herbal infusions and my own hidden memories. She said humans couldn't survive five or six hours in a sweathouse like I could, let alone all night, so she would slip out and back in.

I had asked her if she had a nanny camera hidden in the sweathouse to keep track of me. Her reply had made me laugh: "You need a legion of angels to look over you, but a nanny cam could help."

The rustling of her cotton shift, the sound of her breath, and the crackle of flames seemed loud as she settled across the fire from me and fed the coals. I smelled cedar and burning herbs and heard the scritch-grind of her mortar and pestle. Behind my lids it seemed lighter than before. It had to be near dawn.

It occurred to me that the ceremonial fire was, itself, symbolic. It was parts of this world and the next, the two halves of the universe, energy and matter. It was wood and air and energy, and together they made flame and smoke, the destruction of matter into energy. Then that thought wisped away with the fire.

Aggie said, "Drink."

I opened my eyes against the crack and burn of dried sweat, and studied the small pottery cup she held. On the third try I managed to croak, "Eye of newt? Ragweed? Mold off your bathroom floor? Peyote?"

"That never gets old," she lied, amusement hidden in her gaze. "I have no mold on my bathroom floor."

Which meant the liquid could be composed of the other three. Or not. I took the cup and drained it. The decoction tasted of lemon peel, fennel, wild ginger, something I couldn't identify, and salt. I turned the empty, handleless cup in my fingers. It wasn't traditional Cherokee work, but something fired in a modern kiln and given a bright blue glaze.

"What did your dreams show you?" Aggie asked.

I handed back the cup and said, "Same as last time. The angel's location looks a little like my soul home. Walls that curve in toward the ceiling, dark streaks of water on them. Wings that seem to lie flat across the ceiling and down, as if dripping to the floor. Light that comes from nowhere and everywhere. There might have been a puddle of blood on the floor. Hard to tell. But unlike my soul home, I keep seeing people standing along the walls."

"People or other angels?"

I frowned at the question. Had there been wings behind the people? "Maybe. Maybe a *suggestion* of wings, like shadows. Or maybe I just want to have seen that and so I remember it now."

"Did you see yourself in your dream-state?"

If I watched myself, as opposed to being an active part of the dream, that would tell her a lot about whether this was a vision teaching me about myself and my life path, a prophetic dream portending something about the future, or if it had been a memory. I closed my eyes again and pulled at the fragments. The angel's wings draped, so much larger, longer than in artwork depicting the messenger beings. I heard the faint drip of water, but the echo was different from the usual loud reverberations of my soul home. This place itself was subtly different from previous visions.

In the memory of my vision, I saw myself. My hair was braided into a fighting queue and I was dressed in armor, one of the latest models Eli, my brother of choice, bought these days, now that money wasn't an object. In teaching visions, I usually wore tribal clothing, the kind my father had worn when I was a child.

In addition to the armor, at my waist I was wearing the Mughal blade that Bruiser had given me.

That was interesting.

In the dream-state I did nothing, said nothing, so it probably wasn't a vision teaching me about who I was or guiding my path through life. Seeing myself meant it wasn't a memory. The ancient knife itself was part of a prophecy, and I seldom wore it, mostly for ceremonial occasions when the prophecy did me no good. Only rarely had I worn it into battle.

When he gave the blade to me, Bruiser had said, "A certain wily salesman suggested that the damascene blade is charged with a spell of life force, to give the wielder the ability to block any opponent's death cut. Pure balderdash, but it makes a nice tale." Except that Alex, the tech-genius of Yellowrock Securities and Clan Yellowrock, had traced the blade back to the seventeen hundreds, and there were stories over the centuries about people surviving the death stroke of an opponent's blade.

"Prophecy?" I asked the universe. Or God, if he was listening. Not that anyone answered, not even Aggie. And since I hadn't looked for the future in rain droplets in months, I might not know what this meant until it was too late. However, if I went searching for the meaning in the future, I probably wouldn't understand it anyway, and if I saw danger—and I would—I might feel forced to meddle in time. Meddling in time—timewalking, time-jumping— might trigger the return of the magic cancer. All of which was why I hadn't tried. Seeing the future was like that. Helpful. Until it wasn't. And then it tried to kill me.

I inhaled and caught a familiar scent. He had to be close because I was human-shaped, and my nose in this form was unspectacular. I cleared my throat again and warned, "Werewolf."

"In the vision?" Aggie asked.

"No." There was only one werewolf in New Orleans, and the moon wasn't full, which made them cranky, so he'd be chill and not bite anyone. I wasn't worried. Yet.

I frowned, my thoughts going back to the angel in the vision. "Hayyel was Angie's . . . whaddaya call it. Guardian angel. And he helped to deal with Evangelina's demon-calling circle. I'd always thought that he was just in the right place, right time, and jumped in to send the demon back. But maybe dealing with the demon caused him to be partially chained to something in this plane? Chained to the world of matter when he should be a being of energy? That doesn't make sense. Sending demons back has to be part of his job, right? So maybe he had *already* been chained here?"

That was a scary thought. It meant that either an unknown person with more power than I understood was currently involved, or that an unknown someone in the past had that power and had chained an angel.

I accepted and drained a bottle of water. "From the beginning Hayyel was close by. He had the freedom to act and intervene in some events, but maybe he didn't have autonomy?" I stopped speaking aloud, following the layered implications in the vision.

I had postulated that Hayyel had already been partially chained, here on Earth, and was, currently, already part of the events taking place. Maybe he had been waiting for Evil Evie's demon circle to manifest . . . and for all of us to be present so he could do . . . whatever he did to us all as he dealt with the demon Evangelina called.

I had sometimes wondered if he had planned it all, planned to change us. Maybe use us. Molly, my BFF, and her family: Evan, her partially-in-the-closet air witch husband, her children, my godchildren: Angie and EJ. Rick (my former boyfriend and now a wereleopard), Kemnebi (another wereleopard), Brute (werewolf stuck in human form). Even my Beast, the other soul who lived inside me.

We were all changed in fundamental ways by the banishing of the demon and the proximity to the angel.

A chained angel? Partially chained?

So maybe Hayyel had been, and was, still close by. Maybe he could help, even if he was chained. Or maybe he needed help to deal with being chained. Or both.

I was glad I hadn't said all that aloud, because there was power in this vision and some kernels of truth. I opened my eyes, not sure when they had closed.

Aggie was sitting across from me, wearing her linen shift. She rubbed something onto her knees, as if they ached. When she saw me looking, she shrugged and reminded me, "Werewolf? Demon? Angel?"

"There were two werewolves inside Evangelina Everhart's circle with a demon. The demon was eating them. The angel appeared and—" I stopped. There had been a burst of light at the demon circle when the angel appeared, Hayyel doing something, changing something. "The angel did something to all of us." But the most obvious change had been to Brute, the werewolf I thought I'd just now caught a whiff of. Brute was bound to the angel in some way, probably even more than Angie.

The memory of the werewolves in the demon circle vision was overlapped with memories and visions of the Mughal blade, the prophecy attached to it, and me in armor. Which was strange unless what I'd seen was a combination of all these three: memory, prophecy, personal spiritual vision.

I closed my eyes and pulled the visions back to me. "What do you need?" I whispered, not fully sure who I was talking to. Hayyel? Aggie One Feather? God? "What do you want me to do?"

The memories and visions shifted, as if being shuffled like cards in a deck. In the overlapping of it all, things came clearer, almost as if the sun rose and shone light into the space, ruby and sapphire light, like a prism. In the vision, in the strange place, the people who watched the angel came clear.

The people standing along the walls wore brightly colored clothes—robes. Like people wore in Biblical times. I inhaled in shock. Not a vision. Not my soul home. The red and blue light seemed to flow across the walls, brightening the angel wings. I took it all in, memorizing everything.

Something scratched on the sweathouse door.

"He's here," I said. "At the door."

Aggie tensed. "The angel?"

"No." I'd been out awhile again, and my voice slurred. I swallowed to try and moisten my throat. "The werewolf."

Aggie swore and dumped a bucket of water on the fire. Smoke, sparks, and filth shot out like miniature fiery thunderheads blooming. On the far side of the firepit, the elder was standing, a wicked blade in her hand. "You bring an abomination to my door?" she spat.

"He's not feral," I said, pressing against my scalp to put out any sparks. My hair made crunching sounds from dried sweat salt. I crawled to my feet, hearing the salt crack and feeling it crust painfully in places best not mentioned. I was salty and sweat-streaked and now sooty. My braid swung forward, stiff as a stick, filthy.

"All werewolves are rabid *beasts*." Aggie hissed the last word and I blinked at her. She didn't look like herself. Dressed in her handmade, undyed ritual shift, her hair cut short to her shoulders, her feet bare, Aggie held a single-edged vamp-killer—fourteen inches of steel, silver-plated on the back of the blade, one that would poison vampires or were-creatures.

A weapon in the hands of a Cherokee elder, in the midst of a sweathouse ceremony. Aggie, furious. Her mouth twisted down in fear.

I stared at her, trying to decide if what I saw, the terror I saw on her face, was real or part of a drug-induced ceremonial hallucination.

Is real. Elder smells of fear, Beast thought at me. *Aggie is afraid of werewolf. And is afraid of the I/we of Beast. Aggie has feared since she first saw us in half-form.*

Yeah. And werewolves are evil in post-white-man tribal tradition, I thought back. *Evil.*

A shiver of shock raced through me. I tried to lick my lips, but they were cracked and I tasted blood. "Not all werewolves are rabid. And this one travels with a grindylow who'll kill him if he so much as opens his mouth to lick someone." I stepped slowly to the door, my eyes on Aggie and her weapon, one that could kill me as easily as the vampires for which the blade had been designed and named. The reasons an elder might be armed in a place where no such weapons were allowed flitted through my mind. Her fear, her need to protect herself from me was the best possibility.

She no longer trusted me to keep her safe.

I unlatched and cracked open the door.

A huge white snout tipped with a black nose poked into the crack. It snuffled and snorted.

Aggie smelled of terror, even to my human nose. She raised the blade higher. So far as I knew, she wasn't trained in fighting with a vamp-killer but I had never done a deep background on her. And lack of skill didn't make her any less dangerous. "He won't hurt you, Aggie. Hey, Brute. You got a grindy with you?"

A kitten-nose appeared over Brute's and a neon-green-furred face followed. The grindy was sitting on the white werewolf's head, which even in my dehydrated state was adorable. The grindy tilted its head and made a *meep* sound.

Brute shoved the door wider and peered inside. He stopped, watching Aggie. He wagged his tail and sat, perking his ears forward, tongue lolling out one side of his mouth. At a quick glance he looked like a bleached-out Great Pyrenees dog, maybe one whose bloodline included moose or elk. Then you saw the wolf fangs, icy eyes, and high-set predator ears. No sweet Great Pyrenees at all. He whined. The grindylow said *meep* again, and pulled itself higher on Brute's head, holding on to his ears with both paws.

Aggie lowered the weapon, but her eyes were still too wide, her stance uncertain.

"Let's step outside," I said to Brute.

Moving slowly, I bent and picked up a few bottles of water, one of which I opened as I left the sweathouse and guzzled, crunching the plastic to force the water out and down my throat fast. I drank two more and swallowed a salt tablet with the last one.

Talking to a werewolf in wolf form was difficult. At the house, we had a soundboard that Beast could tap on to communicate. It was new and it made our lives so much easier, but out in the wild we were still stuck with the Q and A, yes and no, method of communicating, a series of questions to which Brute could respond with a no head-shake or a yes nod.

"Brute. Is there trouble?"

Brute nodded.

It was daylight or near enough, so that meant the trouble was not likely a vamp. "Is one of my humans in trouble?"

Head shake.

I asked my way through the list: witch, were-creature, cops, ICE (who had, lately, gone after vamps because the long-lived ones didn't believe in documentation), para-haters, PsyLED—the Psychometric Division of Homeland Security—and half a dozen others before Brute made a disgusted chuffing sound and stared at the sweathouse. I turned to see Aggie, standing in the open doorway, her right side hidden, probably carrying the knife. "One of the tribal people?"

Head shake. He looked from Aggie to the firepit, now with only a few glowing coals left.

"Oh," I said, feeling stupid. "You know something about the angel?"

Brute nodded.

"What is it?"

He turned and disappeared into the gray light.

"Crap," I sighed out. "Not a yes/no question." I looked at Aggie. "He doesn't usually run away when I mess up."

Aggie frowned and turned her back on me, picking up a leather scabbard and sheathing the blade. Her shoulders were hunched, her head down. I didn't know if her posture was angry, exhausted, shamed at drawing a weapon, or something worse.

"Aggie?"

She shook her head, the motion weary, and asked, "Could your vision be in a graveyard? You've fought battles there before, and blood drinkers frequent them."

I frowned, thinking. Watching her move, the stress

and uncertainty in her jerky movements. Fear, again. She was afraid and I didn't understand.

She turned to face me, the scabbard nowhere in sight. "A church?" she asked. "A cathedral?"

"It didn't look like a graveyard," I said. In the Deep South, few burials are beneath the ground because the water table is so high the air-filled coffins float to the top and have been known to float away in the next flood. Coffins are secured on the surface in brick or stone mausoleums and statues of saints and angels are common in them.

My vision didn't look like a church either. It looked like a cave. But in a vision, who could tell? There were dozens of graveyards with statues and hundreds of churches in and around NOLA, most with paintings, murals, stained glass pictures in the windows, angel statues, saint statues.

I thought about the curved, domed ceiling, the strange light and the sloped walls, as if something was dripping down them. "If it's a real place then maybe a small Roman Catholic church in NOLA?"

"Or farther away," she suggested, her voice tense, her eyes looking away from me. "In France or Rome. Anywhere, if it's a church or cathedral."

That was a daunting thought. "The darker streaks on the walls could have been mold and the odd light could have been from stained glass windows, I guess. I didn't see any, but the lighting was red and blue. So I'll hope that Hayyel is trapped in an old ruined church somewhere close and not thousands of miles away. Maybe a local one, moldy, damaged by hurricane." I could plan for it to be close, though trusting in luck and flying by the seat of my pants hadn't gotten me many places in life except in trouble.

Aggie didn't reply, but her body was still stiff and jittery, as if preparing to be hit.

I let the memory of the vision fill me again. The last two hurricane seasons had left the landscape scarred and hundreds of buildings, homes, and churches dilapidated. Hayyel *could* be trapped in a building somewhere. "Yeah. Maybe a church. I think I need to see it again. When can I come to sweat again?"

"Not today. Not tomorrow. Not this week." Aggie was

still not looking at me, her eyes off to the side, staring at the floor.

I opened my mouth, stopped, closed it. I had a feeling that the answer was going to hurt, but I didn't have much of a choice. "Aggie? Was the knife for me?"

She raised her head. Her face was drawn down, etched by dread and fatigue. "If you shifted into a dangerous creature. Or if you shifted into a different person."

"*U'tlun'ta.* You think I'm liver-eater. Spear-finger."

She shook her head, her shoulders slumping. "Not today. Not yet. But someday. All the elders agree. We have talked. The Choctaw. The Western band of the *Tsalagi.* Walkingstick. My mother. And now you bring a werewolf to my door." She raised a hand to stop my comments. "Not intentional, I know. But it came here only because of you. Because of what you are. Of what you may become. Spear-finger. Raven-mocker. You are a dangerous creature, or you may become one. You are a killer, and you know this, yet you do not seek to mend your ways and search for peace."

As she spoke, my eyes burned. A faint tremble started in my fingers and ached into my chest. It hurt to take the next breath. "By my order and my command, two of the three skinwalkers I know of, my grandmother and a clan member, were jailed when they became liver-eaters. And my people know to kill me if I ever—" I stopped.

Back when I was looking into the possible futures, I saw a vision in a waterdrop, a vision of an aged Eli killing me for taking the dark path that skinwalkers often finally trod, when they are old and insane. In that vision, my chosen brother's face had been full of sorrow and anger and fear. *Fear.* Like Aggie's.

Elder is full of fear, like prey in chase, Beast thought, sadness in her mental tone. *Elder fears the I/we of Beast.*

My breath caught. My heart fluttered in my chest like the wings of a dying bird.

Aggie wasn't just afraid of the werewolf. Aggie was afraid of *me.* Brute appearing had just been a catalyst that set off the fear. I closed my eyes for a moment and tried to breathe through the pain. A woman I looked up to and admired was afraid of me, of what I might do, might become. From the look in her eyes, Aggie had been afraid of me for a long time. And because she was an elder and I was still in need, she had continued to be afraid of me because I needed her. Which sucked.

Savannah Walkingstick was the only other elder I might trust to lead me into sweat. But she wasn't here. And clearly she wasn't my friend.

My eyes ached, my head pounded as the truth of our relationship settled inside me. I had thought Aggie was my friend.

We were not friends. Aggie One Feather was afraid of me. The tremor and pain in my chest slowly died as I watched her, the coals hissing as she wet them down again.

I had learned a lot about ceremony and formality and the proper words to say in difficult situations during my time working for vamps and being led into the healing paths by Cherokee elders, but I had no idea what to say. How to handle this. Except that it was gonna hurt. A lot. I clasped my hands in front of me and bowed deeply from my waist, held the position, and then stood upright.

"Elder of the People. *Egini Agayvlge i*, of the *ani waya*, the Wolf Clan, of the Eastern band of the *Tsalagi*. When I came to you the first time—" My throat closed in a sudden wave of grief. I stopped and took a shaking breath before continuing my sentence. "—you asked, 'How may I help you?' the traditional words of the shaman. With your guidance, your patience, and your wisdom, I have found a path through the darkness, one that has led me into long-lost memories, into the past and into the present, into a family of the heart, and into a family of tribe and clan. In return, without knowing it, I have caused you to experience fear. I have caused you to bring a weapon into the place of ceremony."

I blinked, my eyes too dry to cry out the pain in my soul. "You did this for me. Continued to bring me to sweat and to circle. Despite knowing who and what I am, right now, in this moment, you fear what I might someday become. You fear me, spirit deep, soul deep. I understand your fear and I will not burden you with it any longer.

"I thank you for your past kindness. I thank you for all the knowledge, the tribal lore, and the gift of myself. I never would have found so much of myself without you. You are my *uni lisi*. And you are the beloved woman." I bowed again, more deeply this time, and when I stood tall, I stepped away from the open doorway.

"I honor you," I said, my eyes taking her in, her body bent and tight, her arms wrapping around her as I spoke. "If you ever need my help, know that I will come. I will stand between you and any enemy. I will guard you. I will fight any battle for you. I am your servant and your war woman, for as long I live. And know this, that should I step from the path of healing and wholeness, my people will kill me."

Her eyes swept up to mine and away, hers wide and red-rimmed, as if she were crying, though she wasn't. She tightened her self-hug. Aggie One Feather said nothing in reply to my formal words.

"You will never be in danger from me."

When she didn't respond, or even look as though she might be searching for words, I stepped from the sweat-house and closed the door. Without bothering to wash away the stink of an all-night sweat, I pulled the filthy shift off me and yanked on my jeans, T-shirt, and sneakers. Undies, weapons, and a cell phone were in a gobag, which I grabbed, and sprinted up the white-shell-paved road, faster than human. Skinwalker fast. Needing to be away.

When I reached the street, I turned and ducked into the brush, under the long-leafed pines, and let the sobs escape. Deep. Racking. Painful as they ripped up my throat. I dropped butt-first onto the ground, leaned against an old pine tree, and cried. Not with tears, because I was too dry for them, but with the rough, hoarse, ripping howls of anguish and loss.

I cried until my chest ached. I cried until the sun was high. Until I was empty and I could see and feel the shattered, jagged edges where Aggie used to reside, within me. A ruined, bleeding, abandoned place in my soul. Leaning against the tree, sap on my cheek, the grief finally spent itself, leaving me hollow and broken.

Time passed. The sun was over the horizon. I couldn't stay here, like a stray animal haunting Aggie's home.

Beast has den. Beast has family, like puma and sisters and kits. Jane is not alone.

And how long before they fear me too? I questioned.

Beast will not eat family. The I/we of Beast will not eat the soul of another.

I wrapped my arms around the tree, pulled myself to my feet, and called Bruiser, asking him to come get me. I didn't answer when he asked what was wrong. I simply said, "I'm walking away from Aggie's house, toward NOLA. You'll see me." I ended the call, relieved myself on the pine tree's roots, then patted it in apology. And I walked down the road, away from Aggie One Feather's home, away from a place of refuge as the day lightened around me.

CHAPTER 2

I May Be a Glorified Guard Dog, But a Guy's Gotta Get His Beauty Sleep

I heard the SUVs before I saw them. Bruiser hadn't come alone. The lead vehicle passed me and executed a three-point turn before pulling up to me, Bruiser behind the wheel. I got into the passenger seat as the other two SUVs also made three-point turns and jockeyed for position, one in front, one behind us. My protection detail, drivers and passengers armed to the teeth. My Consort, armed, a shoulder rig and a thigh rig. Nine-mils, with interchangeable magazines and ammo. Being the Dark Queen—the queen of the vamps, whether they, or I, liked it or not—came with perks, like money, political power, and excellent weapons. The job also came with enemies, and keeping my people safe wasn't one of the perks. Keeping friends wasn't one of them either.

I felt Bruiser's eyes on me as I belted in. He held out a bottle of room-temp water, which I guzzled, but he didn't ask any questions. I looked down at my arm. It was crusted with salt and dirt and my skin hung on me like an old woman's. He could tell I hadn't showered as was custom after time in a sweathouse. I hadn't fully rehydrated. I probably needed a couple gallons of water and a lot of minerals. And some time with a stiff brush and some strong soap.

Absently, I rubbed at the tree sap on my cheek, and I felt more than saw Bruiser hold his hand out to me. I curled my chilled hand in his warm one, leaned my head against the window, and closed my eyes. It would be easier saying this when I couldn't see his face.

"Aggie was afraid of me. Of me going *u'tlun'ta* and trying to eat her." Bruiser said nothing, but he squeezed my hand gently. The tires sang as we turned off the secondary road and onto a state road. "I thanked her for her help. She didn't send me away, she didn't tell me to go exactly, but I won't be going back."

Bruiser still said nothing, but his hand was warm, and he interlaced our fingers, as if giving me a signal that he wouldn't be leaving me. Not ever.

I said, "I don't think I ever told you, but, in one of the visions of the future, I saw me as *u'tlun'ta*, and Eli, an old man Eli, killing me." I opened my eyes and swiveled my head to see his face. His lips were soft though not smiling and his brown eyes were intent on the road. His Romanesque nose gave his otherwise pretty face a sense of strength and determination and purpose. "That doesn't bother you?" I asked. "Me being a feral people-eater?"

Those beautiful lips turned up slightly. "How many potential visions of all the potential futures have you seen?"

"I don't know. Couple thousand? Maybe more?"

"And in how many were you ever *u'tlun'ta*? In how many did anyone ever have to kill you because you became evil?"

"One?"

"One. Out of thousands." His lips became a full smile, tender, kind. My heart melted. "The futures show us what might happen if we walk a certain path, if everything we do, every battle we fight, every friend we lose or gain, every good or less-than-good deed we do, results in just one particular choice and outcome. The future isn't composed of just one path, one single decision, one event. The present may be composed of those things, but not the future. The one butterfly we step on today doesn't make us who we are going to be tomorrow."

There was an old science fiction story about some man who went back in time and accidently stepped on a butterfly. When he got back to his own time, the death of the butterfly had changed the entire social-political outlook of the planet. It was a time-travel story we had talked about often, a story we had shared with my godchildren and my whole family-of-choice. It was a story of warnings about playing God. Bruiser was telling me that even though I had been a monster many times in my life, I wasn't destined to remain one or to become a bigger one, and that the choices I had made had resulted in positive consequences as well as negative ones.

I squeezed his fingers.

He released mine and hefted a six-pack of electrolyte water into my lap. "Drink."

It was gross, but I drank it all and felt a lot better because of that. "Imma take a nap now, okay?"

"Shall I leave you asleep and carry you to bed when we get home?"

I lifted my arm and caught a whiff of stink. "Yuck. Not smelling like this. I foresee a long hot shower in my immediate future."

"I'll join you. I can imagine nothing better than to lather you in your new shower, massage away the grime and the salt and the exhaustion, and . . ." He paused, and then said slowly, "And leave you moaning and smiling."

Which sounded totally wonderful.

The shower in our home—formerly known as the freebie house and still referred to that way though it was now *officially* titled the Queen's Personal Residence in New Orleans—was big enough for two, Bruiser in it with me. That shower was healing and tender. It took forever to get all the filth and sweat and stink off me. I lost count of the necessary, essential, mandatory latherings, but it was lovely, and afterward, I was very, *very* clean.

Sadly, the moment I fell onto the sheets, a shift hit.

Sharp pain pricked into my brain as Beast's mental

paw shoved me down and down inside our twined souls and toward sleep. My last thought as the pain hit and my bones snapped was that I'd have to be in Beast form all day.

Rolled over and put paws on Bruiser chest. Bruiser scratched Beast ears. Beast chuffed softly and closed eyes in happiness. *Bruiser is best mate. Is strong and smells good. Smells like Onorio.*

"Hey there, Beast. Jane still awake inside you?" he asked, fingers scratching deep into fur.

Am not Jane. Beast showed killing teeth.

"I'm taking that as a no. You want steak?"

Beast hungers. Licked good-smelling Onorio. Did not taste as good as cow, but tasted good. Licked again.

Bruiser slid from mattress and stood naked. Pulled on human clothes. Onorio should grow fur. Was warmer than stupid human skin. Beast stretched slowly on mattress, scrunched back and shoulders and hips into sheets, getting much puma-hair on Jane-bed. Was cat-claiming. Mate laughed. Beast rolled. Reached with body and draped front paws to floor, body and legs pulled long, slid off. Landed. Shook pelt. Yawned.

Beast followed mate out of bedroom, into kitchen. Sat on floor and curled tail around paws. Bruiser got dead cow meat from cold place called fridge and put in small white box to run around and make warm. Smell of cow was good on air. Licked jaw. Would not be much blood. Stupid humans did not like to drink blood. But cow was still good meat. Had hunted wil-de-beest and longhorn cow with sharp pointed trees on head with Edmund and Eli in big truck. Was better than warmed cow from fridge with water-blood. But was much work to hunt cow, and Beast hungered.

Bruiser took cow meat from small box and placed on plates. Two plates. Beast smelled cow meat and werewolf. Brute was behind Beast.

Snarled. Beast whirled back, front legs over own shoulder. Shoved off with back legs. Spun in air, lithe and lissome. Jane's words for Beast.

But Brute wavered and was not there. Beast landed

where Brute had been. Brute was beside table. Brute chuffed dog-chuff. Beast snarled. Looked at Bruiser. Mate was standing, plate in each hand, watching, strange look on his face. Bruiser had not seen Brute timewalk before. Brute had been at sweathouse. Brute only came when needed something, when was important. Must be important for Bruiser to see Brute timewalk.

Snarled again. *Is Beast cow from cold place and white box to make warm. Is Beast's.*

Brute lay down, belly to floor, panting, tongue hanging. Brute was big werewolf. Was twice the size of Beast. But was not acting male-wolf-alpha.

Is Beast cow. Showed another glimpse of killing fangs.

Brute licked own jaws and muzzle in submission. Put jaw on legs. Watched with sad, calm eyes.

Bruiser put dead-cow on floor in front of Beast. Beast tore off chunk of cow with killing teeth and swallowed. Ate another bite. Looked at Bruiser and made whistle sound of kit. *Is good cow.*

Bruiser asked, "Is it okay if I feed Brute too?"

Beast chuffed. Turned head away from both mate and dog, but watched from corner of eye. Ate more.

Bruiser put plate in front of Brute. Cow piece for dog was smaller than Beast's. Was good for Brute's to be small.

Brute ate in one bite, choking on cow. *Stupid wolf-dog.* Beast finished cow and licked jaw with rough tongue, cleaning off water-blood and small bits of cow. Cleaned paws, sitting with head high. Stared at Brute. Waiting.

Werewolf stood to paws, but crouched close to ground, eyes looking away, head down. Was properly submissive to alpha big-cat. Beast stared. Stopped cleaning paw. Wolf stepped closer with one paw. Beast did nothing. Brute crept close and stopped; extended head to Beast. Was cat gesture, to touch heads. Was strange to see on wolf.

Beast leaned in and touched wolf head with Beast head.

I know where Leo is. You and Jane probably need to know too.

Beast reared back. Skittered into next room, living room, and to far side of couch. Wolf had talked to Puma concolor mind to mind.

Brute was there-not-there. Then was standing at big-cat door at side of house. Brute chuffed out dog-laugh and ducked through door. Beast raced across living room and outside, predator eyes on wolf.

Bruiser opened door and came into yard to tall metal cage gate that led out to street. Said, "It's fully daylight. Don't be seen. If you can slip through time, I'm quite sure the angel gave you the ability to remain unnoticed."

Beast looked at Brute. Brute was man, stuck in were-wolf form by angel, Brute had angel magic powers. But Beast was best hunter. Beast shoved off with all feet, leaped. Cleared tall gate and landed near street. Chuffed in challenge and thought, *Can wolf-dog jump gate?*

Bruiser opened gate. Wolf strolled out and looked at Beast, using bored cat look. Was good cat look for human man stuck in white wolf. Brute stood beside Beast and small silver lights danced out of wolf, like sparks into Beast's nose. Beast sneezed. Looked around to see Bruiser mouth was open to speak, hand on gate, not moving. All things stopped moving.

Brute was in timewalk. Beast was in timewalk with Brute, with angel's wolf. Brute bumped puma with hip and started walking. Beast walked. Together, walking slow but fast, Beast and Brute, passing humans, dogs on leashes, bikes, and cars, all not moving. Then more changed with silver lights. Got bright. Too bright for Beast eyes.

Smell changed. Was no longer near Jane house. Blinked eyes to see place of death for humans, place humans put bodies to keep scavengers from picking bones clean of rotting flesh. Beast did not smell rotted humans; smelled Lake Pont-char-train, stinky-salty-fresh-dead water. Had not been in this place before as Jane or Beast.

Wolf did not go into pathways between tall, stone graves. Wolf bumped puma again and walked across street and to porch of house, still walking through time. Took much effort, but wolf pushed open door. Walked inside.

House had no furniture, no rugs, no paintings on walls. House had no fresh smell of humans. Was empty.

Timewalk ended. Brute trotted upstairs and Beast followed wolf into empty bedroom. Into empty closet. Brute looked to see if Beast watched, then wolf scratched on piece of wood near floor. Wall opened to show stairs back down into darkness. Brute pranced stupid dog-walk down into dark, tail wagging. Beast followed more slowly. Smelled Leo on air of stairs. At bottom of stairs, found small room with no windows, space for bed, chair, table, and weak light at top of tall pole. Leo was lying on bed, not breathing, heart not beating. Black hair was spread over pillow. Skin white. Was wearing black pants and black shirt with white spot. Black jacket was over chair back.

Beast stepped onto bed and walked up and down, sniffing Leo. Vampire smelled not-alive-not-dead. Still smelled of pepper and what Jane called papyrus, but also smelled different. Did not smell of fear and blood and sex and violence. Beast lay down on top of Leo, muzzle and killing teeth to Leo neck, sniffing. Was what Jane called flehmen, pulling air over air sacs in roof of mouth. Used brain of ugly-dog-good-nose Beast had taken from other form. Leo smelled different from Leo before being more dead than now dead. Vampire death was confusing.

Leo smelled of ocean and wind in trees. Smelled of clean earth.

Bed and Leo smelled of Brute. Sniffed more, harsh sound of flehmen. Smelled Brute on mattress, much wolf smell. Brute lay beside Leo many days. Brute had been guardian of Leo. Brute jumped to small mattress and lay beside Leo, head on paws, eyes on Beast, touching Beast with leg and side. Beast swiveled ears and narrowed eyes in cat-stare to show displeasure. *Wolf will not touch Puma concolor,* Beast thought.

Brute lowered head, asking Beast to touch. Beast did not want to talk to werewolf, but was important. Beast blew out breath, snuffling, thinking.

Touched Brute head. Brute thought at Beast, *The angel said a bunch of gobbledygook crap I didn't half under-*

stand. What I got was that some witches have been doing dark magic shit, calling a demon, borrowing its power in return for some big mojo curse they have planned, and binding Hayyel closer. He's nearly bound.

Jane has to find the angel and free him before the Heir binds him fully, and before Mainet becomes the master of all the suckheads. If that happens, Leo will be totally bound too, and if the bindings are all finished, we're all screwed. Jane will have to kill Leo to keep him from going over to Mainet. War will come.

What the fuck else? Brute thought. *There was something. Oh. Right. You have to burn the Heart of Darkness after you kill Mainet. As soon as you kill him. Not before. If the Heart of Darkness is destroyed first, the timelines show war. And the angel said Leo is important, but he didn't say why.*

Beast thought, *Leo was master of the city. Then Leo was dead. Then Leo was not dead. Leo smell is not same Leo smell. Why is Brute with Leo? Why is Leo here? In this empty den.*

I'm his fucking guardian. Can you believe it?

Beast pulled away, thinking, wondering why master vampire needed a guardian to mate. Saw spot of white on Leo black shirt, between paws. Moved paws to see white band on collar. Leo was Leo but not Leo. Leo was different. Leo was outclan priest. Angel wanted outclan priest kept safe. Did not know how to tell Jane this. Did not know what this meant. Was confused. Looked at wolf and chuffed.

Wolf put head back and touched Beast. *That's all I know, cat, and I'd a told Jane if she could hear me. Unfortunately you're the only part of her who can talk like an animal. Shit's about to get real, you asshole cat. Be safe. Be smart. Stop acting stupid. Jane's in danger.*

Anger rose in Beast. Beast thought, *Beast is not stupid cat. Beast is not prey. Beast is best ambush hunter.*

You better hope so, stupid cat, or this city is about to be overrun by a world of darkness. Now get outta here and close the door behind you. I may be a glorified guard dog, but a guy's gotta get his beauty sleep.

Beast stood and stepped on Brute before sliding to floor. Wolf-dog-human grunted with weight and prick of claws but did not fight. Brute was human in wolf shape. Had been biker human. Used to like to fight but did not fight Beast. Beast trotted upstairs, scratched on wood. Door opened and Beast left lair, shutting door firmly behind. Then Beast realized. Was a long way from Jane house. Brute had left Beast here. *Stupid dog.*

Keeping to shadows, Beast began slow walk getting back to Jane house. Was glad was not summer-hot. Was glad was not raining. Was glad to have time to think as Big Cat and slide from shadow to shadow.

Her claws in my mind, I woke up in Beast's body at dusk. I was still puma, and Beast was silent.

My bed was full of cat hair and the fitted sheet had been scratched and torn. Beast's paws were filthy with what looked like asphalt and the sheets were stained with dark smears.

Dang cat, I thought. *What did you do today? Where did you go?*

The cat didn't answer. I could feel her inside with me, but she wasn't talking. She wasn't even running her body. She was letting me be in charge. Weird.

I caught a whiff of werewolf and Leo, and tried to sit up too fast. My paws were trapped in the twisted sheet.

A knock came at the door and now I caught a whiff of Eli and Alex. I chuffed for them to enter as I worked to get my paws out of the grimy sheets. As I landed on the floor, I pulled the flat sheet and comforter off the bed, and heard something rip. I'd damaged Bruiser's good sheets. *Dang cat.*

"She's still puma," Alex called back behind him, to others I could now smell in the living room and the kitchen. He shuffled on his socked feet, back toward his desk. Alex was the younger Younger, the electronics specialist of Yellowrock Securities, and Eli was the elder Younger, and he was pretty much everything else—weapons specialist, tactics guy, the one who helped me design security protocols, and my second in duels that didn't require him to fight for me. The Youngers were the only people I totally trusted to be in charge of my security. Eli was also not quite healed from the very bad injury that had nearly taken his leg and his life. He had worn an external pin support for a week, removed sooner than expected due to the copious and steady amounts of vamp blood he'd consumed, but he wasn't a hundred percent. He still limped when he was tired or cold. He suffered from pain he tried to hide. Worse—saving his life and his leg had bound us together in some weird way I didn't know how to fix.

Molly, my BFF, and a powerful witch, called it being soul-bound, which was a little like being an *anamchara* but without the volition and desire to be able to share experiences and thoughts and emotions. In fact, whatever had happened between us when I saved Eli's life, this new communion was often way too personal. And kinda icky.

"Are you Beast?" Eli asked me. When I shook my head no, he asked, "So do you know where you went today?" I shook my head.

"I'd hoped it might have something to do with the attack we're watching at the null prison. Come see."

I padded after him to the big screens where the security cameras for Vamp HQ and all the vamp clan homes were displayed. On the biggest center screen was a nighttime shot of a house I recognized. It was the NOLA witch council's maximum-security null prison.

In the middle of the street, in front of the house, were three witches in a circle. To the side of the circle was a short male. Behind him stood a row of warriors, all heavily armed. The dark of the night and the quality of the cams (never good enough unless they were Eli's multi-light cameras) made it hard to tell if the fighters were human or vampire, and impossible to identify anyone by facial features.

The witches in the street turned toward the camera, which, from the angle, appeared to be mounted on the corner eave of the prison, and held out their hands. As one, they said a single word, their mouths open wide.

Even on the mid-quality cameras I saw flashes of scarlet light. Each witch gathered light in their hands and swirled it, as if each of them held a ball made from sunset storms and lightning. Beast rose and stared through my eyes. *Is danger*, she thought.

Yeah. And who's in charge, the witches or the warriors? What are the warriors? Vamps or humans?

The witches threw the balls of light. The camera feed died.

Beast thought, *Shift.* She reached into our skinwalker energies and pulled at the silver mist that powered my shape-shifting. I overrode her for just long enough. We raced to the bedroom and slammed the door. Pain hit, as if my muscles were being sliced from my bones with a blade. My joints cracked and popped and I fell to the floor.

When I came to, I was half-form, starving and very furry, dang it. Beyond the door I heard shouting and clanking and the snapping, clicking sound of weapons being checked.

I stood and stuck my head out the door and demanded, "What?"

Eli barked, "Witches and a group of non-witches— possibly vamps—are attacking the null house."

"Have they called the Dark Queen for help?"

"Negative. Not yet. They will. And even if they don't call for assistance, vamps attacking witches falls under the purview of the Dark Queen's duties and the Master of the City's duties. You have to respond, Janie. *My Queen*," he added in what might have been snark.

I closed the door and opened the closet.

Shoving aside the low-power magical trinkets and amulets I kept at the front of the high shelf—the high-powered ones were stored beneath the small *hedge of thorns* at the back of the shelf or in the not-so-secret weapons room beneath the stairs—I grabbed the Glob and mundane weapons, and yanked a set of armor off the hanger, on the rod below them.

Dressing fast, I strapped the armor into place, aware that armor, any kind of currently available armor, had weaknesses, places between the Kevlar layers and the Dyneema where a bullet or a blade could penetrate. Armor wasn't a full safety measure. It just made most core-based instantly mortal wounds potentially more survivable. For me and for my people.

I braided my hair into a sloppy pigtail and tucked it into my armor neckline, out of the way. I didn't have time for anything fancy. Wrapping the Glob in a big hanky, I shoved it into a padded pocket.

Since I was never the exact same shape when I went halfsies, all my fighting clothes were made to be adjustable, including the boots. I was furrier than usual today, with a full muzzle and cat ears high on my head. I snarled at the mirror and decided the uber-cool fangs made all the fur worthwhile, though positioning my big knobby fingers on the trigger of most handguns was difficult.

I wondered how my people would handle me going into battle again. The last time I was in mortal danger, I'd come so close to dying that I might have been legally dead for a while. Prior to going through the rift—a magical or maybe dimensional opening—my magic had always healed me in a shift change when I was in danger of death. Post-rift, it had failed me several times; I could no longer count on shifting shape when I received a mortal wound, and healing.

My people had all but imprisoned me for a while, trying to keep me protected. In the intervening months, I had spent a lot of time practicing fighting techniques, practicing shifting, and pushing my skinwalker magic. My magic seemed to be growing more reliable. Probably. Maybe. Sometimes.

But either way, my potential mortality put us all in a dilemma because now I had to think first, act later. Not my strong suit.

To keep my people safe, I had to walk a fine line between being protected and also being front and center in fights so I didn't come across as weak enough for enemy vamps to successfully challenge me. I had to be visible in dangerous situations or I'd look like a coward. No Dark Queen or leader of fangheads could survive a label of *coward* without serious challenges, or even all-out war.

For my security teams, that posed a need for balance, offsetting my safety from ambush attack against looking like I had a coward's yellow stripe up my back, one with a target in the center.

I strapped on the double thigh rig with the matching nine-mils and snapped out the medium grips for the extra-large ones, but pocketed the mediums—just in case I shifted back to fully human form while in the middle of battle. Satisfied with the picture I presented in the mirror, I strode from the room to find the organized chaos of a well-prepared team gearing up for battle. Eli tossed me my Benelli, already in its spine holster. I buckled it on too. The ARGO shotgun had kinda become the trademarked weapon of the Dark Queen.

I checked the loads of both semiautomatics and gave Eli a small nod when he held out a gobag with extra mags and extra ammo for the shotgun. I strapped it on a utility ring at my waist. Everything inside the bag was color-coded for not-vamp and vamp, the ones marked with red for mundane kills, the silver-Sharpie-coded ones for killing most kinds of paranormal creatures. Vamps and weres had lethal allergies to silver. "Wanna tell me what bullets are going to do against a game of magic dodge-ball?" I asked.

Eli grunted and pointed to Koun.

Koun, the Dark Queen's Enforcer and Executioner, aka the chief strategist of Clan Yellowrock, answered for Eli. "My Queen. We have flashbangs, null cuffs, and new null sticks that appear to act as personal protection." Koun strode to me and threaded two brownish metallic sticks about the size of a hair stick into slits in a leather surface layer of my matte black armor, near my shoulders.

I had thought all the little slits were decorative but apparently not. I didn't ask where the null sticks came from. They were restricted to military and law enforcement use and the less I knew the better. But these looked different from the null devices I had seen before. "Copper?" I asked.

"Yes. The Seattle coven has acquired the services of a

metal witch," Koun said, as he checked and secured my defensive armor. That should have been Eli's job as my secondo, or my personal security's job, but Eli was giving orders into his comms, and Quint was off tonight. She would be ticked that she missed the fighting.

"Metal witch?" I asked.

Koun's blue Celtic tattoos rose out of the neck of his modern armor and from his sleeves. His armor was black inked with blue to match the tattoos beneath. His long pale hair was braided back into a tight fighting queue. But his weapons were totally different from mine. He carried an ax, two swords, and, on his belt, what looked like fragmentation grenades. He knelt at my feet, which I hated. I opened my mouth to tell him to stand up, but he wasn't doing the subservient thing. He threaded another null stick near my waist before spinning me around and adding one above my butt, below the Benelli.

Alex, bent over his tablets in the living room, answered my question, "Metal witch. Pietro Gonzalez. Twenty-seven. Survived three childhood witch-cancers. He was born a stone witch but after chemo discovered a special affinity for ore-bearing rocks. He made your null sticks and the latest version of the silver null cuffs. His coven added full coven null workings to them and the coven has described them as being *exceptionally robust*."

Koun said, "They make my undead flesh ache simply handling them."

I touched one to find it had a very sharp end. Stakes? To nullify a vamp, maybe? "Full coven workings are expensive. Are they really worth it?"

"The local coven has been impressed with the quality and efficacy of the devices. Pietro also makes amazing solid silver athames, which they are praising," Koun said, as he strapped another blade around my calf.

"Ducky. Hey," I called out. "I need food. And somebody give me an update. What are we looking at?"

Eli slapped a platter-sized piece of naan folded around a sirloin steak into my hand. I bit in and grunted with appreciation. It was still warm. *Holy moly, this is good.* A little bit of heaven.

"I got into a nearby resident's security cams, as well as the null prison's cams," Alex said. "Three witches appeared at the edge of a camera view at the null prison. The streets were empty one second and the next second a woman was standing there, then two more. When the three women stepped aside, people began popping into place in groups of three and walking into the shadows. I'm thinking maybe an *obfuscation* working for dramatic effect. Like magic. Get it?" Alex chuckled at his very small joke.

I stared at him.

"Right. So. I had to get into the prison's system to adjust the angle of a camera before I could detect a magical circle in the middle of the street, with the pavement all churned up. An unknown group of attackers spread out into the night and gathered up the street. Then you came in. I was still counting heads and trying to determine species when the witches threw magic workings and knocked out some camera systems.

"As of this time, I have no video from inside or outside but I'm working on it. I have programs open to access more private doorbell and security cameras up and down the street." Which was technically illegal, but . . . I didn't tell him to stop. His fingers danced across the keys and he whispered something I couldn't make out. "Audio from inside the null prison is coming through, but it's staticky. As far as I can tell, they're still under magical attack, with the assumption that the attackers are trying a jailbreak. The prison's wards are not down. Yet. The witch guards are patching holes in their outer ward but it's crumbling."

"How many layers of wards?" I asked.

"Three. And then the null house itself, which should be enough to incapacitate most magical beings."

"Bruiser?"

"He was at HQ," Alex said. "He's securing the premises, turning everything over to Wrassler, and heading to you ASAP with two teams."

Alex hit a key and Bruiser's voice came over the speakers. "Gamma team. Two lanes of cover fire when my teams exit. Then immediate lockdown, everyone stays in their rooms. No one in. No one out. High alert and roaming teams inside."

"Roger that," Wrassler said. "Voodoo, get your team to the airlock doors—"

"Hey, Bruiser," I interrupted, speaking loudly to be captured over the other's mics.

"Yes, My Queen?"

"Don't get dead."

"Same to you, my Queen." The warmth in his voice was like the touch of his hand in a dance, intimate yet formal.

Alex hit another key and the sound cut off, but I knew Bruiser was okay, so I could think about other things.

My cell dinged and I saw a text from Alex. Who was sitting like three feet away from me, so he wanted this private. I read: "Just got a text. Number untraceable. Reads: 'Hey Money Honey. Cover your six. Shit's going down. And I could use a good saving about now.'"

I texted back, "Reach calls me Money Honey."

"No way to prove it's him," he texted, "but he disappeared some time ago. If Reach is in NOLA, and the Heir's prisoner, he would want a rescue."

"Not high on my list, but I'll keep it in mind. Let Eli know."

"Copy that."

Reach. In the hands of the Heir, against his will. The Heir, the successor of the two Sons of Darkness, whom I had killed. The one person who might have access to their power. Who might be able to defeat me, behead all my vamps, and then take over the world.

Or . . . Reach was covering his bases so that if Mainet lost, he'd be set free. The former data-whiz of the paranormal world would think ahead. And who knew what his ultimate intentions were, except freedom (assuming he was a prisoner) and money. With Reach it was always money. But Reach wasn't my problem.

Eli read Alex's text about Reach and the Heir and looked at me. I nodded slightly. He said into his comms mic, "Attention, all team members. This attack on the null house, and what appears to be a jailbreak attempt for

one or more of the witch prisoners there, could be the beginning of the attack on our queen by the Heir. Alex, no-
tify all clan Blood Masters to get to safety and lock down.
There could be a multi-pronged attack in progress."

"Roger that," Alex said.

CHAPTER 3

Diplomacy Was Supposed to Be My Main Gig Now

"Team Koppa. Load up," Eli said. "Lethal and non-lethal force weapons. Full gear, max defensive and offensive kits."

Koppa was the special security unit he had been training. Koppa was the Greek letter for Q, as in Dark Queen, which he seemed to find amusing. I knew all the team's faces and even though Eli had been working with them personally for only a week, I felt comfortable going into battle with them. If they let me participate, that is.

That delicate balance of keeping me safe yet visible meant that my crew tried to keep me out of the line of fire, under shields, and uninjured. I understood it. As Queen, I was supposed to give orders, observe as they were carried out, and be vampy diplomatic. I was better at busting heads than I was at diplomacy, and diplomacy was supposed to be my main gig now. Which sucked.

From the corner of my eye, I saw Eli press a small stone into his pocket over his most recent wound. A healing or pain-reducing amulet from his girlfriend, Liz.

"My lady," Koun said, leading the way outside and into the street. "You will ride with me."

"Uh-huh. And will you drive me away from the fight?"

"I do not drive away from any fight," he said, his tone full of insult. "In my human life, leaders led the way into battle."

Black SUVs were double-parked blocking the street, the matched make and models of the fleet of armored SUVs owned by the Dark Queen. The traffic had been stopped by SUVs on either end of the block, to wait or take a detour. My . . . freaking entourage. Bet that made the commuters happy.

Horns honked with unexpected outrage. Unlike in other parts of the country, born and bred Southerners didn't honk much. Not usually.

Koun opened the passenger door of one of the black SUVs. It was parked so close to the next car that I had to slide in sideways. Still not completely trusting that he'd drive me toward battle, I adjusted the Benelli M4 and strapped myself in. Koun closed the door, got into the driver's seat, and started the vehicle.

Before he continued his commentary, he turned off his mic. Mine was still off, my headset in my lap as my chief strategist pulled down the road behind Eli. Two other vehicles fell in behind us and the traffic along the street opened up. In the privacy of our vehicle, Koun said, "This modern method of kings on horseback directing from safety at the rear of battle, or, even worse, generals sitting in a protected situation room, directing the warfare from microphones and video, is cowardly."

Our vehicle passed four photojournalists hiding in the thick foliage in alleys between buildings. Even if they had low-light cameras, they wouldn't be able to get pics through the heavily tinted windows. But they had to know that the Dark Queen was on the move.

"I understand your need and desire to participate," Koun said. "I recognize your fighting skill. I will protect you as needed, but will not impede you." He speared me with a glance, his cool eyes sharp as icicles. "Unless, my lady, you do something stupid." He turned his eyes back to the street. "I reserve the right to stop you should you attempt something foolish."

I thought back to getting into the car, and realized Koun had parked the car so no one could get a good shot

of me—photographically or weapons-based. Protect but
not impede. And he called me "my lady" not "My Queen"
when he had something to say that he considered private.
Got it. I liked that kind of forethought in my Enforcer and
Executioner. "Goodie. Comms."

"*Goodie,*" Koun repeated with something like delight.
He didn't smile but his eyes did glint happily as he turned
on his mic. "In my experience queens do not say *goodie.*"

"I'm not a regular queen, dude." I put on and activated
my specially constructed comms earbuds and headgear,
adjusted the shape for my high-placed, rounded cat ears,
and toggled my channel to private. I said, "Alex. Address
and floor plan on screen."

"No updated floor plan on file with the city since 1967,
but we know work was done when the house became the
prison. We have to assume they handled any construction
stuff under the table. Old floor plan and address to follow." He texted the address, which was near the Garden
District, near the corner of Philip and Constance Streets.

I had been inside when Tau, a *senza onore*, had been
imprisoned, but it had been a while, so I pulled the location up on my tablet and studied the layout. Yeah. The
floor plan had been totally different from the city's original. For a house on the outskirts of the Garden District,
this one was pretty fancy: two stories with a wide, L-shaped
porch with a matching second-floor gallery, an atelier with
livable space, and a private alley-driveway. The house had
upscale landscaping in a postage-stamp-sized yard, was
painted gray with lots of white trim, and looked to be
about five thousand square feet. Maybe more.

Alex also sent me video feed from a camera in the
prison's security system, one in the yard that hadn't been
hit with a witch bomb intended to kill electronics. This
camera was a low-light model and there was enough ambient light for me to see the front of the house and part of
the street. Three witches were standing in a circle that
had ripped up the roadway. As poor as New Orleans was
these days, it would never get fixed. Which was a stupid thought but the only thing I could focus on while my
eyes and brain tried to figure out what was happening on
the cam.

"Alex?" I said into my comms. "Have the witches at the prison called us for help?"

"Negative. Not yet. They're arguing about calling for backup right now."

"Crap." I shook my head. Alex was listening in on the witch's internal electronic security system. It was one of the brands with a trademarked name, a rudimentary AI, and the ability to make phone calls or give orders to the house system with a verbal request. Those things were a piece of cake for someone like Alex to hack into, which he had clearly done a long time ago.

My cell rang just as we turned down St. Charles Avenue. The name on the face said "Lachish Dutillett." I hadn't known she was in my contacts, and I certainly hadn't known she had my official Dark Queen number. I also thought Lachish was an inmate at the null prison, and therefore unable to make calls. I slid my eyes and the cell sideways to Koun so he could see her name.

"Interesting," my Enforcer said.

I tapped the face, put it on speaker, and answered casually, "Yellowrock here. What can I do for you, Lachish?"

In my earbud, Alex said, "Lachish?" sounding as surprised as I felt.

Lachish said, "We're under attack. Can you help?"

"The Dark Queen has sworn to protect her city and the sentient beings in it," I said, which was the proper protocol for my political position, but also wasn't exactly a yes. Because I wasn't supposed to know anything about their danger, I asked, "Who is the 'we' under attack, who is attacking, and where is the attack taking place?"

"Vampires and humans are attacking the null prison. An unknown number of unidentified black magic witches are assisting. They've broken through the outer ward. We're taking heavy magical fire."

"Location," I said, already knowing but keeping up the pretense.

She gave me the address, and I said, "Koun. How long to that address?"

"Two minutes, considering the traffic, My Queen."

"We're close by," I said to the witch. "Two minutes."

"We'll hold on."

Through the cell's speaker, I heard a low-pitched boom, and the cell vibrated in my hand. It was so deep and heavy, it was as if the Earth itself had been hit by a sonic weapon. Lachish gasped, a strangled sound. The connection ended.

Koun tapped his headgear and informed the others in the team that we needed to "progress with all speed."

Moments later, Eli's vehicle, which had ended up in front of us, pulled onto the street and slowed. Koun matched his vehicle's speed.

Our SUVs' positions provided us with an excellent field of view. Clearly visible were three witches standing inside a circle.

With Beast's vision, I could see the witches and the magics that entwined to make the circle and a protective ward over and around them. The energies were unfamiliar and sickly toned, a glowing yellow-green. The attacking witches weren't the kind pictured in fiction, neither old crones nor buxom beauties, but rather, they were strongly built, sturdy women wearing dresses, sweaters against the chill, and stout leather walking shoes. If I had passed them in a grocery store, I'd have pegged them as upper-class grandmothers who loved to bake, had huge gardens, taught Sunday school in the local Baptist church, wore pearls, and kept cats. None of them were familiar to me.

Some energies screwed with pixels, but I set my cell to take close-up pics and sent them to Alex. "If you can get anything through the magical energies, start facial rec," I ordered.

"Roger that."

"For now, left to right, we'll call them Ursula, Fiona, and Endora." All the names were witches from TV and movies and Alex chuckled as he passed along the designations to team Koppa and to Bruiser's teams, with the close-ups, so their designations would be consistent. I tapped my mic, went to the general channel, and noted Koun did the same.

Redheaded Ursula turned her attention to our vehicles, reached down to the broken pavement, and gathered a ball of power between her hands. She was handling raw energy, which was dangerous, sometimes deadly, for even the most powerful of witches. The threat was unmistakable. Eli's vehicle slammed on brakes and only Koun's vampire reflexes saved us from rear-ending them.

I felt Eli's battle-readiness settle over and through him. "Drones are in flight," he said. Our connection snapped into place inside me and I took a deep, calm, cold breath.

Koun whipped the wheel and pulled into a drive as Eli's vehicle backed down the street, passing us. I caught sight of Eli in our headlights; he slipped out of the driver's side and into the foliage near the street as whoever was in the passenger seat slid across and took over driving. It was a slick move.

Koun was a third of the way into a fast turn when I opened the door.

"Find us," I said to him and leaped into the street, my body protected by the SUV. Beast-fast I moved, pulling my ARGO shotgun.

"Be safe," Koun snarled. "Do not make me regret allowing you freedom to lead." The SUVs pulled away. The headlights had hidden my escape, just as Eli's had hidden his, and unless the witches in the street had some sort of low-light *seeing* working and were scanning the foliage, none of the attackers knew we had escaped the vehicles.

The Benelli cradled in my hands, I followed Eli into the low trees and shrubs, pulling on Beast's night vision to augment the weird bond Eli and I had ended up with not so long ago. It wasn't an *anamchara* mind-bond, but in battle it clicked into place like being whipped with barbed wire. In daily life, unless we suppressed the connection, we always knew where the other was, and had a sense of the other's emotional state. Which had been uncomfortable the first time Eli got lucky with Liz Everhart, his . . . lady? Girlfriend? . . . after he was mostly healed. *Yuck. TMI.*

After that, I figured out fast how to block Eli and he me, using biofeedback and meditation techniques. Or target shooting. Or a really loud violent sci-fi film.

Neither of us liked the bond, but we were stuck with it, and in battlefield conditions it was handy, the sensation intensifying, along with the rise in adrenaline. Eli was just ahead, waiting on me, attuned to the link we shared, knowing I was coming. Catlike, I slid through the leaves of banana trees, lemon trees, and elephant ear plants and to Eli's left.

In the street, Ursula threw the ball of energy at the house they were attacking. It gonged into the middle ward, a low tone that ached through my bones. With Beast's night vision, I could see the effect even as the sonic vibration hit and thudded through me. The energy ball burst and shivered over the center ward, spreading like viscous slime and eating into the magical protections. Energy and sound consumed and countered the ward, a high-pitched buzzing, like white noise but more annoying. It grated along my nerves as if a floor sander had been applied to my skin.

The ward was quickly repaired, but in Beast's vision, it was already mostly a patchwork of repairs. It wouldn't last.

As the tone of the sonic attack decreased, the witch I had named Fiona gathered power, rolling it into a ball. But she didn't toss hers at the house. Instead, she threw it along the street. Confused, I watched as it moved, only realizing at the last moment what its target was. An electrical transformer exploded in a shower of sparks. A bolt of electricity shot like lightning into the sky.

Up and down the street, lights flickered; the entire block went dark.

Taking advantage of the change in illumination patterns and the deeper shadows, Eli and I moved closer to the house. His focus on the witches in the street was icy cold and sharp as a laser, while he also maintained a broad and wide attentiveness to the entire street, the yards around him, and every being nearby. It was a mindfulness, a situational awareness I could never emulate. He had acquired it surviving one or two Middle Eastern wars and dozens of black-ops missions with Uncle Sam's Army Rangers.

With his left hand, he pointed at his own eyes and then at the house. My eyes followed the direction.

Inside the middle ward, standing with her back to the

front entrance, was a witch I vaguely remembered from
the witch conclave in NOLA some months past. She was
siphoning earth energy and moon energy and slamming
little silver and iridescent-green workings into the middle
ward. It was her work that was holding the ward together,
and she was powerful, precise, and skilled. But it was like
trying to patch a sieve. The ward was still failing.

The high-pitched white noise increased, a sensation
like fire ants biting. I wanted to scratch my pelt off my
body. Ursula, Fiona, and Endora were drawing up more
power, starting to make a ball-shaped *attack* working
from it.

If Eli was having any sonic-fire-ant problems with the
sensation, I couldn't tell. Stoic warrior.

Koun was suddenly at my other side, equally austere.
But then, he and Eli were wearing proper headsets, unlike the one I had to wear to fit my hairy upright puma
ears. I had less sound protection than they did, and this
magic was high-pitched, like fingernails on a blackboard
over loudspeakers.

Four more Glinda witch prison guards raced out the
front door of the null house and took up positions in a
circle pattern with the lone defender, adding their energies to her patch-job working. Five witches on their home
turf against three. It should be enough.

It wasn't. Endora threw the *attack* working bomb. The
sickly green energies hit, boomed, and spread, eating
through the defensive measures of all the Glindas.

Eli gestured to the street again, this time indicating a
location farther down. He whispered into his mic, "Attacking mixed paranormals are confirmed. Three witches,
six vamps, and six humans are among the attackers. The
front door of the house is center clock. At its eleven are a
group of three vamps and six humans. Three more vamps
in the foliage at the house's nine o'clock, providing cover.
We are at three o'clock. I want a man at the prison's six,
next to the house behind. A man at nine, behind the
guards, and a shooter farther down the street to cover the
large group in the street. Acknowledge."

Three voices acknowledged.

"Tango and Delta team leaders, what's your twenty?" Eli asked.

"South of you. ETA ten," Bruiser said.

"Koppa Team," Eli said. "When you are in place, target vamps. Fire on Koun's command or mine. Non-lethal weaponry against humans except in self- or collateral-defense. Do not target witches. Repeat. Do *not* target the attacking witches. We do not have termination orders by the U.S. Council of Witches. Repeat, no termination orders for witches."

Overlapping voices said, "Copy."

I added, "We do not have termination orders *at this time*. The night is young."

That got some laughter over comms.

"Carmine," Eli said, speaking to a new team member, "do you have remote viewing ready?"

"Affirmative," she said. "Uplink to Alex is operational. All remote units are airborne. Video to follow."

Unlike Eli and the human team members, I wasn't wearing infrared and low-light headgear, which let them differentiate between the body heat of various paranormal beings, but I could make out the groupings of the attacking warriors, all silvered in Beast's puma vision. Three witches, three vamps, six humans in the street. Someone had multiples of the Rule of Three in mind for this attack, which made this situation even more dangerous in ways I probably didn't fully understand.

I considered calling my BFF, Molly, of the Everhart witch clan, for info, but before I could, Fiona began to ball up another magical bomb. I guessed it took time to regroup, so they were trading off. Good to know. If I was right.

"Hold your positions," Alex said. "I have Brandon and Brian on my cell, advising."

Crap. Right. The laws regarding paranormal beings and creatures were constantly evolving. I wasn't sure what I could legally do at this point. As the Dark Queen, I could attack enemy vamps if they were doing harm to humans. Ditto on witches who were attacking humans. But witch-on-witch attacks, with vamps as glorified spectators, was out of my political wheelhouse, especially on a city street with human witnesses probably standing at nearby windows, cell phone cameras active and uploading to news services and the web.

I switched channels and whispered through my mic, "Alex. At what point can we legally intervene?"

The IT boy-wonder said, "According to the Dark Queen's attorney, as long as the Wicked Witches and vamps stand in the street and don't actively injure or kill someone, and are not physically on the premises, you cannot legally attack *anyone*. Repeat, can*not*. The moment any attackers break into the house and/or threaten the security of the prison that houses black-magic witches, the Dark Queen can intervene because the city's populace could be at risk from paranormal activity that might result if the prisoners got free.

"And while I'm quoting legal crap, as per the Robere twins, *if* the Wicked Witches get through the wards, the null energies inside will make it impossible for the prison warden witches to mount magical defenses and also impossible for the attacking witches to use their own magic, so it isn't likely the witches themselves will try to get inside. I sent the Roberes the real-time sit vid and they said the non-witches will likely enter the building. The moment a vamp steps on the witch property, it falls under the purview of the Dark Queen's diplomatic and political responsibilities to protect her city. In addition, should one of the attacking vamps hurt our city's witches, you are a go under your status as Master of the City to kill the fanghead. That part's my words, not theirs."

In frustration, I slapped my own head with my palm. Again. Again.

Koun, at my left side, gave a dry chuckle. Eli never took his eyes from the warriors and witches.

"Until then," Alex said, "all we have is witches attacking witches, and so far, no danger to the security of the prisoners or the human populace. Hold your position, stand down, and do nothing that might constitute overstepping your legal authority."

"Team Koppa," Eli said, "disregard order to stand

down. Follow battlefield and rescue protocols. Choose a target. Hold fire. Fire on our command."

The Roberes were the Dark Queen's lawyers. They were saying that any rescue might never be completely legal, despite the call for help, therefore we had to wait for paranormal exigent circumstances or a no-witness moment. I wasn't an unknown rogue-vampire hunter anymore. I was fully recognizable no matter what form I was in, and the humans along the street were taking video on cell phones. If I stepped from the shadows, I'd be seen.

"Flashbangs?" I asked. "Hit them with beanbag cannons?"

"No legal right to attack," one of the Roberes said into the headset, his voice scratchy. "A no-danger situation at this time. This is a lawsuit waiting to happen, against the moneybags Dark Queen. Worse, if you act unprovoked, and outside your legal rights and responsibilities, it gives the witches standing in the street the right to toss magical energies at you and your people."

"Holy crap," I muttered, disgusted. "It doesn't look like a no-danger situation to me."

"It could be a setup," Eli murmured, "trying to get you on camera doing something illegal, something outside your responsibilities and authority."

Inside me, Beast growled low, and I got the feeling of her pacing, tail twitching.

Koun said into his headset, "Hold positions."

I swept my gaze along the street, spotting a few of our people, human and vamp, all behind line-of-fire cover. But not necessarily behind cover that would protect them against magical weapons.

At the prison, Endora threw another magical *attack* working bomb.

The middle ward fell in a shower of sickly orange and green droplets that hit the earth and splattered. The defending witches retreated inside the inner ward.

No one had been injured. *Crap.* It was the first time I'd ever wished someone had been wounded in battle, just so I could attack. Watching this made me ache and seethe and want to bash something.

A harsh, burning scent, like acid, reached me, something new, stinging my nostrils, as if the magic had changed. It smelled as if this working now had physical properties. Maybe it did.

The witch I'd dubbed Fiona began to draw up magics.

At the smell, Beast came alert, flooding my system with her unique fight-or-flight response. *Danger*, she thought at me. I/we pulled in a breath through my cat-nostrils, filling my chest.

Through our bond, Eli must have felt my reaction. His heart rate sped, his breath deepened, and his entire body simultaneously tightened and relaxed.

"What?" he demanded.

"I don't know," I said, pulling in air over the scent glands in the roof of my mouth. *Crap, crap, crapola*. "This working is different. A spell with a weird . . . scent? Taste?"

A second weird sensation rushed over me, and this time it came with memory. It was the feeling I got when a ward was opened and closed, almost in the same instant.

The vampires and humans standing near the witch circle moved toward the prison. It wasn't a rushing attack, not a measured advance, nor was it the elegant motions of the vamp Sangre Duello challenge. But it was steady and determined. The advancing party divided, leaving the front of the house clear. But no one stepped on the property. Not yet.

Koun said, "Prepare to fire."

The three witches remained in their circle in the street. They began to draw up power again, though it was obvious they were tired, and nearly at the end of their power reserves. This magic was dark, a sickly, vile orange/green tint stained with a lightless black, like soot. It stank of battlefields and graveyards and rotted meat, with the overlay of acid.

Ursula, Fiona, and Endora said a *wyrd* in a language I didn't know.

It didn't sound like Irish Gaelic, the spell language used by the Everharts, nor did it sound like a Romance language. But it was magic for sure, black magic. Not that I could prove it, not without a visible sacrifice. The blood sacrifice had to be hidden under an obfuscation working, a really effective one.

I couldn't act without solid proof. I also couldn't act in the mere presence of black magic. It had to be used in violation of witch law, and without the sacrifice I had no idea if the law had been broken.

Crapola again.

They said the *wyrd* again. And a third time.

The power of the *wyrd* shivered along my limbs and through the lush trees and foliage along the street, through the yards. Sucking life and light from everything. Black sparks hissed and sizzled all around me. The three witches drew in the rising power and rolled it between them into a lightless ball filled with orange motes of power with a shimmer of green, manipulating magic into a sphere as big as a beach ball. All the energy in the world seemed to shift toward them, all the light, all the warmth. The magic stank of acid and old bones. And brimstone.

I knew what this magic was. And it wasn't just black magic.

"We got a problem," I managed to say.

I nearly fell. Koun caught my arm. "My Queen?" he asked.

"Aw, crap," I said, trying to think of words to explain what was happening, yet knowing that nothing could stop it. Nothing. "Oh no . . ." If I told Koun what they were doing, he would rush in and he would die true dead. I wasn't sure how I knew that. I just knew it, as surely as I knew Koun would be dying true dead for me.

I clutched his arm to hold him in place.

I knew this magic, knew how it could take over and destroy everything.

The witches rolled the power, three witches. Rule of Three. This was gonna be bad. Holding the ball of dark magic, lifting it above their heads, they turned.

The Glob, in my pocket, heated, sucking in all the random bits of energy. Protecting me, protecting Koun and Eli. But doing nothing for my unit hidden all along the street.

From overhead, leaves fell, dry and brittle. "Oh *shit*,"

I whispered, seeing the future as clearly as if I were seeing it in droplets in the shower.

"Jane?" Alex said, startled at the profanity.

I drew in a lungful of air and shouted, "Retreat! Retreat! Fall back!"

Before I could say another word, the witches threw the ball of energy at the house.

The dark power hit the inner ward. Black sparks flew through the air and shivered through the yard, down the street, through me. Draining even through the power of the Glob. Dark power ate into the ward, green and orange and the black of hell. Static lightning crackled across the ward. The stench was acidic and acerbic and the smell of roasted bones mixed with brimstone as the working attacked it.

I staggered. Caught myself on Koun and Eli.

The Glob in my pocket grew warm. Then hot. And . . . even without *le breloque* on my head, my crown was active. I could feel my own Dark Queen magic dissecting the working, protecting us, protecting my people like a wall made of sheet steel. A thin barrier I hadn't known I could draw on. And didn't know how I was doing it now.

Not knowing how I did things sucked.

But we were okay. That was good. I'd take it. If that was really happening.

"Alex, is everyone okay?" I asked.

"Yes, according to armor suit readouts. Except you. According to the overhead drone, your pocket is showing a heat source."

I shook my head to clear it, remembering the drones. Right. Eli had made sure they were launched before he left his SUV.

"The Glob," I said. "It's hot."

In front of me, the vamps who had been standing to the sides of the attacking witches stepped forward. I still held Koun close, as the last of the dark magics quivered and dissipated. I could feel the desire to rush into battle quiver through his body. Eli stared into the night, ready to fire, but waiting for the moment when we legally could defend the prison.

I looked away from the action and swept my eyes around

the battlefield. The foliage that had been verdant and green was now dry and brown, brittle and flaking away. Dead.

"Contact the Roberes on a separate channel," I said to Alex. "Open a conference call between them and alert the national council of witches, the governor, and the mayor. We're going in."

"Rationale?" Alex asked.

"The attacking witches just used a death magic *wyrd*, one that destroyed the neighbors' property." I said. "Using death magic is an automatic death sentence. It's flimsy, since we haven't been giving sanction by the U.S. witch council, but it gives us an opening."

Alex said, "Copy that." A moment later he said, "The Roberes say to move in."

CHAPTER 4

I Felt the Punch of the Shot in My Left Arm

"Eli and I will secure the asset. Protect the prison," Koun ordered his men.

Me. I was the asset. They moved me back, farther from the action. We were practically on the front porch of the house next door to the prison.

I glanced back to make sure the occupants were safe. Place looked empty. No lights, no movement. Dead foliage. I caught a view of rotting pumpkins on the porch and a big turkey made out of thatch, wearing a red hat with Mardi gras beads and a banana hammock. *Only in New Orleans.*

In the street, the witches and their protective circle had vanished, leaving behind the churned and ruined pavement, a stink of tar, and glowing embers of magic. It wasn't an *obfuscation* working; they were really gone. They had either done a group timewalk or a vanished through a *transport* working and those didn't exist outside of a witch-time circle.

So far as I knew.

We had seen the bad guys show up, but the witches

doing a vanishing act was enlightening. Their disappearing told me the attackers might have a mini transport circle.

Or they had opened a demon-calling circle. I sniffed the air. There was no fresh scent of brimstone.

I stepped forward just as the prison's inner ward fell.

Our people fired. No one fell. They missed. All of them.

Vamp-fast, with little pops of sound, the attacking fangheads and their humans had raced to the house. One vamp burst through the front door. Two others leaped through the windows, glass shattering. Their humans raced in behind.

"Go," Koun said to his unit.

Lachish was in there. People I knew. Witches. *Family* . . . My *u'tlun'ta* grandmother. Ka N'vsita, another *u'tlunt'a* skinwalker, and also a distant cousin.

I wrenched my arms free. Shoving through the dead trees and elephant ears, I sprinted for the door. My team was left behind.

"This was not our plan," Koun murmured to Eli. He did that vamp *popping* thing and appeared just ahead of me.

"Tell that to Jane," Eli muttered back, catching up at my left side and slightly behind, his weapon and eyes covering the street, the foliage behind us.

One of Koun's swords left its scabbard with a soft *shhhsh* of sound, his ax already in the other hand. My Enforcer took point. Eli drew a vamp-killer in his left hand, handgun in his dominant hand, following me. He was limping slightly from the wound he was still rehabbing.

I glanced back. Two other forms, ours, were on our six, sticking close. Thema. Kojo.

Three of the enemy's humans stepped into the street.

Their weapons aimed at my small party.

Eli fired. Two shots in quick succession, just as Koun said, "Fire."

Two more shots rang out. All almost overlapping.

Three enemy humans dropped where they stood guard. My heart tried to race. Eli's heart pumped hard, pulling me into his battlefield state. Cold. Emotions frozen. Time

changed, everything going bright and sharp-edged. The
awareness we now shared was crystalline and cutting.

Sirens sounded in the distance. Screams echoed from
the prison house.

"Koun. Null energies have been known to leave vamps
woozy and dizzy until their undeath balances with the
null," I said. "We also have to cross any lingering death
magics they threw. There might be some left active, and
they might affect our vamps. We don't know if the enemy
vamps have protection against the same, so be prepared.
I'm the best one to survive simply entering the house." I
had survived Molly's death magic. Molly's secret. And no
time to explain all that even if I'd wanted to. "Going to
point."

No one argued. Koun stumbled. Vamps didn't stumble.

I sprinted ahead and across the threshold. The death
magics crackled across me and were sucked into the Glob.
Traces of death magic and the prison's dying null energies
fell across me like waves of scalding water and splashed at
my feet. I slowed. My limbs felt heavy, clumsy, leaden. I
moved to the left of the door. Out of the way. The sensation passed.

Eli took the right. Glanced at me. Pointed down.

The house was dark, but Beast's night vision was nearly
as good as Eli's tech-augmented vision. There was a
woman on the floor at his feet. A witch. Throat torn out.
Dead. Vamps had killed sentient beings in my city. I was
fully justified in *any* response.

"Witches are down," I growled into my mic. "Death
energies are down. Null energies are still in place. Use
caution. No mercy to the vamps or their humans."

Eli said, "Koppa team, lethal response required against
all enemy fangheads."

I stepped over her, my combat boots grinding on the
broken window glass. Grunts and the sound of breaking
wood came from the back of the house.

Eli entered, moving right, away from the doorway.

Koun stepped in, moving slower than normal, to the
left, in front of me. He staggered again at the null energies, regrouped, and slid into the left hallway.

Eli gestured for me to follow Koun. I moved through the lower floor.

I had been here before, but I'd had light then. Nothing looked familiar.

I stepped over another dead witch, into a hallway. A vamp appeared just ahead. Koun materialized out of the dark and took his head. Arterial blood spurted across the wall. My Enforcer slipped into the blackness again. The vamp-body fell.

Two shots rang out. I reached for Eli's mind. He was ahead and to my right. Firing. In danger. His heart beat, hard thumps I could feel.

Knees bent, ready to fire, I moved forward, along the dark hallway. Movement to my right. I fired before I even knew I needed to. A vamp slid down the wall, gasping silently, trying to breathe. Left-handed, I drew my vamp-killer and took his head. A human stepped from the dark. She fired.

I felt the punch of the shot in my left arm. Nerveless, I dropped the vamp-killer. I fired my Benelli again. The human fell back. She landed in an open doorway, on top of Koun's legs. He was sprawled, faceup, his armor out of place, his abdomen exposed. A wood stake protruded from his belly. Even if Koun had been fighting vertigo, it had to have taken at least two people to get the drop on him and find belly flesh. I yanked the stake out and dropped it beside him. If there weren't other injuries, he'd make it.

I looked at my arm. Close range, even armor was useless against some gunfire, and no armor had full Kevlar on the sleeves or legs because that stuff didn't bend well. I worked my hand into a fist. It was numb but it didn't hurt and there was no blood, so . . . Go Kevlar.

Pain. Not mine. My heart rate sped. Adrenaline shocked through me.

Eli's in danger.

I pumped my fist, shook my open hand, willing the nerve back into working order. The stench of battle filled my lungs. Nitrocellulose. Vomit. The contents of bowels. Vamp blood. I fought off a sneeze.

Gunfire sounded. Crazy, ammo-eating, fully automatic weapons fire. That was a lot of firepower and damage for such a small team in such a small space. They had planned and practiced this scenario. Beneath the automatic gunfire was the specific three-shot, pause, three-shot, pause, employed by Eli.

Another barrage of automatic gunfire, churning through walls. I dropped low.

Eli. Pain in his thigh. Intense. Wounded.

My hearing was damaged. I had no directional hearing to sense the danger, but I had Eli-sense. Ahead. There. *Reinjured. Same thigh.*

I tried to lift my left arm. Saw a trickle of blood, but not bleeding bad. Mostly numb from the impact on my armor. Useless.

I was down two rounds in the Benelli, but I had nine-mils if needed. Moving on down the hallway, I stepped toward what looked like a T-intersection of another hallway. The null working grew stronger. Walking was like trying to walk underwater, pushing against a current. I must be near the most heavily warded cells. Ignoring the pain in my left arm and the blood now dripping down my fingers, I snugged the Benelli against my body, my knobby finger on the trigger.

Reaching the end of the hallway, I squatted. Peeked around the opening, left, then fast back into protection. That way was empty, closed doors on both sides. Three housecats, eyes gleaming in the dark, were crouched up high, on carpeted shelves that ran along the walls above the doors. I peeked right, ducked back into protection. Right was also doorways, several open. One doorway had a group of what looked like three humans holding a battering ram. I leaned out again for a final quick look. The humans reared back and swung the ram against the door. Beyond them was a vampire. I stood and swung around, partly into the hallway. Fired. Fired. Fired.

The booms were deafening. Humans fell or raced or crawled across one another, trying to get away. The vamp was gone. The ram lay in front of the splintered door.

I moved into the narrow hallway. One human on the floor fell over, dead or out cold. With the side of my foot,

I slid her weapons out of easy reach. Ahead, the gunfire stopped. Eli was . . . *there*. Just ahead. The next room. The door was open. I positioned the Benelli on its strap and tapped my mic. "Alex, we need vamp healers and human medics. And whatever law enforcement you think. The Dark Queen's defenders injured or killed a bunch of armed, attacking humans and at least two enemy vamps inside the null prison. We have injured of our own. They get first priority."

"Roger that," Alex said. "On the way."

I tapped the Clan Yellowrock channel and said, "Eli. I'm coming in."

Eli gave a breathy grunt.

I repositioned the Benelli again, counting back to rounds fired. And how many were left before I had to reload. Peeked into the room, taking in everything with a single glance. Back out. Considered. No lock on this busted door. The furniture was piled inside the room—chests of drawers, chairs, mattresses propped on their sides where they had once pressed against the door. Barricade. I bent and duck-walked in. Eli was on the other side of the furniture. On the floor. Blood everywhere.

Beyond him, on the floor in a tight ball, was Lachish Dutillett. She sat up. Appeared uninjured. Eli had been protecting her. Lachish had called for our help. Lachish was supposedly a prisoner here, being held for a crime I had never learned about. In an unlocked room. Whatever she had done had happened around the same time as the Sangre Duello, when Leo "died." Her crime and punishment had to be involved with that. Except there was no door lock. She wasn't wearing null cuffs.

I dropped to my knees, facing the door, and put the shotgun on the floor, easy to hand. I shoved Eli's hands out of the way and took over tightening a pressure bandage on his thigh. Same dang thigh he was still rehabbing, same thigh that was full of steel from a bad break and muscles and tendons that were weak from being cut from the bone. But this was just a gunshot. *Just a gunshot . . .* Going by the empty oversized syringe beside him, he had already inserted the Xstat to control the bleeding.

With this many injured, we needed an Infermieri, but

I had sent Florence back to visit her kin in Lincoln Shaddock's territory. I needed healers.

Koun staggered into the doorway, one hand over his belly. "My Queen," he said.

"Eli needs vamp blood," I said.

Koun went to a knee and cut his wrist, holding it to Eli's mouth.

"How bad?" Alex asked over comms.

"Bad enough," I said. "He needs an ambulance and surgery. Again."

Alex cursed.

"As do you," Koun said. "I smell your blood."

"Jane?" Alex asked, his voice cracking slightly with anxiety.

"Fine," I groused. "I'm hit. Get someone in here for me."

"Kojo was at the back," Alex said, "He's in. Bringing reinforcements."

Maybe five seconds later, Kojo popped into sight and knelt at Eli's side. The ancient African vamp pulled a small steel blade and cut his wrist, placing the bleeding wound at Eli's mouth. "Drink," he commanded.

Alrighty then. That was new. Kojo and his wife, Thema, resisted giving their blood to anyone except by direct order. This was the first time either of them had actively volunteered. "When you're done, I need help. And Koun needs a little topping off."

Kojo chuckled, his teeth white in a face so dark I could barely make it out in the lightless room, even with Beast's night vision. "I will feed your pet," Kojo said, looking up at Koun as he insulted my right-hand vamp. Which was a lot more like his usual uncompassionate self. "But the Dark Queen should know. The attacking Naturaleza are gone. They took their dead and some of the prisoners with them." Vamps knew Natureleza by their smell and the speed with which they moved. That was important. But my vision was going dark and kinda fuzzy around the edges. "Uhhh," I said. The world whirled and spun sideways. The room darkened. I was passing out.

Thema popped into the room and caught me as I fell to the side. She righted a chair and placed me into it. Like

Kojo, she cut her wrist but she held hers to my mouth. I drank. Power flooded into me, along with the tart, nearly bitter flavor of the ancient vamp's blood.

I hated drinking blood.

Inside, Beast said, *Good strong vampire blood. Want more.*

I didn't reply. My heart rate was a little odd. Too fast. Kinda stuttering. I looked down at my arm, which looked silver and gray in the dark.

The lights overhead came on. I blinked as the silver and gray of Beast's night vision resolved into scarlet. Blood all over me. All over the floor where I'd walked and stood.

I had lost more blood than I thought.

I had thought my armor had deflected the round and it had just nicked my arm, the thump of impact numbing my hand. Had thought my weakness was sharing Eli's symptoms of blood loss. Nope. I was bleeding a *lot*.

Nausea made my mouth water, a sour slime mixed with the taste of Thema's blood.

Thema cursed in a language I didn't recognize and withdrew her wrist. "I thought someone had killed the witches' housecats," she said, peeling off my armored jacket, exposing the thin long-sleeved T-shirt I wore beneath. The reek of my sweat and my cat blood hit me. Thema had a point, one I had never noticed. My pelt was gummed with clotting blood. My upper arm looked yucky.

I looked away as Thema licked the wound, her saliva clotting my blood. She recut her wrist and began to smear her blood into my wound, healing it. My vision cleared now that I was sitting down, and I took in the room.

Lachish fully uncurled from her place on the floor, revealing something squarish and brown. A wooden box. I kept half an eye on her.

Eli made a soft sound, not quite a groan but a sound of pain. Kojo was applying his blood to Eli's thigh. Koun, who had only recently been belly-staked, sat heavily onto the floor, a barely controlled fall.

From the sight of his armor, Eli's Kevlar had stopped several lethal rounds. He was gonna be bruised.

Lachish came to me, standing in front of the chair where

I sat. The box she carried was maybe eighteen inches by twelve, and twelve deep. Even over the stench of battle, Eli's blood, Koun's, witches', humans', and my own, I smelled the familiar scent. I knew what was in the box. Things that hadn't made sense suddenly did.

I raised my eyes to her. "You aren't a prisoner here. You're the guardian of the heart of the Son of Darkness."

I had killed both Sons of Darkness, but from one of them, I had kept the heart and sent it to Jodi Richoux, a human born from a witch family that had been decimated by vamps, as a show of peace. Unfortunately, I discovered after the fact that the heart didn't decompose. It began to regenerate and add tissue. Now it was in a null house. To keep it undetected and not growing.

Which hadn't worked to protect it. Nope, nope, nope.

Lachish sagged and Thema caught her too. I had thought she was uninjured, but I was wrong.

"You are bleeding, you stupid witch," Thema accused. "You have been shot. Sit." She flipped another chair upright and placed Lachish in it, the heartbox in the witch's lap. The vamp cut her fingers this time and placed them at Lachish's mouth. "Drink. And know that I dislike sharing my blood with a fool." She looked at me. "The ambulances are almost here to take the injured to Tulane. This one is not dying immediately, but she will if not taken to a hospital. My blood will help to stabilize her injury and survive the ministrations of the paramedics until a surgeon can get to her."

My newest and most independent vampire not-quite-scions were doing a lot of healing today, something they were not fond of, were not particularly good at, something they had once considered beneath them. Compassion was clearly still not their strongest asset, but I appreciated the efforts despite the sucky bedside manner. Moments later the vamps, including Koun, vanished into the shadows, leaving the non-vamp patients behind.

Human paramedics and firemen made their way into the suddenly too-small room and took over triage and stabilization of the patients, two men working on Eli and two women on Lachish, who refused to let go of the box. No one came toward me, not one person, even though I was clearly wounded, blood clotted in my pelt and all over my detached armor.

Everyone knew who I was. There was no mistaking the Dark Queen in any of my forms. But the medical community had no protocol for me, and I was currently too non-human-shaped for their ministrations. One of the men bent over Eli muttered under his breath, "That one needs a veterinarian."

I laughed, a growly sound, which made the man flinch. I pointed to my ears. "Cat hearing."

"Sorry. Your . . . magister."

Magister. A version of majesty. "Jane is fine," I said, but he didn't look at me again. He was starting an IV on Eli. I met Eli's eyes and he gave me the minuscule battlefield nod, followed by a glance at the door. That meant *I'm good. You should leave.* I nodded back, slung the Benelli around my good shoulder and into the spine holster, and walked out of the room under my own power.

My arm hurt like crazy now that I knew I was really injured, but the wound was closed and mostly what I needed was a shape-change, or a lot of water to rehydrate and time to heal naturally if I intended to stay in this shape. One-handed, I worked my arm back into the armor. The pain from the movements nearly brought on a fainting spell again and left me panting and nauseated. Mostly dressed and using my uninjured hand, I tucked my left hand into a pocket to keep the injured arm steady, and *crap*, that hurt. I wasn't leaking blood, but I wasn't a hundred percent.

When the agony eased, I began a recon. With my cell and my good hand, I took pics of everything I thought might be interesting, wandering the house until I found a kitchen—a chef's dream kitchen—and raided the fridge for fluids. I discovered that witches drank a lot of wine. Like, a *lot* of wine. There were five previously opened bottles of red on the counter and eight open bottles of white in the fridge. In the back of the fridge was a bloated plastic half gallon of old, mostly-cheese whole milk and a gallon of blue Gatorade. I drained the blue stuff, burped softly, and left the empty plastic bottle in the sink, on top of all the stemmed glasses piled there.

This was not a prison like I had expected, though there were closed doors with numeric security locks along the hallways. Feeling better after the blue fluid, I finished my perusal and photo-taking of the null prison's public rooms and wandered back to the hallway where my people were. The paramedics were taking Lachish out on a gurney and I pressed my slender bony hips against the wall to make enough room.

As the women wheeled her away, the witch shoved the heartbox at me, and I caught it one-handed against my belly, nearly dropping my cell. "It can't leave," she said. "Only the null workings are keeping it in stasis."

Except that the null workings were not protected by wards, or even a front door now. A vamp could walk in and take whatever they wanted. I had a feeling if I said that, Lachish would refuse medical help and bleed out. "Okay," I said. "Null. Stasis. Got it."

"Give it to Ailis Rogan." Then she was gone.

Like always, it took a sec for me to put the name together with the person. Ailis Rogan had been one of Katie's Ladies when I first came to NOLA. She went by the name Bliss back then. And she was a witch. And . . . Ailis had once been Lachish's protégé. And Lachish wasn't really in prison as an inmate. "Oh yeah. Right." I tapped my mic. "Alex, is Bliss here?"

"Out front, behind the police crime scene tape. She hasn't been allowed in," he said.

"Okay." Gingerly, I tucked the box under my injured arm and when I caught my breath after the torture eased said, "Will you ask the cops politely if they will please allow one Ailis Rogan inside to take over the workings of the null prison. It's fine by me if you hint that more dangerous prisoners might escape otherwise."

"Copy that," Alex said.

While I waited for diplomacy to work, I continued to wander, this time deliberately, to the long hallways with locked rooms. In one room—thankfully still sealed—I smelled Tau, a crazy witch who had been really hard to take down, and Marlene, her mom, who was nearly as strong and crazy as the daughter. A battering ram had been abandoned in the middle of the hallway and Tau's door looked as if it had been hit several times before the effort had been forsaken.

The next two rooms had busted doors and when I leaned into each, I smelled witch, familiar witch, though I couldn't place them in my memory, and I hadn't been here when they had been imprisoned. It looked as if the occupants had left in a hurry, taking little or nothing. I wasn't even sure if them leaving had been voluntary or kidnapping, but then I didn't know who was missing yet. I stepped over the doorways and the null energies wrapped around me like a frozen woolen shroud. It hurt. *Crap*, it hurt.

I stood just inside the door and breathed, waiting the pain out, and when the pain eased enough to think and move, I snooped through the rooms. They shared a bath. Both of the connecting rooms contained a full-sized bed, craft things—one with a sewing machine and quilting frame, the other with yarn out the wazzoo—clothes in small closets, dinner trays on table-desk combos (partially eaten roast beef and mash with broccoli and a side salad for both missing prisoners), recliners, side tables, and laptops. Cell phones had been left behind too. The TVs in each room were on, one to a gardening show, the other to a news channel.

I gathered all the electronics and slid a pillowcase off a pillow, stuffing the cells and laptops into the improvised carrying case, and knotting the case to my left thigh on my weapon harness. I wouldn't be pulling offhand weapons anytime soon. Carrying the heartbox in the crook of my injured arm hurt with each step, the shift of weight drilling into my nerves. But I could tell the arm was still improving, and I had my uninjured arm free to draw a weapon if needed.

In one bathroom niche was a prescription bottle containing meds for high blood pressure. I took a pic of the bottle, patient name, doctor name, pharmacy info, and texted it to Alex with the word "Research" beneath it. Gratefully, I stepped out of the null energies and into the hallway.

If I hadn't been in such pain, I'd have shaken my pelt

and scrubbed my ears to get rid of the null effects. Instead, I just breathed, leaning my back and the spine-holstered Benelli against the wall.

The other rooms were still locked from the outside, with big modern locks, both digital and mechanical. From inside them I heard TVs, music, or silence. I wondered if the occupants of the silent rooms were leaning ears against their doors, listening. They had to have heard the gunfire and the battering ram.

Upstairs, the layout was nearly the same. The last two doors on the hallway opened opposite each other, and, from them, my Beast-nose recognized two scents. Familiar. Pungent. Fetid. Rank and rotten and all the filth of the world in the stench. Black magic skinwalkers. *U'tlun'ta.* Family. My grandmother, Hayalasti Sixmankiller. Across the hallway I smelled a distant cousin, Ka N'vsita.

A cold slither of fear wormed through me. The doors weren't busted open. They weren't closed either, but open a sliver. I pocketed the cell and drew a vamp-killer.

CHAPTER 5

I Was Not Now, Nor Had I Ever Been, Nice

I pressed a shoulder against the first door and it swung open. Null energies coated everything. Forcing myself to enter, I cleared the first room. Then the second.

The rooms stinking of *u'tlun'ta* were empty.

Holy crap. They weren't after just some witches. They freed the u'tlun'tas. *What the ever-freaking heck could anyone do with insane skinwalkers?*

Jane knew bloodline skinwalkers were here, Beast thought at me. *Jane hid from skinwalker cages.*

She was right. I had been both avoiding and moving toward these rooms from the moment the call for help had come in. And I had worked hard at not thinking much about the skinwalkers imprisoned here, hadn't really believed that they would be taken.

Yeah, I thought at her.

Jane is not afraid. Why did Jane hide?

Relationships are complicated.

Humans are stupid kits, she thought back.

I can't disagree.

I took pics as fast as I could and moved back into the

hallway, putting together what I had seen. There was nothing personal in the last two rooms. No crafts. No books. TVs were off. No mess anywhere. Even their dinner dishes were scraped clean, the utensils placed across the plates. Their closets contained nothing, bathrooms clean and empty. These two rooms were cleaned out. They had known they were leaving. They had packed. Eaten well. Been ready to move out.

On the private channel, I reported my findings to Alex. He was silent for too long before he acknowledged my words, saying, "I got a bad feeling about this, especially with Reach possibly being a part of Mainet's IT team, willing or otherwise."

Because Reach *could* be a captive of the Heir of the Sons of Darkness, Mainet Pellissier, Leo's bloodline creator and master. Or he could be faking being a captive, to give him an out, should we win against the Heir. "Yeah? Why?"

He briefed me—the quick version—on Bliss, the local witch coven politics, the things I hadn't known about Bliss's and Lachish's positions in the coven, and the steps the Roberes had already taken with the U.S. Council of Witches. Half politics, half gossip, but Alex needed to chatter, his nerves and worry over Eli clear beneath his words, but some of it explained why Bliss was here. Listening, I went back to snooping and made sure I had a good feel for the place, sending plenty of pics to Alex, just in case he needed them. Mostly I was waiting for Eli to emerge.

Before he did, Bliss walked down the hallway. The lady of the evening who once fed vamps had become a VIW—very important witch—and Lachish's personal protégé. With Lachish in jail, I had assumed Bliss had fallen out of favor with the New Orleans coven and out of power. Except I had been wrong about a lot of things.

Bliss had nearly vamp-white skin, wore her black hair pulled tightly back in a bun at the base of her neck, and her face could have been carved from vamp flesh, it was so still and emotionless. Where once the witch-in-hiding seemed to slide among the shadows, avoiding notice, now she strode, confident and radiating energy, even surrounded by the null workings.

I almost called her Bliss, but altered her name at the last second. "Ailis. Thank you for coming."

She gave me a tight smile, as if she had seen my mouth make the *B* shape before I altered it to the *A* shape. "Jane," she said, ignoring my change in status, reducing me to what I had been when she first met me. "I spoke to Lachish outside. You have the box?"

Holding my breath against the pain, I hefted the box in front of me. Bounced it a little. Her eyes followed the motion. "I have the heart of the Son of Darkness." I smiled, showing my killing teeth, testing the woman who had been elevated to the high position of Lachish Dutillett's protégé, and—now that I thought about it—likely heir apparent of the NOLA coven. Because Lachish hadn't been demoted at all. She was still in charge. That meant Bliss had a lot of power. A freaking lot of power. I bounced the box again. "The witches were incapable of protecting it."

"It's still here. Therefore we were capable," she said, her tone even and without inflection. She wore a high-collared blouse, tight black skirt, and a matching short jacket with black pumps. Pale makeup included a neutral pink lipstick. A large leather tote rested beneath her arm, the straps over her shoulder. She looked like a businesswoman in total control, a human CEO, unless you could see the energies tightly leashed around her.

With Beast's vision, I could see a lot of what Bliss was now, the energies wrapped around her. After ignoring her magical potential for years, the witch had accepted her gifts, trained hard, had learned to command her magics, and had become much more powerful, all in the course of months instead of the more typical years.

I said, "The wards are totally down. The doors and windows are busted. Some of your prisoners are missing. Witches' guards are dead. Doesn't look very capable to me. This piece of organ meat was my responsibility. Looks like it is again."

She said, "You need a *hedge of thorns* and a sufficient null space to keep it in stasis, and this prison is the only location in NOLA where you have access to strong null energies. How will you keep it safe without wards?"

"I have an army," I said softly. "And a portable null space."

She pursed her lips, her expression speculative, as if thinking through all the potential permutations of this conversation. She said, "I've hired armed guards to patrol the grounds. I've called in backup to restore the wards and add extra layers of protection. Meanwhile, I beseech the Dark Queen of Mithrans for guards at this prison to repel any attackers who might make a second attempt tonight."

That was an excellent move, I thought. *Ask me for help. Nice.*

Witch is good ambush hunter, Beast thought.

I said, "Without the mayor's and NOPD approval, and unless there is further violence against your people, my people can only fight inside the house. Not on the grounds."

"I have spoken to the mayor, the governor, and three leaders of the New Orleans coven," she said. "I have approval from all to protect the grounds. Your Mithrans will be allowed to fight as needed."

"This is a crime scene. Multiple witches are dead. You had to step over them when you entered."

Ailis flinched ever so slightly at the memory, as if I'd poked her with a sharp blade.

"You lost four prisoners," I said, pushing the blade deeper. "Two witch prisoners and . . . two other prisoners." My heart clenched at the thought. Did Bliss know who the skinwalkers were to me? I hadn't personally arranged for them to be imprisoned here. That had been Ayatas FireWind, my bio brother and a big shot in PsyLED. Had he given the witches the relationships and bloodlines when he brought the skinwalkers to them? I had no idea who knew what about the missing prisoners. But usually when there was trouble in NOLA Aya stuck his nose in. It was odd he hadn't called already, wasn't he.

"I would like a dossier of each missing person," I said, "a list of crimes and transcripts of court proceedings—should such transcripts exist—for each missing person, and a breakdown of their abilities and power signatures."

"All pertinent files have been sent to the IT and security department of the Dark Queen." A faint smile softened her harshly beautiful face. "It was nice to talk to Alex again."

As opposed to talking to me, implying this conversation wasn't nice. Okeydokey. Fair, if a little mean. I was not now, nor had I ever been, nice. However, this was a change in how Bliss/Ailis acted to me. Harsh, stiff, a tad bitchy. I wondered if she was being difficult because I had the box and she didn't, or if Lachish had been talking behind my back, poisoning the waters. And if so, why? Or . . . yeah. There had been some hot Bliss/Ailis on Eli dancing at a party not so long ago. Maybe Bliss/Ailis had wanted more and not gotten it and blamed me? Or, worse, they had done the dirty deed, but Eli had pulled away and she blamed me? People were weird so it could be anything, but no way was I asking Eli about his sex life unless I absolutely had to. *Ick.*

Since I didn't quite know what was happening, I let my cat lips curve into a small polite smile, one that hid my fangs, and didn't reply.

"The circle in the street," Ailis continued, "may be a problem. It isn't active, but it isn't dead either. There is some kind of passive, waiting energy involved. I've directed the NOPD to put hazard cones up and police tape around it until the guard-coven is up to checking it out. The ones not dead or injured are down for the count. The wardens expended personal energies defending the wards. They need to spend time in full circles, recharging themselves and their amulets."

I grunted and said the proper phrases I feared might come back to haunt me. "Whatever the NOLA witch council needs from the Dark Queen, whatever is in our power to provide, is yours. Except for this." I rapped on the heartbox.

"The witch council of New Orleans is honored to have the attention of the Dark Queen."

Attention, not assistance. Yeah. A little snark in that last bit. "My people bled to save yours and to save this." I tapped on the heartbox again. "They could have died, along with your witch guards and friends, and this would have been lost. My emissaries will make certain that the witch council is made aware of our sacrifice, and why it was necessary."

Bliss's eyes went wide. "Emissaries?"

"Before you get cheeky with the Dark Queen, you should make sure what diplomatic channels are already open," I said. "The Roberes have been in contact with the USA witch bigwigs. Seems no one in NOLA told them about the Heart of Darkness being in the city, let alone in the prison. And they were also not informed about a vampire attack on the prison, in an attempt to regain said heart, until my emissaries told them. So why don't you take care of your house and I'll take care of mine. And the vamp heart." Again I gave the box a single tap.

"You tell her, Janie," Alex said into my earpieces.

Beast shoved her ability to tamp down pain into me and I twisted my hips, slinging the pillowcase holding the electronics behind my legs. I managed to get my bad arm repositioned on the heartbox, all without showing the agony of the movements. "Just so we're clear," I said, sounding only a little breathless, "I have access to a small portable *hedge of thorns* and several null amulets. I'll keep the heart of the SOD safe until this place is repaired and the wards properly strengthened."

Ailis/Bliss reached out both hands for the box. "But—"

"No buts," I interrupted. "You want to play on my battlefield, you want my people to defend you and yours, then you'll play by my rules and you'll show proper respect to my office, even if you can't show it to me personally."

I turned and walked from the house as Alex said, "Meee-ow."

"Alex, my arm feels like it's being mangled and set on fire all at the same time."

"Roger that. Sending someone to bleed and feed you. Eli's on the way to the ambulance," he added.

I waited at the front door, hearing the gurney and the tramping of loud human feet, feeling my brother-by-choice move as his gurney was pushed along the hallways and into the foyer. His dark eyes found mine instantly, our connection still strong even this long after the battle. He held out one hand and we gripped palms for a moment as he went past, his armor blood splattered, his dark-skinned thigh tightly wrapped in multi-colored sticky wrap. "I'll need surgery," he said, his tone matter-of-fact.

"I'll see that someone new is standing by to donate." I meant a vamp to feed him, and he gave me a curt nod. Every time a human drank vamp blood, they stood at risk of becoming addicted, and every time a human drank from the same vamp, they stood a chance of being rolled by the vamp and becoming a human blood-slave or blood-servant.

Eli had long passed the safe threshold for drinking any vamp blood at all, but without the blood, he would take forever to heal, and rehab might not work this time, not if the injury had damaged the metal nuts and bolts holding his leg bones together. With the blood, he would be healed and in a safe place in a day, two days tops.

That might accelerate his change into whatever he was becoming, but he and I had talked about it several times, and Eli had long ago weighed the consequences of drinking more vamp blood against being permanently maimed. Recently, he had signed the papers to drink, even if it meant accidently being turned. We both knew he was no longer just human.

I released his hand and the paramedics pushed him outside. I tapped my mic. "Alex. Update on my Infermieri?" Infermieri were vamps who could donate forever without making humans into slaves, and whose blood was such a potent healer that a single drop could heal a human from most mortal wounds.

"Negative. I sent a formal request to Lincoln Shaddock and another to Florence herself, asking her to return to NOLA to feed Eli. No reply yet."

Koun came online to the comms, and said, "Have there been attacks on any of the clan homes or the Mithran Council House?"

"Negative," Alex said, "but I do have news about the null prison. Interior and exterior cams are now back online. And, just so you know, Leo Pellissier is standing in the shadows of the banana plants where you and Eli were positioned before the death magic bomb exploded."

"Really," I said, deadpan. Louder, I called out to the paramedics, "Hang on!"

I loped across the tiny yard to the plants, trying not to grunt, gasp, or moan with every step as gravity banged my arm around. I dove into the dead plants and, with my uninjured arm, grabbed Leo's shoulder and shook him. "Get over there and heal Eli."

"Yes, my . . . queen," Leo said. It was a version of the line he used to say: *"Yes, my Jane."* That had been a subjugating and possessive line and I'd hated it. This was better. Or at least I thought it was. With Leo—even thrice-born Leo—I never really knew.

The former master of the city walked slowly across the lawn, in front of the headlights of the ambulances, his legs throwing sharp but graceful shadows. He bent over Eli's gurney, the night obscuring what happened next. Two minutes later, Leo backed away and Eli was loaded into the ambulance. In minutes, it and the other emergency vehicles pulled away, leaving several NOPD cars, the DQ's SUVs, and the avidly watching neighbors.

Leo rejoined me in the dark of the dried-out plants, the big leaves crunching with his movement and with the breeze blowing in off the river. "He will live," Leo said.

I said nothing. I had learned from Leo himself how effective silence was.

Eventually he said, "You are angry that I did not fight beside your people."

Again, I said nothing.

"Angry that I stood by and did not assist." He turned in the dead foliage and said, "Mainet Pellissier is the maker of my bloodline. He named my family. And he is the Heir of the Sons of Darkness." He said it like it was a title. As if he found it terrifying.

"Heard about him. Heir to Sons of Darkness. But I don't know for sure where he came from or how he became the heir to the creators of the suckheads."

Leo smiled faintly at my use of the insulting term. "Mainet Pellissier was originally named Aram Bar Ioudas." He stopped, his black eyes on me, letting me put it together.

I had heard some of those words before. "Bar means son. So, Aram, son of Ioudas," I said. "Ioudas means Judas in Hebrew. Or maybe Aramaic?" The understanding swept

through me. "Judas Iscariot. Iodus Issachar. Aram . . .
There was another brother?"

The channel noise softened, going crisp as Alex opened
a private channel. "What did you say?" he asked. "Repeat
that, Janie."

"Aram Bar Ioudas, son of Judas Iscariot," I said, staring into Leo's eyes. "Son of Ioudas Issachar. We knew
they had a sister they sacrificed in the black magic that
made their kind. But they had other siblings, didn't they?"

"One brother," Leo said. "The youngest child of their
father, the betrayer. Aram was still a child when the Sons
of Darkness attempted to bring Judas Iscariot back from
the dead."

"No," Alex said over my earbuds. "There's no mention
of a baby brother in any of the bloodlines of the Sons of
Darkness. No Heir was ever named. And Mainet Pellissier
appeared in the twelve hundreds."

"'There is always an heir,'" I whispered, repeating something I'd heard once. "An Heir, a secondo Heir, and probably a tertiary Heir. Why didn't I think about that?"

"Only one heir to their power," Leo said. "The Heir,"
he repeated, speaking it like a title, because it was.

Alex swore softly. The sound of keyboard keys being
hit came over the channel. "There was a baby brother?
Maybe the SODs kept him under wraps, in a cave, chained
to the wall or something until they felt he could be used?
And that baby brother chose the name Pellissier?" Alex
demanded. "That baby brother just *happened* to make
Leo's bloodline? There's no such thing as a coincidence,
except—" He stopped, keys clacking harder.

"Wait," Alex said. "The surname Pellissier, and a
dozen other spellings, actually meant fur cloak or armor,
and was worn into battle. And one of the SODs was called
the Flayer of Mithrans, like a military title. Maybe there's
a connection."

I knew Leo could hear Alex. Vamp ears, but I didn't
expect him to answer. Until he did.

"My master chose the name when he escaped from
Rome, where he had indeed been kept in chains, to France.
He chose the name Pellissier to imply to the Mithran world
that he wore the same skin, the same power, the same"—he

twirled his right fingers in the air as if searching for a word—"potential . . . yes, as his brothers. He passed the name to his children of the body, as the way of designating his descendants. Few lived through the blood challenges presented to them. But there were a very few."

Leo cocked his head and held my eyes, his expression imploring and yet demanding. "*Think*, my Jane. Why do you think all the Europeans flocked to New Orleans?" The look on Leo's face said his words were deadly serious. "Why not Buenos Aires, or New York? Or Mexico City? No. They came after me."

Crap. "You're the secondo Heir now. And you didn't tell me. You did not tell me that *very important bit of info*." But it makes all the dang freaking sense in the world. Why NOLA? Why here? Because of Leo and his bloodline. Which meant it was one of the deepest, most closely held secrets in the vamp world.

"These things did not matter until now, my Jane. And also, your Alex had Reach's data bank. I presumed Reach had uncovered this secret long ago."

But . . . in the back of my mind I had known there had to be a reason why Leo Pellissier and the city of New Orleans were so important to the rest of the vamp world. It hadn't been the presence of the SOD in the subbasement of HQ because the vamps kept coming even after there was nothing left of him there.

I had never looked for a reason.

This Heir made Leo's bloodline one of the most important vamp bloodlines in the world. But Leo, keeper of secrets, creator of layers of plans and multiple possible outcomes, was still talking.

"When Joses hung in the basement, and the Flayer of Mithrans was alive, there was a balance of power. Now? There is the Heir, the Heart of Darkness"—he tapped the box under my injured arm, a single soft rap, much as I had done—"and a Dark Queen." He gave a tiny shrug. "I am a young outclan priest, with extremely limited Mithran power and even more limited resources. I cannot fight the Heir and Blood Master of my line unless it is your intent that I die yet again."

"No." I didn't want Leo dead. I didn't want anyone else, anywhere, dead.

"Good." He reached up and traced the central vein of the nearest dead leaf. It was so brittle that it crusted into dust at the touch of his pale fingers, and he caught the dust in his palm. "I do not think even the creator of time, nor his minions, will permit a timeline where I might live a *fourth* time." He extended his hand and let the dust float down, as if seeing his next death there, dust to dust.

I said, "This is no longer your city. No longer your fight. I get it. Fine. My people have been expecting Mainet to arrive. But we didn't know why. And we didn't know that NOLA was a . . . a last stand. But you have to know that you being still alive changes everything about the fight to come."

Mainet had come to the witch prison for more than one reason: two imprisoned witches had been broken out, two *u'tlun'ta* were gone. Two powerful witches, Tau and Marlene, had been intended for rescue but the attackers had to stop their jailbreak. Timing.

They hadn't expected us to show up so soon, or maybe at all. We defended the prison, and two of their targets, the two powerful witches, had been abandoned. And they had failed to get into Lachish's room for the heart. So far as I knew, no one was supposed to know it was here. So how had Mainet known it was being guarded here? Had Leo known as well? Could Mainet read Leo's thoughts? Had Mainet *himself* been here, one of the vamps hiding in the night? And if so, how much control did Mainet have over Leo? If he got his claws and fangs into Leo, could he bind Leo and turn him against us?

Inside me, Beast murmured, *Leo called vampire* master. *Leo is bound to master. Has been bound for moon times. Can only be more bound.*

My cat half was being logical. *Crap. Crappity crap crap crap.* "So if he gets the Heart of Darkness," I said to Leo, "finishes binding *you*, kills me, gets *le breloque*, and all the other magical thingamabobs, he can own the world."

The former master of the city lowered his head, his black hair falling across his face, hiding either a smile or his fangs. From the shadows of his darker-than-midnight hair, Leo said quietly, "He is my master. He is the Heir. You carry the Heart of Darkness.

"The oldest tales speak of the ancient seer who once served the Sons. When her prophecies did not please them, they killed her, but before she died, someone wrote them down. It is said that when the last Dark Queen came, she would destroy the sons of the creator of the Mithrans and Naturaleza. They took great labors to prevent such a thing, yet here you are, and you killed them.

"There is power in that box you carry, unimaginable power. You could have destroyed the heart. Instead you saved it. You gave it to the witches to look after." Gently, he added, "None of the timelines have been stable since that moment."

My entire body tightened. *Timelines* . . . How did Leo know about timelines?

He raised his head, his eyes on the heartbox. "My Jane. Hear me. You must keep the Heart of Darkness safe until you have bound the demon, set the messenger and judge free, and killed the Heir. Only after the Heir is true dead may you destroy it."

My heart did a little jig at the words *demon*, *messenger*, and *judge*, which were all terms used for angels, fallen and not, in ancient writings. Reflexively, I tightened my bad arm around the heartbox. Pain shot from my wound to my spine and brain, and down to my fingers. My breath stopped at the shock.

Leo lifted his black eyes to meet mine. "The Heir and the maker of my line has magics and amulets and powerful beings in his thrall—beings that only Sabina knew were his."

I followed his eyes to the null prison as if seeing the *u'tlun'tas* who had been set free—the *u'tlun'ta* who ate and absorbed Sabina (the outclan priestess), and the *u'tlun'ta* who ate a vamp and the Onorio called the Firestarter. Gramma probably knew all about the powers of the Heir. She and Ka were working with Mainet? Maybe she had been part of his plans, more or less, for centuries, yet with her own agendas, pulling her own strings and hoping to take over. I should have killed her when I had the chance.

"For centuries, when the Sons of Darkness yet ruled, the authority of the Heir was barely seen, little more than threads, delicate, secretive, hidden filaments, glints and glimmers in the darkness, like a spider's web. His influence was no more than gossamer loops and knots, his power invisible until the light landed upon it, just so, or until one was poisoned and trapped within his snare.

"With the death of Joses Santana, the eldest Son of Darkness, he came into much of his power as the secondo Heir. He could not have known about the heart you saved because he did not come to take it from you. He only knew that he was not as powerful as he had hoped."

Leo wasn't guessing at all this. His tone said he *knew* all this. Yeah. Mainet and Leo were connected somehow. Or Leo had a mole in Mainet's camp. That was possible too. Maybe someone in the Heir's IT department? Maybe Reach?

"Mainet, while not as strong as he had hoped, stretched out his hand and sowed discord in Europe, his influence and control reaching across the land, from city to farm, from mountain to swamp, across the ocean from shore to shore. I had feared his power would be uncontrolled, uncontained, except that my Jane, my wild card in all the timelines, had brought love to the empty heart of Edmund." Leo smiled at me, his face too pale, though otherwise looking fully human. "Your Edmund and my Grégoire fought and defeated the followers of the Heir. They broke the back of Mainet's power in Europe before he could take the reins and force his will upon them all, gather an army, and bring war to these shores."

"That sounds like a good thing," I said, my words hesitant as the ambulances left the area, as local cops and city official vehicles changed out shifts. And the coroner's van pulled in.

"Perhaps. But when my Jane killed the Flayer of Mithrans, his power fell upon Mainet. Yet it still was not the full power that should have been his. When he did not attain his complete power, he searched for the reasons and he discovered the existence of the heart you carry. As long as the Heart of Darkness still survives, he cannot achieve his full power."

Suddenly I understood. "I can't beat him if he has his full power, can I? So I have to kill him before I destroy the heart."

"If he attains his full power, he will have twice the strength of either of his brothers. He will be power incarnate."

"Well, crap."

"Indeed. He discovered that the demon and the messenger had been partially bound here, in this city. And so the Heir comes here to take your city and your crown, to fully free the demon and fully bind the messenger. He comes here because here is where his bloodline resides. Already, his power and reach grow at an alarming rate, trapping and using and feeding upon all he has ensnared. When he has the Heart of Darkness, no one will be able to stand against him."

Leo's sclera bled to vamp scarlet and his pupils dilated until they were wide and black. In vamps, this was a sign that they were highly emotional or very hungry. He said, "Because I am no longer master of the city, able to protect the beings who reside here, able to draw on their energy, their collective power, he has come to gather the last amulets of power that my uncle brought with him when we came here. Power that my uncle, and then the outclan priestess Sabina, safeguarded for all these years. And your crown. He will have that as well."

I had Sabina's amulets. "I—"

Leo interrupted, now speaking fast, as if he had a hot date waiting. "His mastery is draining those of his line. He is choking the un-life and undeath from all of his line and storing our life-forces within himself. When Mainet is ready, he will kill those sworn to you, and he will kill you."

Everyone wanted to kill me. No surprise there. But that other stuff was problematic, especially since Edmund, the Emperor of Europe, was coming to NOLA for his coronation, bringing the most powerful vamp warriors to witness his crowning. Like Grégoire. And soon. Grégoire was supposed to be the biggest, baddest fighter of all fangheads in the world, and from what Leo was saying, Mainet could soon have the weapons to take both of them and the Dark Queen over. And worse, all that magical stuff Mainet wanted? It was stored in NOLA. It was stored at my house.

"Holy moly. But, wait. Draining and storing vamp power? As in siphoning life-force power from you?" I glanced at the dead leaves around us as all sorts of terrible probabilities flittered through my mind like ash on the wind. "He's using death magic? And storing it, like in a battery?"

"Yes. Except his *battery*, as you call it, is alive and partially bound to him by ethereal strands of interdimensional power. He requires another being, from the opposite dimension, to complete his seizure of power. And the Heart of Darkness. All in one place."

Angels and demons could hold power in multiple dimensions. *Hayyel.* The angel was partially trapped. Opposite dimensional could mean hell and a demon. Did Mainet have a demon trapped already? "Are you trapped in his web?" I asked. "Are you being drained?"

"Oh, yes, my Jane," he whispered. "Just as are all of my kind who dwell in this city of death. Heed these words, for I will soon be unable to speak to you." He looked at my hip. There was a tiny popping sound and Leo vanished.

CHAPTER 6

Nice Riding, Too. Very Rodeo.

"Crap," I muttered. Louder, I added, "You coulda been less mysterious." Leo didn't answer. Didn't mean he was gone, just meant that if he was still around, he was done being helpful. As usual. But that look at my hip. He had been staring at the pocket holding the Glob, the only magical weapon I fully owned, one that had been made from part of my own body.

Death magics. Demons. Angels. And the Glob. And . . . I had drunk Leo's blood. I wasn't a vamp, but technically I was Leo's scion. Was I being drained? "Alex. You still there?"

"Affirmative," he said softly.

"Is that why I'm having trouble with my shifting? Through the preexisting relationship with Leo, as his Enforcer, so that this Heir, Mainet, is draining me enough to make me lose control?"

"I don't know, Janie."

But Leo had pointedly looked at the pocket holding the Glob. That look had seemed expectant. Purposeful.

As if the Glob might be the only thing standing between me dead and Mainet as king of the world.

Leo had shown me that I had a valuable weapon. More, he had mentioned my crown. As long as I had them and the heart, I stood a chance. My people stood a chance.

Koun appeared far down the street, his armor discarded, his blue-tattooed body mostly naked, a sword unsheathed in one hand, walking toward me up the street. Fully vamped out. I had no idea how he got out of the house. If I hadn't seen him paralyzed with a stake in his belly, I'd never have guessed he had been wounded. His belly was healed now, his body reflecting the red and blue lights of emergency vehicles, his pale hair long and unbound, blowing around him in the swirling river breeze, a veil that rippled like fine silk. He looked exactly what he was—a Celtic warrior, fearless, vicious, death in vampire form.

Along the street, cops turned and placed hands on the butts of their weapons. Two stepped behind engine blocks and aimed over the hoods of cop cars. This was the kind of situation that could go bad in a hurry.

I stepped out of the shadows. Using all that formal mumbo jumbo I had learned, I shouted, "Here stands the Dark Queen. Here walks our Enforcer and Executioner. We seek peace."

The cops looked from the mostly naked Celtic vamp to cat-snouted me and shook their heads. Their body language said, *Only in New Orleans*, but they relaxed, guns went back into holsters, and one of them actually smiled.

I blew out the breath I was holding. Koun glided up to me, his bare legs moving with that vamp grace and elegance I had envied for so long. His expression told me he had news, but with that vamp stillness he habitually wore, I couldn't tell if it was good or bad. My heart stuttered.

Eli's response of panic shocked through me. I sent out thought of, *Wait*, and felt him settle, uneasy, worried.

To Koun I said, "Bruiser?"

"He is well, My Queen."

Eli felt my relief and we both pulled away from that battlefield connection, erecting walls as best we could this close in time to the concluded deadly danger.

Koun held his sword close to one side, and with his other, bloody hand, he covered my mic. Softly, for my ears only, he said, "This attack at the prison had two waves, which Alex's drone cameras discovered. They were moving in, to surprise and decimate us in the quiet after the attack here. Your Consort's team encountered the second wave two blocks away and engaged your enemies. I joined later for the mopping up. Your Consort and I and the teams with him dispatched fourteen Mithrans and incapacitated as many humans. No casualties on our side. The injured are being dealt with.

"Your Consort allowed one Mithran and four humans to escape. I understand that his people carried tracking devices and had tagged the vehicles used by the second wave."

"And?"

"Alex's flying drones are currently attempting to track the escapee's cars. One is heading downtown, but there seems to be a glitch on its tracker. The other disappeared out of range into uptown before the drone could lock on."

I heaved a sigh and tapped my mic. "Alex, I know you heard all that and know all this. Update."

"I have research started, security programs running"— he meant hacking into more cameras, but he didn't say that—"additional drones flying patterns, and, with any luck, the drones will pick up the vehicles. I'll try to have something for you when you get back."

Before I could respond, Koun stepped in front of me and lifted his sword to the sky. It wasn't some symbolic gesture, but a defensive stance. I followed his gaze and saw coils of rainbow lights, the shimmer of frills, pearlescent horns, and the glint of dragon scales. In the night sky I recognized Pearl and Opal, two arcenciels, dancing in flight, fully visible to human eyes.

The cops called in a paranormal sighting. The neighbors turned their attention and cell phones from Koun and me to the night sky. I was sure there would be half a dozen vids of arcenciels flitting and glimmering, which would likely go viral. I clutched the heartbox to me, wondering if this was what the rainbow dragons wanted. Wild guesses were both my forte and my undoing.

Softly I said to Koun, "What now?"

Koun took a breath that he needed only to speak. He raised his head to the sky and called out, "Do the arcenciels seek an audience with the Dark Queen?"

"We are sent by She Who Guards the Rift to request a boon of the Dark Queen."

"The Dark Queen and her Enforcer and Executioner recognize the arcenciels Pearl and Opal," Koun said. "Speak."

I noticed he left out his title of chief strategist of Clan Yellowrock. I guessed that was a lesser title than being the queen's killer.

"She Who Guards the Rift claims *le breloque*," Opal said. "She lays claim to the heart you carry and to the vampire who seeks it. It is her destiny to wear the corona. It is her destiny to devour the heart. It is her destiny to watch the vampire burn in the noonday sun."

She Who Guards the Rift was Soul, the most powerful arcenciel I had ever met. She was also one of the head honchos of the Psychometric Law Enforcement Division of Homeland Security, and my bio brother's direct upline boss. Her natural form was a dragon made of light, but she could shapeshift into a four-hundred-pound tiger and a small, very curvy human. She was scary and she hid her monster tendencies well, which made her even more scary.

To rainbow dragons, the words *claim* and *destiny* meant very different things from what the words meant to humans. Arcenciels could see into the future, timewalk, bubble time, and skip forward and back through time in ways I had never been able to, even back when I was risking death doing that. When arcenciels laid claim to something, it meant that along some specific timeline, they had seen that those items belonged to them. When they used the word *destiny*, it meant many timelines foretold this event. So at some point in the future, Soul could probably be the Dark Queen, eat the heart of the Son of Darkness, kill Mainet Pellissier by letting him burn in the daylight. Unless I got in her way. So . . . maybe? No. Not. That felt wrong, felt like a ploy to avoid some problem that stood between now and some future they wanted.

Unlike my usual flying by the seat of my pants, I hesitated before I responded, because what I was about to say might get me killed if the two young rainbow dragons interpreted my words wrongly. Before I could open my mouth and probably insert my big paws, Bruiser called out, "*Le breloque* cannot be given away, nor claimed by another being."

He walked down the middle of the dark street, his matte black armor throwing off all reflections, making him part of the Mithran darkness in which he had walked all his human life. "The corona chooses to whom it will be bound, and it has chosen Jane Yellowrock. It alone has made her the Dark Queen. Until it releases her, no one else may take her throne and her power."

Bruiser stepped in front of the cop cars' headlights. Behind him, I caught glimpses of the reinforcements he had brought. According to Koun, my Consort and he had been in their own battle, proven by the wide spatters of drying blood across Bruiser's chest and one leg. The blood on his armor suggested that someone had died badly. Because of Alex and Bruiser, the second wave hadn't made it to the house.

My breath caught as Bruiser angled through the cops and cars, his body gliding like a vamp, balanced and purposeful. Bruiser looked mighty dang excellent in his armor, in a tux, in jeans, and naked, can't forget naked. In bloody armor, he looked regal, stepping across the sidewalk and toward us. Yeah. Sex on a stick.

As if he heard my thoughts, Bruiser found me in the shadows and smiled. It was a claiming sweetness, as if his soul thought, *There she is. There's my love.* And I heard his soul inside my own. My heart melted into goo.

Bruiser glanced to the porch of the null prison and abruptly changed course, stopping, bending, and . . . He lifted one arm. In his hand was *le breloque*, the corona, the crown of office the arcenciels wanted, and which I had not brought with me.

Into my earbuds, Alex cursed and a moment later added, "Just saw some fresh doorbell feed. The crown appeared on the front porch when you first went inside and the null energies hid you."

Great. Now it was chasing me down.

"Behold, *le breloque*, which seeks its chosen queen!" Bruiser shouted, all dramatic, holding the crown high, letting the cop car lights reflect off the gold, letting all the civilian cameras and the reporters' cameras get a good look, because there were at least ten reporters and paparazzi on the other side of the police tape.

Gently, Bruiser pressed Koun's sword to the side and stepped behind me. His shadow cast fractals across the ground as he raised the circlet of gold laurel leaves and the gold band it was wedded to over my head. "Behold," he shouted again, lowering the crown on my head.

Le breloque, which was too big for my head, contracted and snapped into place on me. It made an unexpected cracking-grinding sound of hard plastic and rubber breaking. "Ow!" I said, flinching. Bruiser had forgotten to remove my headset and it squealed into my earbuds as the connection was lost. I yanked out the earbuds, a reflex I couldn't stop, despite the fact that I knew it wouldn't happen again. That squeal was *loud*.

The arcenciels dove at me. Their bodies flashed into light and back into solid, mass to energy to mass. Koun's sword slashed through the light. Pearl smacked Koun with her tail. He went flying, leaving behind his sword. Claws raked my head. Scoring deep across my skull. I bellowed.

Opal's claws caught in my hair, tangled in my braid, hooked under the gold rim. Which tightened against her as she back-winged. Lifting me off my feet. Pain pierced through my brain. Radiated through my skull. Zinged like lightning down my spine.

My crown didn't release. And she had her claws under it.

Opal shook me like a cat shakes a rat. My teeth clacked and clattered. My bones rattled and popped. The Benelli fell. Faster than sight, Bruiser grabbed the shotgun out of the air and fired point-blank into the dragon, beneath her wings. The shotgun boomed the world into silence.

Silver flechettes, I thought. *Not iron. Good. No interspecies international incidents.*

Stupid thoughts as the arcenciel snapped me back and forth. Agony shattered through me. My limbs waggled like a rag doll's, boneless. Then bones snapping. Dislocating. The scent of my blood filled the air.

I was hurt. Bad.

In a single glimpse I saw Bruiser firing. Another shake and I saw his arm back, throwing a blade at the dragon. There was blood in my mouth.

I caught a flash-vision of Koun. A second image of him as he leaped upward and landed on the serpentine back, like a bull rider but twenty feet in the air. He stabbed down, his mouth open in a shout.

The silvery, glistening arcenciel blood spilled and splattered over me. Into my eyes. Into my mouth. I tried to spit but just bit my tongue again. Dizziness spun though me.

I had a single rational thought that Opal had dropped me. *Oh crap.*

I hit the ground. Chin first. Stars, entire galaxies rotated through my vision. I had forgotten that about being hit on the head so hard—stars.

The world went black except for the bright points of light.

And then nothing.

I woke in the SUV, Koun trying to feed me from a cut in his wrist and Thema smearing her blood all over my scalp and all over my crown. *Le breloque* still hadn't let go of me and some of the headache I was experiencing had to be from the too-tight crown and the plastic headset that was broken and trapped underneath.

Oh yeah. And Opal's claws.

My stomach roiled. Nauseated. Sick. My tongue felt scalded and there was a horrible taste in my mouth. A burning sensation like I'd sucked on a thousand hot peppers.

Arcenciel blood had been in my mouth. Had I swallowed some? Gotten it in the cuts where I'd bitten my lips and cheek? Was it toxic like their venom? *Crap.* Had one of freaking dragons bitten me? Again?

If so, as usual lately, I hadn't shifted when in danger. *Crappity crap.*

"My Queen. Drink," Koun said, implacable and yet kind. He cupped the back of my head and placed his wrist against my lips, and I sucked it down.

Cold gross blood.

Good vampire blood, Beast thought. *Strong blood.* Before I could stop her, she bit into his wrist, killing teeth lightly piercing his skin.

I swished Koun's blood around in my mouth, letting it heal my tongue and take away the bitter taste of arenciel blood. I tapped his elbow and he twisted his wrist to disengage my killing teeth from his blood supply without tearing his muscle and tendons. "My lady," Koun murmured. "Are you well?" I pointed at my mouth and he held out a glass. A champagne glass he picked up from somewhere in the SUV. This had to be Bruiser's personal vehicle. I spat into it.

Arenciel blood wasn't venom, but I wasn't taking chances with it doing something weird to me. I'd accidently gotten high on Arenciel blood once. Not happening again.

I drank a few sips of his blood, enough that my head cleared, and strength eased through my strained muscles and bones. Pain from being shaken like a bunny in a dog's teeth flowed out of me too. Cold blood was still gross, but it had its place in my diet.

I tried to stretch and knew I wasn't healed yet. Not enough. "I got shaken by an arenciel."

Almost casually, Koun said, "And clawed, and dropped. You dislocated your right shoulder, damaged your left hip, have a lovely pattering of bruisers down your right ribs, visible beneath your pelt. You will not feel your best until you shift."

I grunted. I remembered most of it. I needed to shift, but until I could, I drank vamp blood, which made a world of difference to my pain level.

When Koun's wrist healed on its vampire-own, I pulled back.

"Did they get the heartbox?" My voice sounded vaguely like rusty nails being pulled from a coffin lid.

"No, my lady. I have it here." Koun tapped something that rang with a hollow wooden sound.

I patted the cold flesh of his arm with three fingers. It hurt too much to move my entire hand. "Good work. Nice riding too. Very rodeo. Did you kill the dragon?"

"No, My Queen. I had armored you with a silver-bladed athame on your left calf, in case witch ceremonies were necessary or in case you needed to kill some witch-spawned evil. I borrowed your blade before I tried to ride the dragon."

"Oh. Good for you." I didn't remember wearing a silver-plated blade, but I did remember that riding an arcenciel was considered the best way for anyone to time-walk. "Did you timewalk? And where are the dragons?"

"I remained in current time, astride, until they vanished," Koun said, an odd timbre in his voice, "at which time I fell a very long way to the ground."

"How far did you fall?"

"I would estimate two hundred feet. Or so."

I thought about that for a while as Thema finished healing my scalp, got up, and walked away without a word. I realized that my head was on Koun's bare thigh. Way too close to things I did not need to be close to. I tried to figure out where to put my hands so I could lever myself up, and I couldn't figure out a safe place. Instead, I asked Koun, "Are you broken?"

"Yes, My Queen. I have two broken ankles."

Ouch. Tentative, I asked, "They hurt?"

"Yes, My Queen."

No wonder he was so self-contained and formal sounding. He was in pain. I tilted my head, as a logical question presented itself. "And Thema didn't offer you her blood?"

"No, My Queen." His tone changed. "I believe she is in what the Consort calls 'a snit.' The Consort has called in two Mithrans of Clan Arceneau and a dozen humans have volunteered to feed me. Soon, I will drink my fill, sleep, and be healed. However, before I can deal with my healing, we have another problem."

I grunted again. I felt the car seat under my shoulder and put my other hand on the leather, just there, pushing up. Koun braced me and provided some muscle. "Go on," I said, pleased that I didn't puke on Bruiser's fancy leather car seats or Koun's naked self.

"Your witch believes the circle that damaged the street

is a transport circle. Alex has security camera footage
that seems to support this speculation."

Yeah. I had figured that was likely. I leaned against the
headrest and felt my scalp. Healed. Hair matted and full
of dried blood. It would be a misery to wash it all. And
the stupid crown was still stuck to me. And it hurt. In fact,
I hurt all over, though it was a low-level pain like the flu
or something. Gently, I wiggled to see if I had broken
bones, but it felt like soft-tissue damage, not bones. Everything bent and stretched, for the most part.

"The witches disappeared from the center of the circle, right?" I asked. "Like a vamp goes poof, but this was
more like *Star Trek* teleporter than vampy-ness?"

"Yes. How did you know this?"

Calmly I said, "I went through a transport circle once.
It kinda sucked."

Koun tensed, as if his entire body became a coiled
spring.

I figured he had put two and two together and come up
with fifty-eight. "I doubt the circle in the street is for me.
Chill out, dude. Let's get me a shower, and you some blood
to heal, and go over the footage."

"Chill out, dude," he repeated happily. "As My Queen
desires."

Koun wasn't snarky. No vamp who had lived so long
was snarky in the modern sense, because a bigger, more
powerful vamp would have taken offense at some point
in the centuries and killed him for disrespect. However,
the final short phrase held just a hint of something close
to it. A faint tang of mockery with a haze of . . . affection?
Maybe? He'd lost his pal Helgebert not so long ago, and
had been mourning, so the affection seemed like a good
thing? A sign of healing? I chose to consider the touch of
attitude as a good thing too.

All that white tile in Leo's—now my—personal shower in
HQ made the pale, pinkish, watery blood and the occa-
sional clump of dried, dark-red goo really stand out. The
pounding hot water dissolved the dried blood out of my pelt
and hair, which was especially difficult because the stupid

crown still wouldn't come off and the plastic was still crushed between it and my head. It freaking hurt. But eventually the water ran clear. It took an hour to get clean.

I was grateful that Quint, my lady-in-waiting and personal psychopath bodyguard, wasn't here, or she'd have climbed in with me, taken a scrub brush to my head, muttering curses under her breath about me not taking care of myself and not protecting myself, while she tried to scalp me, abrade my skin off, and get way too personal with her scrubbing. I'd likely hear enough complaints when she got back from her two days off. Quint not being here for a major battle was going to result in either an elaborate tongue lashing or a scathing silence. I looked forward to neither.

Once I was clean, I turned off the hot water and suffered through an icy shower to kill the pain and decrease the swelling and bruising. I hated cold showers. But since anti-inflammatories did little for me, I didn't have much choice.

It took a while to dry off. Pelt that had gotten wet to the skin was hard to dry, and if I didn't get all the water off, I'd smell like stinky wet screamer-cat. Not something I desired. As I applied the hair dryer to my body, I considered the possibility of having a dozen heater-blower units installed to speed things up. There was room in the corner. It could work. It would blow a dozen breakers somewhere in HQ or a transformer out in the street, but it could work.

My hair in a single long plait, I considered the offerings in the closet. Everything was custom made, adjustable for the different shapes my body acquired and was predominately—as Quint put it—"winter attire suitable for the subtropics." Which New Orleans was. There were three slender evening gowns, three dance skirts, a dozen tank tops, black pants, thin-knit long-sleeved tops, and a selection of sweaters and tops to wear over the thinner stuff. There was even a black business suit with slacks, a matching pencil skirt, and a white button-up blouse. Madame Melisende, the vamp couturier I had brought back into fashion (haha), had been busy. There were also two sets of armor and a nice selection of shoes and battle boots, a versatile mix of clothes and armor. Unlike the last time I looked in here for something to wear, everything in the closet was black, scarlet, or gold, matching my color preferences, "Coolio," I said softly.

I pulled out white cotton undies and a super-soft set of black oversized velour sweats, lined in silk, that seemed to slide across my pelt. These particular layers were not something I would have expected to find hanging in any closet filled by the vampire fashion designer, so someone had been talking to her about my pelt.

Two of the pockets were false, leaving space for quick draws of weapons strapped to both thighs, and there were plenty of other pockets for phone, recorder, any comms unit I might be carrying, a key-fob pocket, and an ID and credit card pocket. With pockets left over. I *loved* pockets. Quint had clearly been working with Madam M to refine her designs to my bodily needs, weapons needs, and color choices.

Dressing from the pelt-and-skin out, in clothes I hadn't chosen but that fit perfectly, had become commonplace, and I really liked these sweats. Also, the sweats matched a pair of expandable plushy house shoes, also in black, and they were so comfy. I feared I could get used to this whole "being taken care of" thing, though there was something missing. Weapons. Which I had tossed to the bed pre-shower. They had been bloody and thanks to my stripping in a hurry, there were blood smears on the coverlet. Duvet. Whatever.

I considered the weapons on the bed, and decided the Benelli was overkill for inside HQ, and the semiautomatics were still uncomfortable for my half-form fingers even with exchangeable super-sized grips. There was a time when I'd have cleaned the weapons before I showered, but it hadn't even crossed my mind.

I had . . . *people* for that now. I had servants and minions and scions and I didn't have to dirty my pretty little—huge knobby?—hands cleaning my own guns. I had forgotten my weapons. Once upon a time I *never* forgot. Forgetting my weapons was the difference between life and death. I stared at the bloody mess of the bedspread, blinking, thinking.

Thinking back to what I really was. A rogue-vamp hunter for hire. Yeah. That. That thought grounded me. All this servant stuff? The protocol and pomp and circumstance? I could learn it. I could do it. But that wasn't me. Biker-chick, rogue-vamp hunter, monster killer for hire. That was me.

This queen stuff was weird.

I cleaned off one harness, as well as I could without a good cleaning kit, and felt nearly human once I strapped a vamp-killer over the sweats, to my left thigh. Looking in the mirror, I chuffed a laugh. I wished I had my human face so I could wear lipstick, the one kind of makeup I could reliably apply on my own, but the idea of lipstick on my cat lips was ludicrous. The crown stuck on my head and the up-pointed, rounded puma ears were bad enough.

I turned to leave the room when my eye caught a glimpse of dark gray-blue and black coiled on a pillow, at the head of the bed, heavy enough to dent the pillow deeply. My hindbrain instantly saw a snake, interpreted before my modern brain saw a different pattern. I sniffed. The scents in the room hadn't changed since I entered, though I hadn't noticed the thing when I came in, covered in blood and still talking on a handheld comms unit. I hadn't looked around. Which was stupid and totally outside of both training and instinct.

The thing was heavy, denting the pillow deeply enough that I hadn't seen it. I eased across the room in case it was an ambush, but I caught a scent of gun oil and Eli.

The thing on the pillow was a semiautomatic handgun. From the deep dents, it had been on the pillow awhile. And Eli . . . Eli was in the hospital. So he had put it here some time ago for me to find. Like a present. Tears filled my eyes.

I eased the weapon out of the holster, and placed it on the bed, whispering, "Ohhh. My." If a gun could ever be called *sexy*, this was the gun. It was an HK45 Tactical. The weapon had a large trigger guard and a long grip. It was only a .45, but it would be sufficient for most of my needs. I tilted the weapon and saw that the barrel was threaded for suppressors and had rails for accessories. Lights or lasers. Cool stuff. Eli-approved stuff. Heckler and Koch had a solid name in both military and law enforcement. Plus it was a freaking cool gun. "Hey there, baby. Get a look at you."

Wrapping my hand around the oversized grip, I seated it carefully in my half-form hand, trigger finger on the frame, and released the magazine. The grip fit my knobby fingers and odd-shaped palm, and was heavily crosshatched to make it stay in place when it got sweaty or bloody. The grip was ergonomic, comfy, and easy to hold, and the grip could be changed out for a smaller one for my human-sized hand. I had other weapons with convertible grips but this one was . . . not pretty. It looked . . . effective. Yeah. That.

With my left hand, I pulled back the slide. There was no round in the chamber, not that I'd let that make me any less cautious. People had died for less. I sighted the weapon on the closet doorknob and wished I had requested a gun range be built into one of the unused subbasements. I could still do that. I was the queen. I could have a shooting range if I wanted to. I grinned like a madwoman.

I checked the ammo in the mag. These were silver-lead Radically Invasive Projectiles 2.0, called RIP2 bullets, designed for paras. I hated them. The frangible rounds were designed to fracture into very small pieces after impact, once they were inside flesh, and were like hollow-points on steroids. A single round could utterly destroy a human body cavity. These rounds were a grade above standard human lethal, and the added silver made them lethal to vamps, were-creatures, and any other creature with a silver allergy.

Still. One round into Mainet's belly and he'd be down, laid out for a beheading. My worries about what he might be up to would be gone. *Temptation, thy name is gunfire.*

The magazine snapped into place slick as goose grease and the holster accepted it like a lover. I strapped the thigh-rig on my right side. The straps would crush the velour. Madame Melisende would be ticked. Or maybe not. She might just make me another soft set of sweats that wouldn't crush. That would be nice.

Feeling more like me, I opened the door. Saw three forms. Without thought, I grabbed one by the throat and slammed him into the second one. They both fell. I reached for the third, who stepped back fast, hands up, and disappeared down the hallway.

They were all wearing black with a gold embroidered crown logo on the left side of the chest, over the heart. *My people.* The third one had turned and vanished so fast I might have imagined him. Her. Whoever.

Neither of the two at my feet was breathing. Had I just killed two of my guards? Panic threaded through me. "Holy crap in a bucket," I muttered, and knelt beside them. I took a breath and smelled vamp and my own scent, but also the stink of human, human blood, and sex. Hands shaking, I gripped the jaw of the one on my left and forced open his mouth. Inch-and-a-quarter-long fangs rested against the top of his mouth. The one on my right had fangs a little longer. *Vamps.* Out cold. Not dead humans.

I closed my eyes as relief sang through me like electricity through high-wires.

I hadn't killed anyone.

I gusted out a breath, thinking. I hurt all over from the too-fast, sloppy, defensive moves. The one who had run? I pictured his face. Long-Knife? The not-quite-a-vamp sent to me by Ming of Knoxville. He had turned tail and run, not that I blamed him. Probably scared I'd whack him too. But what had he been doing outside my quarters?

"Hey, Aunt Jane."

Aunt Jane. Adult voice. No immediate attack.

I opened my eyes and looked up from my crouch to see Shiloh Everhart Stone. She was standing with her hands laced together below her waist, shoulders relaxed. No weapons on her. No weapons visible on her. Standing a good twelve feet away. Addressing me as Aunt Jane, not My Queen. That alone made this a social, personal meeting.

Since when did I have to analyze every single freaking thing everyone said to me? Every nuance of expression or tone or body position? Since when had I become so paranoid?

I stood slowly. I towered over Shiloh, but she didn't alter position or scent. She wasn't scared of me. She didn't smell of prey or predator, no more than any witch or vamp did.

The young, witch-bred-vampire had learned to apply

makeup well enough to add years and sophistication to the fifteen years or so she had been when she was forcibly turned by Renee Damours. She was dressed in elegant black pants and a jacket, her blouse the same dark red as her long, straight hair. She carried a haze of witch magics about her, visible in my altered not-quite-human eyesight.

Shiloh had been studying with the outclan priestess, Sabina, before the very ancient vamp had been consumed by an *u'tlun'ta*. Now, oddly, Shiloh's magics were leashed in a way similar to the magics of Ailis/Bliss, the other young witch I had seen tonight. I wondered if they were studying magics together. If they were in a coven together. Were lovers or something. *Aunt Jane.*

Shiloh was my scion. She had sworn to me. She was also the child of Evangelina Everhart, my BFF's sister, the witch I had killed for summoning a demon. Shiloh was tied into my entire history in both New Orleans and Asheville. And in a small way, to the angel Hayyel, who had helped banish the demon. And, therefore, to the mess I was in.

I let a small smile cross my cat face. "Hey, Shiloh." I toed the vamp on the left. "You saw that, I guess."

She chuckled, the sound far too mature for her teenaged looks. "Nice move. I'm sure Alex caught it on the security cam. Those two will take a lot of bloody ribbing for letting their own queen knock them out." She crossed her waist with one arm and propped the other elbow on the hand, the fingers of her raised hand on her chin. She lifted an eyebrow, amusement in her eyes. "Alex says he's sending the vid to Eli in hospital, so his brother can enjoy seeing the results of his sparring with you the moment he comes out of surgery."

I glanced at her ears and saw the earbuds both exactly the same color as her perfect, vamp-white, Irish-gene-gifted flesh. "Update on Eli?"

"The surgeon isn't happy to have a vampire in the surgical suite," Shiloh reported, still amused. "But Kojo convinced him it was okay."

Convinced him, in vamp-speak, meant rolled him and forced him to agree. Kojo had rolled a surgeon and was in a surgical suite. I might have to pay off the surgeon once he came out of the mesmerism.

I said, "Alex, I know you can hear me over Shiloh's mic. You make sure Kojo knows that I'm properly grateful for his blood to heal my brother, but that if the surgeon makes a mistake because of being rolled, I'll hang his head on a pike at the entrance to HQ."

A moment later, Shiloh chuckled. "Alex already threatened Kojo, except he told the vampire you'd hang his skin on the front door."

"Whatever works," I said.

At my feet, the vamp on the left took a breath and groaned. I toed him again. His eyes fluttered and he looked pained.

"Come on, Aunt Jane. I'm your escort to Security."

Escort? I didn't need an escort. I started to object, but sighed instead. I had been shot, been shaken by a dragon, dropped a few feet to the street, dislocated some joints, thought I'd broken some bones, which, considering how much it hurt to breathe deeply, might have been ribs, and I hadn't shifted and healed on my own. I was still sore and aching and bruised, probably the way a rabbit felt after being shaken by a big dog. I remembered thinking a similar analogy when it was happening. My people had seen that happen. They would be edgy for a while. "Sure. Why not?"

CHAPTER 7

So You Got Your Panties in a Twist

Shiloh opened the doors of Security and my eyes found Alex. "Eli?"

"He's good. Out of surgery just now, and in recovery."

"Bruiser?"

Alex's expression went stiff and formal. "Politics. Better him than you. My Queen."

Because I have a big mouth and am known for hitting first and—maybe—being nice later. Right. I blew out a worried breath and took in the room. The main security room was packed with people: Alex to the left with a couple dozen security cams on his personal central monitor, many of the same views up on the even bigger monitors overhead, the stench of scorched coffee coming from the coffeemaker, a lot of chairs around a huge table in the middle of the room with food boxes in its center—Krispy Kreme donuts, pizza boxes from two different restaurants, and a platter of boudin that had been grilled, sliced into blackened two-inch lengths, circled with cheese and crackers and fresh fruit. I ignored everything but the meat, pulling the platter closer and eating several pieces, which were unfortunately cold, before I tuned in to the activities. Or maybe it was the name that tore my concentration from meat and spices to the conversations around me.

"Who is Bruiser having to deal with?" I asked.

"Clan Arceneau. Grégoire's clan," Alex said without turning around. Without the proper fancy deferential mumbo-jumbo.

I felt the surprise in some of the vamps at his lack of kowtowing. I felt the speculation that I wasn't strong, dominant, capable of ruling. I remembered the fact that Kojo and Thema said I was too *laissez-faire* for a vamp royal. I tried to figure out what I'd need to do to keep the lines drawn, to keep respect from the vamps and yet keep me as me, accessible and not a horrible person. There had to be a way other than cutting off heads.

I took my seat, my back to the coffeemaker and the solid wall there, and popped another length of charred boudin into my mouth and mushed the spicy food around while I considered my conundrum. Boudin was basically heavily spiced ground-up meat and didn't need my killing teeth at all. This one was crawfish-based and had no rice filler, and my salivary glands practically moaned with delight. So freaking good.

I swallowed and took a drink from the water bottle that had appeared, almost magically, at my side. I showed my teeth. "Start at the beginning, Alex Younger. Little brother. Head of Communications for Yellowrock Securities, for Clan Yellowrock, for the Master of the City, and for the Dark Queen," I said, naming his titles. Reminding the vamps present who he was to me and what power he wielded.

Alex's head jerked up and around. He took in the room before he met my eyes, his already knowing, because we had talked about the line I walked with the older vamps. He knew how hard I worked at being accessible and still keeping the vamps in their places, subservient to me and therefore forced to follow my rules and the new vamp laws in the Vampira Carta of the Americas. "My Queen," he said, the words sharp, but a hint of laughter in his eyes. "Forgive me."

I inclined my head, all regal-like. "Put up the photos of my kills before I became what I am today."

Alex managed to hold in his grin. With the push of a button, a series of heads—heads without bodies—appeared on the screens. There were quite a lot of them.

To the vamps who had reacted to Alex's lack of subservience, and now probably to my lack of table manners, I said, "I am the Dark Queen. I'm also a really good fighter. That head in the middle there?" I pointed. "That's de Allyon. He used to be the MOC of Atlanta. I cut off his head after I chewed off his assassin's head with my teeth." I grinned to show them off, wondering if I had meat stuck in them. "Okay, Alex. Let's view the prison attack."

"Yes, My Queen. Missing from the null prison are two lower-level witches and two of your *Tsalagi* clanswomen."

"Tell me about the witches."

"A low-power mother-daughter team who called themselves Butterfly Lily and Feather Storm."

The names were instantly recognizable. Most witches didn't go for the sixties' Sex, Drugs, and Rock and Roll names. The true honor was to have been named with a known witch clan—like Everhart. Women with a little power but born outside of a clan sometimes named themselves, like the very low-power witches Butterfly and Feather.

I didn't know why they might be in witch jail. The two were weak, mostly powerless, but helpful and sweet. I liked them.

When Rick, my former boyfriend, went furry the first full moon after he was bitten by a were-creature, they had tried to help him control his magics. They hadn't succeeded, and since then, had clearly gotten themselves in trouble with the witch council, enough to be in lockup for a while.

I owed them a boon for trying to help Rick. It was my job, therefore, to rescue them.

"Well, crap," I muttered. Louder I asked, "Why them? They don't have enough power to interest another witch, let alone a vamp putting a coup together." I remembered the medication in the cell at witch-null central. "They aren't powerful enough to make their own healing potions or amulets. They don't have enough power to do anything illegal. There were witches with a lot more power in that prison." I remembered Tau, the witch and dis-Onorio, or *senza onore*—a dark Onorio, and others I'd fought and beaten since I came to NOLA.

Taking them didn't make sense, unless the attackers didn't know which prison room each witch was in, which would mean they had less-detailed data than we had thought. Or, maybe they were more interested in getting the heartbox and abandoned the witches to help the team trying to take out Eli. I shared all my thoughts with Alex.

"Don't know what they knew about the jail part, My Queen," Alex said. "As to the reason why someone might take weak witches and not stronger ones, I took the liberty of calling an Everhart."

By his tone, I knew he meant Liz, Eli's girlfriend. Liz and I weren't besties, but we were getting along better. We had even hit Café du Monde for beignets and coffee and a convo one day a week or so ago before she flew back home to Asheville. I wasn't a girly girl, not one to "do lunch" or "do coffee" with anyone not in my little circle of friends, but I had decided I needed to make an effort with Eli's girlfriend, especially as she might be long-term, but also because she was Molly's and I claimed Molly as one of mine.

The two hours at Café du Monde had flown by and cleared the air between us. We had laughed a lot, something I didn't do enough.

"She called her sisters," Alex said. "They think the bad guys were snagging the witches as a twofer while they were grabbing your clanswomen and going for the box and maybe had to abandon it when Eli set up a serious defense. The witches, even the weaker ones, could be used for the transport circle. Apparently, they might need weak witches at the home base working like conduits to funnel their life-force through as a power source. Or maybe they were taken as bait because they're yours. Or maybe they thought Tau and the other stronger witches would be hard to control, so they took the weak ones first. Or some combination of all that."

I knew about circles. I'd survived some doozies. That gave me possibilities my people might not think about. Plus, I had seen weak witches used in a time-circle in Natchez, and another time-circle in Asheville. Being in that kind of circle as a conduit could be lethal. Weaker witches were half buried alive in a circle, their magics used to link between stronger witches, their own life-force used to power the working as they slowly died and were absorbed by the ground and the power-drain. *Dang.*

I swiveled my chair and ate more cold meat. "And the *Tsalagi*?" My clanswomen had been aligned with Mainet's people. They were in jail as much for that as for eating people, going *u'tlun'ta*. They had stolen the bodies, memories, and power that belonged to others. We had thought the skinwalkers would be safe and protected there, behind witch wards, but they had apparently just walked out, their doors not damaged, simply opened, allowing them to walk free. That settled inside me. "The attacking witches have someone on the inside. Or had."

"Past tense, My Queen," one of the human guards said. I whirled my chair around and saw Blue Voodoo standing honor guard behind me. I nodded for him to continue. "One of the witches killed in the attack had used her prison guard ID card and her passcode to open the doors."

I spun back around to the table and screens overhead. "Interesting. They used her and then they killed her because she was a loose end. Bad for her, but good to know how they operate. That way if any of the people who are sworn to me have secretly changed sides, they can know what the so-called Heir does to his people."

There wasn't a flicker of response in the room, but I knew my words would get around. It was a nice warning, but maybe I needed to make it clearer.

I added, "Upon my honor and my crown. Anyone who is getting pressure to join up with the unwelcome visitors, the cowards who fled from Europe and Edmund and Grégoire, can come to me for help in escaping their influence. I don't kill people who are loyal to me or who come to me when they get in trouble."

I sent my eyes to Alex. "Any update on the *u'tlun'tas*?"

"Negative," Alex said, his own greenish-brown eyes calculating, watching the room.

I thought about the armor in my closet and what weapons I had in HQ, to do all the things I might need to do.

A pop of air blew past my face. Everything happened fast.

Thema was suddenly standing inches in front of me.

Her eyes were vamped-out, black pupils the size of dimes in scarlet sclera.

Her mouth opened, jaw unhinged. Her fangs snapped down. Big-assed fangs.

My feet shoved me away from her. Instinct. Rolling out of the chair. But reacting, not acting. My left hand landed on the vamp-killer strapped to my left thigh. Right shoulder to the floor with a crunch, legs slinging over my head. Pain sang through my joints and ribs like the roar of wildfire. Right hand went numb, missing the new gun. My vamp-killer clattered away.

My guards' weapons *schnick*ed and clicked and aimed at Thema.

"Hold!" I shouted.

A little slow, a lot stiff, I rolled to my feet. Stepped to the right. Picking up the knife. Pulling the H&K.

Though she reeked of fury, Thema hadn't attacked. "Hold your fire."

"My *Queen*," Thema said, only slightly strangling on the title. We'd made a lot of progress in the last weeks on her position in my clan, but the queen part was still hard for her to swallow. "I am your Consort's *messenger*."

My growl stuttered. Stopped. I hadn't even noticed I was growling, but the vibration still rumbled in my chest, like an echo of threat. Beast's golden eyes glared back at me, reflected from Thema's black ones. Behind me, the room had gone still as death, the stink of threat and attack strong on the air. There were weapons of all sorts aimed at Thema. She ignored them.

Thema didn't look angry. Or hungry. She looked . . . insulted?

Ho-ly crap. "So you got your panties in a twist because the Consort asked you to deliver a message."

Softly, she said, "Your Consort has requested that you await him here, and not go—and I quote—'traipsing back to the null prison and attempt to go through the transport circle alone'—end quote. And I am no *messenger boy*," she finished, her words a hiss of insult.

Bruiser had given her a job to do that she felt was beneath her. On purpose. Interesting.

Calmly, I said, "Messages are delivered by whomever is available. And whomever has no other job. By your own choice, you and Kojo have been predominantly fighters. There is no current fight. Therefore you are put to work as we need you." I dismissed her by turning my back. "Alex. Update on the circle."

His eyes were too big, but he answered calmly enough. "Liz and the other Everharts suggested that taking the people they did might be a trap, and that was the reason those specific witches—weak ones—were taken. Because you would care, and they could use the witches as hostages to make you more compliant. Ditto on the skinwalkers. Which means they have a really in-depth dossier on you."

Yeah. To know about the witches trying to help Rick, and then the circles they had participated in, all the good and bad. Intel. Really good intel. Tilting my head to Thema, I said, "The Everharts. Are they safe?"

Thema moved her eyes around the room and took note of all the weapons aimed her way. Including mine. She looked . . . *discombobulated* was the right word.

Her eyes bled back to human, her jaw unhinged in that snakelike thing the older vamps do. Her oversized fangs clicked back into the roof of her mouth. She ducked her head in what almost looked like respect. "According to your Consort, they are, My Queen."

"They've beefed up their defenses," Alex said. "Lincoln Shaddock sent guards to protect Bedelia and her mom at their house. They're as safe as we can make them, as spread out in the mountains as they are. I contacted PsyLED SE, and informed them of the threat. Got a polite, 'Thank you for the info,' but no quid-pro-quo info in reply."

I frowned at that. I hadn't heard from my bio brother

nor from my ex-boyfriend, both of whom worked out of the Tennessee PsyLED office. There had been a violent attack in the middle of the street and at the witch prison, and PsyLED hadn't contacted my office? The two nosy-bodies hadn't called? Hadn't shown up?

Littermate in danger? Beast asked.

I didn't know.

The golden gleam of Beast's presence in my brain faded, and the normal amber of my human irises reflected back from Thema's eyes.

I shoved my own weapons back into their sheath and holster. Without taking my eyes from my unlikely not-quite-scion, I said, "Weapons down."

My people put away their weapons, but they didn't look happy about it.

I rolled my right shoulder and things popped inside me. Some of the pressure eased. "I'm the only one here who's been through a transport circle. It sucked. If the open witch circle is a lure and an ambush, with some kind of reversed *hedge of thorns* working at the other end, it would be an excellent trap. But if I had been planning to go through it, I wasn't going alone. I was taking help." *Liar, liar,* I thought. I would have totally gone alone, without even thinking about it.

Alex snorted delicately.

Thema slipped to the side and lifted my chair upright. Turned it so I could sit easily. "My Queen," she said gently.

I sat. The weapons around the room had been holstered, but I knew all the eyes would remain on Thema. For a warrior, she had miscalculated gravely, giving in to temper and perceived insult.

To my side, the door opened, and Deon entered, pushing a tea trolley laden with trays and those round metal tops that keep food warm. The smell of boudin and spices and fat and grease flooded the room.

I swiveled in my chair and watched the small man. Deon was dressed conservatively, for him, in a red, skin-tight catsuit and a chef's short white jacket. He shoved the trays already on the table to the far side, saying, "Old and cold. Good enough for the help but not the queen."

Someone nearby snorted in amusement.

Deon placed three trays on the table in a nice semicircle in front of me and removed the tops. One tray had salmon tartare on toast points topped by leaking egg yolks and caviar, another held broiled or roasted crawfish boudin and fried pork boudin balls, the balls still sizzling with hot oil, and the third was decorated with fancy sliced breads, several spreads and dips, and sliced cheeses. No fruits, no veggies.

Deon nestled a pot of tea into several cozies near my left side and a tea mug to the right printed with the words, "If Queenie Ain't Happy, Ain't Nobody Happy." He stepped back and studied the placement of the trays, nodded, and leaned into me. He kissed the top of my head. Tears flashed into my eyes at the kind gesture. Blinking away the tears, my eyes followed him as he left, sashaying once to make the glittery words on his butt sparkle. They said, "I'm the Queen's Bitch."

I laughed and relaxed, catching a whiff of satisfaction from Deon as the door closed. He knew me and he knew just how to disarm me. His method was similar to the way I used to disarm Leo—the unexpected, the not-respectful, the fun. Deon made HQ a lot less boring and he had a knack of doing just enough to show he wasn't dissing my position but showing love.

I popped a boudin ball in my mouth and it was still sizzling, hot enough to blister my tongue. I breathed in and out to cool it, and when I could stand the temp, I crunched down. The flavor was amazing and seafoody and greasy. Perfect. I looked around the room. It was still too quiet. My growl must have been something new in a place where new stuff always meant problems and trouble. I swallowed and asked Alex, "Do you have the neighbors' cell phone vids queued up?" Because no way had he not obtained copies of every security video tied into every doorbell camera and every cell phone Wi-Fi system from the houses around the null prison.

"Center screen," the Kid said calmly, as if violence hadn't nearly happened, and the food hadn't been delivered. He was turning into a mini Eli, except Alex's main arsenal was electronic and program based.

I ate crunchy boudin and raw salmon on toast with drippy, nearly raw eggs and salty-slimy fish eggs, and piles of cheese. It was a messy little bit of heaven as I watched the scenes on four screens above the table, scenes that shook and tilted weirdly, and moved from the witch circle to visions of me in the bushes to shots of the front of the null prison, as Alex arranged them in order and replayed the pertinent ones.

The salmon tartare was wonderful on top of some kind of bread made in a swirl, soaking up the egg yolk. The tea was hot and dark and had been brewed just a hair too long, giving it an edge of bitterness. No cream. No sweetener. The bitter note paired perfectly with the raw meat and sloppy egg and the bread and the scenes on the screens where none of my people died.

When my plates were mostly empty and we had seen all the footage, I said, "Show me just the footage of the abductions. And if you can line up the time stamps, that would be nice."

Alex made a "Mmmm" sound. Keys clacked. The scenes all started at the same moment, when a female vamp raced from the front door of the witch null prison, dragging two women behind her. She raced to the circle and threw the women at the witches inside. Butterfly Lily and Feather Storm were shoved across the boundaries of the circle.

"Again," I said. We watched the replay and I asked, "Did the circle fall or did Butterfly Lily and Feather Storm pass through the working without it exploding?"

"Unknown," Alex said, sounding like his warrior brother and not the kid I had first met. "According to Liz, if the witches had bio material, a circle can be calibrated to allow anyone to pass through, including the two kidnapped witches."

Biological material meant fingernail clippings with some skin attached, hair with a root attached, and anything a woman might flush. "Check finances of every person who's had access to the prison or the prison's garbage. We might still have someone inside. And for that matter, the dead witch might be a plant to hide the identity of the real traitor, who stole the dead guard's ID and security number and then sent her to die."

"On it already. Program's running in the background and I got Bodat working on it from home. So far nothing."

Bodat was his stinky gamer friend, a computer-nerd-gaming-geek who now worked for the U.S. government tracking and busting Russian and Chinese programs built to destroy the power grid and interfere with various intelligence communities. Bodat was now a VIP to the government.

"Also check with the city and see if anything has been going on with the rainwater runoff system or the sewage system in the area." Because they could have used one of them to transport through.

Alex made a sound like, "Huh," as if that was a good idea and he was reading my mind on the reasons why I suggested it. "Yes, My Queen."

"Okay," I said. "Next up."

The center overhead screen lit with two vamps walking behind two women. I expected it to be Grandmother and Ka; instead it was Sabina and a redheaded vamp. The vamps in the room inhaled in shock.

Someone to my side whispered, "She's alive . . ."

Sabina looked around and stared into the camera. And she smiled. Except it wasn't Sabina's own cold smile, it was hard and heated and a little bit crazy. Her eyes tracked to the side and she smiled again. And again. She was seeing the humans in their windows with their cell phones and she was grinning at them, making sure she was on camera everywhere, and that the vid would make it back to me. To my people.

And this right here was the main show.

Almost as bad was the redheaded vamp, standing beside Sabina/Gramma. She was familiar. Alex had run a facial rec and discovered her name was—or had been, before she was eaten alive by Ka—Gertrude Grun, a vamp who once was in the household of one of the Sons of Darkness, Joses Santana. Gertrude had been a powerful vamp, and she too had been eaten alive in a black magic ceremony by an *u'tlun'ta* who now had the ability to shift shape and look just like her. And on top of being an *u'tlun'ta*, Ka had also been bitten by an arcenciel, the venom of which had been known to make the bitten nutso.

Two *u'tlun'ta*, both of whom had eaten powerful vamps, working with the bad guys.

"She isn't wearing her white robes," Shiloh said. "Sabina would never wear jeans."

"That is not Sabina," I said calmly. "*That* is a glamour. Look at the smile. It is *not* Sabina."

The vamps exhaled. They might not be totally convinced, but the ones who knew the priestess personally would be. Word would spread to combat the gossip I could practically hear already. Gossip that said Sabina was still alive instead of eaten and taken over by an *u'tlun'ta*.

"If you see Sabina, do not approach," I said. "Do not let her get close to you. Call the sighting in to HQ and stay away. Koun?"

"My Queen," Koun said.

I had smelled him, but not searched the room for him. "I need two special units assigned with equipment and gear, ready at all times, to take down those two women. Heavy on the null sticks and personal anti-magic protective armor."

"Yes, My Queen."

"Alex, when you notified PsyLED, was Ayatas FireWind informed about the identities of the escapees?"

"I requested he be so informed," Alex said.

"Mmmm." That meant exactly nothing. Aya might not know Gramma was loose and wreaking havoc. "Lemme see any good shots you have of the vampires who attacked the prison."

On the main screen appeared still shots of the vamps, ones who were likely in supporting roles. Shots taken before the null prison was breached and we killed some of them.

In the center, a larger still shot appeared. The guy in charge of this attack. Leo hadn't specified that this was Mainet, but dollars to donuts it was. So far as we knew, there were no pics or portraits of Mainet. This guy wasn't pretty, like most fangheads, turned because they had caught the sexual interest of some vamp, but just average looking, which meant he'd had another kind of value to whomever turned him. If this was Mainet, then the importance would have been his bloodline, matching his brothers, the Sons of Darkness.

He was short with beefy shoulders and muscular thighs. Olive skin, black hair, dark eyes. His hair was long and braided out of his way. His face reminded me of a plainer version of Leo, and not just the hauteur and regal arrogance, but his actual face. His chin was Leo's chin. The width and depth of his brow was Leo's. The shape of his hairline—Leo's. The totality was all just a little plainer, the features a little less sharp. But that family resemblance was there—human genetic family resemblance.

"Okay," I murmured. I ate some cooled boudin balls while I studied the others, committing them to memory. "Names and dossiers to my computer when you get them. I also want to see everything you obtained from security cams from inside the prison."

"There's not much. The system went down when the outer ward was taken down. Up on screen," Alex said.

He was right. There wasn't much. Watching useless video footage, I caught the scent of papyrus, black pepper, and that unidentified, unrelated, something new I had smelled before. He was in the room with us. I hadn't seen him enter, hadn't smelled him until now. I followed the scent to the corner of the room. There was nothing there.

I didn't see Leo standing there, silent, watching everything, but I knew he was there. My body clenched for battle. Beast shoved adrenaline and skinwalker fight-or-flight chemicals into my bloodstream.

I heard a faint click as an unseen pair of fangs *schnick*ed down.

CHAPTER 8

I Knew Better Than to Get My Skin Anywhere Near His Fangs

There was no pop of air.

No attack.

I thought back to the last two times someone had come through the door. Thema and her theatrics and emotional reaction to being ordered around. After her, Deon had entered, preceded by an air blast full of spicy food. Leo came in then. Must have. The smell of the food and vamp emotions had overpowered Leo's familiar yet new scent.

"Video off," I said. The screens stopped, then went black. Every eye in the room turned to me and I knew I needed to do or say something lavish and political—preferably before Leo made himself known or someone else smelled and identified him—but I had no idea what.

"Alex, room cameras on, please."

The Kid whirled, met my eyes, and punched a key on one of the keyboards. He searched the room electronically and with his eyes. Leo had chosen a spot where Alex's cams, even the ones that could detect beneath an *obfuscation* working, couldn't spot him, maybe in front of the weapons cabinet. Frustrated, Alex shoved back to his desk and punched keys, searching through camera views. The vamps and humans were confused, looking from Alex to me.

Alex whirled his chair again and pointed a finger that suggested I was right about where Leo hid, behind a witches' *obfuscation* working. Listening in? Planning an attack? Planning a practical joke? Leo didn't joke. But he did play games.

No one else's fangs were down. Leo hadn't attacked.

Softly, I said, "The Dark Queen recognizes and honors . . ." Not *our guest*. This used to be his HQ. He had titles out the wazoo. I needed something better. Something fancier, but nothing came to me. I settled on, "the clan Blood Master, Mithran, and outclan priest, Leo Pellissier."

"Ah, my Jane," he said, just as quietly. Leo suddenly appeared, just about where my nose had suggested he stood.

The sounds of shifting bodies and soft gasps were suddenly loud in the emotionally charged room as the vamps and humans found and focused on Leo. In the aftermath of the shock, the room fell oddly quiet. I met Leo's eyes in the shadows. He looked vaguely amused. He was also fully vamped-out. I hadn't noticed in the dark of the null prison attack, but his hair was longer, a little straighter, curling only slightly at the ends. His suit was severe, his black shirt of fine cotton or linen, not the silk he used to favor. The little white priest's collar he wore threw me again, despite the certainty that he wasn't the vamp he had been before he died the second time.

"Forgive my unannounced entrance, My Queen," Leo said, bowing slightly, that pretty hair flowing forward and back. "I present myself to the Dark Queen and the Master of the City of New Orleans, in your place of power, unarmed, as is customary among visiting Mithrans."

Leo Pellissier, former MOC of NOLA and most of the United States, had just acknowledged and recognized not only me, but also the power he had arranged for me to wield, and he'd laid no claim to anything or anyone, not even his own clan and bloodline.

Knowing that everything we said and did would be interpreted and reviewed by vamps for decades, if not forever, I stood and walked around the table to Leo's corner. His irises were so dark they had always looked black, even when not vamped-out. His skin was whiter than I had ever seen it, bloodless, the result of either his healing or the *fame vexatum*, the enforced hunger that Mithrans, and especially the outclan, practiced, to build their psychic powers, as opposed to the drink-'em-till-they-die Naturaleza. His expression was grave (the thought of which almost made me laugh), and when he met my eyes, he made no attempt to roll me or take me over. There were no feeding or sexual undertones to his gaze. It was just . . . nice.

"We are graced with the presence of the former master of the city," I said, using the royal *we*. "May we offer you refreshment?" I asked. "Both human and Mithran would consider it an honor to feed the thrice born. Or if you want"—I let a small smile crease my muzzle, not exposing my fangs, which would be a sign of aggression to a vamp—"some boudin balls," I finished. Vamps didn't eat much in the way of food that might feed a human, and never boudin balls. Like, not ever. My eyebrows went up as I gestured to the greasy, nearly empty tray again.

Leo returned my smile and chuckled, his fangs still down and his eyes still vamped.

A second wave of shock swept through me. Vampires couldn't laugh and be vamped-out at the same time. It wasn't possible.

Except for thrice-born Leo Pellissier.

Even Katie Fonteneau, also a thrice born, but in no way a priest or priestess, hadn't been able to vamp-out and laugh. So far as I knew he was the only one. And I didn't know if that was a good thing or a very bad one.

"Sooo," I said into the silence. "Boudin with extra hot sauce and a chaser of beer?" I'd sorta tricked Leo into eating super-hot sauce once and his reaction had been less than happy.

His expression telling me he remembered the event, Leo shook his head and said softly, "Only you, my Jane." Louder, he said, "I would be honored to listen to the security update. My Grégoire and your Edmund are returning soon, to my—your city."

I studied Leo as I considered his request. Grégoire was my Warlord and had once been one of Leo's lovers and his best friend. Blondie hadn't come home when Leo rose from the dead. So far as I knew, they hadn't seen each other, and I thought my warlord would have come home to see his lover. Ed hadn't been back either. They were still in Europe, until the coronation, the night I formally crowned Edmund Emperor of Europe. Like, soon. Real soon.

Between Grégoire and Edmund, the NOLA vamps had killed every European suckhead opposed to Edmund's ascension to every fanghead throne of Europe. Those beheaded vamps were also the ones who might have opposed my ascension to Dark Queen. Two birds, one war, a cleansing set up by the now-outclan vamped-out priest standing in my security room. Before he died the second time.

Leo had made sure Edmund was bound to me, was my primo, was also acting Emperor of Europe, and I was master of Clan Yellowrock and MOC of NOLA. Convoluted, layered, twisted, braided, and complex as possible. And weirdly, Katie hadn't come home either. None of Leo's closest lovers and political cadre had come to visit. Part of Leo's layered plans? If so, it was a political situation that gave all the advantage to me, Leo's wild card who, sadly, knew next to nothing about politics.

Of course, I did have access to other forces: arcenciels—some of whom didn't want me dead on sight—an angel-blessed werewolf, three Onorios, powerful witches, possibly Gee DiMercy, though he was less certain, and others, as well as the aforementioned werewolf-blessing angel, Hayyel. Not that any of them were bound to help me, and the angel might be in trouble. There was always that.

"Have you talked to Grégoire?" I asked. Because the

last time I saw him, Blondie had been homicidal and probably suicidal from the loss of his life in NOLA, the banishment of Katie (Leo's other favorite lover) to Atlanta, and the death of Leo. Leo was back but he was not Grégoire's Leo. Leo was a changed vamp.

I had to wonder if the diminutive blond swordsman knew that. Would Leo's changed personality and status turn Blondie into a danger to himself and non-enemy others? Did Grégoire have a new love? What was his emotional state? Would he flip out when he came back to face NOLA and all the changes he had left behind? I had no idea if there was a way to find another Anzu, one who could stay by his side to help keep him sane. If Grégoire came back, would he try to kill me?

Yeah. That. Probably. I needed a spreadsheet to keep things straight, but I didn't say so out loud. Some eager-to-please vamp would gift me with a thousand-page spreadsheet with footnotes and links to other stuff. *Gah!*

"No," Leo said. "We have not spoken." He smiled. "I do not have a cell phone." Which might have been a joke of sorts? Two older vamps in the room chuckled.

One of Grégoire's many titles was the Blood Master of France, a position he had claimed after Grégoire killed all other contenders. Would Blondie even show up here for the coronation or would he stay in France? Was he avoiding Leo? That could be bad. We had made all our plans with the assumption that Grégoire would come back with Edmund, but nothing was certain yet.

When I officially crowned Edmund, his new, formalized position would cement peace and allow Edmund to recognize the current MOCs he had endorsed across Europe, vamps who had allied with him, and to appoint newer ones in the cities that no longer had a master, bringing an end to any lingering vamp war there. But if Edmund died on the way here, or died here, or on the way back, everything Leo had created and planned would go up in smoke. And the war Grégoire and Ed had stopped cold, by killing all the Naturaleza enemy leaders of said war, would revive. There would be no stopping it as young, less powerful vamps duked it out and set themselves up as warring kings of every small town and city.

And the European humans would go to war as they almost had before Edmund forced peace on the vamps there.

Except the peace there had sent all fighting enemy vamps west, to the Americas, and their leader now had an ongoing alliance with three witches, two liver-eaters, and a bunch of fangheads and humans who wanted territory and power. All in the middle of a coronation and plans and constantly evolving security measures.

And Eli wasn't here. He was in hospital. Eli, who was managing the ongoing plans and security measures, including the fact that Edmund and his entourage had been intended to stay in the old Rousseau Clan Home, now the Yellowrock Clan Home.

On second thought, a spreadsheet could actually be handy.

I hoped Eli and Bruiser had already figured out where Edmund and his people were staying and where Blondie and his entire clan were staying. The Arceneau Clan Home had been rebuilt after the fire, while Blondie was in Europe, but wasn't fully furnished yet. Therefore— Grégoire would be staying . . . anywhere he wanted. He was the silver-backed gorilla in the room, the one from the old joke, who sat anywhere he wanted.

The silence had gone on too long. I could smell the human sweat and the suckhead aggression starting to build in the room. "The Dark Queen is honored. If the outclan priest has advice to offer, it would be most appreciated." I gestured to the place beside me at the table. "If the outclan priest would join us?"

Leo gave a small bow. Nobody died. Yet. Things were going swimmingly, if awkwardly, due to my uncomfortably long silences.

We took our places and I nodded to Alex, who had turned his attention from his screens to watch us. Alex's right hand relaxed and slid from beneath the keyboard drawer. *Alex with a gun? Okaaay.*

He knew how to shoot, Eli had made sure of that, and also made sure the Kid spent a lot of time on the range. He was an excellent shot. Maybe better than Eli, and that was saying a lot, since Eli had been trained by Uncle Sam and had been an Army Ranger. But. A gun in the Kid's hands in the security room? I took my seat, movement jarring my ribs. Leo took the one beside me.

"Start over with the null prison attack footage, please," I said, "specifically any shots or footage of the attackers: vamps, witches, and humans, with any IDs and info you have on them."

"Yes, my lady," Alex said. He queued up the video of the null prison attack again. On every screen was the scene in the street and in the shadows of the null prison yard. In most scenes a man stood behind the attackers, the man I thought was Mainet.

Leo's mouth twitched down very slightly. Enough to let me know he had seen this man at the prison, knew him, hated him, but hadn't tried to kill him.

In the deeps of my mind Beast whispered, *Jane is killer only. Should kill vampire.*

For a moment, I didn't know if she meant Leo or Mainet.

His voice pedantic and emotionless as Eli at a debrief, Alex stared, saying, "This man is believed to be Mainet Pellissier."

I slid my eyes to Leo. "Yes?"

Leo nodded once, a graceful movement, and his fangs clicked closed. His sclera bled back to human white. I'd never do the regal nod thing well. Leo was a master at it, despite his expression being oddly full of grief. "The Heir," he said, his voice oddly soft.

Alex continued. "There's no previous mention of Mainet as a human or vampire in France or Spain prior to the early twelve hundreds, though he could have been around a long time before that."

Leo set his eyes on Alex, predator eyes. His hands tightened as if to form into fists or claws until he forced them to relax. "Continue," Leo whispered.

"He first appeared in twelve hundred–ish, as a Mithran, during a local recurrence of the Black Plague. Mainet was given rights to start a blood family in AD 1450. He turned Amaury. He owns the Pellissier vineyard in France. He is believed to be *very* powerful but also very private. We don't have much in our files except that he was capable of having children in the human manner for at least three hundred years after his first appearance."

Leo lowered his eyes to his hands, which he clasped loosely together in his lap, to all appearances, calm. But I had seen that reflexive clench. Leo had some bad mojo about Mainet. "Children of the body," he said, "are precious and rare among my kind."

Leo had had two children of his body that I knew of, and his daughter had been among the long-chained, stuck in the devoveo. When the Mercy Blade had attempted to dispatch her, under his authority as the vamp misericord, Leo had nearly killed him, and had driven him away. Later, much later, Leo had killed his centuries-old, insane scion himself.

Leo took a breath he didn't need, blew it out, and seemed to study the gold ring on his thumb. I wasn't sure, but it kinda looked like the Pellissier seal ring, the one that was pressed into hot melted wax for official clan pronouncements. While Clan Pellissier had ceased to exist when Leo died without a real heir, the clan had never been officially disbanded. It was interesting that he still wore the ring. I smelled his grief. He still grieved for his children, one he had been forced to kill, and one an *u'tlun'ta* had killed. He turned the ring around, his head bowed, his long hair shadowing his face.

Frivolous thoughts raced through me. I was the titular leader of Clan Yellowrock and I had no seal. Did I need one? Did the Dark Queen have a seal ring? If so, where was it? Mental note to self—check on seal rings. Get one or more seal rings made. Don't react to the pain and grief on Leo's face. Don't. *Don't.* He'd hate that, here in front of the people who had once been his.

Finally, Alex went on. "In the years following the formation of Clan Pellissier, Mainet turned several of his descendants, including Rudolfo and Amaury Pellissier. Amaury was Leo's maker and the former Master of the City of NOLA." He gave a rolling motion with his hand and added, "For the newbies and anyone who's been living under a rock for the last hundred years."

"Who is Rudolfo?" I asked.

"Leo's father's cousin," Alex said.

"Rudolfo did not survive devoveo," Leo said quietly. "Gee DiMercy gave him the mercy strike before we came to the colonies."

"Leo," I said gently. "I know that Mainet is draining his blood scions of magical mojo. But does Mainet have some additional hold over you?" He had been able to talk to me at the null prison, but now he seemed different. Almost as if he was in some kind of pain.

Leo's fingers twitched. All ten of them. His mouth opened and then closed. His jaw unhinged slightly, the way the old powerful ones did when they wanted to drink down and kill prey. His three-inch fangs again clicked forward on their little hinges, like a viper, and his eyes began a slow change, the sclera bleeding scarlet, his pupils dilating to vamped-out black.

He was fighting it. And he was losing. Leo sucked in a gasp of air as if to speak and then swallowed several times. No words emerged. His throat seemed to close up and he never exhaled. His mouth twisted oddly, as if he wanted to speak and couldn't.

"Tell me about a celestial being, half chained," I whispered to him.

Leo's shoulders went back. His lips turned down hard, making grooves on either side of his mouth. But he didn't answer. Instead he swallowed, his throat moving as if it burned. His hands clenched, his eyes landed on me. Fully vamped out. And angry.

"Interesting," I said, holding up a hand to stop two of the newer guards who reached for weapons. I considered Leo. I had used all the magical power of the Dark Queen to summon Leo, not so long ago. He had appeared. When I demanded he help, he had saved Eli's life. Responding to a magical summons and a direct order meant I was . . . *Holy crap.* At that moment, I had been Leo's master. And yet, now, I had given him a request—an order?—he couldn't obey for some reason. And not being able to obey one's master was a problem. It meant he was psychically bound to silence on certain subjects.

This had happened in the hours since the attack on the null prison house. If Mainet had been behind that attack, and he had gained some magical energies after the attack, had his claim on Leo already deepened? Could it work so fast?

"What if we stuck you in a null room? Could you talk then?"

Leo's eyes went wild with an expression I had never seen on his face. Fear. Terror.

"I retract my questions and request," I said.

Leo blew out the breath he had taken, and his shoulders slumped. His hands relaxed to stillness.

"Go on, Alex," I said.

"Over the next few decades, Amaury Pellissier turned his sons-of-the-body and his nephews, including Leonard Eugène Zacharie Pellissier and his brother, known as El Mago, in 1525."

Leo's eyes bled back to human and his fangs retracted, but only for a moment before they clicked back out, and back in, back and forth, as if he fought a compulsion. Something or someone wanted him to be vamped-out. He was fighting it.

Alex said, "Amaury Pellissier and his scions came to the Americas and started the colonial branch of the Pellissier blood family, under the proprietorship of Clan Pellissier and the French Blood Master, Mainet Pellissier, in the French countryside. Then there was a break between Amaury and Mainet."

That made sense. Amaury had already been a powerful vamp when he came to the Americas. Once here, he found freedom enticing. He had an opportunity to take control of his own fortunes and so he did. "He dumped his maker?" I asked.

Leo's eyes widened.

"The records of the cause of that break in the power of the clan are missing," Alex said.

"But somehow he broke the link between master and scion." I thought about the angel. About all the magical amulets in the city. About all the vamps who had come here, to a small, tired city on the Gulf of Mexico. Why here? Why not New York?

Leo tightened his lips and didn't meet my eyes, the frown again pulling down his face.

Yeah. Leo knew why Mainet and Amaury parted ways

but couldn't say. Couldn't say anything about Mainet, or the angel, leading me to conclude that the two, and Mainet's break with Amaury, were related.

If Leo was bound and under a vamp blood compulsion, that binding had to have deepened between the time he appeared to me at the null prison and now. Maybe Mainet hadn't just gotten stronger. Maybe he had caught Leo.

I took Leo's icy-cold undead hands and pushed up the sleeves of his black suit coat. There were bloodred abrasions circling both wrists, five inches wide. Fingerprints were deeper. Fingernails had broken his skin. He had been held down and . . . and he hadn't healed. I looked at his neck. There was nothing there, no bite marks. But there were other places a vamp could be drunk from.

"He caught you. You got away," I whispered, "even after he had you."

Leo's shoulders slumped. He took a breath he didn't need and blew it out. His eyes met mine and his were damp with tears. This close, I saw a white hair on his suit coat and I plucked it free, twirled it. I had a pretty good idea what had happened. "Brute appeared, didn't he? And he got you free."

Leo blinked away tears and I understood.

"But not quite in time. You've been rebound, or your binding has been partially strengthened by your old master." And yet, Leo was here, clearly in defiance of this new compulsion. I wanted to hug him. But I knew better than to get my skin anywhere near his fangs.

Alex cleared his throat to warn us he was still on the comms and continued his info. "Mainet lived in seclusion in France on the Pellissier winery until Grégoire started challenging and killing vamps who refused to participate in the change of leadership," Alex said. "The reasons why the Heir came here are obvious: to run away from Edmund and Grégoire and a conflict he didn't want to engage in, to get the box everyone wants"—meaning the heart of the SOD—"to take power over the U.S. vamps, to take over as the new SOD, and to take over the Dark Queen."

Leo met my eyes. In them I saw agreement to the

words Alex had just stated. Yeah. Power. That was what all the old vamps wanted. They had lived so long that they had inevitably buried their loved ones, their unchanged human children, their scions stuck in devoveo, all their blood-servants, all who perished, the years passing too quickly. They had loved and always lost. Broken and lonely, they had drunk and sexed their way through all the other humans, and burned through all the passions that a young vamp was prey to. All that was left was power, control, remaking the world in their own image.

And there was still the blasted heart.

I didn't say it, but it seemed obvious that the heart belonging to one of the creators of the vamps could possibly be used in any ceremony to finish binding the angel and maybe bind a demon. And with those two bound, use their power to affect changes not only on Earth, but maybe in heaven and hell as well.

That made sense, as Earth was the place where heaven and hell met.

Leo stood, shoving back his chair. It wasn't the smooth graceful motion of the Leo I knew, but rough, clumsy, and inelegant. Oh yeah. Bound. Fighting it.

Stiffly, Leo gestured. It was a little like the sort of hand gesture one would give a dog, and I grinned. It was the kind of thing the Leo of old would have done and it sent an unexpected sense of release through me. He walked to the door, into the hallway, leaving the door open. He didn't look back. The former MOC appeared to be heading to the elevator. I looked around the room for Eli. *Right. In surgery.* "Any news?" I asked Alex, one eye on Leo.

Alex, the mind reader, said, "Eli: awake. Drinking from a lower-level vamp and acting all stoic and ranger-y. Bruiser: in video conference with the governor but will join you at any moment should you need him. Koun: His bones were set by one of the Roberes, and he's healing. Alex: My drones sent back good vid and info, are all back safe, and I'm going through to cut out the unusable and enhance the necessary useful stuff. Nothing else happening."

I stood from my chair and followed Leo through the

open door. Two of the security team fell into place just behind me, though not the same two I had coldcocked. One of these was a vamp I had seen around, an older, more experienced one, if his smooth gait was an indication. His name was Jermaine. With him was a human, Blue Voodoo, one of the security guys hired when Derek was still with us.

Voodoo looked older and harder, a little thicker through the chest, and he walked with a firm stride, his eyes landing on the vamp at his side as often as they did on the surroundings. Since Derek died at the hands of enemy vamps, our humans were having a little trouble trusting vamps they didn't know well, and this guy was fairly new. Or maybe it wasn't Derek-related, and Voodoo just didn't like vamps in general. Integrating vamps and humans in security teams had worked well for us, but that didn't mean they always got along. There had been a few bitings. And a few shootings. So far no one had died.

When we got to the elevator, Leo was holding the door for us, his face impassive, the lack of expression one he had worn when he rode his power over most of the vamps in the nation, making NOLA the stronghold of vamp power in the Americas. We got on and Leo pushed a button, not speaking. Voodoo seemed uncomfortable with the silence, his partner, Leo, and probably puma-faced me, his eyes moving between the two vamps.

When the doors opened, we were looking at subbasement four. This level hadn't been used a lot when I first came to NOLA, as most vamps stayed at their Clan Homes with their Blood Master and human dinners. Then there had been some violent clan rearrangements and the eight vamp clans had become four, leaving four Clan Homes empty and overcrowding the remaining four. Near the same time, Leo's Clan Home had burned to the ground. Leo, as MOC, had opened the Mithran Council Chambers to house many clanless vamps as well as the overflow from the suddenly much larger clans. Around that time, parts of sub-four began to get a makeover. Leo walked along the hallway, opened one of the storage rooms, and peeked inside.

"You organized it," he said mildly. "My people always wanted me to assign the chore to someone, but there was sensitive information in the records, and magical trinkets were stored here, locked in trunks, hidden in the safe. Some out on the shelves for the taking."

"Derek's guys organized it," I said, my heart in a spasm at the name. "Your enemies killed Derek."

"My enemies will kill us all if they can," Leo said. "And you have far more enemies than I ever did."

Point to Leo.

He didn't ask what had happened to the info or the amulets and I didn't volunteer. He moved on, stopping at one of the newly refurbished suites. He placed his palm on the door, as if giving it a blessing, but he didn't try the knob. "You finally killed her, despite my best efforts to keep her alive."

I knew this room. It had been dusty and abandoned when I first came here. Now it was a suite for a vamp or two and several humans. Before that, the room had been used by Adrianna, and I had killed her several times before Leo stopped saving her. Eventually I took her head and she stayed dead.

"There is nothing here now," he said, which made no sense. Leo turned and glided back to the elevator, his motions as smooth as they had been before the weird jerky movements and the inability to talk in the security room. There was something almost feline about his movements now, predatory and hungry, like a hunting big-cat. This was the Leo I knew best.

Back at the elevator, we stepped on, the unit rose, and we stepped out, me following Leo's lead to the gymnasium. The lights were off, which was a surprise. I wasn't sure I had ever seen the gym with the lights off, but it was near dawn and the vamps would be heading to bed soon; the humans would be changing out shifts. It smelled of the new synthetic workout mats and unknown vamps: the floral of wilted funeral flowers, a little nutmeg, a hint of lemon, the scent of raw earth, like a newly turned field. Blood from their dinners.

Leo entered and the lights came on, motion sensor or

Alex following us on the security cameras. "You changed little," Leo said.

"New mats. And we added landing mats so our people can learn more advanced moves without getting hurt."

A faint smile tugged at his eyes. "You treat my people as if they will easily break."

"Yep."

Leo shook his head. "A little blood, a few bruises never hurt anyone."

I didn't respond to that.

Pensively, he said, "I remember when the Dragon appeared here for the first time. You fought it."

That was an odd memory. An odd tone. I shifted my eyes from the far wall to Leo, and something clicked in my brain. We weren't just taking "an old home tour," letting him revisit his former HQ. Leo was using this excursion to tell me something. Maybe several somethings. Adrianna, a nutso and a traitor, who had been saved by Leo on several occasions. Her possessions, which had included a magically empty snake amulet armband, had been kept in the storage room along with lots of other amulets. An angry arcenciel named Opal had invaded the vamp gym and been badly injured. Arcenciel blood . . . Timewalking? Was he trying to tell me something about timewalking?

Leo sighed, another totally unnecessary breath, turned, and left the gym. This time I followed a half step behind instead of walking next to him, watching him the same way the guards did. We took the elevator to the main floor and walked toward the front entry. Just beyond the hallway, he stopped.

He was looking over the place, taking in the changes made when he died and I became the Dark Queen and the MOC of his city. The walls were still the soft dove gray of the Pellissier clan. Also unchanged from his tenure were the carpet, rugs, security nook, and the high-tech, bullet-resistant entry. But not everything was the same.

His eyes were drawn to the white-and-gray marble tile on the floor of the magnificent foyer. His crest had been inlaid there once. Now mine was there. Something in Leo's stance changed, tensed, and his head tilted to the side in that improbably birdlike way vamps have. His scent changed too, growing sharper, more acerbic.

Blue Voodoo reached for his weapon. The vamp beside him placed a pale white hand on his arm, preventing the human from drawing. I held up a hand to stop him too, and mouthed, *Wait.*

Leo walked into the foyer and stopped at the edge of the circle of my crown, staring down at it.

From the security nook, Wrassler appeared, one hand out of sight. Wrassler had been Leo's man, but none of us really knew who Leo was now.

The former MOC dropped to one knee and held a hand, palm down, half a foot above the gold-toned circle, as if testing the temperature or feeling for magic. He lowered his left index finger and gently touched the brass that had been inlaid in the middle of the white-and-gray marble, the circle six feet in diameter, representing my crown, centered with the Glob, a puma fang, and a feather in different-colored marble. My crest.

"I didn't make the changes," I said, feeling slightly uncomfortable when he held that position, unmoving as stone, not breathing, staring at the Dark Queen's crest in the middle of the wide space that had once been his. "I didn't even know the work had been done until Bruiser told me about it."

Leo looked up from the marble inlaid crest. "My George," he said softly. "Yes. It is customary for the master of the city, the most powerful Mithran in the territory, to have his crest inlaid in the entry floor of his city's Council Chambers headquarters, to remind friends and visiting enemies alike who they would have to fight and conquer. I am not displeased." He stood and looked to Wrassler. "I am gratified you survived your injuries, my friend."

Wrassler blinked in surprise. I was dead certain that Leo had never called Wrassler *friend* in his previous life. "Thank you, sir," Wrassler said.

Leo turned and took the stairs this time, meandering

to a different floor. We trailed behind. When Leo opened the door to the vamp library, the lights again came on. *Oh yeah*. Alex was following our progress through the building.

The former MOC walked slowly to a shelf of dusty books. His scent and gait changed again and I realized that Leo was fighting internal bonds to keep going forward. Leo was in trouble and wasn't able to tell me what kind or who to kill for him. He looked at one shelf of old leather-bound books, at me, and again back at the books. Without a word, he left the room, moving fast, and then with that vamp speed that displaced air, he disappeared, making a little pop of sound.

I studied the shelf. The books had the look of vamp journals, which were always musty, handwritten, and seldom in English, most written in French, Italian, Spanish, or any of dozens of languages. They shouldn't be here. I was pretty sure they hadn't been here the last time I looked for journals.

I was taller than either of my bodyguards, and I reached up high, pulling one book down at an angle, tugging on the rounded edge of the leather binding. When I opened it, I saw the fancy handwriting, like calligraphy, and not in English. I held it out to the vamp. Jermaine. "Can you read this?"

He frowned and carefully turned the pages. "No. I read only seven languages, and this looks like Gaelic. I read no Gaelic, though I know a few spoken Scottish Gaelic words."

He reads only seven languages. Oy.

I pulled down all the old journals on that shelf, stacking them in the vamp's arms. When he was laden, though not showing the weight, because vamps have that extra strength that comes from being dead-ish, I led the way back to the security room. On the way, I texted Alex with the words: "Our clues are: Adrianna, her magical belongings, an arcenciel and her blood, and some old books. And maybe something about my corona, since he touched the brass in the marble entry floor."

Alex texted back: "Brass. Right. I'll find vamps we trust to translate. Protocol Research means the books will not be allowed to leave the security room except with written permission of a member of your family (that's you, me, Eli, and Bruiser) and no notes or pics are allowed. No one can take off with something they want."

I glanced up at a camera as we passed and nodded.

CHAPTER 9

Only Cold Iron Would Hurt a Rainbow Dragon

Back in the security room, my guards settled against the wall behind my back, on either side of the coffeemaker. I had half noticed people standing there before, but there were people all over the room, so I hadn't realized the two were there for me. I glanced back at them, giving them the kind of attention I should have given them before. Voodoo and the vamp were wearing black dress slacks, black dress shirts, and black jackets, with a gold crown embroidered on the left pec, not black jeans and long-sleeved T-shirts. *Dang.* The fancy duds meant they were as much an honor guard as bodyguards.

I hope they didn't plan on accompanying me to the toilet. That would result in the same kind of head-banging injuries as the two vamps outside the door to Leo's suite. My suite. Whatever.

I looked around the room, estimating maybe thirty people, all dressed in black, though most in black tees and jeans. All the shirts had the gold circle on them. Soooo. Black was my official color and the crown claimed them as mine, taking over from Leo's dove gray. I figured he had noticed that. I wondered who had made that decision, and guessed Bruiser, who was not present yet, and was probably still dealing with the governor and law enforcement and the problems vamps made for New Orleans.

"Jane," Alex said, pointing over my head.

I looked to the security screens and spotted Leo and Wrassler (dressed in black, which I hadn't noticed) outside the MOC's office, as the head of HQ's security unlocked the door. "Cameras inside?" I asked.

"Negative," Alex said as the two entered and vanished from the screens. "Wrassler informed me that Leo had appeared in his security station and requested—politely— that Wrassler accompany him for a few moments. I sent Angel Tit, one of the Vodka Boys, up fast to take over the station and Leo and Wrassler went straight to his old office."

The scents in the room changed as tension wove through the people assembled there. I might be the only one who noticed the descriptive word *politely* Alex had used. Leo was never polite and he almost never asked; he ordered and he demanded—elegantly, yes—but asking was so rare I could count on one hand the times I remembered it happening.

I watched the clock on the bottom of the screen, and two minutes and change later, Leo left the room, Wrassler and Gee DiMercy behind him. Alex cursed half under his breath. I wasn't the only one who hadn't seen Gee enter. The Mercy Blade, aka the Misericord of the Mithrans, was a magical creature who could cloak himself in glamours, look like most anything he wanted, and could probably go anywhere, even with all the paranormal-detecting equipment in the hallways. He also often called me little goddess, which was always a little weird.

Wrassler closed and locked the door behind them. Leo was carrying a tiny silver box. They stopped and turned, seemed to be chatting, so I got a good look at the small but deadly swordfighter. Not for the first time, I realized Gee (in this form) and Leo could almost be related, the misericord and the vampire both olive-skinned, dark-haired, dark-eyed, and lean as slabs of beef, though Gee wasn't a vamp and was more olive-skinned than the ivory-toned fanghead.

Gee wasn't wearing black, a distinction that stood out sharply now that I knew what to look for. He was wearing a scarlet shirt and sapphire pants, a sword strapped around his hips. Once again, Gee carried the red-striped flying lizard on his shoulder, though the lizard was now bigger than only a few weeks past, its tail wrapped around Gee's neck and across his shoulders and chest. The flying reptile was a good thirty-five pounds. Maybe more. The men stopped talking and started walking.

The security room was silent except for the soft clacking of keys from Alex's desk area as he followed the pair on video through the hallways. Wrassler glanced up at each camera, knowing we were watching. The huge man's face and body language were tight, though his limp was much less noticeable than once before. He'd lost a leg in a battle inside HQ. I hadn't thought he'd survive, but he had, and then had married my friend Jodi, of NOPD. Wrassler was tense. Worried. Trying to tell us something by body language alone, but I didn't know what.

The scents of agitated people in the security room with me went up another notch.

"Ready a team?" Alex asked me. Meaning a security team of armed and dangerous former active military to head that way. Half a dozen men and women in the security room instantly pulled and checked weapons. *Ready a team* to . . . do what? Race around and try to shoot Leo? Maybe accidently injuring Wrassler? Try to shoot Gee? Bullets wouldn't hurt Gee. And why would we do that anyway? Nothing was happening, nothing except Wrassler's unease.

And then it hit me. Dawn. The vamps would be no help. Even as I had the thought, the fangheads filed out of the room and popped away, leaving only humans in security.

"No," I said, settling back in my chair. "Wait." Instantly the tension in the room went down a notch. *Oh. Right.* I had to remember that as the DQ, my emotions affected the emotions of my people. A calm queen meant calm teams. *Weird.*

The three men walked to the front entrance, through the airlock, and started down the stairs to the oval parking area that diplomats and important guests used. Multiple screens showed the scene from different angles. Dark out. The night just beginning to lighten as dawn threatened the vamp-world.

On one screen, two arcenciels appeared overhead. Opal was iridescent in blues, silvers, with faint trails of pinks, cool and bright all at once. Pearl shone with the hues of nacre, pearly white, pearl pink, black pearls. I hadn't seen them since they tried to steal my crown and hadn't seen them here since we fought Shaun MacLaughlinn. The fact that they appeared twice in one night was odd, suspicious, maybe dangerous.

Leo extended his fist, holding it high in the air. A reflection glinted between his fingers, from the security lights and the faint dark gray of dawn. Which Leo should not be able to withstand without being a lot more powerful than he let on.

He opened his hand to reveal the silver box, cradled in his palm, and the two arcenciels dove closer. They hovered in the air above him, wings flashing in all the colors of the rainbow, capturing the dawn light. I watched as Leo waited. Opal altered shape, growing a human-shaped limb that hadn't been there a moment before. Fingers, thumb, palm, at the end of one full arm. *Crap.* We had never caught vid of arcenciels partially shapeshifting before, and here we had one growing an extra limb. Opal took the box from his hand and darted back a few yards, as if fearful he might demand it back.

Gee then stepped down three steps and lifted the flying lizard into the air, over his head. The arcenciels flew closer again, their translucent wings batting at the men's hair, sending it flying. They sniffed the lizard's belly the way dogs might scent another. The red flying lizard flapped its wings and puffed out its throat in some kind of display, the throat an unexpected sapphire blue.

The arcenciels' wings fluttered faster and they began to shimmer all over, as if excited. Or angry. Wrassler drew his weapon, not that it would do him any good. Only cold iron would hurt a rainbow dragon. The dragons twirled in a complicated acrobatic flight pattern, their colors changing to darker hues that seemed to reflect a darker emotion—maybe anger? Huge heads bobbing, they flailed their wings, gyrated their bodies in serpentine spirals, and flew out of sight. Gee and the lizard disappeared, like poof, instant gone-ness.

Leo vanished, just as poofy as Gee, but in a vampy way. Wrassler stood there, his weapon still drawn, taking in the front parking area and closed gate of the Mithran Council Chambers. The day grew brighter, grayer. He holstered his gun, trudged up the stairs, shaking his head.

I pulled my cell and found Gee in my contacts. He didn't answer, so I left a terse voicemail. I texted Soul asking if the leader of the arcenciels knew about the silver box Leo had gifted them, asking what it was, asking if she knew about the flying lizard and why the others got so upset, and asking if she knew her people had tried to steal my crown, claiming it was at her directive. Okay. It was more like a long rant, but calling it a text made it seem better.

Soul didn't text back, but now that I knew she could grow an arm in her dragon-form, not using her cell phone wasn't an excuse or the result of an unfortunate shape, it was deliberate. And Leo? I had no idea what was going on with Leo or what he had given the rainbow dragons.

An hour after dawn, my cell rang, displaying Angelina Everhart Trueblood's number. My goddaughter used to call me on Molly's line, until her parents gave her a cell and limited access to people she could call. I couldn't help the way my cat-shaped face softened as I answered, the cell held up tight to my cat ear, to keep others from over-hearing. Angie was private godmother business, not queen business. No one's business but mine. Plus, Angie called with weird news sometimes. "Hey, Angie Baby," I said softly.

Alex rotated his chair, watching me, his long curls bobbing against his darker-skinned face.

"Hey, Ant Jane," Angie said. She used to call me Aunt Jane and I had no idea where the Ant thing came from, but it was adorable. "Don't tell Mama I called. But I saw my angel. He's close to you. He wants to talk to you."

I sat straight up in my chair, scanning the room and checking all the screens. No Hayyel. But that might not be what Angie meant. "Close as in location?"

"Close like in time. All the futures say that Mama and I'll be coming to visit, but I haven't told Mama yet." I could almost see the eight-year-old's eye roll when she added, "Mama gets upset when I know things."

My breath hitched. Everything in my body clenched. I was glad the vamps were gone because I knew my scent also changed and that would have caused trouble with them. Alex reacted to whatever he saw on my face, his eyes going wide. Voodoo put a hand on his weapon.

I waved them both down and shook my head once, a tiny motion, hoping to tell everyone not to worry just yet. Angie was one of very few double-X-gene witches in the world, meaning that she had gotten the witch gene on the X chromosome from both parents, and therefore double of the usual witch power. Angie Baby had come into her power—way more power than most witches—far too early. She was still a kid and yet she was becoming prescient, seeing potential futures. It worried me, as seeing the future was something like timewalkers could sometimes do. Angie and I hadn't talked in depth about her time-sense yet, mostly because it scared the bejeebbers out of me to think she might get cancer like I did from messing around with time.

But . . . I wondered *how* Angie saw potential futures. Was her way safer? Or was it the way I used to, before the cancer and the healing and before I stopped trying to see potentials? If I tried to look at the futures again, I wondered if I could still see possibilities in water drops, and if that would be safe, provided I only looked and never used the gift to slow or alter time.

But, if I could see the possibilities, would I be able to restrain myself from messing around in time? Could I resist? Should I resist? There were worse things than dying if I could save the people I loved. I needed to talk to Angie about her futures and how she saw time.

"Ant Jane?"

"I'm here. Why haven't you told your mama about the trip?"

"Because Cassy was fussy last night. Mama says she might have colic, like a horse. She kept Mama and Daddy up."

That made sense.

"I'm getting ready to stick waffles in the toaster for me and EJ. We're gonna eat breakfast out at Mama's rock garden. And don't worry. The new *hedge* is still up."

The Everharts were back on their land, in their new house. Their first home had been destroyed by Angie Baby's emerging magic, the second one had been attacked by one of my enemies and burned to the ground. I had spent personal money to expedite getting their house finished and their stuff (as much as possible) replaced in record time, though I'd not been able to replace Big Evan's compositions or his one-of-a-kind collection of rare, hand-carved flutes. Or Molly's houseplants. Being my friend was hard and dangerous, no matter how I looked at it, so I helped where I could. "Okay. You be safe, Angie."

"Okay, Ant Jane. I love you."

"I love you too." I ended the call and looked up to see Bruiser standing in the doorway, his eyes on me, his mouth soft. He was wearing a plaid shirt, jeans, and brown casual shoes, his hair styled back, away from his face. He wasn't wearing black, which made me all kinds of happy. My honeybunch looked nothing like a scion or someone sworn or bound to me. He looked like a guy dressed for a casual date. Maybe dinner. And also he looked like sex on a stick.

"Angie?" he asked, of my phone call.

My face always gave that away. "Yeah. How 'bout you take me away from here, Consort?"

"I can do that. Who's on duty?" he asked the room.

Six humans stepped forward.

"Three vehicles. To the queen's personal residence." Bruiser checked his weapon and replaced it in a spine holster. "Alex, you ride with us."

"As long as you don't neck in the car, fine."

I spluttered with laughter.

The trip back through the French Quarter was uneventful, except for seeing all the homeless people on the streets, which was a sad juxtaposition with the city's

Thanksgiving decorations everywhere. The homeless slept in doorways, under foliage, the lucky ones in small tents. We passed one guy sleeping with his head on his shoes as a pillow, his winter coat on and buttoned tight, a heavy stick clutched in his fingers. "Make sure the church who was doing all the good work with the homeless gets a donation. If they're not any further along in negotiations with the city about a location for the permanent individual low-income homes they were talking about, see if a nudge from us and a promise of financial support will help."

"Yes, My Queen," Bruiser said. It was the same tone he had once used to Leo, when Leo was giving orders and his primo was replying.

I turned in my seat, caught his amused and placid smile, and scowled at him. Knowing I sounded bitchy, but unable to stop it, I demanded, "What!"

Bruiser laughed. "It's okay, Jane. As queen, when you make an official request, especially one that has to be handled through diplomatic channels, it requires specific verbiage to acknowledge the order."

"It wasn't an order. It—" I stopped. Actually, it was an order, and it would require diplomacy and access to the queen's accounts, which was part of the reason why the Robere brothers were back in town and not with Grégoire in Europe—to handle the queen's diplomatic affairs. My Consort and the Roberes were the best of the best when it came to politics and diplomacy. And yeah. I had given an order. "Holy crap." If I used stronger words, I'd use one now.

"Precisely," Bruiser said. He kissed me on my furry cheek. "I'll also see to it that the church and the homeless shelters all have sufficient funds for Thanksgiving feasts for the homeless and indigent. You are a good queen. You are *my* queen. You are also my love. And I hope sex is still on the table for later."

I leaned against him and let my body relax, breathing in his scent. "I love you," I murmured. "I love that about you. That you can keep the two parts of me separate. Queen and Jane."

And Beast, she reminded me.

"Always and forever," Bruiser said, his lips against my hairline.

"But maybe not sex on a table."

Bruiser chuckled again, this time with a tone that let me know he was envisioning us on a table.

"We have a perfectly comfortable bed. And we might break a table, which could hurt."

"My love, you are eminently practical."

Mate, Beast thought, longing in her tone.

All three of us remained silent the rest of the way home and when I crawled into bed, it was with the pseudo-night provided by the steel shutters that had been mounted on the house sealed closed. They told the world that "the Dark Queen is in residence. Go away."

I fell into deep dreams, my half-form body spooned against Bruiser's.

I woke alone, in human form, my crown on the mattress near my hand. The scent of bacon was wafting under the door and I was starving, having shifted in my sleep and without calories to replace those used up in the transition from one form to another. I started drooling, before I remembered that a late breakfast was being prepared by someone other than Eli. That killed my appetite and sent an ice-water shock through me.

Reaching out to him, I felt his heart beating, slow with sleep. The relief was so intense my muscles went limp.

I left the bed, fingers rubbing my aching head, picking plastic bits from the crushed headset out of my hair. I put the crown away, beside the heartbox on the shelf of magical doohickeys, and showered. Very late fall in NOLA usually meant highs in the seventies, sometimes in the sixties, but today was chilly, the heat wasn't on, and once I got over being worried about Eli, I was hungry enough that my bones felt the chill.

I studied my human self in the mirror as I dressed, pulling on thick stretchy yoga pants and a sweatshirt over a tight tee and wool socks. No weapons. Not to start my day. I braided my hair again, this time clean and tight, as it had come unbraided when I shifted.

I wasn't as skinny as I used to be. I had taken on forty-five pounds of mass from the street, and left a big hole behind that had to be patched by the city. I was muscular and shapely, which was a nice body change, and was presentable enough that my security team, whoever they might be today, wouldn't see me naked. I also, according to the mirror, still looked like an eighteen-year-old human. Not that appearances mattered to vamps, who maintained the superficial age at which they were turned. Heck. I fit right in.

I made my way to the kitchen, expecting to see Alex at the stove, and stopped short.

My new personal lady-in-waiting, security, and bodyguard, Quint, was standing at the stove, removing a piece of bacon from the griddle. The stone-cold killer was back from two days off, was dressed in thick-knit yoga clothes that looked a lot like mine, and was armed to the teeth. She was also dancing in place, earbuds in both ears, and singing along softly to a musical, some song from *The Lion King*. Before I could announce myself, a nine-mil was centered on my chest. The bacon, held in tongs, dripped onto the hot iron skillet. I stopped short and she didn't kill me. The weapon slid back into her offhand rig.

"Jane's up," Alex said, his tone laconic.

"You were supposed to tell me when she got up," Quint said, nearly a snarl.

"You were supposed to be working on modifying your reaction time to add in a split second longer for judgment. Look, evaluate as you are reaching for your weapon," he said, "then don't. Not when it's one of us."

"I know how to do my job," she said, and this time her words were low and deadly.

"You drew on your asset," Alex said, ignoring her tone. And maybe goading her a little.

"Asset?" I asked, taking her attention from my brother to me. "I'm not a *thing*. I'm a person."

"You are Quint's asset. And she just drew on you in your own home. Bad Quint," Alex said, his voice not teasing.

"Stop it, you two. Quint, if you drop that bacon on the floor, I will personally break some body part," I threatened her. "Bacon is precious."

Quint's posture altered instantly, as if a switch had been flipped. She put the bacon strip on a paper towel, her back to Alex and me. Alex grinned as if this was all a good joke. I shot him a warning look and he just grinned wider. Male, young, and amused at the antics of the females. I'd seen that look before on men. I'd probably have to beat his butt in the gym someday to remind him being male did not make him invulnerable or right. And then spar with Quint to garner the respect she wasn't used to giving her . . . *assets*.

I sat at my place at the kitchen table. Centered in the table on the round serving thingy was a pot of tea under a pink knitted tea cozy. I was certain that I did not own a pink tea cozy, and that no one in my household would ever have purchased such an item. If Eli had purchased a cozy, it would have been in camo colors. If Bruiser had purchased it, the cozy would have been dove gray or black. Alex would have rolled his eyes at the thought of giving me a cozy. Therefore, Quint, sociopath and killer, had brought a pink knitted tea cozy to my house. "Ummm. Nice cozy?" I asked. Because I hated the color pink, which she knew.

"I crocheted it for this teapot. It has roses and gilt and the pink is a perfect match," she said, sliding a full serving platter in front of me. It contained two pounds of bacon, at least a dozen scrambled eggs, and two tall stacks of flapjacks. "Real maple syrup, warmed, and local hand-churned goat-milk butter, which is why the butter is white and not yellow. I know you like protein or gruel after a shift, but Eli warned me you like that nasty stuff fixed only one way and I haven't been told how. And oatmeal is disgusting. So you get meat."

Quint crocheted. And cooked. Someone had been messing with timelines or I had waked in an alternate dimension. Except she was carrying more weapons than Eli did, so that hadn't changed. At a glance I counted two nine-mils in a double thigh rig, a .32 at her spine, a nine-mil under her left arm, and a tiny .22 on her left ankle, over the yoga pants. She also was strapped down with five vamp-killers and three throwing knives. Same Quint.

Just . . . dang. Quint had crocheted me a pink tea cozy. She knew I hated pink. If I reminded her I hated pink, would she shoot me? Why had she made me a cozy? I touched the little hat-for-a-teapot and found it to be soft. Lacy work. Pretty. *Okay. Fine.* "Thank you."

"It's also pink so that if we ever need to hide a listening device in it no man would think to look in the fibers. Most men hate pink and avoid it. I added a tiny pocket on the edge to hide a mic."

"Ah," I said. Now that made Quint-sense.

I tasted the eggs. They were perfect. So was the bacon. I poured maple syrup over the thin pancakes and the bacon and dug in as if I were starving. Which I was. My hands were bony, and when I touched my abdomen, I could feel my hip bones jutting against the skin. I still had mass and muscle, but I lacked fat.

"Edmund is due to arrive any day now," Alex said, taking his chair next to me. "And we're not ready." The Kid was lean and muscular from workouts with his older brother, and he smelled good, meaning he had showered. He was also growing a moustache, which was patchy and thin, but was thicker than the last time he tried to grow facial hair. Growing up. Quint slid a plate in front of him. It contained the same kind of food, but not as much of it.

"Eli?"

"Not happy to still be in the hospital." Alex frowned and his expression told me I wasn't going to like what he said next. "He lost a chunk of muscle and his PT will suck this time, even with vamp blood."

This time. Because Eli had been wounded so very often in his life.

"Percentage of expected return to normal function?" Quint asked, pouring tea into my mug. The mug was white with red lettering that said, "Touch My Tea, Lose a Hand." It was new; I liked it.

"Eighty-five percent," Alex said, his voice hard.

"Unacceptable. We need an Infermeri," Quint said, pulling her cell. "I'll get my uncle to contact and intercede with Florence, and with Shaddock, and convince her to return to New Orleans. Then I'll get him to locate more healers seeking permanent placement."

"Why would Quesnel know about Infermeries?" Alex asked. Which meant there was something missing from his research files.

"My uncle knows everything about Florence and her bloodline. He was one of the soldiers she saved in World War Two, and he figured out what she was. He didn't run screaming into the dark. He accepted what he saw and helped her do her job. He was there the night she healed eighty-seven soldiers, and after the war he served her for a number of years before he went to Clan Pellissier. Excuse me." She turned away and began speaking softly to someone on the other end of a call.

We kept eating. I finished off everything on my plate before I sat back to enjoy my tea. Black and strong, no sweetener, no creamer. Just a nice burst of caffeine, and bitter enough to work as a counterpoint to all the maple syrup. I was drinking more plain tea since Bruiser came to live with me and I was learning to appreciate the unmodified taste.

"Good afternoon, Unc. How has your day been?" Quint asked Quesnel as she circled back into the room.

With my bodyguard busy talking and staring at the security screens someone had mounted along the walls near the tall ceilings, Alex leaned close and murmured, "We need to compare notes about why Mainet wants the heart. I mean, I know what I think, but I have no idea what you think."

"Hayyel is partially chained. I smelled a burst of brimstone during the attack on the prison. And then there's the stuff Leo said. So, I'm guessing that Mainet has a demon chained. If so, he intends to use the heart to complete chaining the angel. Maybe force a binding between the angel and the demon, and then . . . I don't know . . . destroy the heart or eat it, and then he'll have access to all the power in both spiritual domains and on Earth. I have no idea what he intends to do with all that power, but whatever it is, we won't like it." I wiped my plate with the last smidge of toast and popped it in my mouth. Around the gooey bread, I said, "I've been told not to destroy the heart until Mainet is dead."

"Mainet probably doesn't intend to bargain for vamp redemption and make things right in heaven," Alex said, which was what some vamps wanted. Redemption and the return of the souls they lost when they rose on the third day, batshit crazy, starving, and ready to kill any nearby human for their blood. "And if Angie is right, the Everharts will be here," he said. "Eli will—" He stopped, his face contorting as he took in that Eli wasn't available to do his usual jobs. "*I'll* have to move some of our people to the Yellowrock Clan Home so there's room for the witches if they want to stay at HQ."

Alex, taking over for Eli. *Crap.* He knew how to do the job. We both did. But *crap.* I poured another mug of tea and this time added sweetener and creamer. "If we get a vamp healer, how long before Eli can get back to us?" I asked. "And will he be better than eighty-five percent capacity?"

He shrugged. "Can't hurt. Could help. The Consort already offered to send the Lear to Asheville to bring Liz here, to be with Eli as he recovers. She accepted. The rest of the Everharts and Truebloods could come too, and Florence, if it's night, or if she's willing to fly in a coffin. The jet's already taken off. Once it lands, they can load and be back in three hours, give or take."

"Yeah. That works," I said. "Push for Florence. If Quint and Quesnel have muscle, use it to get Florence. And while we're talking about healers, ask the Roberes about protocol for getting more healers for the U.S. I agree that one isn't doing it."

The Kid tapped some instructions on his tablet and looked back up at me. "Done. And I've begun a background search for demon-calling and demons themselves. I've also checked the updates to the fanghead files, the ones I turned over to the most tech-competent of the security team. The updates say that Mainet is an unknown. He never flaunted his power in any public way, but he's the heir of both of the SODs and the closest thing to the current master of all the Naturaleza. Possibly with more political power than the Dark Queen herself, because he has allies in Asia and Southeast Asia. There aren't a lot of vamps in that part of the world, but the few there are powerful."

That would be bad.

"So, what if Mainet can force the angel to manifest in physical form," Alex said, his tone hypothesizing, "and instead of eating the heart of the SOD himself, to obtain power, he forces Hayyel to eat the heart? How much would that change an angel? Could Mainet force the angel to destroy the arcenciels? And everyone on our side? Could he take over time?"

"Too many possibilities," I said.

"Yeah. Okay. What's with the red lizard?"

"No idea. Opal and Pearl were not happy." I checked my cell and no one had replied to my texts. I re-texted Gee and Soul, then called both and left new voicemails. No one was paying attention to me. Being the DQ wasn't giving me the control I wanted, and the position meant only more headaches. I felt my belly again. Now it was a round little ball just below my ribs, so that was good. Being DQ might suck, but the food was excellent.

My cell tinkled; Molly's number and name appeared on the screen. I tapped and said, "Hey, BFF."

"Lachish called and told me what happened at the prison. The NOLA witch council has requested the Everhart Clan to come help restore the wards and help protect the heart, since our clan has the newest *hedge of thorns* ward."

All sorts of possibilities flashed through my mind. The Everharts had devised the original *hedge of thorns* and had been upgrading it constantly since, as enemies found ways to magically break them. It was a lot like high-tech hacking into well-secured institutions, an attack and the defensive measures taken by the owners to protect sensitive info from others. But in this case, it was magical energies and protections that were being created and then attacked by outsiders, not electronic. With the exception of the Seattle coven, the Everharts were the most powerful witch clan and coven in the U.S. because of the *hedge of thorns* and its diverse applications.

But, having that many Everharts in my city spelled trouble, danger, and more trouble. It also meant I had to know if they came as friends or as a diplomatic mission. I decided I had to bite the bullet and ask.

Casually, I said, "If you're coming as *my* guests I can offer some of you rooms in my house." I dropped my voice and tone into formality. "Molly Megan Everhart Trueblood, earth witch of the Everhart clan, if you come as the *Dark Queen's* guests, *we* can offer you rooms in the Yellowrock Clan home, with the understanding that Edmund and Grégoire will be here soon, and Edmund will be staying in the clan home. Grégoire might be staying there also. Or we can offer you rooms in the Council Chambers, though you would of necessity be in contact with many Mithrans."

"It's pretty cool how you do that. Switch the role on and off." She exhaled quietly. "Proximity to that"—she hesitated—"that *man* . . . is not what . . . some of us need on our plates just now."

I grinned. Despite her understanding that a marriage between a centuries-old vamp and a little witch wasn't going to happen, Angie had a major crush on Edmund and still secretly fancied herself his fiancée. "It's not the way things are *supposed to be done*," I said, accenting the four words the way my older vamps might, "and I hate to divide and conquer, but you and your family could stay here, in my personal residence, and the others could stay at the clan home. Or HQ. Accommodations would be both official and not."

"Yes," she said quickly. "That would work. I think the clan home would be best."

That put the twins, Cia and Liz, and Carmen if she came, in the Yellowrock Clan Home or HQ, whichever they decided, which would work nicely, though when Eli came home Liz would likely spend a lot of time here with him. "Okay. I'll also have a suite made available at HQ in case anyone has to crash there for some reason." Knowing vamps and trouble, there would always be a reason someone might have to stay over. "I'll have three rooms at the clan home prepared and your rooms here too. And

CHAPTER 10

He Thought I Was Going to Die

Alex said, "Whatever Quint and Quesnel did, it worked fast."

We both glanced at Quint, who was washing dishes, and who glanced over her shoulder at Alex and me, her face faintly amused.

"The Lear will be in Asheville and ready to depart for NOLA in four hours," Alex said. "Shaddock took my call himself. He was still awake and fully coherent and is working with his primo making arrangements."

Which said a lot: That Quint was handier than I expected. That Shaddock, the MOC of Asheville, had more strength and power than I expected, to be awake in full daylight. Something I often neglected to remember. It also said something about the value of Quint and her uncle's contacts in the vamp world. The annoying man hated me, but I had to be nice to him because he knew wine—which vamps loved—and because I might need him someday. Like today.

I hated that about the job. The false appearances and relationships built on power, bartering, and negotiating.

Alex pursed his lips and looked at his screen as if there were things he didn't want to say aloud. He settled on, "Florence will be shipped to the plane inside an airtight, light-safe box. The Shaddock Clan is also handling security at the airport."

I studied the Kid. He was so unlike the doughy, moody, unwashed, garlic-stinky teenager I had first met. He was still super smart, but now he was strong, dedicated, clean, and had made himself fit. He didn't look up from the tablet at his side, but his lips twitched. "If you cry over how wonderful I am I might get spoiled."

"True. I'll be sure to take my weepy self off then." I socked his shoulder gently as I left the room. Back in my bedroom, where someone had made the bed and straightened my things (which was just so freaking weird), I settled into the new comfy chair and ottoman with my laptop open. I had some business to attend to, all the minutiae of Yellowrock Securities, my personal emails and messages, and the DQ's stuff that had been approved by my secretary, lady-in-waiting, and handler, Quint, and had reached me personally. Handlers. I had handlers in every part of my life.

Jane is in cage but not metal cage, Beast thought. *Beast was in metal cage once. Remembers smell of hunter and captors. Stink of cage-place. Will never forget. Will run and die before cage again.*

I wondered if I'd ever be free of the DQ cage. And if I did put my personal freedom in front of all the responsibilities, would the world I knew disappear? If I stepped on a butterfly on my way out, would the past be changed by a group of timewalkers? Would the arcenciels vanish? Would vamps vanish?

It was dark when I finished my computer work and Bruiser came in. We crawled into bed and were asleep in seconds.

Two hours or so later, my cell rang again. A sense of fear lashed through me like an electric whip.

Beside me, Bruiser came awake, from asleep to total awareness, as I picked up my cell. He was also aiming a weapon at the door. Fast reflexes, my Onorio/Consort.

I held the cell up to him.

Angie's photo and name were on the screen. "Angie?" I answered as Bruiser put the gun away.

"We're all coming in the morning, Ant Jane. My angel is callin' me, telling me there's danger when we land. You have to protect us or we're gonna die bad." The connection ended.

That electric terror thrashed me again, as if I was being struck with a whip made of lightning. I was up and running before I even realized it. Naked. Gasping. Stopped at the door. The cell in my fist made a soft squeak where I held it too tight.

"Jane," Bruiser said, gentle, kind, as he eased out of bed and up to me. "There's nothing to do right now. You need sleep."

I stopped, a low growl of frustration stuck in my throat.

I had nowhere to go. Nothing I could do in this moment would fix things.

Except trying to see time, trying to timewalk. And if Angie and Soul and the other arcenciels were timewalking, I'd just muddy the waters and die trying. I cursed inside my own brain as Beast growled.

The I/we of Beast will save kits, she thought.

Dang skippy, I thought back.

"Back to bed. You need your rest," Bruiser said.

I crawled back into bed, into his arms, snuggling in close, knowing he was right about needing rest, but knowing I'd never get back to sleep. Fortunately, Beast shoved me under, deep into dreamless dark.

My last awareness was of knowing we were all, right now, safe.

I was armoring up, human-shaped, hungry, alone in my bedroom in my own freebie house. The sounds of straps slapping and armor bumping were loud in the silent room. I had gotten a few hours of sleep and felt clearer-headed but still a little sleep deprived.

The tiny door latch was engaged to keep Quint away, not that the latch would keep her out if she decided to break down the door. It was more along the line of a request for privacy. I could smell her frustration on the air as the heat came on and the scents in the house moved through the vents. She was ticked off that she had missed all the excitement of the previous day, and she hadn't bothered trying to hide her irritation.

I was the only nonhuman awake in the house.

Koun and my vamps were all asleep.

I had no witches on the payroll.

Eli was going to be discharged from the hospital in a few hours, to be driven home by one of the Vodka Boys, and he hadn't been informed about Angie's warning for fear he'd try to divert the SUV to the airport to help us. Alex and I were afraid he would succeed in getting himself killed for real this time, since he could barely walk.

Instead of Eli's steady hand running this op, it would be Bruiser. My Consort was perfectly capable of running an op, and he'd taken part in any number of training exercises with the teams over the years, something I never even thought about. But . . . before, on ops, we'd had Eli. And Derek. And right now, the one going into danger was my love, my Consort, Bruiser. My heart did a funny leap that actually hurt.

I smoothed my hair down and separated it into three parts. Breathing. Letting the spiritual act of braiding my own hair calm me, even as I tied it off and coiled the plait into a queue for fighting. I had to stay calm. If I let things upset me, I'd alert Eli, and he had to be kept calm in the hospital. If he knew an op was about to begin he'd be ticked off that he'd not been included.

Bruiser had left while I was dead asleep for HQ to begin coordinating with Alex on comms and the human teams Tango and Delta on the ground, along with the Everharts and their own magic as the flying steel vehicle descended and landed and they got to safety. Or that was the plan.

And there was the human half of team Koppa and me, a skinwalker with uncertain control over her shape.

Alex would be coordinating everything, a long-distance human electronics whiz—one I still thought of as a kid—and any toys he could bring to bear. No vamps due to daylight. Just us humans against any attackers, the enemies all unknowns with unknown strengths, armament, and weaponry. But I was pretty sure they would include my *Tsalagi* clanswomen, witches, and humans.

I had talked to Molly and her sisters on the flight—without mentioning Angie—explaining that I had intel that suggested they could be attacked as they landed or as they debarked the plane. They had plans to protect themselves, knew what to do as the Learjet landed. They had magical defenses ready to counter missiles, rockets, small arms fire, lasers, magic that might affect the jet's many working parts, death magic bombs, flocks of birds an enemy might startle into their path, and, for all I knew, defenses against balloons, clowns, and circus animals. They had other magical defenses ready for their debarkation, but that was also the most likely moment for an attack: the minutes it would take them to climb down the steps, cross the tarmac on foot, and drive to safety.

At this moment, Yellowrock One's flight plan still listed Lakefront Airport as the destination. Just minutes before the plane landed, the pilot would be alerted and the flight plan would be changed from our usual landing site to Greater St. Tammany Regional Airport, a tiny place we had never used. While the unfamiliarity would make it hard to secure, and the length of the runway was not ideal, it would also throw off any attackers.

One team, led by Bruiser, was already on site at Greater St. Tammany Regional, checking out the area, hoping (and it was a hope, not a likely reality) to set up drones that would fly low, far away from the landing area, sweeping the trees in the distance, the roads nearby, and all other access points. *If* the airport personnel and FCC regs allowed drone use. Despite ongoing discussions, no drones had yet been allowed. That meant humans on foot, moving slowly, employing other, less-effective scouting equipment, would be solely responsible for gathering intel and securing the grounds.

I buckled the Benelli to me, the waist strap snug though still looser than when I was in half-form. If I shifted unexpectedly, the shotgun would hang on my half-form's smaller waist, bumping my hips, and the armor would be tight across the shoulders until I adjusted, but everything was designed for expandable areas. I added a single thigh rig for the new H&K and adjusted it a bit higher than usual because my half-form's hips were wider than my human shape and might hurt in any unexpected shift.

I swung a double shoulder rig into place for nine-mils, and added two gobags of color-coded magazines that hung on my hips, nine-mil ammo in one ammo bag and .45 ammo in a much smaller bag. I might clank when I walked, which made me smile. As usual, some mags were marked in silver in case I had to aim at paras; the others were standard for humans we needed to kill. Defensive use only.

We also had rubber bullets, rounds Eli called rubber baton rounds, that could be fired from either standard firearms or dedicated riot guns, which Eli kept stored under the stairs, which Koun, Quint, and some of the others knew. The baton rounds were intended as a non-lethal alternative to standard metal rounds, but placed wrong they could maim, blind, and, though only rarely, kill.

I might have to shoot humans. Which I hated. Humans could have been rolled and forced to fight us, attacking without the ability to measure intent and purpose. I straightened the rigs. Tightened them on my thighs.

Those same humans would kill Angie with no qualms.

Again I pushed away the emotions I had no time to deal with right now.

I checked my cell to see an update from Alex. It told me that the Robere twins were driving everywhere, to city hall, to HQ, to Grégoire's clan home. They were also on the phone to the governor and the local NOLA PD, the various sheriff's departments and highway patrols, as well as local, small-town law enforcement near the airport, trying to mitigate present and future DQ problems with politicians and cops should there be an attack. That meant the airport switcheroo wouldn't be secret for long. I sent back a text acknowledging that I understood. Talking with the law used to be my job, back when I was a lowly rogue-vamp hunter.

Now I had people for that.

I scrutinized myself in the mirror. I was still human-shaped, and I was fully aware that I might shift without my own intent and control into one of my other natural forms: various half-form shapes or fully to Beast. Half-form would be okay. The armor was designed for that in mind. Puma concolor was a different matter entirely. A big-cat in this gear would make me a target, a big-cat trapped in clothes, like a net. I shouldn't go. But. This was an official visit by VIWs—very important witches. And—Angie had said I needed to be on site, so I'd be on site.

I was part of the welcoming team, and despite Quint's furious demands that I be kept safe at HQ, I would be at the airport, carrying enough firepower to make even Eli proud. Not that I could figure out what kind of attack might come.

There was no record of Mainet being able to daywalk, but who really knew. Including vamps in daylight, the danger could be anything. What kind of weapons would come at us? Magical, surely, which I couldn't stop anyway. Mundane, which would injure us all. Killing some of us. "Crap," I whispered as I pulled on a super-comfy pair of custom-made adjustable battle boots.

I had poured over the sat maps of the small airport. There was no protection for debarking passengers, little security, lots of danger, but it would be an unexpected place for Yellowrock and NOLA visitors to land. Unexpected meant safer. Maybe. Unless the enemy had access to time . . .

Through the postulated time circle.

Even without trying to see the futures, I could envision possibilities. Angie was a witch. She could see time, almost like a . . . like a scryer. A time scryer.

Did the enemy have time scryers?

What if the Heir or his scions and slaves could scry? That could allow them to act outside of, or ahead of, time. They would have plenty of time to put one of those transporter circles on site, and no human or drone would see it until it popped into existence. *Crap.* I was tired. I didn't have Eli to bandy ideas back and forth. I hadn't thought through all the possibilities.

I was securing my human feet into my battle boots

when my cell pinged with a text. It was Bruiser, telling me, "Security is in place and the airport is locked down. All other flights are being diverted, and the officials have allowed the Dark Queen's drones to make two passes around the airport. Everything seems safe." My terror eased until I read the next line. "Now only time changes and the roads into NOLA present a danger."

And that part made me nearly shiver. I texted back, "If Mainet has time scryers, they may have a transport circle in place under camouflage. Something that would let them send attackers there at the last possible moment."

Bruiser texted back, "Understood. Re-evaluating."

We needed Eli.

We didn't have Eli.

I needed the Infermeri. The vamp who was locked inside the nearest thing to a coffin, strapped into the cargo hold, on the plane that might be attacked and destroyed, along with my friends.

My armor had special sheaths for sharp pointy things. Into them, I added throwing knives and knives of various lengths and for various purposes. I threaded in the null sticks. I checked myself in the mirror again. The matte black armor was cinched to allow for body-shape changes and the battle boots were laced tight. My amber eyes glowed with my Beast.

I/we are best hunter. Will keep witches and kits safe.

Yeah. Dang skippy, I thought again.

Beast does not skip.

I chuckled and smeared on scarlet lipstick, shoved the Glob into a padded pocket, flipped the light switches off, and left my room.

At two p.m., my driver, Wrassler, who surely had admin duties and should be shuffling paperwork or talking to staff or something, and my three-person security team, each member armored and armed top to toe, sat in my SUV, which was also armored. To keep the four black vehicles, part of my motorcade, from standing out like extra thumbs, we were parked between two metal buildings, one of which was an office, the other a brand-new hangar. The vehicles were impossible to see except from

specific narrow angles, making them difficult targets. All
the other SUVs were empty, as the team I had brought
had dispersed to provide additional protection for the jet.
The other vehicle drivers were positioned at either end of
the narrow passage where we were parked.

I had learned that airport security had been dead set
against weapons and former military, but the possibility
of magical attack, especially seeing the video of the null
prison attack, had changed their minds. That and the
charm of my Onorio Consort. He wouldn't roll humans
the way he could a vamp, but when he turned on his power
of persuasion, learned as primo at the feet of the former
MOC of NOLA, he was more than formidable.

All around the tiny public airport and scattered in
trees off the runway were the rest of the teams. Bruiser's
two teams had arrived in staggered batches, on motorcycles, and had been outfitted on site, so there wouldn't be
so many SUVs parked all over and visible from overhead.
Two snipers in desert camo armor were on the roofs to
either side, each with a good firing vantage point. Even
knowing my people were there, I hadn't been able to spot
anyone.

Alex, sitting in the main security room in HQ, had
access to the tower's audio both here and at our usual
airport, which I knew he wasn't supposed to have access
to. He had been giving us a running commentary, up to
one minute ago. Then zilch. I adjusted my earbuds and
repositioned my mic. Still nothing but the quiet chatter
from the teams in the field.

On the small dashboard screen were thumbnails of each
of the vest cam images. On two of them I spotted the black
hoods of our SUVs, meaning they were in our narrow alley,
covering us. One showed the roots of a tree. Another was a
close-up of a section of a metal wall. Bushes. Dirt. Boots.
A view of an open area near the runway. Nothing useful.
And I hated being stuck in the SUV, away from everything.

Being DQ sucked, but I kept my sulking to myself.

"You should be able to hear the Lear," Alex said into
my headset. I nearly jumped at his voice. Quint almost
smiled, as if I was cute. I narrowed my eyes at her in threat
and her smile went wider as if taunting me. I eased the

window down a bit. My hearing in my human ears was far less acute than in my other forms, but within a few seconds, I heard the distant hum that quickly became a roar. This was where the danger increased. Magic might bring down the plane. Or rockets. Explosions. Bombs bursting in air.

I had a mental image of Angie Baby's body falling from the sky. Arms and legs flailing lifelessly as she plummeted to the ground. The visual wouldn't blink away.

I pulled on Beast's speed and strength, opened the door, and leaped out. Quint grabbed at my shoulder rig and tried to stop me, but I twisted my body against her fingers and slipped into the shadows cast by the hangar. Cursing, telling Alex I was on the move, she followed.

I inched into a better angle and watched the runway. The Lear appeared, seeming to float in midair. Slowly it dropped lower, its engine sounding different. Did engines always change pitch when a Lear landed? I couldn't remember. After too long, after *forever*, it touched down. Reversed with a great rumble I could feel in my bones. Grew quieter. Taxied around and closer. Stopped.

Faster than was probably regulation, the hatch opened. Two women in Yellowrock Security garb rolled the stairs up to it and took up places beneath the belly of the plane, long-rifles pointing at the distant trees.

Molly, carrying Cassy (*Holy crap*. How had I forgotten she would have to bring the baby?), with EJ and Angie right behind her, started slowly down the stairs. Her husband followed, his bulk a protection hovering over them all. Molly's sisters were right behind, bunched close. Big Evan, the air witch, was whistling a bright tune. In this form, I couldn't see magical energies unless the casters of the working allowed it, and while there was nothing visible, I knew the Everharts were clustered together because they were manipulating a moving *hedge of thorns*. I might not like their lack of speed, but I accepted it was for a good cause.

My heart was beating too hard. It hurt in my chest, as if it hammered against my ribs.

The tight group walked down the stairs and right into the brand-new hangar. I blew out a relieved breath. In seconds, surrounded by a small security team, they were all hustled out the side door and into different SUVs in my motorcade. As they were divided and positioned, the drivers materialized and slid into the vehicles.

"Activity in the west quadrant," a voice said into my earbuds.

Liz was shoved at Quint. My lady-in-waiting grabbed the curvy witch and heaved her into my SUV, then tossed me in on top of her. Cia followed, landing on top of both of us.

"Drive!" Bruiser shouted into comms' earbuds.

Wrassler took off. So did three of the other SUVs.

Liz, Cia, and I pushed apart and struggled for our seat belts, the twins now side-by-side. Wrassler drove like the hounds of hell were after us and he was dodging their teeth. As SUVs pulled out of the pickup area, someone screamed into comms, "Incoming!"

I twisted in my seat. Got a glimpse of someone jumping off the roof of the new hangar—the one the Everharts had just walked through. An enormous *whomp* sounded. My ears popped even through the SUV's armor. The walls of the hangar blew out. The roof caved in. The vehicle rocked and bounced. Behind us, debris flew and fell. Quint hadn't gotten in any car. I didn't see her. Just clouds of dust and smoke billowing.

The witches still weren't buckled in. I shoved them into the floorboards.

My connection with Eli woke up. He felt my adrenaline spike. I felt his fury, that he hadn't been informed about whatever I was facing.

The SUVs had all pulled out, tires shooting gravel. All the vehicles going in different directions. White motorcycles were everywhere.

The Lear made a good target. The vamp-hatch in the belly was open, a coffin-sized box being offloaded by a four-person team. A small *something* exploded just above the Lear, debris flying. The team hit the dirt. Untouched. No concussive force, no debris touched the jet or the team. How? The witches were all on the ground. In SUVs, moving. No circles. No—

Angie's magic?

My jaw bones popped. My head ached. I could suddenly see as my half-form did, which included magical energies. There was a blue glow around the jet. A second blue glow covered the four humans again holding Florence's travel box. Now with no place to go. No SUVs, no hangar. I looked at my hands. I was still human except for part of my face; the shift had stopped there, leaving the rest of me human. A helpful shape for once. When I looked back up, the jet and box were no longer in my sightline. White motorcycles sped after us. I counted three on my tail. I yanked the witches up. "Seat belts."

"No shit," Cia said. The moon witch was shaking.

Inside me, Eli raged. I tried to send him calm, but all I got was that he was on the move. On the way home from the hospital? Trying to get to us? *Of course. Idiot man.* Into comms, I told Alex to find his brother and tell him we were all okay.

At my side, Liz was doing something with her hands, a weird reddish glow gathered in her palms, leading back to the chunky stone necklace she wore, her amulets all glowing. The witch was a stone mage, her magic strongest when she was in a circle, sitting on a fully charged boulder. She'd be limited in the moving vehicle. She reached to her sister and they joined hands. Cia's moonstone necklace glowed a vibrant silver, though she too was limited as the moon wasn't in the sky. I scooted closer to the door, trying not to touch them and interfere with their working.

The motorcade SUVs were headed out fast with no prearranged route. That was on purpose in case a time scryer had been watching. One vehicle gunned it toward I-12, one toward 190, circling around, scattering. Wrassler used back roads, taking the long way home. Everyone avoided crossing the bridge over Lake Pontchartrain, where every vehicle would be a sitting duck. We'd regroup near Slidell. Bruiser, in the earbuds, ordered the white crotch-rockets to gather around the vehicles, my three closing the gap.

Someone said, "Transport box is undamaged." A moment later she said, "Asset is secure. SUV and driver are on the move."

My Infermieri was still with us. Undead, not true dead.

The woman said, "LZ injured require medic, civilian ambulances, and first responders. Also will need ATF and parish coroners."

After the briefest hesitation, Alex said, "Understood. ETAs to follow."

That chatter told me the airport had injured and dead.

I checked my weapons, listening over the headset, which still fit my ears. The drivers checked in. Bruiser had Molly and Evan and the kids. Quint was currently shouting into her mic, the scream of a motorcycle nearly overpowering her voice.

Eli had joined the comms. He was angrier than I had ever heard him, talking to Alex. Eli was claiming that we either had another mole, or someone even better than Alex (Reach and his possible return? I remembered the Money Honey comment) had drilled into comms, or the entire security system was compromised. Alex said to him, "Janie has a different thought." One of them cut the feed on the general channel. My thought was the time scrying, which we weren't sharing with my own people. Just in case.

The plan was for all the SUVs to converge again on U.S.-11, as we entered the outskirts of Slidell, heading toward Front Street. One of the DQ's SUVs appeared. Then another. Three out of four in front of us. Where was the other one? The one with Florence, in her coffin.

Mismatched, brightly painted motorcycles raced in behind my SUV, enemy bikes, the riders firing weapons. The attackers might be great shots, but the car armor was built to resist all small-arms fire, and decrease the effectiveness of even bigger stuff, up to a small rocket. The crotch-rockets wove and danced, two of our riders, on white bikes, fired back, but the chance of hitting their targets was low.

"No collateral damage," I demanded into my mic. "Alex, tell the motorcycle protection to peel off."

"Belay that order," Bruiser said. "Countermand that."

I blinked. *Belay?*

"Team Tango," Bruiser said. "Cut out all civilian vehicles."

"Copy that," team Tango's leader said. Sugar Tit. I was pretty sure it was Sugar Tit. "Let's ride, boys and girls. Traffic laws are for sissies."

"Traffic laws are *not* for sissies!" I said.

No one responded.

I changed it, repeating, "No collateral damage."

No one countermanded the order this time, and I got some muttered "Copy, no collateral damage" in reply.

In the rearview, I saw a civilian car dodge a motorcycle and hit an electric pole. The airbags deployed. So much for "no collateral damage." I'd need to make sure the vehicle was replaced. *Dang it.*

We entered Slidell city proper. Citizens scattered.

I felt a working from outside, magic prickling over my skin. Comms cut out. Static sounded for too long before Alex came back on. He was cursing, trying to find a workaround. I heard him say, "Magic interf—" and then he was gone again. "Got it," he said, and I heard voices shouting and giving info. We couldn't afford to lose comms, not now, but—

Comms went down again. This time Alex didn't come back on. Freaking dang magic.

I looked back to see SUVs behind us in the suddenly decreasing traffic. Spotted Big Evan's head and body and Molly's and Angie Baby's faces in the vehicle behind mine, about fifty feet back, Bruiser driving.

A beige van pulled from a side street behind my vehicle, cutting off the others. Swerving. Orange magic burst from it, orange energies, tinted with a slimy green.

Each vehicle behind me was hit with a working, except Molly and Angie Baby's. The attack parted and went around that vehicle. Their SUV was fully engulfed in Angie's raw blue-white witch power, so intense I could have seen it with human eyes. The raw magic coalesced, shimmering into Big Evan and Molly's moving *hedge.*

Raw magic meant Angie was powering her mom and dad's working.

The orange blast coalesced and whipped-ricocheted our way. It hit our vehicle. Hit *us.*

The pain was so intense it was like getting tased and flayed all at once. I felt as if my skin sloughed to the floor and my bones bled. The witch twins and Wrassler screamed in pain. From somewhere far away, Eli sent a shaft of cool quietness into me. Time did that battlefield change. Slowed. Slowed.

The SUV engine spluttered. The vehicle rocked as if it hit something. Skewed in a circle as if it slid on ice.

As if moving in slow motion, I rammed against the side window. The front airbags deployed. The SUV encased in the blue glow raced past, Bruiser driving. Our eyes met for an instant. His were wide and broken. He thought I was going to die. But he was saving the children. I gave a nod, and then he was gone. It was the right call.

CHAPTER 11

Her Skin Caught Fire

The orange magic surrounded me. It was splattered with thousands of green motes. It slashed and carved inside me, like claws. Grabbed the place where the silver haze of my magic resided. It sliced deep.

My skinwalker energies didn't defend, didn't seem to know how to defend. But I had other power, other defenses. If I could make them work without the crown on my head. I thought about *le breloque*. Drew on the Dark Queen power that was mine, and felt it gather inside me, a rising tide of light and heat and frigid cold. I could . . . With a thought, the energies formed into a silver point. "Yes," I said. I thrust the silver point into the orange energies. My power pierced the assault. Energy exploded out of me.

I shifted. Fast. It felt as if I was being turned inside out.

I opened my eyes, seeing my hands. Knobby, long fingered. Half-form.

The vehicle was still sliding.

The orange magics were gone. The twins were gasping.

Weeping. When I looked at them they were holding their own defensive magics around them and Wrassler, like a tapestry of lights. There was a broken space in their circle, where I had been. Wonderful crazy witches had been trying to protect me too. My *attack* magic had broken through and punctured the defensive working, damaging their ward before it killed the orange green attack spell. That hadda hurt.

The SUV died. Slid to a stop.

Wrassler slumped over the steering wheel and airbag. I hoped not dead.

The white motorcycles were down, my people lying on the street. The enemy bikes shot toward us, two red, one black. The beige van followed.

The hedge in the SUV snapped back closed, with me outside it. Still shielded by Everhart magics, Liz and Cia were holding an undulating ball of purple-and-white power. With one finger, Liz opened the SUV door at her side. Cia shifted the weird ball into Liz's sure grip. The *hedge* fell. Liz threw the magic at three enemy motorcycles. The *hedge* whipped back up. The bikes crashed as if they had hit a wall. Flipped into the air. The attacking humans were flung from the bikes as if whapped by a huge hand. Wheels screaming, the beige van spun around backward and hit a building. The bikes landed.

The twins fell to the side, exhausted.

The attackers lay in the street, twitching.

Holy crap.

A whir sounded. I looked up. Approaching overhead was a drone, a remote viewing aircraft. Before I thought, I ripped the Benelli from its spine sheath. Stepped out of the SUV. Gauged the distance and its speed. Not more than fifty feet away and slow. I braced. Brought the weapon up. My finger squeezed the trigger. Fired.

The drone exploded. I ducked. It had been carrying a small bomb.

My hearing was ruined, but I somehow heard Wrassler cough and mutter, "The SUV is done for."

Two of our white HQ motorbikes pulled up to the beige van. One rider fired point-blank into the van. Emptying mags. Rubber rounds, I hoped. Something went *whomp*.

Smoke boiled out of the van. Tires screamed. A white bike rode up to us. Stopped.

Quint glared at me through the faceplate. Cold, hard, and furious. "Get on the bike," she said to me.

I twisted to the side and picked up Liz. I carried her to Quint's bike and sat her on pillion. I returned to Cia and put her on the other bike with one of the new security people. "Go."

"You're my asset," Quint said.

"That's an order," I said.

Quint cursed but both bikes took off.

Over the earbuds, between staticky bursts, I heard Wrassler call for pickup of our people who had been hit by the magical attack and the enemy combatant humans, who were still twitching and clearly alive. A third white crotch-rocket wailed up the street. Braked hard. Skidded, rubber on asphalt. Stopped. Eli. Battle face. Expression colder than Quint's. No armor. He pulled a semiautomatic, pointed it up. Fired twice. Debris fell. He had taken out two more remote aircraft. I hadn't seen or heard them approaching.

Eli had just saved our lives.

Wrassler opened his door. Coughed. There was a smattering of blood on his lips. Eli cursed and called again for a medic. Wrassler coughed harder. There was more blood. "Can you ride?" Eli asked him.

Shaking his head no, the big man pointed to a stairwell between two buildings, one a warehouse with an exterior staircase and a second-story door under a metal roof. Eli dropped his bike, got an arm under Wrassler's shoulder. Both men limped to the stairway. Wrassler crawled up to the top of the stairs to the protected landing. I was useless, so I covered the still-twitching humans and kept an eye on the skies for more drones. From farther down the street, more of HQ's bikes converged.

When one of my helmeted riders tried to get me on pillion, I turned the Benelli on him. "No." Not without Wrassler. Wrassler, who was too big and too injured to ride pillion on a crotch-rocket.

The anonymous guard spun to another SUV and all

but carried Carmen out of it and roared off, the witch riding behind, holding on as if for dear life. It looked as if she had left her kid in Asheville, or maybe the kid was in Angie's SUV. The drivers and the men and women who had been riding shotgun in the SUVs behind me also got rides. None of them were coughing blood.

My hearing was coming back online, but my SUV was . . . melting. It had received special treatment, a death magic bomb. As if the attackers had known which was mine. Or maybe my magic had done something to the attack spell. Could be.

"HQ SUVs will be here in ten to load up Wrassler, the rest of our security people, and the three humans taken out by Liz's magic bomb," Eli said, speaking to me but not looking at me. His eyes and hands were checking out one of the enemy's crashed bikes. Mad as a hornet. Limping badly. Shouldn't even be walking.

I felt his rage and his pain like my own fury and aches in my own flesh.

"Alex," he said. "Can you tell who's running this attack against us? General location? Because we're shutting them down."

"Affirmative. Maybe." His voice cracked slightly with strain and I could hear clacking of keys and tapping of fingers on tablets, banging against the surfaces like castanets. "Hang on."

Still holding the Benelli, nominally covering us all as Eli half carried Wrassler up the exposed stairs, I studied the enemy humans, who were now trying to make coordinated movements. One vomited. By the stink, they had peed themselves.

Eli made it down the stairs to them and dug around in their pockets, finding key fobs for the bikes. He removed IDs and weapons. He rolled them over and applied zipstrips to their arms. Which I should have done. Except one of us had to stand cover.

Feeling useless, I ran my eyes over the SUV. It had stopped melting. Using the edge of my uniform sleeve to keep death cooties off me, I opened the SUV hatch and took out a modified long-rifle, ammo, a first aid kit, two bottles of water. Climbing the steps to Wrassler, I handed him the weapon and gear. "Per the Dark Queen's order. Kill our enemies if they come for you."

"Yes," he said, the words gurgling, "My Queen."

I raced back down the stairs. Eli turned on a bike once ridden by an enemy human and handed me its fob. He had taken the last of the weapons from the SUV. I holstered the Benelli and adjusted my headset. I had no helmet, and I wasn't taking one from the enemy. They probably had death cooties too.

"Pickup in eight," Eli told Wrassler. "Stay alive or your wife will kill me."

"True dat," Wrassler said, sounding more like himself. "If I die, she'll slap me alive, kill me all over again, and you all too. That said, I'll keep these guys down and try to keep the area clear with cover fire. I don't wanna kill a human today. The cops frown on that."

Magic and rubber bullets and smoke bombs had taken out enemy humans. If humans died, that was going to be a problem for the Roberes to handle. Still. I didn't care enough to ride by and see if our enemies needed help.

Over comms, Alex said, "I'm inside one of remote aircraft. Enemy security sucks. It's moving away from y'all. Assuming it's heading back to the remote handler."

"Coordinates," Eli said.

"Head west from your current twenty." He gave us street names. Eli and I took off on the unfamiliar bikes. Not Harleys but Suzuki Hayabusas. Fast, well-balanced racing bikes, but real whiners sound-wise.

I was armed, but firing was pretty much a useless exercise from a bike. I trailed Eli, feeling his too-fast heart rate. He shouldn't be here.

Eli wasn't wearing armor. He had a thick bandage around his thigh. The sticky wrap was stained with watery blood. I said nothing. Followed him. Feeling his rage.

Alex said, "The drone is high enough that I can see a good ways around. Ahead is an eighteen-wheeler, parked in a large concrete parking area. Truck has a shiny, slick paint job." He told us where to turn. Three turns later, he said, "There are three witches sitting on the street beside the truck in a protected circle. Drone is dropping to it.

The back of the vehicle is open." He told us to turn, saying, "If you want to go in unheard, you'll have to do it on foot. You're half a mile."

"No stealth," Eli said. "These are their bikes. They have magical tracking amulets on them. They think friendlies are approaching."

"Copy that," Alex said. "I'm getting some good footage of the witches and the inside of the eighteen-wheeler. There are two people in the trailer."

"Get out of the system before they sense you," Eli said.

"Withdrawing. Leaving a back door in case I happen to need it again."

"Are all our people secure?" Eli asked.

"Negative," Alex said, "but the assets are undamaged and converging on NOLA. The sleeper is stored in an SUV and on her way."

Sleeper. Florence. Good. We might need her sooner than expected.

"How many of our people are still in the Slidell downtown area?" Eli asked.

"Four."

"Send them to us."

"Already done. They're thirty seconds behind you," Alex said.

We slowed and seconds later four white crotch-rockets fell in behind our red bikes. Together, we converged on the location of the eighteen-wheeler and the witches. We sped into the drive of a warehouse. Along the side of the huge building. And into an even bigger concrete parking area with loading docks every few feet along the back of the warehouse.

The witches sitting in the circle stood and disappeared. Just vanished. Like a magician's act. But . . . "Their circle is still working," I said, "still active. It's glowing with the same weird ugly energies they attacked us with." A half second later I shouted, "The energies are growing."

"Abort!" Eli shouted, looking up. He gunned his bike to the right. "Abort! Abort! Disperse!"

I turned to the right, following Eli, my turn too hard, too fast on the unfamiliar bike. My boot grazed the concrete. I almost—*almost*—put my foot down. Which could dislocate my ankle. At the last second, I corrected my lean and accelerated. We all took off, down the drive to the street.

I glanced at the driveway in front of me and back, following Eli's eyes, even as I gunned the unfamiliar Suzuki Hayabusa. Above the open space at the eighteen-wheeler was a drone. A BIG one. Carrying something that glowed orange. Another magical bomb.

Below it, the concrete in the witches' circle buckled, as if something was trying to come up from beneath the ground. The circle was a portal of some kind. Just like the transport circle in the street at the null prison. And probably at the airport. And in Natchez, way back when. This was a trap.

The HQ bikes veered into the street and scattered in different directions. Alex was giving directions to Eli and me. Just in front of me, Eli turned hard right and down an alley. Took a left. Eli veered into a tiny alcove, braked, and spun out in a squeal that hurt my damaged ears. I laid my bike down to avoid hitting him. The wheels rammed into the wall at the end of the nook. My body followed. I slid against the pavement and was thrown high. Into the wall. I shoved off the wall with my half-form strength and landed on top of Eli. Covering him with my body. We both opened our mouths and covered our ears, preparing for the detonation.

There was a massive explosion. Even so far away, protected by several buildings, the concussive wave hit us. It was like being hit by a truck.

Eli pushed me to his left. Before I could pick myself up, he aimed over my shoulder, his arm against my ear as partial protection. Fired. A remote aircraft crashed onto the roof of the building at our side. No explosion. Eli said, "Their bikes are tracked. Useful to us until they realized our people had them. Ditch 'em."

Through the battle-bond, I felt his pain, his exhaustion. He was nearly spent. I adjusted my headset and pulled Eli to his feet. Placed the Benelli in his left arm and pulled his right over my shoulders. The angle was odd, but with my left arm around him, he had support, and I could fire with my right. He met my eyes, his expression telling me he could shoot just fine, offhand.

I pulled my new H&K and put a finger in place along the frame, above the trigger. "Alex. Which way?" I asked.

"Back the way you came," he said. "The sat maps didn't show the alley you're in as being closed off. That wall is new since the last upload of the sat maps. So you have to backtrack to the road and then right. I have people en route to you. Local law has been notified to stay clear, that this is a paranormal attack being handled by the Dark Queen's special forces. They've cleared the streets and have barricades going up. If you see a cop, stop and take shelter before they see you until I can contact them and assure your safety."

"Roger that," I said. Because some cops would shoot my monster self on sight. Taking most of Eli's weight in my arm around his waist, we moved back toward the street. Without signals or words at all, Eli was watching above us and covering our left. I was covering in front, our right, and as much of our six as I could. There was some overlap, so if one of us missed something, the other one might spot it. We reached the road and spent plenty of time making sure no one was watching and no civilians were around. We headed right.

I could smell the sour sweetness of Eli's wound, the pain and the battle stink of his sweat, a combo of adrenaline and determination and the drugs that were still trying to clear his body from the surgery. But mostly, with my cat nose, his blood. Glancing down, I saw thick, almost gelatinous fresh blood on Eli's bandages. *Idiot man.* "You die on me and I'll have a vamp turn you and then I'll kill you again," I threatened.

His laughter was mostly breath. "Love you too, babe."

After his last injury, Eli had signed the turning papers, so I could do it too.

In the far distance my cat ears picked up the whine of motorcycles. "I hear bikes," I said to Alex. "Friendlies?"

"If it's from Front Street, affirmative. Six of our finest heading to you. Four up front and two more a block back."

"Roger that," Eli murmured.

The bikes grew closer. Eli and I stopped in an entrance doorway that was set back in the wall, giving us cover from behind and above, but making us visible to our rescue. Eli said, "Sorry," and slumped in my arm. I grabbed the Benelli and let Eli down to lie across my feet. His bleeding was much worse, the bandage soaked and mushy. "I need a medic," I said to Alex, holstering the handgun, the shotgun sweeping everywhere.

"Can he ride a bike?" Alex asked. "I can set up a rendezvous site with an ambulance."

"Negative, unless I strap him to the rider." That told Alex more than I wanted to on the open line. The connection went silent except for static that shouldn't be there. Equipment damage from concussive waves or magic.

A moment later, he said, "I just checked about Florence's coffin. They're still en route. I'm going to Kojo and Thema's rooms. They're the oldest on site. If they're up, I'll ask for help. If they're asleep, I'm staking them both and having their undead bodies brought to security." Entering a vamp's lair was an unforgivable insult, whether they were awake or asleep. If Alex had to break in and stake them, they would kill him later. No question. So the insult had to come from me.

"By the order of the Dark Queen, make it so, number two. They should be awake-ish, so knock first. Loud," I said. "They might be able to stay awake long enough to help."

"You know how much I hate being called number two, right?"

"I do. Suck it up, buttercup."

Any reply he might have made was drowned out by the six white motorcycles that turned the corner and sped to us. Four bikes moved out and Chi-Chi, wearing goggles, pointed where he wanted the other bikes. They took cover positions, weapons raised and tracking up and down the street. The other two stopped, turned off the bikes, and shoved back faceplates. "Hey, Legs," Blue Voodoo said.

Legs. Not *My Queen.* All of Derek's guys had stayed on after he was killed, and they were part of HQ's and the DQ's security. But they were here for me, as a person, not because of my title and position. I smiled, and some of the tension lifted from me.

Angel Tit and Chi-Chi glanced our way and both gave that military nod that said they acknowledged me but were busy covering the surroundings.

Voodoo said, "Let's get you two out of here."

"Pressure on that leg," Angel Tit said.

Voodoo asked, "Evac?"

I slid the Benelli into its sheath, repositioned Eli's body. "You'll get on your bike," I said to Voodoo. "I'll strap him to your body. Alex is setting up a rendezvous with medic. If that isn't possible, you'll get him to HQ. Alex is waking a donor to have on site."

"No shit?" Angel Tit said. He glanced at me. "No offense, Janie, but the Kid's got balls. Hope they let him keep them."

"Funny," Alex said, breaking into the channel. "Hang loose on the bike evac. One of our SUVs is a mile away, driving like a bat outta hell. Cia tells me Liz is missing so I'm guessing it's her. ETA in seconds."

An armored SUV made the turn a block up and roared to us, Liz at the wheel. She was furious, her magic barely in check, her amulet necklace glowing bright even through the tinted windows.

I picked up Eli like a baby and carried him toward the street.

Liz braked hard and opened her door. "You stupid—" She stopped shouting when Eli shifted, unconscious in my arms. "Son of a witch," she cursed, whirling to open the hatch. "I can't keep you alive, can I?" she demanded of his unconscious body.

"He's a man," I said, as if that was explanation enough. I laid him inside the back, gently positioning his leg. "And a warrior. Born and bred to run toward trouble, not stay safe."

Angel Tit removed a first aid kit from the back of the HQ vehicle and ripped open a plastic package, removing a high-strength trauma pressure bandage, a kind I had never seen before, with a handle to create or release pressure.

Before he could wrap the seventy-inch-long dressing on top of the existing bandages and around Eli's leg, Liz unhooked her amulet necklace and pulled three stones off. She shoved them under existing bandages, next to Eli's skin. "Healing amulets," she murmured, "calibrated to him."

"Good," Chi-Chi and I said at the same time.

As Voodoo and Tit worked, Alex said to me, on a private channel, "Cops won't let the ambulance through. Not for us."

He meant not for paranormals. Not even for the humans who worked for us.

"Yeah?" I said. "We'll see about that. Call the Roberes. Get them to call the local mayors and the governor. Remind the elected officials that I can move my headquarters anywhere in the States I want. I'm sick of making that threat, and this is the last time I'll say it. If Eli dies, or the next time they refuse assistance, or get in my way on official business, I'm outta here. I'll move my headquarters to Asheville. And New Orleans can sink into the Gulf for all I care." Pulling the MOC and the DQ headquarters out of the city would leave NOLA and the entire South to the strongest vamp warlord who could take and keep the hunting territory. "Tell them they can explain to their constituents that they're responsible for the blood running in their streets because they chased us off. And tell them I'll go onto national media to explain why I'm moving."

"Yes, My Queen."

"Dang skippy, *My Queen*."

I said, "Liz. You. In back with Eli. Voodoo. Drive. I'm taking your bike."

I pulled the Benelli and waved away his helmet. I wanted people to see my Beast face. "Everyone rides behind me and surrounding the SUV. Down any drone, stop any vehicle that chases after us. Alex," I said. "Be ready for us. Medical protocol. We're closer to HQ than any hospital I trust."

"Yes, ma'am."

Medical protocol was brand-new. Trying it out on Eli meant working through problems on the fly. *Holy crap.*

I straddled the shiny white bike. Turned it on, happy for once to have an electronic start. Mad as I was, I might have broken a kick-start. "Move out." My weapon clear and visible, my mouth open so my fangs showed, I pulled into the street.

Six blocks later, we came to the first barricade. The OIC—officer in charge—was on the phone, his body language confused and yet obsequious to the person he was talking to. Holding the cell away, he waved his men back, yelling, "Stand down! Stand down. Move your vehicles. Do not, repeat, do *not* impede the Dark Queen's progress." The cop cars moved and the man waved us through, nodding at me. I snarled at him. He took three steps back.

There were no more stoppages. No traffic light problems either. The cops on the streets stopped traffic for us, waving us through.

As we motored toward HQ, I listened to Alex's reports and updates. Wrassler had been picked up and was safe at HQ. The other Everhart witches and families were safe at HQ, standing on the grounds marking a ward around the entire property for a *hedge of thorns*. The vehicle with Florence had heard about the attack on me and had taken the long way to throw off our enemies, across Lake Pontchartrain, despite orders not to, and there had been an accident. She was sitting in traffic. My people were all alive. Some injured, banged up, a few with busted eardrums from magical and mundane explosions, and some with road rash from fast-stopping, sliding bikes.

Eli's heart was still beating, slower now, in time with my own. Relief and fury danced through me like a rumba, grinding, both hot and cold, and putting an end to the politics. *Now.*

All the way through to the French Quarter, I ground my teeth because there was nothing to shoot, nothing to kill, and Eli was . . . Eli was bad.

It took forever, but we rounded the corner and I gunned the motor, racing into the back entrance of HQ, where a gurney and a line of security personnel, housekeeping, and even kitchen staff were lined up, ready to help. The

Everharts were standing with them too: Cia, Carmen, Big
Evan, Molly, and . . . Angie Baby. I didn't see EJ and no
Cassy, which was good, because seeing Eli's condition was
probably too much even for little Angie.

Under the roof of the porte cochere but out of the way,
I killed the bike's engine and slung my leg over it, standing. "Angie doesn't need to see this," I said to Molly.

"I'm supposed to be here," Angie said, her expression
mulish. She crossed her arms and glared at me, her straw-
berry curls bouncing. "I'm not a little girl anymore. Eli's
hurt, with lots a blood and guts and I'm not gonna cry or
act like a baby," she said. "And something's gonna come
from over there"—she pointed at the back-left corner of
the property, above the twelve-foot-tall fence—"when
you open the trunk door."

Evan cursed. A word he had probably never said in
front of his kid.

"We don't have the *hedge* ready," Molly said.

Crap. I needed to look at time, if I still could, even if it
made the cancer come back. "Probable bogey from the
back-left quadrant," I said into my mic. "Fire on sight. Do
not allow a drone near HQ. Get Eli and the civilians inside. Take cover."

My people raced into cover positions. The few steel
shutters that were still open in daylight clanged and
banged shut. Big Evan picked up his daughter and carried
her inside, Molly and her sisters on his heels. The SUV
carrying Eli turned in, made the small circle, and came to
a stop under the porte cochere.

The hatch opened. Liz slid to the ground, bloody, shouting, "Evan! Help!"

The big man was suddenly just there, whistling, his
hand over Eli. There was so much blood. Angie grabbed
me by the thigh rig and pointed. "There, Ant Jane!"

She pointed to the tall brick fence as a big honking
drone moved slowly, unerringly, toward HQ.

My team opened fire.

The drone didn't go down. It was wrapped in an orange magic ward. A freaking portable, flying defensive
ward. In midair. Even the Everharts hadn't created that
kind of ward.

The sound of small arms fire was intense. Deafening. The drone paused and then headed straight for us.

I glanced at the SUV. Big Evan was lifting Eli. The sorcerer's lips were pursed, probably whistling his heal-ing magic. Molly and Cia were there too, Moll's hands covering the blood-soaked bandage, her earth magics like a golden glow, her fingers stained with Eli's blood. The Everharts headed inside with Eli, his leg unmoving, supported. I looked back at the drone.

There was no one to help with the drone wrapped in magical energies. How much of a load was it carrying? Enough to take out HQ entirely? I aimed the Benelli and took a shot. Nothing.

The steel doors clanked as they closed.

"I'm sorry, Mama!" Angie yelled.

I got my head around fast enough to see her barrel through the narrow crack of the steel doors. Outside.

I caught a glance of Molly's mouth open in panic.

Big Evan's hand shoved into the cracked opening.

My godchild wrapped her arms round my waist and *pulled* my magic to her. A silver-and-blue glow of raw power shot throughout with purple, red, and black motes surrounded us. Visceral, primitive, undirected power.

"Angie, *no!*" I screamed.

In a single instant, her clothes caught fire.

Her skin caught fire.

Her magic shot around and through me.

My armor flamed. My skin blistered where she touched me.

My own power joined the working, silver and black and red.

Angie swirled the power into a ball just like the witches in the beige van had. She threw it. Straight at the attacking drone. Screaming, *"Squash!"*

"Down!" I grabbed her. Dropped. Covered her magic-burning body with mine.

The drone explosion was massive. I lost time for a bit, coming to when the pain hit. The concussive wave had . . . busted something inside me. My body was on fire. So was Angie, the flames of her raw magic glowing between us. My armor was smoking.

I shifted. Fully to Beast. Faster than I ever had. My
armor was in flames and pieces.

Beast is best hunter. Beast is best mother of kits.

Beast crawled out of the gear and ruined clothing. Burning. Angie's magic was still scorching, smoking. Pelt was
on fire. Flames crawled up snout, across fangs. Beast
picked up Angie by her clothes, fangs tangling in them. Big
Evan was shoving against the doors with all his might.

Beast raced, dragging Angie, slinking through the
opening crack in the steel doors.

Dropped Angie at Molly's feet. Molly snuffed fire. Took
her daughter and followed Eli's blood trail up the stairs
into the security room. Pain eased as fire died, but . . .

Beast was hurt. Was burned by raw magic. Burned
bad. Paw pads were agony to walk on. Each foot left watery bloody fluid in the paw prints behind us. Beast nearly
fell, caught self against wall. Followed Molly and kit to
security room.

In middle of big table Eli was sprawled. Bloody. Skin
ashen, gray, blue, Dead?

Thema and Kojo were vamped-out. Awake. In daylight. On top of Eli. His bandages had been ripped off.
Vampires cut their arms, bleeding on wound.

Jane woke. Peered through eyes, watching as vampires
bled into Eli mouth. I/we watched. Beast shoved down on
pain. Jane did not know how bad we were injured. Yet.
But it had to be bad.

CHAPTER 12

Kindness Is Hard. Being Mercy Blade Is Hard.

Bruiser stood on the table, overseeing the EMTs and paramedics on the team that composed medical protocol.

Eli's arms were outstretched. IVs were being inserted by medics, with human donors of O-negative blood type ready and waiting to provide person-to-person transfusions from prescreened donors. It was a transfusion like in the eighteen hundreds. Worrisome. But . . . necessary.

The witches were on the table in a circle around Eli, hands linked. Magic covered the trio in the narrow center circle. Eli. Thema. Kojo.

Molly shoved her child into the tight space, landing her in Thema's lap. Moll took her place in the rudimentary circle. The Everharts' magic grew.

"IV in right arm," someone said. "Ringer's lactate infusing."

"IV in left arm. Beginning transfusion," another said.

The Everhart magic flared like the sun. Someone cursed. Everyone, even the humans, looked away from the brightness of the power.

The electronics overhead smoked; an acrid stink of heated metal and melting plastic filled the room. Alex swore and powered down fast. Someone opened the door to the hall and people left. Fans came on, pulling the smoke out of the room. "Jane. Let's go," Alex said. Then he swore again and knelt in front of us. One hand reached out, stopped, and dropped to his side. "You're as bad as my brother." Louder he called, "Bruiser, we need a stretcher for Jane. She's burned."

Pain hit.

Holy crap.

I/we whimpered. I/we had never been burned on our face and belly before.

"Send Kojo and Thema as soon as Eli is stable," Bruiser demanded.

This sucks, I thought.

Beast lost kits to fire once. Found bodies later. One kit survived. Burned. Beast dropped it over cliff. Beast was Mercy Blade to Beast's kit.

Suddenly we were in my soul home and I was pretty sure I had passed out in real life. Wearing my male warrior clothing, I was sitting cross-legged, elbows on knees. Beast lay across from me, a well-contained fire between us, her eyes reflecting the flames. "You had to kill your own kit?" My whispers echoed through the tall-roofed cave.

Did not have vampires to heal with blood. Did not have doctors or witches. Did not have grown-up Jane to know how to save kit. Kit was in pain. Would not live.

Beast's ear tabs flicked. Her tail tip moved slightly, barely visible in the flame light. She thought to me, *Before Jane, when kits would not live, Beast shoved kits out of den to die. Was mountain lion way. After wesa came, Beast learned was kinder to drop kit from great height. Mercy. Was way of Jane. Like way of Gee DiMercy.*

Holy crap.

Jane taught Beast kindness. Kindness is hard. Being Mercy Blade is hard. Being Dark Queen is hard. Being I/we of Beast and Jane is hard.

The smell of vamp blood drew us back. I got a good look at Beast's body. Pelt gone, weeping blisters. Places where the blisters had ruptured already. Underlying tissue was seared. Not third degree that I could see, but bad.

The pain was beyond anything I/we had ever known. We snapped and snarled. Beast shoved me down, into the quiet and the dark.

"Jane? Jane, you with us?" The voice was shrill, a sharp, piercing pain in my ears and brain. "Beast?"

"Janie, you in there?" The echo was a bass drum beating on my ears. I mewled.

I opened my eyes and the agony shoved deeper. Alex and Bruiser were with me. I/we were lying in a bathtub filled with cold water, ice cubes floating around us. I nodded, the movement feeling like I had been burned again. The pain was in our face, paws, and our belly. I lowered our muzzle and mouth into the water, up to our nostrils. Water filled our mouth. Our lips were burned away. Even our gums were burned. The cold water eased the pain and took away some of the heat. Our feet were blistered. Second-degree burns that would heal with a shift. But we could see the burned patches on our snout. Raw witch magic had burned deep. That had never happened before. We were in dangerous shape.

"The witches tried to help, but there was too much residual magic in your body. It just made it worse. And you snapped at the Mithrans who tried to assist. Can you shift?" Bruiser asked.

There was a time when we couldn't shift from Puma to another form in daylight, but the half-form had given us options. Sometimes. Like when the moon was more full than not. Or when Beast was well fed and in the mood to shift. But today, we had shifted twice with insufficient calories, and we were injured. We whined, closed our nose flaps and ducked our head under water. The pain was beyond description. Cold water and over-the-counter medical supplies were not going to be enough.

Shift? I thought at my Beast.

Can try. Am starving. Like in Hunger Times.

Inside us, I felt her reach out and tug, gently, on our magics. They rose, tattered, and holed where Angie had used them. But there, and there, were small patches of silver skinwalker magics. We gathered the magics and I pulled on *le breloque*, wherever it was.

Pain like a tornado formed of razor blades and barbed wire wrapped around us. We were caught up in it. Sliced and torn. Mercifully, everything went dark.

I woke in bed, snuggled into something so soft it was like the love child of silk velvet and goose down. The lights were low, the silence so deep I could hear my heartbeat.

Someone's arms held me; Bruiser's scent wrapped around me, identifying the man. My Consort. I tried to speak and managed only a ragged cough. He eased me upright into a sitting position and moved around the bed, offering me a bottle of fluid, pink. Electrolyte stuff.

I took it in a skeletal hand and drained it. "Thanks," I whispered. I touched my torso, my bony fingers finding ribs like a washboard and sharp hip bones. I still had most of the muscle I had gained when I took mass from the street, but without the fat I had worked so hard to put on. "Well, that sucked," I managed, my voice so rough it sent me into a coughing fit.

When it passed, his hand stroked down my hair, coiling it on my shoulder, and down my bare back. His hand was warm, and my skin was icy, as if I'd been outside, naked, in a snowstorm. "Can you eat?" he asked.

I wanted to ask about Eli and Angie, but when I opened my mouth, fear caught me. I couldn't speak the words. Cautiously, I rolled down and lay flat, saying, "I better start with something easy. Broth?" I met his beautiful eyes, which were full of worry and things he didn't want to say either. I batted away a sheen of tears. "And eggs?"

Bruiser called the kitchen and I heard Deon's voice answer with, "What does our Queenie girl want? I will make her anything."

Bruiser repeated my request, and then added, "I imagine she will need something meatier soon after."

"I already made eggy soup with my world-famous wine-bone-stock. On my way up. Oh. And you tell our Queenie her Thanksgiving spread is going to be outstanding. I have twenty-four turkeys on order, and that's just for starters." The connection ended.

Thanksgiving. Right. A holiday that would be totally

different this year because I'd still have very important vamps in the city after the coronation, and I'd have to deal with a changing political structure and . . . the DQ would have to entertain.

"Help me get dressed?" I asked with a smile that felt all wrong. "I don't want to blind Deon with my scrawny femaleness."

"You didn't lose your muscle tone, only all the softness of the scant fat you had accumulated. And besides, my love, you are beautiful. You will always be beautiful." His voice sounded of truth, which could only be love talking, because the mirror in the corner showed me that I was nothing but dried-out flaky skin stretched over bones and muscle and dry, nearly crispy hair. Bruiser went to my closet, bringing back undies and stretchy yoga-style pants and a velour tunic that would probably hang on me. Silent, he helped me dress and was braiding my hair when a knock sounded and Deon entered.

"Girl, you look like death warmed over three times." Deon set up a tray on the small table in the corner and pulled it close to the bed. My mouth watered at the incredible aromas that filled the room. He took my wrist, *tsk*ing at the bones pushing against my skin, and placed a bottle with an oversized straw in it into my hand. "Suck it down," he said, "like a baby. This is the fastest way to get calories and protein into you."

I took a sip and the most amazing flavor of eggy soup filled my mouth. I drank it down fast and handed back the empty. Deon placed another in my hand, saying, "This one has extra yolks stirred in it, if you can keep it down." There were five more bottles on the tray. I emptied them all, strength flowing into me from the marrow and joint protein, the raw eggs he whisked into the boiling broth just before serving, and the sugars from the bottle of wine Deon cooked into his bone stock. When I finished the last bottle, I was stuffed so full I was nearly drowning. I said, "This stuff is heaven," and tried to hide a burp. I wasn't successful.

"Of course, it is, Queenie. Because I made it full of love, and because I am *pure magic* in a kitchen."

"I love you too, you wonderful, weird little man. And yes, you are. Now head on back to your personal fiefdom and sear me a steak, heavy on the fat."

Deon picked up my hand and kissed the back of it. Casually, he said, "I'd die for you, you know." He turned and left my quarters.

My mouth was hanging open. "What did he just say?"

The corners of Bruiser's lips lifted just a hair. "Deon says you saved his life when Katie left and you gave him a job as your personal cook. He had lived hard before that, on the streets from time to time, then as a blood donor and sex toy before he took over the kitchens at Katie's. Then she left for Atlanta, left her people with no one to care for them. You gave them all a new life with a future when you offered them a place in your clan. And then you brought Deon to HQ and put him in charge of the kitchens. He has a home, a job he loves, and people who accept him, even love him. He really would die for you."

"Oh," I said. "Ummm. Oh. Crap. Let's make sure he never has to, okay?" I pulled the soft blanket back over me. "I think I can handle it now. Update, please."

"Enter," Bruiser called out.

Alex, laden with tablets and a laptop, opened the door, looked at me once, and averted his eyes. He put his electronics on the table, pulled out a chair, and sat before looking at me again. I had a feeling he wasn't happy with the way I looked. The flaky skin and dry-as-straw hair had to have been a shock.

"Eli is alive," he said to Bruiser and me. "So is Angie. So is Wrassler."

I had expected bad news. The relief was so intense that I nearly threw up the broth and eggs. I pressed down on my belly, hoping to keep the food down. This time, there was no stopping the tears that rolled down my cheeks. That meant the fluid had gone a long way to hydrating me. "Okay. Go on."

"Florence's travel coffin was undamaged," he said. "We chose not to open it until dusk because she'd been banged around so much she might be pissed and we might damage her if we had to defend ourselves against her.

She's in a secure location at HQ, under guard. There were injuries among the team on the way here, and outside when Angie detonated the bomb carried by the drone. They are being attended to. No deaths. Thema and Kojo waked other Mithrans to assist in our people's healing. No Mithran resisted them, and the injured security personnel will all recover." A ghost of a grin passed across his lips. "Apparently those two scared the Mithrans into helping."

It's about time. I nodded for him to continue. Sipped my water. Breathed. The relief pulsed through me with my blood, doing as much to soothe and heal as the wine-bone-stock.

"Under the new Emergency Medical Protocols, Eli received infusions of blood donated by three O-neg humans who had been previously tested for, and found negative for, atypical antibodies. He drank from Kojo and Thema, and they bled all over him and all over Angie. With all that, and with the Everharts' healing magic, both are feeling better than anyone expected. The other vamps they waked fed the others, no rolling, no non-consensual attempts at sex, and the vamps didn't kill anyone."

"Where are they? Eli, Angie, and Wrassler."

"On premises," Alex said, sounding very Eli-like. "Liz is with Eli. We moved some humans around for Cia and Carmen, and Angie is with her parents in a suite with a—I guess a playroom?—for as long as they need. Wrassler is recuperating. I called Jodi and she's on premises as well, ordering people around like a drill sergeant."

"Is Angie going to scar?" I had seen her burns. She had been blistered deeply, the blisters already busted and the cooked tissue beneath visible.

"Not much, if any, for Angie, and much less long-term damage than previously for Eli. Evan, Molly, and Liz had been working on healing magics and amulets. Molly said two of the new ones for trauma flew and are now proven."

I managed a breathy chuckle. Magic was mathematics and geometry and mental control of energy. When the math went bad, Molly made paper airplanes of the calculations and flew the failed working across the room. The fact that Moll could heal with her earth magic and hold down her death magic, in the midst of a major crisis, was a good sign for her future mental health and magical control.

"Security teams are stationed everywhere," Bruiser said, "with good sight lines of the air, the property, and the rest of the block. There are additional teams at each of the Clan Homes and your house. We have team leaders available to give you an update if you want."

"What I *want*?" I looked at my Consort. Now that my worry was gone and I was feeling a little stronger, my anger flared. "What I want is for what happened today with the local emergency responders, led by the politicians, to Never. Happen. Again." We had all nearly died because of the Heir. But Eli had nearly died because the locals played politics in the middle of a paranormal war. *"Never."*

Bruiser tilted his head and his smile grew. There was a mean edge to it, as if in answer to my own rage. "My love and My Queen, Jane Yellowrock, studied under Leo's tutelage. She understands the power of a threat that is backed up by proof. I left messages with the town and parish leaders after the null house attack. The messages were clearly ignored. I am prepared to carry out the orders of the Dark Queen."

"Good. I want a press release drafted that states the Dark Queen was impeded in her protection of her territory and local human law enforcement, by local politicians, who instructed law enforcement to that end. I want it stated that our humans nearly died protecting the human citizens in the area and that several of our people were injured, including a child. I want it to be stated that I'm considering abandoning NOLA and the entire Gulf Coast. To hell with just talking nice to the politicos. I want the public informed that I'll withdraw my political protection of New Orleans and its citizens and leave the way open for a takeover by a local warlord. There'll be war in the streets as the European vamps fleeing the war there fight it out for control here. Let it be known that my people and I are the ones standing between peace and dozens of events where our enemies prey on the populace and eat them like a buffet. Send that press release out through every media outlet you can think of.

"I want teams at the mountain house, getting it ready for the permanent residence of the Dark Queen, with more garages, an expanded landing pad for the helo, steel shutters on all windows and access points, including all the cottages. And finish the underground bunker. All those plans you and Eli talked over? Finish them. Put some money into it. Whatever you need. Use local companies so word gets out fast. Good ol' boys talk. A lot.

"Then I want a serious, nationally recognized press personality given secret access to the inn and property, as if that access was being done without our knowledge. I want it to look absolutely positive that I'm moving HQ permanently to the mountains. And when that press person calls HQ for comment, I want them transferred to you. And you can tell them the details of what will happen to this city if there's no vamp presence here. Make sure they get directed to the YouTube vids of the vamp war in Europe, and what happened to entire towns that were taken over by warlords. If I, personally, have to do a live interview, fine. Set it up. I'm done playing games."

"Yes, My Queen," Bruiser said. "Leo would be proud."

"Yeah? Leo should have done this years ago."

"Leo could never be seen in public in the daylight. He was never perceived as human. He was secretive and seldom let the public near him. Leo drank blood and kept blood-servants and blood-slaves. He hunted humans in his city for centuries, a creature whispered about and feared. That alone made him more than simply non-human, it made him *in*human. There was a time after he killed his daughter when he was a monster. And then you came and turned his world upside down. When he discovered that there might be a bloodline that could potentially save the long-chained, even his own child, who was by then true dead, he lost a great deal of his control for a time. Because he had killed her *himself*. Knowing that they had killed their own? Every Mithran mourned."

That had never crossed my mind. That every vamp who had dispatched a long-chained scion would have to mourn all over again because if they had waited, it was possible to have saved them with the blood from Amy Lynn Brown and others like her.

"You?" His smile softened into pride. "You can pull this off. Leo never could."

"Yeah?" I had never thought about any of this, not the way he stated it. "Okay," I said. "Set it up. Fast. Make the people and the reporter believe it."

"With pleasure, My Queen."

It was late afternoon and most of the security team members were gathered in the security room, silent, the humans eating from the platters of food on the table or leaning against the walls. No Everharts were present.

I was sitting in my chair, a two-pound rare steak on a platter in front of me, and a serving bowl full of loaded mashed potatoes beside it. A large bottle of water and a teapot with mug, sugar, and creamer were to the side. I cut a wedge of steak with a thick layer of fat and shoved it in, chewing. Being human-shaped meant I had to properly macerate and masticate the protein. The taste was amazing, but then, starvation makes everything taste better.

As I ate, Alex was talking, explaining the screens overhead. The largest one was divided into smaller sections, showing the events of the day gathered from our people's vest cam footage, security cam footage, and some video posted by witnesses onto the Internet. Two screens were blank, marked "Police Audio," and showing that jagged line that meant either an earthquake or decibels, hertz, whatever. He looked at me, and asked, "Which first, My Queen?"

I swallowed a hunk of steak down. "Audio," I said, cutting another slice.

We listened to the cop chatter about the explosion at the airport that took down the new hangar. We also listened to their chatter about the Dark Queen, armed and dangerous, and how one politician wanted her in jail for endangering humans. I expected there to be a lot more of that until Bruiser set our plan in motion.

The audio-only parts were broken down and hashed

over by Wrassler, Bruiser, and Alex. The other team members were mostly quiet. Derek's teams had seen combat and they understood the danger their brothers in arms had faced today.

We watched the video of everything Alex deemed worthy of my time. The cop vest cam footage of me riding up in half-form, full Beast face, Benelli to the fore, was impressive, if the scent change in the room was anything to go by. I did look kinda scary. One particular angle showed our fangs catching the sunlight; that one was Beast's favorite.

Beast is best hunter, she thought.

Yes, you are, I thought back.

"Make a few stills of that," Bruiser said. "We can use it to our advantage."

Last, we studied the vid of the bombing caught on the airport security cams. The bomb hadn't been some movie version of an explosion, all slo-mo and flames. In real time, one moment there was a hangar, the next there was a view of dust and a hole in the ground. In slo-mo so slow that it amounted to still shots, we did get a few out-of-focus shots of debris flying, crumpled sheet metal, and twisted steel.

Our SUVs had barely gotten away in time. If they hadn't been armored, the last two vehicles wouldn't have survived.

At the end, Alex said, "We have an alphabet soup of agencies interested in this because it appears that a rocket or missile was used on the hangar. Until they tell us whether there was a guidance system, we'll call it a rocket."

I asked, "Casualties?"

"There were three deaths from the rocket, all human, all airport employees."

I put down my knife and fork with hard clanks. All the faces turned to me.

Humans in my territory died on my watch, because I moved the landing site. I wondered how many would have died had we used Lakeview Airport. More? Fewer? No one? Had I made things worse? "Make sure the families are taken care of," I said softly. "Whatever Leo used to do, plus a little something." I frowned, thinking back. "I remember seeing one of our guys jumping from the hangar roof. How is he?"

"She," Bruiser said. "Sarah Spieth. Sniper."

Sarah was being groomed to be the new head of communications. She was former military with active duty wartime experience, was insightful, and didn't waste words.

"How bad?" I asked.

"Broken right lower leg, compound. Broken left wrist, both bones," Alex said. "Both eardrums blown. Concussive injuries. But she made the doctors at Tulane laugh when she described what needed to be done to the people who blew her up."

Dark humor was a good sign. I twirled my fingers at Alex to continue.

"She underwent surgery at Tulane, and although an ordinary human would stay in the hospital overnight, she will receive vamp blood at dusk, as fast as I can get someone to her. Hopefully she'll be released afterward. Once back here, she'll receive regular donations of vamp blood and PT until she heals fully. The Roberes sent someone to her hospital room to make sure that when the officials show up to get her statement, that's all they do."

"Why are we having trouble with the officials?" I asked. "Leo didn't have this much trouble."

"They feared Leo," Bruiser said. "And the elections changed our sphere of influence. We lost a lot of our political supporters."

"Hmmm. I didn't financially support any of the political contestants in the last election. I need to set up support for both parties and make sure that, no matter who runs, I'll have influence of some kind. Alex, do some digging into the current batch of politicos and ferret out their secrets. Everyone has skeletons."

I stopped, my hands frozen. Forgetting to breathe.

That was not my usual kind of thought. Those were Leo's lessons in how to run his city.

"Do some digging?" Bruiser repeated, gently, reading my mind. Reading my shock at the words that had come from my mouth.

I hated hearing Leo's influence come out of my mouth.

But if playing the political game got me what I needed to keep my people safe, I'd play all day. And I'd freaking win. I nodded, my eyes on Alex, his widened as he understood that he was being asked to use his skills to dig up dirt on politicians. He bobbed his head once, his eyes still surprised.

It wasn't my usual use of his abilities. It was Dark Queen stuff. *Dang it.*

My hands had formed claws and I forcibly relaxed them. Knowing that I could come to hate myself as part of keeping my city safe, I said, "Then find out what their cities, towns, and parishes need. Get the Roberes to make overtures. Provide some assistance. Not a lot. And nothing to individuals. Maybe parks. Sidewalks. Replace a water line. Something the people need. And make sure it's known it came from us."

"Yes, My Queen," Alex said, sounding mollified.

"And the donations to the homeless shelters?" I asked.

"Sent."

I hated politics but I was getting better at them. And sometimes politics meant being able to be compassionate and do good work. I'd take it. And if there was political dirt that kept my people safe, I'd take that too.

Alex said, "The various municipal police, parish sheriff's departments, Homeland, TSA, FAA, and ATF are trying to find where the rocket came from.

"It looks as if a shoulder-mounted rocket launcher was used. Someone found a witch circle in the woods on airport land, with the ground churned up inside. All around the circle were signs that a lot of people showed up in the woods and then disappeared like a Vegas magic act—out of thin air—at the witch circle. Law enforcement has stayed away from the circle until someone can check it out and make sure it's no longer active. Carmen Everhart is on the way there now to make sure it's disabled." A faint ding sounded, and he checked his tablet. "Huh. I just heard from one of Eli's contacts. She says the ordnance used on the hangar was U.S. military, but that's all she can find out right now."

Rocket launchers, bomb-carrying drones, transport

circles, death magic, and the potential of timewalkers meant no place was safe from attack. I stuffed a chunk of meat into my mouth and chewed. Thinking. I ate several more. Somehow the two-pound steak had disappeared. I dug into the mashed potatoes, bacon, cheese, and butter. *Holy cow*, that was good. Of course, bacon made everything good. When I swallowed enough to speak, I said, "Most of our people will be safest at HQ, under the Everhart protective ward. Once it's up," I amended. "Make sure anyone who wants to bunk here can.

"Do we have an update on the people who disappeared from the null prison?" I asked.

"Nothing new. I have a team working on it. And while we're talking alphabet soup," he added as an aside, "I'm researching why PsyLED Southeast hasn't replied to our overtures."

The hallway door opened and Quint stepped into the room. She was armed with a single nine-millimeter semiautomatic under one arm. Under her clothes and in her boots there were undoubtedly more weapons. Quint was always armed to the teeth. She closed the door behind her and took up a position where she could shoot anyone in the room. When she looked at me, her eyes were cold and lifeless and yet communicated her displeasure. I had foisted Liz onto her, forcing Quint to leave me in danger, and Liz had driven back to save Eli. Without her. Badass assassin lady-in-waiting bodyguard had been outdone by a curvy, sexy witch. I'd likely hear about all that later.

"For now," Bruiser said to me, ignoring my bodyguard, "the grown-up witches are securing a ward around HQ, one that leaves one entrance unwarded so people can get in and out. They are also trying to address ward security for the Yellowrock Clan Home and get the ward at your private residence back up."

I nodded, swallowing a huge mouthful of food. The Queen's Personal Residence in New Orleans had a permanent ward around it, laid into the grounds, but it needed to be powered often and hadn't been while the Everharts were in Asheville. "That's secondary to getting the ward up here," I said.

Bruiser tilted his head, not agreeing, not disagreeing. I might be the DQ, but when my orders countermanded my own security, they were generally ignored.

"Because all the Everharts are dealing with the null prison wards, the open witch circles, and other witch security measures, Angie has asked for you, My Queen, and for pizza for supper. Deon is sending two large pies to the temporary playroom." He chuckled when I looked at my empty plate and bowl. "You ate it all. Even the mashed potatoes."

"It was full of cheese and bacon," I explained.

"And so you'll turn your nose up at Deon's homemade pizza?"

I bobbed my head side to side as if thinking things through. Casually, I said, "I could eat."

Which is how Quint ended up standing guard in the hallway while the Consort and the queen spent the rest of the afternoon babysitting, curled on a wide, plushy couch, as Beast purred with happiness.

Together, Bruiser and I, tangled up with Molly's kids, relaxed for the first time in what felt like forever. We read books to the kids and played a game that involved monkeys and a barrel. Then several rounds of Go Fish. EJ was great at the monkey game and he loved Go Fish. He had no idea how to play it, but he loved it.

Angie Baby spent a lot of time braiding and rebraiding and finger-combing my hair, EJ was often wrapped around Bruiser's neck like a spider monkey, and Cassy slept on a pallet at our feet. When her diapers had needed changing—that stink was familiar from Moll's other kids. *Yuck*—Quint did a competent job, though she looked at Cassy the way she might a peculiar little doll instead of a baby human—with vague curiosity. Pizza appeared off and on all afternoon, delivered by Deon to the coffee table nearby. I ate most of it.

The kids regaled us with tales of KitKit (Molly's notfamiliar cat) and George, the kids' basset hound. My godchildren had no idea that Bruiser's real name was George, and didn't understand why I fought laughter every time George's farts were described as "Dis-*gus*-ting!" or

"Gaggy." And why I was brought to tears at descriptions of his "potty training" failures. My Consort didn't seem to mind the stories or my not-so-muffled laughter, watching me fondly as Angie Baby chattered. She never mentioned the incident under the porte cochere, and never seemed to be in any pain, but she was also content to sit and listen to books, not something the little magical troublemaker usually wanted to do for extended periods.

When not making fart noises with his mouth or strangling Bruiser, EJ played with a small wood and plastic train set and miniature village on the floor. He was intent on the moving pieces and the sounds they should make, especially the train whistle.

When not screaming or sleeping, Cassy was fed and burped by Quint or older blood-servants. Cassy also tried repeatedly to stand or crawl away, which I thought was way too soon for a baby—she was still technically a baby, right?—to be mobile, but what did I know?

Near dusk, Carmen appeared, which let us know that the Everharts were at a stopping point with the current workings, the *hedge of thorns* around the null house and around HQ. She chased us out with the words, "Your presence is requested in the security room." When I tried to find out what she had discovered about the circle at the airport, she chided me with the words, "War Woman Big Ears," meaning Angie was listening avidly.

"Ant Jane's a war woman, but she ain't got big ears," EJ said, pulling his ears out to the sides. "I gots bigger ears than her does."

Bruiser tousled the little kid's red hair.

Angie glared at Carmen. "Aunt Carmen," she said, pronouncing it properly, "was talking about *me*. I saved everybody but because I got burned, they won't let me help, even though I am *totally healed*." She held out her arms to show me. "See?"

"Ooookay," I said. "Family business, not mine." Which was the coward's way out, but I didn't care if it kept me out of Angie Baby's bad graces.

Bruiser and I left the room, allowing Carmen the pleasure of dealing with her stubborn niece. But we never made it to the Everhart debriefing in the security room. Instead there was a muted alarm on both of our cell phones, on Quint's headset, and softly spoken over the security speakers throughout the building.

The alarm said, "Intruder at the front gate."

CHAPTER 13

I Wanted to Clap. Slowly. With Sarcasm.

Dressed in the casual clothes I had worn while eating pizza, I stood in the tiny secondary security room, a nook in the foyer, near the bullet-resistant, explosive-resistant (but not rocket- or missile-proof) front airlock entrance, staring at security cam screens positioned to show the front drive, stairs up, and entrance. A vamp was standing in the street, about twenty feet away from the closed gate, his hands up and out, as if in peace, or showing himself as if part of a circus magic show. *Nothing up my sleeves . . .* However, his face was in full shadow, his dark hair free and covering him to the middle of his back and chest.

I couldn't see his face, but I knew this was the Heir.

Carefully, he walked to the heavy steel and titanium gate, which was, currently, the only thing keeping most people out. A foot and a half away, he leaned forward and braced himself on the gate, arms still outspread.

"The ward?" I asked Wrassler.

"The foundation of the Everhart *hedge of thorns* is in place but hasn't gone up yet. They need to wait until the moon is above the horizon—which will happen in an hour or so—to raise a ward large enough to cover HQ."

Cia, the moon witch, would be at full power when the moon rose. Got it. So the ward would go up the moment that Cia could draw on the source of her power.

This vamp might know that. The Heir was powerful, with a gift for the dramatic. He certainly knew he could put his hands on the gate and not suffer from a blast of witch magics. In the cameras positioned across the street, mounted on the buildings owned by HQ, we watched as he laid his forehead on the metal. It was almost as if he was praying, and with his arms stretched out and up, there was more than a hint of symbolism in the position—the view of the Christ on his cross as seen from behind. The cross that the Sons of Darkness had mixed with all the other bloody wood from Golgotha's murderer and thief to create the first blood drinkers. All the vamps standing with us in the foyer recognized the imagery. He was saying he was now king, that he would die for his people and his mission, that he was the way forward. And that the Dark Queen allowed him to get this close. It was a mark of the position he intended to take and proof of my failure.

I wasn't a master vamp in the sense of the blood tie that bound scions to a Blood Master, but I knew Koun was standing behind me. I could feel his presence and his power through all his blood that was in me. He felt at full power, which meant he had taken in a lot of human blood to heal his broken ankles. I could feel Thema and Kojo, who had also clearly fed well. And I could feel Eli and his girlfriend, Liz, in one of the entrances to the foyer, the battle bond awakening between my secundo and me. There was no way Eli was ready to fight, and he hadn't talked to me yet, but I felt his heart rate, steady, calm. I figured he was still mad at me. But it was only fair. He and his warriors kept me safe because I was mortal, so I kept him safe for the same reason. Or tried to.

I put on a headset and accepted weapons from Quint. I even let her strap the rigs on my thighs and hips, kneeling, working around me. "ID confirmation?" I asked Alex, who was in the lower-level main security room.

"We got one view of his face." A fuzzy still-shot appeared on the upper corner of the screen. "Probable ID, Mainet Pellissier."

Just as I figured, the guy who wanted to take over the world, starting with killing me, was at the front entrance playing God. "Oh goodie," I said. As I watched, Mainet stepped away, threw back his head, his black hair flying, revealing his face, and leaped straight up. It was like levitating but fast, as if the ground had been a trampoline.

He landed on our side of the twelve-foot-tall fence with ease, dropping to his toes, one knee, and the fingers of both hands in the circular parking area before standing and again outstretching his arms. Doing the Christ thing and at the same time indicating he wasn't armed. He was also proving that he could walk into my territory unmolested.

Fanghead protocol said they were supposed to present themselves unarmed when entering another vamp's territory, but this felt more like an invasion than obeisance. Mainet was apparently alone, not that I trusted what I was seeing, not with a vamp who controlled transport-circle witches. He could have backup anywhere. My vamps moved toward the entrance.

"Hang on," I said. They stopped with that preternatural stillness vamps could achieve, not breathing, not blinking. "Let's see what he does."

On the screen, Mainet vamped out slowly, so very slowly, showing his control of his powers. His jaw unhinged. His five-inch-long fangs slowly swept forward and down with that click I couldn't hear but knew had to be there. The sclera of his eyes bled scarlet and his pupils widened into the black pits of hell. I wanted to clap. Slowly. With sarcasm.

Beast can jump higher, she thought at me.

The vamps in the room vamped out too, almost as if he was calling to them. Mainet Pellissier was reaching out to the vamps through . . . through Leo's bloodline. Ahhh. I stepped from the security nook and spotted Leo, once again standing in a corner, his hands clasped in front of him, his head bowed. He was wearing a gold cross with tiny holes in it on a gold chain around his neck. Okaaay. A vamp with a cross, not burning and on fire. So maybe it was protection?

Yet, Leo slowly vamped out too.

As if choreographed, all the vamps turned toward the front entrance. *Crap.*

I needed to be the DQ. I needed that power. I needed the crown.

Behind me, a soft clatter sounded and when I turned around, *le breloque* was sitting on the security desk. Wrassler whispered a curse word.

I had either called *le breloque*, or it knew it was needed and came on its own, proving it was a magical AI . . . or sentient. Either possibility was coolio or scary or both. Right now I was going with coolio. I reached back, grabbed the laurel-leaved gold band, rearranged the headset so it wouldn't get smashed against my scalp, and put the crown on. It snapped tightly into place on my skull with an *ow*-worthy speed.

I didn't know what I was doing, but I had to start somewhere. Why not at the top?

I concentrated on Leo, reaching out to him, willing him to think of me. Slowly, the former master of the city turned to me. He took a breath and blew it out. An instant later, every vamp in the room breathed. Leo's fangs retracted and his eyes returned to human normal. There were multiple clicks around the room as all the vamps returned to looking human.

They all pivoted in place and looked at me.

Something weird happened in my chest, a heated, sinuous gathering of power. With it came an emotion that defied immediate description beyond a burst of . . . something like . . . joy. I laughed. "Holy crap."

The vamps around me smiled, because it was happy human laughter, not vamp mockery or cynicism. Oddly, they seemed, for the moment, tranquil and calm. For vamps.

Bruiser moved from me to Leo, and my heart did a little skip of fear. Fear that he might be leaving me for his old love, before I saw the null cuffs in his hands. He held the wide bracelet out and Leo extended his hands. Bruiser clicked the cuffs onto his former master's wrists and adjusted a second cuff until it fit around Leo's head. Leo closed his eyes and his shoulders dropped as the power being exerted by the maker of his bloodline was cut.

"I am sorry, my old friend," Bruiser said. Faster than

I could follow, Bruiser's arm came forward. Leo grunted and dropped to the floor, boneless. There was a wood stake poking from his belly.

Bruiser had just paralyzed Leo.

Instantly, I schooled my face and my emotions to neutral. No shock. Hiding my surprise. Instinctively I projected a placid calm, like a still lake beneath a full moon. I took a breath and shoved it out into the room as well.

All the vamps looking at me took a second, unneeded breath and visibly relaxed. *So. Okay. Yeah.* They were being called through Leo's old bond. But with Leo out and the corona on my head, we were safe. Safe-ish. For a while, anyway.

"Let's go see what the unwelcome visitor wants," I said.

Before I could move to the airlock, Liz, Cia, Big Evan, and Molly stepped into the center of the foyer. Evan motioned everyone back and the Everharts and Truebloods took places in a small circle. I realized they were standing on my crown, the six-foot-diameter symbolic version of it embedded in the gray and white marble. They all sat inside the band, too close for a good circle, knees touching. Molly said, "Begin."

An Everhart/Trueblood witch circle sprang into being. It wasn't balanced, because they needed five to act as a full circle, and Carmen was probably staying with the children, and Cia still lacked the power of the moon. But it was a bloodline circle, all of them joined by genetics and love in one way or another. Molly touched the brass band in the floor and light blazed up, so bright all the humans turned away. This circle was way more powerful than I expected.

And the Everharts had known it was here—a permanent witch circle in the center of the Mithran Council Chambers. And none of the vamps seemed surprised. That meant the two para groups had achieved some kind of rapprochement around the time the floor had been amended with my crest.

Bruiser had been very busy for a very long time.

I nodded to Molly, who inclined her head at me and began to speak in Gaelic, opening a working they had already prepared. I wasn't sure what working they were beginning, but I knew they had my back, and HQ's protection in mind.

Stepping to the front entrance, I accepted my Benelli from Quint and felt Eli at my side. He wasn't trying to keep me safe, which meant he knew I had to combat the Heir's symbolism and be seen as powerful. I glanced at him and he looked pretty dang good to have been walking through death's door only a bit ago. "Good to have you back, bro."

"Good to be back."

"Are you eighty-five percent?"

"Vamps and witches working together? I'm better than before I was shot this time. Closer to ninety-five percent." He waggled his hand. "A little sore still."

"Try not to get shot again. Or bitten."

"Roger that. You too. We're neither of us at full speed yet," Eli said.

"Yeah." I knew that. I felt it in my bones.

The inner bullet-resistant airlock doors opened and we stepped into the airlock cage, up to the outer doors. I looked down on my visitor. Without the big ol' fangs and vampy eyes, Mainet could have passed for human. Again, I realized that he wasn't drop-dead gorgeous, but he was pretty enough, and in person looked even more like Leo than I had expected.

The Gaelic chanting behind me stopped and Molly said, "The inner *hedge of thorns* is now active. You're safe as long as you stay on the landing at the top of the stairs. Go down one step and you break the ward. The outer ward will be up in five minutes, give or take, when the moon rises."

I smiled slightly and nodded. "And we trap him?" I asked.

"That's the hope," Moll said.

Bruiser, Eli, and I pushed through the outer doors to the landing and stopped at the top of the stairs that led down to the parking. Over comms, Eli gave orders to the mixed vamp/human teams.

Behind us, Quint and Koun both cursed. There wasn't room on the front landing for anyone else, but Quint elbowed to my side anyway.

The rest of Team Koppa, my security team, gathered, filling the airlock, bodies pressed close. They were touching and . . . through a dark joy still beating in my chest, I counted them. Fourteen loyal vamps and humans at my back. Two sets of seven. Something mystical about that number.

Included among them, Quint, Bruiser, and Eli, with me. Nothing mystical there.

Mainet met my eyes.

It had been a long time since I'd had to worry about being rolled by a vamp, but this was different. Mainet had intense power behind his will, something dark and demanding. *Le breloque* heated on my head, and I thought at it, *Don't burn me this time, for pity's sake.* The gold band continued to grow hot, so I guessed it wasn't listening to me now. Through our bond, I felt Eli lower his eyes, looking at Mainet's hands and then his shoes, to avoid the power that seemed to boil out of the vamp.

"Jane?" Bruiser said, the word a warning about the power of Mainet's mesmeric call.

I needed the Glob to absorb the attacking energies. Unlike the crown, the Gob didn't translocate when I need it. "Crap," I muttered. It had been in a pocket when I last stepped out of my armor. I had no idea where it was and hadn't thought to find it.

"Hold," I said softly to the vamps behind me. "Look away from his eyes. Look at me. He's drawing power from his bloodline and it's hitting you. Hold." All my vamps obeyed, working to stop Mainet's power over them. The bond of dark joy between us all strengthened, which was something I had never experienced. And would have to wait to think about.

"Do you know who I am?" Mainet asked me.

"Sure do, dude," I said.

At my side, Eli spluttered with laughter and his tension diminished. I felt the amused reaction pass through all the others. *Good.*

I said, "You're Leo's ugly bloodsucker gran'pappy. You coming to ask my permission to be in my city? If so, you're late. Shoulda been here the night you arrived. Bad fanghead. Shame, shame, shame." I rubbed my right index finger along the length of the left index finger in a child-hood gesture of reprobation. "But then, few visitors to my city have any kind of manners or breeding. You'd be surprised how few show up and present themsel—"

Mainet threw his head back and shouted, "I challenge the pitiful female for the crown and title of Dark Queen."

I laughed again. "Tough, Manny-boy. No can do. The title can't be passed and *le breloque* chooses its own heir. It tells me when it likes someone and right now it's calling you all sorts a bad names. Bloodsucker. Fanghead. Murderer. Eater of humans. Things that have to do with your mother and sexual contact. I mean, really. You did all that?"

Mainet's vamped-out eyes blazed. "You will not refuse me. I challenge the Dark Queen to Sangre Duello!"

"Seriously, dude. Can't help you there," I called back. "You can't challenge the Dark Queen. It's not in the Vampira Carta, the original or the new one. You can challenge me for MOC of NOLA, but before you get to me, you'll have to fight your way up through my minions, including my primo, the soon-to-be-crowned Emperor of Europe, Edmund the Great, when he returns to the U.S. But he might foist you off to Grégoire first. Oh. Wait. You already ran away from Europe and from Blondie with your tail between your legs. *Chicken.*"

"What are you doing?" Eli whispered.

"Annoying an uninvited guest."

Bruiser called out, "The Dark Queen is correct. There is no recourse for challenge of a Dark Queen. And it is well known that you removed yourself, via clandestine means, from the territory of Grégoire of Clan Arceneau, Master of Paris and all of France. And it is confirmed that no one has or can defeat the swordsman—the Warlord of the Dark Queen."

Over comms, we heard Alex say, "You've been targeted. Move!"

In multiple pops that stole the air and made my jaw ache, the vamps were suddenly just gone. Except for Koun, who picked me up and then *moved*. Inside. Fast.

As he leaped, I was somehow looking over his shoulder and saw Bruiser and Eli in transit too. The outer doors slammed shut. The men were speeding through the airlock and with the inner doors still open. *Safe.*

Beyond the airlock, a brilliant, scarlet light flashed into place at the twelve-foot-high wall. The outer *hedge of thorns* had been activated.

The new steel entrance doors slammed closed. The inner doors closed on the heels of Koun and me, my Consort, and my brother.

A single explosion rocked the earth. I didn't have to ask. I already knew. A rocket had hit the brand-new outer *hedge* and exploded.

But what had happened to Mainet when the outer hedge closed? Was he still inside on the grounds with us?

Koun dropped me at the security nook as Eli and he began to give orders. Over Wrassler's shoulder, I watched cam vid from the other side of the twelve-foot-high gate, enemy men and women dressed in dark clothing with a single white stripe along the left shoulder. They raced into the street, firing weapons at the walls. One woman wearing a white-stripe uniform dropped to a knee, positioning a tripod with what had to be a rocket launcher. How many of those things did my enemy have?

From cover, my people on the far side of the street fired down on the woman. She fell to one hand and her knees in the street, still trying to reach up toward the launcher. Sirens sounded from everywhere. Flashing blue lights approached. The enemies in the streets began to retreat, laying down cover fire. My people, our team at our outer perimeter, under cover, hidden and at least somewhat protected in the buildings we had purchased across the street, returned fire.

The woman at the launcher took multiple shots, her body jerking with each.

Injured, she still managed to reach her weapon. She triggered the launcher. It fired.

A second explosion juddered against the *hedge*. A display of red sparks and black oily smoke filled the screen. The woman was dead in the street.

Cop cars and two firetrucks came from everywhere as emergency services responded, parking at angles blocking the streets.

The other white-striped soldiers retreated into alley-ways. A single magical ball of energy hit the outer *hedge*. Orange and green sparks shot into the night sky. Magics twisted in the darkness, brilliant as shattered diamonds.

The outer *hedge* fell. Smoke billowed up, black clouds of sparkling power.

But the attackers didn't swarm us.

Time passed. My attachment to Eli waned and my heart beat fast and hard in my chest. A painful sensation, irregular rhythm.

No more rockets were fired. "Why didn't they cross over the *hedge* when it fell?" I asked no one in particular.

"My Queen," Koun said, "you have not advertised the actions of the Everharts in your city. It is unlikely they knew that the Mithran Council Chambers was so well warded. They expected this to be an easier battle."

"Our people?" I asked.

"All safe. All currently unarmed and making their way back inside the walls," Alex said.

"Mainet?" I asked.

"Gone. One cam showed he jumped over the wall just before the outer *hedge* went up," Alex said. "Otherwise he'd be full of silvershot and headless right about now."

"Well, crap on crackers with toe jam," I said. I looked back at the witches centered in the circle of my crown seal. They were again chanting, trying to get the *hedge* back up. I wanted to talk to them. I wanted to check in on Angie, who had to have felt the magic of the attack and defense. But my needs would have to wait.

"Do you wish to handle the situation outside, My Queen?" Bruiser asked, gesturing to the screens with the cops everywhere.

"No," I said. "If the Roberes are available, get them on it. Right now, I want a very private chat with the Youngers and you. And tea. And maybe some more po'boys. And bread pudding. With Deon's bourbon sauce."

Bruiser smiled slowly. "As My Queen desires."

The debrief was fast, in the little meeting room off the gym. The po'boys and the bread pudding were gone, nothing left but an enticing aroma on the air, when Alex brought up a new consideration. "A few months back, I had Wrassler update the Lost and Damaged Equipment Log. He's been keeping tight tabs on all our gear and weapons and who signs out what and when and detailing its condition when it's returned. He discovered this morning that we're missing a comms set. I think Mainet's people have it."

Eli turned cold eyes to his brother. "Who?" He meant who lost it.

"Two possibilities. One of the newer guys from Knoxville, Long-Knife, had the set last, and placed it on the damaged list. But it's not there and it hasn't been repaired or replaced. So, maybe someone else took it, or maybe Long-Knife just lost it and it made its way to Mainet."

"Maybe Long-Knife *took it* to Mainet," Eli said.

Long-Knife had been sent to NOLA by Ming of Knoxville, for a little attitude adjustment. But part of that adjustment could have been needed because she didn't trust him. He'd been bled and read by Koun, but there were people who slipped secrets through. Some blood-servants were less loyal and harder to read than others.

"If they have the headset, then they can listen in to our communications."

"Not anymore," Alex said. "I shut the mic features off from here. But if I'm right, everything until then has to be considered compromised. That's ten days' worth of battlefield communications lost."

That meant they knew everything that had happened at the null house. They had known about Leo talking to me. That was why Leo had bruises—because they knew he had talked to me. It wasn't my fault. But it felt like it.

And yet, they hadn't known about the hedge at HQ. If they were using the headset for intel, they were getting spotty info.

Bruiser set down his fragile teacup with a delicate clink. "Check back over the list and get someone to look again through the damaged equipment. Then have Long-Knife brought to our queen." He looked at me, his brows raised quizzically. "Jane," he said softly, "we have three options. I can read Long-Knife, in my own way, without forcing a bond. But I don't know how deep such a read will be since he's neither Onorio nor Mithran and yet, something more than human. Or, you could try to bleed and read him, as you did with your crown, with Monique. Or bloodless, as you did with your subjects earlier."

I thought back to the soul-home-style visions I had when reading Monique Giovanni, the evil Onorio. I had forced a temporary mental bond between an enemy and me, using a drop of her blood that I smeared into my crown. The visions had shown me a lot in terms of the evil that clung to her, but little of her actual plans. That form of bleed-and-read hadn't left her chained to me mentally. Life might have been easier if it had.

Then I considered the moments in the doorway, when I touched all my team, mind-to-mind. I shouldn't have been able to do that. It was a Blood Master's ability and gift. Yet, I had opened a bond. I had known them then, all the group at the doorway, touching them through the blood we all consumed and with my power as Dark Queen.

But.

I had sorta accidently bound Edmund to me. And then Eli with the soul bond. And I didn't like either binding at all.

Could I read someone who had drunk blood from the vamps I called my own? Could I read human enemies through their blood? Could I find a traitor and not bind them? Would using my crown to read Long-Knife work? What if I read too deeply? What if I someday decided I liked that kind of power?

That would make me even less human than I already was.

Or. What if Long-Knife was a plant? Someone with a . . . a snare in his mind. One that might trap me? Trap my mind. *Holy cow. What if Long-Knife is a time bomb?*

"I'd rather we hold him and let . . . someone stronger read him tonight," I said. I didn't want to bind anyone. I didn't want to chain someone to me. I didn't want to be attacked by a time bomb. "I think Kojo or Thema would be best."

Bruiser poured us both more tea, his face thoughtful, as if working out moves on a chess board. The tea was the good stuff, the stuff he drank because money was no object. "I'll arrange that." His expression changed, growing canny, approving, and amused all at once. "Ah. This will be interesting." Sounding as pleased as his expression suggested, he asked Alex, "Where is the comms set now?"

"I tracked the missing comms to Marigny, but the battery is so low it barely pings. We get it now, or we don't get it at all."

Eli stood, talking to Alex. "Time to get it back. Text the Everharts that I need to take a small security team out the back doors and through the ward. I want Koun and Tex with me."

Koun and Tex were my two most loyal vamps. I hadn't seen Tex in a while. He'd begun bunking at the Yellowrock Clan Home to keep it safe, and also to have a place for his dogs.

"On it," Alex said, his thumbs already tapping on the cell face. "Though it could be a trap." Eli turned his battle face to his younger brother and waited until the Kid looked up and read his brother's expression. "But then you knew that."

"Uh-huh." Without a limp, Eli moved away, heading to the armory. And that said a lot about our lives now, that HQ had a fully equipped armory. And that Eli was moving without a limp after a devastating injury. Healed by vamp blood and witch magic on top of various screws, metal plates, rods, and the magic of science.

I yelled at his retreating back, "Go tell your girlfriend what you're doing."

Without turning around, Eli lifted a finger at me. It wasn't the middle. It might have been agreement.

Bruiser watched the door close behind Eli. "Didn't Tex turn down the position of master of the city when you left NOLA?"

"Yup," I said.

"Given their violent history, it's odd how so many Mithrans have turned down positions of power just to stay with you." He gave me an odd, gentle smile. "I understand such loyalty and devotion to you, from personal experience. But for so many Mithrans to cling to anyone not their maker is unusual. And delightful."

I might have blushed. Just a tiny bit. I leaned my head to his shoulder, and he kissed the top of my head.

"Gag me with a spoon. If y'all are gonna suck face, I'm outta here." Alex gathered up his electronic paraphernalia and left the room.

Bruiser lifted my hand and kissed my knuckles, mischief gleaming in his eyes. "That boy has no romance at all in his soul."

"True dat," I said, in NOLA style. "That said, wanna make out?"

"Always, my love. Always."

But as usual, there wasn't time.

It was near ten p.m. when a select group, which included two of the Everharts, gathered in the security room to watch live vest cam footage from Eli's small security team. Liz Everhart sat on one side of me, her twin on the other. I wasn't stupid. I understood that the sisters were boxing me in. It was a polite and indirect threat to my life and health, should Eli not come back alive, healthy, and in one piece. Molly narrowed her eyes at her sisters, making sure they saw her thoughts on the subject matter. That was one cool thing about BFFs and sisters. A single look could say so much.

Quint, who had a finely honed instinct for trouble, sat to our right, her back to comms and security control. Her position gave her a clean line of fire toward the armory area, the doorway, and the twins. Only Alex was out of her line of fire, and I was pretty sure Quint didn't know Alex had a weapon, nor how good a shot he was. Yet.

The new chick, Sarah Spieth, sat at Alex's side, her arm in a cast and sling and her leg stretched out on a chair. She was still deaf from the concussion, but thanks to the quantity of vamp blood in her, she was mostly out of pain and on the way to healing, maybe a little stoned on vamp blood. Alex had promoted her to her new position—"Wrassler Jr.," as he dubbed her—would take over in Wrassler's previous position.

When Wrassler married Jodi, he'd been promoted to an admin position, with a big leap in salary and benefits.

We had been looking for a replacement. Sarah fit the bill. Besides being former active duty military, she had good mechanical aptitude, and no problem learning various electronic and computer platforms.

As her military sleeve put it, "Takes no shit; adaptable; responsible to chain of command; speaks three languages and ASL." (Which I figured out meant American Sign Language.) "Self-motivated." Under an aside comment were the words, "Might be psychic." I liked the "Might be psychic" part. Alex wanted her as Active Comms Chief and Head of HQ Grounds Security. That freed up Wrassler to do the admin job of HQ Internal Security, Official Liaison between NOLA and the Dark Queen, and the job of making sure the blood-servants were safe, like an overqualified Human Resources person.

Sarah turned her head, not moving her leg. For someone who had been blown up and jumped off a roof only hours ago, she looked pretty dang good: military highand-tight haircut, piercings, tats, and a great attitude. She looked at Quint and narrowed her eyes. Yeah. Sarah knew her military stuff and she knew people. We were gonna get along great.

Her eyes shifted from Quint, to me, to the overhead map. She typed a note to Alex and he typed one back.

I turned my attention to the sit map—the situation map that showed each unit member and where they were, as well as all private company security cameras and all the doorbell cameras Alex had been able to obtain. Each of the team members were indicated by a different color, with a name in place below each dot.

Eli's team had parked two blocks over and we watched and listened as they moved toward the Marigny address on foot. Over comms, small dogs were barking, loud music played in the distance, and people were singing drunkenly somewhere close by as the four-member unit leaped over fences and threaded silently through alleys and back gardens. They stayed close, no more than twenty feet between them at any time. Their cams picked up firepits and tiki lights and people dancing. No one saw the team, and if a silent alarm went off, no cops or security guys showed up.

Eli and pals finally reached the address, a narrow-fenced lot on Burgundy Street near Ursulines Avenue. Inside the fence was a beat-up delivery truck, the back doors partially open as if it was empty. Or an invitation to be ambushed.

The vamps on the team kept silent watch as Eli knelt and deployed a tiny remote-controlled speedster toy with an even tinier camera mounted on top. He maneuvered the toy closer to the truck and raised the camera on a four-foot-long telescoping handle. Inside the truck was something that looked like big lumps, not attackers. But something about them must have given Eli pause.

"What is it?" Liz murmured.

I shook my head, feeling Eli's interest morphing into a shared worry.

Whatever it was, Eli didn't like it. He retracted the camera and backed the toy away. He said, "I see bags of something, and I'm getting a familiar tickle in the back of my throat when the wind blows this way, something like fertilizer. Exfil to the next block," he said to his team. "Move it."

We figured it out at the same time and Liz's fingers grabbed my arm, tightening, not looking at me. "Please be safe," she whispered. It sounded like a prayer. Waiting for the explosion. The death of her boyfriend.

CHAPTER 14

A Little Bit of Dog Snot

Pops of air sounded over comms. The pad of running footsteps filtered to us. "If the truck's loaded with ammonium nitrate," Eli said, "we'll lose the entire block."

Alex said, "Placing another call to NOLA PD bomb squad, the ATF team leader who was on scene at the airport rocket attack and the explosions at HQ. He's not getting much downtime."

Holy crap, I thought. Ammonium nitrate was the stuff used in the Oklahoma City bombing, and in Beirut, Lebanon. It was the landscapers' bomb material of choice. Large-scale purchases were heavily traced by the government, but . . . New Orleans was a port with plenty of hidden places for smuggling via boat. If you knew how to avoid the authorities and were familiar with the waterways, you could get anything in.

"We'll stick around until the area is evacuated," Eli said, his breathing just a hint more labored than normal, though that might have been the effect of running full out after a devastating injury, not worry. "Just in case NOPD wants or needs our help."

"Also placing calls to the Roberes," Alex said. "Good thing Onorios don't need much sleep. They haven't gotten any in the last few days."

On screens, we followed our unit sprinting through alleys, over fences, and Koun raced through a restaurant, out the back, and over a wall. Eli, showing off, jumped a six-foot-high wall into an alley. He grunted with pain and laughter when he landed. I let a faint smile cross my face. He was having fun. I could feel the sheer pleasure coursing through him. He'd always missed the adrenaline rush of battle.

Alex cut the volume on comms and swiveled his desk chair to me. "And now, My Queen, we need to figure out where our enemies are laired up. And end them."

That was the kind of comment made by a military advisor, not my kid brother. His expression was unyielding, tough as nails, and completely emotionless. It told me nothing except that he was utterly determined.

End them. Right. "Is Leo still staked?" I asked. When Alex nodded, I said, "Have him brought down here. Leave the cuffs on and the stake in place. And get a couple of willing donors to stand by. He'll be hungry when I pull out the stake."

"You will not pull a stake from a vamp, My Queen," Quint said. "That's my job."

"Whatever. I want some more of Deon's wine broth. And a side order of bacon. For me, not the outclan priest. I am not sharing."

I was finishing off two pounds of bacon and a gallon of wine broth when four security people entered. One held Leo's feet, one held the left arm, one held the right, and one followed, weapon ready, the mag marked as containing silver-lead ammo. As if they were swinging a jump rope, they rocked Leo back and forth and up onto the big table, bumping his head in the process. He landed in the same spot where Eli had last been. Bleeding to death. And now my brother was within a city block of a truck possibly full of explosive material.

I fought down my panic. It would only upset Eli. But *dang it all to heck and back.* Why did he find this kind of thing fun? Duty I got. Responsibility. The joy of a job successfully completed. But fun? Uncle Sam's finest were always adrenaline junkies and usually nuts.

Two humans crawled up beside Leo, snuggling close. I deliberately looked away, hating that I contributed to the mental slavery of humans by not killing every vamp I saw. As if she felt the same way, Liz tightened her hand on my arm. "I bruise," I said softly.

She turned her eyes to me and released her hold. Our eyes held. Hers were full of remorse for things not said and done, fear for Eli, and anger at me.

"I'm just glad Carmen isn't here right now."

Carmen's husband had been killed by young vamps. But Tommy wasn't why Liz was upset.

"I am not your enemy. Nor am I responsible for Eli's decisions."

"He'd give his life for you."

At first, I thought it was jealousy speaking, then recognized her tone as confusion and bewilderment. "Girl, you're *still* not seeing it. Eli would give his life for his worst enemy. It's what Uncle Sam's warriors do. They run into the fire. They die for us. Their families suffer for us. You love Eli, you make a life with Eli, that's who he is. That's your future."

Her eyes filled with tears. She jerked her arms to her ample chest, crossing them. Looked down. "Yeah. Save his worst enemy. That describes him to a T."

"And for people he loves?" I said, making it a question. I leaned in close. "I'm not an Everhart, but you and me? We're sisters in his eyes. Worse, we're fellow warriors in his eyes. There is nothing at all that he won't do for us. Nothing. And you need to remember that."

She nodded, the motion jerky and protective.

I looked at Bruiser and nodded. "Do it."

Quint cleared a place around her and pointed two handguns at the former MOC. I sighed as a dozen people drew weapons and pointed them at Quint. My bodyguard needed a discussion about guns in the security room. "Put the weapons away. Everybody," I said, waving an arm in the air. Slowly they all complied, even Quint, but she looked at me with disgust in her eyes.

With deft motions, Bruiser freed Leo from his arm cuffs. Then from his head restraints. Leo lay there unmoving. Gently, pressing a human blood donor in close, Bruiser slid the wooden stake from Leo's belly. It made an awful sound, kind of slurping. Leo did nothing for maybe thirty seconds. Then he took a breath and, almost tenderly, reached up with both arms and took the head of the nearest human in his hands. He pulled her down to him. His jaw unhinged and his fangs clicked down.

I got up and walked into the hallway, carrying a bottle with its last dregs of bone broth. Quint followed. We stood on either side of the doors, backs to the walls, Quint's position giving her adequate lines of fire up and down. I drank wine broth, the best part, with all the spices and herbs a dark cloud in the bottom. Quint watched me.

"Why?" she asked.

"Why did I make you put your weapons away? Why do I allow you to follow me around like a rabid attack dog? Why what?"

"Why do you allow Leo to live? He might try to take your kingdom back."

"Of all the people who actually want it, he's the least monster-ish and best qualified to be MOC of NOLA." I tilted up the last of the spicy herby deliciousness and swallowed. With the gallon flask, I gestured up and down the hallway. "If he wants the place, he can have it."

Quint blinked, which she didn't do much, and looked confused.

"It's this way. I have a love/hate relationship with places and people. I don't claim any place because cities and land and places can be taken away in a heartbeat. Places don't give anyone security. People? That's even worse. They can be taken away too, and it hurts a lot more. People need protecting. It's kinda what I do. So if you protect me, then you need to learn what that means. It means you have to protect everyone around me, because I'll run in to save them when I need to."

"You're even more stupid than Eli." She sounded surprised. "I heard what you said to Liz. And you are just as bad because you don't have the skills to fight some of the things you go up against."

I shrugged. She had a point. The door to the security room opened and Liz stuck her head out. "He's finished sipping on humans. Now he has a glass of wine and half the guys in here need a cigarette."

"Leo had sex on my table?" *Gross.*

"No. But he may as well have."

"Oh. Right." Feeding often made the feedee very happy.

Back in the security room, Leo was sitting at the table, sipping a glass of red wine, listening to Alex's update, watching the screens we had already looked at, and offering nothing. Over comms Eli said, "NOPD and ATF brought in a bomb-sniffing dog and a better camera. Conclusion is that the truck is full of ammonium nitrate. Military and ATF are taking over, and locals are being evacuated for a half mile in every direction."

"Okay. Be safe, Ranger man." I looked around the room, and met the eyes of each security guy, male and female, human and vamp. "I'm heading up to bed. You people try to keep everyone safe, especially the witches. Their ward kept us all alive."

"Roger that," several people said.

Witches had endured a bad rep for centuries, one put in place by the ancient church, when people went to witches instead of priests, to circle ritual instead of church ritual, and the church suffered a loss of power and monies. The church attacked witches and burned them at the stake, killing mostly innocents, but also a lot of witches. The New Orleans coven had suffered more recent attacks because they had been unable to turn Hurricane Katrina back out into the Gulf, and then Hurricane Ida. Were later unable to end a magic storm, and then more recent hurricanes. Seeing our HQ vamps and humans appreciating the witches and recognizing the hard work that had gone into the working that saved them from a bombing was a good thing. Word would spread.

Bruiser opened the door to the hallway, preceding me, with Quint following us. Behind me, Liz said, "Hey. Queen." I looked back. "We're heading out in the morning to the null prison, to re-create the *hedges* there and see what the witches' circle in the street looks like. You're welcome to observe, if you want to go with us." She smiled wryly. "It could be dangerous. I know how much you like that stuff."

"Thanks," I said. "Let my security know the time and if it's possible for me to attend, I'll be ready."

The door closed and Quint muttered from behind me, "You are freaking certifiable."

"She's fun that way," Bruiser agreed.

The dream sucked. I knew I was dreaming, but I couldn't wake up, which made it suck more.

Hayyel was standing in my soul home, wings broken, hanging at odd, painful angles, blood-soaked feathers in fluttering puddles around his feet. A silver chain around his waist. Sabina, now dead and gone, stood beside him, one hand gripping Hayyel's forearm, the other reaching out to me as if for help.

Hayyel was in trouble, his wings were broken, the bones shattered. *Got it, subconscious mind,* I thought.

The two of them were in a witch circle made of ashes and orange flames tipped with green. In my dream, they were trapped together in the circle, though I knew that no witch circle could hold an angel and that Sabina had been eaten alive and so this wasn't a vision of the future. This imagery was symbolic.

Unless Sabina was reaching out to me from inside of Hayalasti Sixmankiller, in an afterlife of spiritual slavery.

Or maybe in some kind of limbo, searching for her soul, which she had lost long before.

Hayyel's broken wings were a different kind of symbol, an image of being trapped and stripped of power. Even if the imagery was all real, even if the request for help was real too, there was nothing I could do to fix anyone's misery. Not a single solitary thing. My old nemesis guilt was like an elephant doing a pirouette on my chest.

Useless. I'm useless.

Hayyel gestured to his silver chain, as if telling me it was my job to free him. Had he been chained all along, from the first time I ever saw him? Had he been trying to get my attention from the very first, depending on me, using me, to get free from a partial chaining? Did angels groom humans to become good servants? He would if he could, I knew that.

I looked around and realized this vision wasn't exactly like my soul home. There was no firepit, and once again there were niches with the suggestion of people standing in them, blurry and out of focus. Bound beings? Bound angels? *Crap.* That would be bad if there were already other angels bound wherever he was. I looked for the suggestion of wings on the still figures and thought I saw some, at least the hint of them. Maybe.

"How am I supposed to free you?" I asked, my voice booming and echoing in the chamber. "This place isn't even real."

My voice still reverberating, the vision shifted, and the echo cut off. There was a heartbeat of blackness before a new vision came into focus.

Hayyel and I were hovering in the air over a different place, over a house from my past, at the time and power that set so much of this in motion. We dove, or fell, though the roof, the upper stories, and into the basement. We were looking at the witch circle in Evangelina Everhart's basement, the scarlet power reflecting on the walls, a glow I didn't remember seeing when Molly's sister called and trapped a demon. The paintings of vampires in the act of black magic, of demon circles, and black magic symbols on the walls, like a map into darkness.

The demon was ramming his body at the walls of his prison, trying to get free. In the circle with him was Brute, when he was a red werewolf, and Brute's well-chewed werewolf friend who the demon had been eating on. And who had died.

Hayyel had been the one to save us then. Hayyel was partially trapped now. Maybe demon stuff required the Rule of Three, and Evangelina's demon-calling-trapping ceremony had been part of a binding. Had he been trapped by her, or before I was even around, or, worse, had he gotten trapped when helping us? That would be bad. That would mean I was beholden to an angel and owed him his freedom.

But I thought not, or he would have used that boon to

make me help him. This, this being trapped, bound, whatever it was, had happened without my input, and hopefully before my time.

With a lurch that jerked my spine and yanked my arms up hard, I was again in Hayyel's soul home. I was swinging as if from a trapeze, or a wrist noose, hanging above the angel with his broken wings, the true-dead outclan priestess beside him. I took a breath that hurt and felt all too real. My wrists ached. I glanced up and saw that I was bound, the rope around my wrists hanging from a meat hook.

Beside me, on his own rope, swung Leo. We were rocking back and forth, like unbalanced pendulums, back and forth, crossing close to each other at the bottom of the arcs.

"This imagery sucks," I said, my words echoing like a beating drum.

Below me, the witch circle that trapped Hayyel and Sabina flamed high. It bore some resemblance to Evangelina's demon-binding circle, though with different colors. The green and orange flames told me that it belonged to the witches working with Mainet.

"Who wants to bind and control an angel and a true-dead vamp?" I asked.

"You know this answer," Sabina said.

"No. I don't. Tell me what you want me to know."

As if the command gave him permission to speak, Hayyel said, "They will soon complete the binding and Sabina and I shall be lost."

"What will they do with you bound?" I asked. "Bargain with God for redemption?"

"Something far less saintly," Sabina said.

"Yeah, yeah. Destroy the arcenciels. Or invade heaven. Or fix time to suit them. Everyone wants control of the timelines."

"You must save us, Jane Doe Yellowrock," Sabina said, making a yanking gesture. "It is your destiny."

Something pulled in my chest, as if she ripped a vital part from me.

The weight on my chest grew. I couldn't breathe. Pain bruised my ribs as if I was being beaten.

Waking, I grabbed at the thing holding me down. "Ant

Jane. Wake up," Angie said. Something slapped my face, hard. "Wake up!" My eyes flew open to see Angie sitting on my chest, her legs bent and her bare feet poking into my ribs under my arms, which were gripping her. I released her shoulders, which I had surely bruised in my grab. She patted my cheeks with both hands, again, not more gently.

"Owww," I gasped. "Stop that." I picked her up and moved her to the side so I could take some much-needed breaths. My hands were human-shaped. I was in my suite at HQ. Bruiser wasn't here, his side of the bed unwrinkled and fresh. He hadn't come to bed. I took all that in as I sat up and met Angie's petulant gaze.

"You wouldn't wake up," she said with a grown-up tone of asperity. She looked at the door, then back to me, and whispered, "Hayyel is close by. I can feel him, but he's hurt." Angie's glance at the door meant she wasn't supposed to be in here.

I remembered the angel's broken, bloodied wings. Sabina yanking something inside of me, or . . . stealing something from inside of me—part of my skinwalker power? Had that thief been the latent soul of Sabina or Gramma? Had she succeeded in getting everything she wanted? Would she be back? Had it been only a dream or something more powerful than a dream? I shook my head, hoping to find some wits.

Angie was wearing nightclothes, a purple and white striped stretchy onesie that had built-in footies. Too cute. And so she had snuck out of bed and through HQ, where hungry vampires roamed and cameras recorded everything, and past my guards and into my room. And no alarms had gone off. No one stopped her. The powerful brat was going to get herself killed.

After checking to see that I had gone to bed wearing some version of jammies—T-shirt and shorts—go me—I swung my legs over and sat on the side of the bed beside her. My hair was a tangled black nest, but I shoved it out of the way, using the time to figure out what to say and what to ask. Before I did anything else, I sent out a group text that Angie was with me, in my suite, and safe. This way, though Angie would get caught by her parents, and that would be my fault, at least I wouldn't die from a misplaced spell thrown by a terrified Big Evan when he came searching. There was no instant reply from the Everharts.

I put my cell away and started with the simple question. "Did you make your parents go into a deep sleep so you could sneak into my room?"

She frowned at me so hard I thought her face might break. "That's Everhart business. Don't tell," she ordered.

"We've talked about this before. They aren't stupid, Angie Baby. How do you know that Hayyel is in trouble?"

She blew out a sigh that sounded like one of Molly's irritated breaths. "I think it was a dream, but it wasn't a nighttime dream, you know? I have dreams sometimes in the middle, halfway awake and halfway not. When I was little, I called it the *between* place."

I used to call the space between being human-shaped and being Beast *the between*. "Like a vision?"

She frowned. "I guess. They come to me when I'm going to sleep sometimes, and I don't remember much about them. But the ones like today, the half-awake ones, are different. I see them and I know stuff, and then they stop and I'm standing by the bed awake. Except this time, in the dream part, I put Mama and Daddy asleep and then I was standing in the hallway outside your door."

I leaned down and looked at the bottoms of her onesie footies. A little dirty, exactly the way they should look if she walked here. As opposed to transported here. So that was one tiny piece of good news.

She looked down at her hands and shrugged again. "You're gonna be mad. But I made your guards go to sleep too. On purpose."

"I see."

"And then I came in and I whispered, and then I yelled but you wouldn't wake up. So I got on top of you and hit you."

"I remember."

"Did I hurt you?" She didn't look very upset about the possibility.

I touched my cheeks and jaw. "Not bad. But Eli's been teaching you some martial arts moves and you're starting to pack a punch."

"Yeah. Ant Jane, are vampires evil? They live in the night, and sunlight makes them sick and die. They drink blood. Evil things do that. And *in between*? There's a dead vampire with my angel."

Dead vamp. Sabina.

Crap. She'd had a vision similar to mine. And *great*. I was going to have to give the whole "nature of evil and good, darkness and light" talk. "Vampires, just like humans, are capable of good and evil. They have choices."

"So Naturaleza are evil and our vampires are good?"

"More or less."

"Beast eats people. Is Beast the evil part of you? 'Cause I love Beast and I don't think she's evil."

Kit, Beast thought, longing bursting up within her, stealing the breath I had almost caught up on.

"Beast is a predator. But Beast is way more than a normal cat. Like vampires, Beast can think and reason and choose."

"Like people? Like she chose to take care of me when my magic came on me and I called the storm?" She tilted her head up at me. "I don't remember it because I was a baby, but Mama told me how Beast saved me when I couldn't control my magic."

Crap. She wasn't supposed to have to control magic at all at this age. I slid an arm around her and hugged her close, remembering the storm Angie had called that had destroyed her home and nearly killed her and her parents. Angie had been a toddler then. A baby for real. She was what, now? Eight? "Yes. Like that. Beast saved you all on her own. She thinks of you and EJ and Cassy as her kits."

Angel made a surprised *harrumph*ing sound. "Are you and Beast gonna save the angel?"

"If we can, yes. First we have to find out where the angel is." Which, if my dream vision was correct, was either in the physical manifestation of my soul home or in Evangelina's basement, one of which was lost to history, the other back in Asheville. Or, if Aggie One Feather's pessimistic idea was right, he was in a church, cathedral, or graveyard somewhere in Europe.

"He's that way." Angie pointed at the wall. In a windowless room it was hard to tell which direction she pointed, but my laptop was on the bedside table. I quickly booted it up and engaged the compass, discovering that it was nearly dawn. "Show me again. As close as you can. Which way?" I asked her.

Angie closed her eyes and thought a moment, then pointed. Adjusted her aim a fraction. "There. Exactly."

I lined up the GPS and compass on my laptop with the map of New Orleans. If Angie was right, Hayyel wasn't in Appalachia, or in a church in Spain or France or somewhere far away, he was between HQ and the deep blue Gulf of Mexico. "Close or far?" I asked.

She wobbled her head in indecision. "Close? Maybe?"

Take kit in Ed's car for ride, Beast thought at me. *Kit can find place of angel trap.*

Angie whispered, "Brute can help sniff my angel out."

I looked at my godchild, who should not know that the white werewolf was bound to the angel who had saved him from being a meal for a demon. I said, "I don't know how to get in touch with the werewolf. He just shows up when he wants."

Beast said, *Brute guards Leo den. Beast has been there.*

And you didn't think to tell me?

Are many things Beast does not tell Jane.

I thought a very bad word.

"Brute is on his way," Angie said. With that, she slid off the bed and walked calmly out the door, her footsies *shushing* on the floor. In the wake of her colorful jammies, I saw the guards shaking themselves alert and trying to stand. Her mama and daddy were gonna have a fit. And guard duty outside my bedroom was gonna require hazard pay.

I called security and when Wrassler answered, he demanded, "Are you okay, Janie?"

"Yeah. Are you manning the cameras? Because I'd like to know what just happened outside my door."

"Until ten seconds ago, your security detail was standing guard. Now they're on their knees and unable to stand. They look like they've been drugged. What happened?"

"Angie happened. I think she knocked them out and looped the security feed."

"God help us," Wrassler said.

"I think we need to update our systems. Again." I instructed him to wake Quint and have a car brought around back. His reply informed me it would be three vehicles, and that Bruiser would be waiting at the back entrance. *Yikes.* I had forgotten to call my honeybunch.

Hurriedly, I dressed and armed myself—jeans and handguns, one vamp-killer. I headed out the door and snapped my fingers at the guards, not the vamps who had been put to sleep by a witch child, but humans who had shown up to take over. "I'm going for a drive. So I don't get my ass chewed, how about y'all follow me downstairs to the back entrance?"

Something brushed my leg and both guards drew on me, weapons pointing at my left thigh. I managed not to flinch at the unexpected touch or the guns. "Put 'em away. Looks like you two haven't met Brute and his baby grindylow."

To the werewolf I said, "You're gonna get yourself shot someday, you stupid dog."

Not having a human mouth, Brute didn't talk back, but he did give a snort and it somehow sounded like a challenge, like, "They can try," but with air and a little bit of dog snot on the floor.

To the guards, I said, "Of the two, the grindy is by far the most dangerous. Don't let the neon green fur and the cute kitty-cat appearance fool you."

The grindy chittered at me. "Pea?" I asked. There was no response, so not Pea. I had no idea if this one was Bean, Sprout, or Leaf. Not that it mattered. Only Pea could speak (sort of), with the ability to say, "Ssss," for yes and, "Nnnn," for no. None of the others responded to the names humans gave them, and other than Pea's two words, they were identical in appearance at this age.

We all got on the elevator and I asked the white werewolf, "You know what I'm searching for?"

He cocked his head, curious, telling me he wasn't sure what I meant.

"One who's winged and broken, one dead twice and eaten alive?"

He nodded his head up and back down once, human gestures that always looked odd on animals.

"And while we're chatting, I hear you've been guarding a very special someone while he sleeps."

Brute tilted his head at me quizzically, as if it was a stupid question and I should know this already, and nodded again.

"Fine. We'll talk later."

The two guards glanced at each other and raised their eyebrows, as if saying the boss-lady was a little crazy talking to critters.

The wolf leaped into the back seat and growled when I held out a harness. Growled again when I pulled out the seat belt. The grindy took its cue from the werewolf and chittered at me indignantly.

"Fine," I said. "But if we have an accident and werewolf and grindy brains get splattered all over the SUV, it'll probably have to be totaled, because brains are sticky and will never come out, and I will not be happy about my insurance rates."

With that smile that told me he found me adorable, Bruiser took the driver's seat and Quint claimed shotgun. That left me no place except with the dog and the neon green kitty-like killer in back.

I glared at the wolf. Brute snorted with amusement and lay across most of the back seat area. The grindy perched herself on his back, extruded her left forepaw claws, and started grooming the hairs at his neck, just like a kitten. Except her claws were steel and little bits of hair flew up as she worked. Sighing, I belted in, knowing my jeans would smell like dog.

Bruiser started the vehicle and our three-car motorcade pulled into the street. I missed Eli, but he was off somewhere with Liz and I hoped he was having more fun than I was. Quint was cold and silent. Bruiser was deep in thought, as he had been for days, restructuring plans for the coronation, trying to out-vamp-think vamps and keep me safe while doing all the other Consort duties, which were a lot like heir or primo duties under Leo, but

with more prospective duels and attacks and battles. Like
at the null prison and the airport and . . . My brain turned
all that over and . . . *Crap.*

Brute was slobbering all over the upholstery, and I had
the weird urge to scratch between his ears, which made
no sense at all. Unless there was something seriously
wrong with me. As we drove, I realized that I was—well,
I might be—lonely.

There was a time when my life was made up of me,
Bitsa—my bastard Harley—Molly, and Angie. Now there
were all these people in it. People I . . . loved. People to
take care of. Had to consider in my daily plans. Which
sucked. I frowned and looked out the window. When this
coronation was over, I was taking a long, hard look at my
life choices.

The cars in front and in back were being driven by the
two guards from my bedroom, and there were two additional shooters in each vehicle. That made eight people
guarding me while I twiddled my thumbs in the back seat
with a werewolf and grindylow. I used to motor around
this city on my Harley Bitsa all the time. Alone. Now I
had an entourage. And . . . I was lonely.

This was stupid. And annoying. Not that I said anything because no one was listening to me anyway. I was
just the Asset. Or better—the Cargo. Yeah. A lump of
clay. I held in a dejected sigh, but I felt it deep in my guts.
Of course there wasn't much room there right now, as
much as I had been eating, so there was that. Being the
DQ meant great food and all the cool toys I wanted. It
also meant that gushy feeling deep inside that said *family.*
If I could keep them safe.

"This a great area of space to search, Jane, for an angel who is unlikely to be corporeal," Bruiser said. "Can
you give me any details at all? Maybe something you saw
in the visions?"

"Curved ceiling, like a cave. There were these people standing around the walls. I keep wondering if they
were angels, if they had wings. And maybe they did. There
were stains or shadows running down the walls. One time
I saw the place, there was some kind of shimmery red and
blue light, like emergency lights but not flashing."

"Possibly an old Catholic church?" Bruiser asked. "A glow like stained glass windows? They might have niches with statues, plaster of Paris saints, angels, some with wings."

"Huh." I frowned. I had been in St. Louis Cathedral. So yeah, though this was smaller. "All Catholic churches have idols?"

"Statues, Jane," he said, and his tone said I was being insensitive.

"What about a *damaged* church? Black mold on water-damaged walls?"

"After all the hurricanes and the financial devastation of the last few decades, there are many churches that haven't been repaired and might never be."

I sat up straight, trying to remember the different things I had seen in each vision. "Could be." I looked at the were-wolf. "Whatcha think, doggie? An old church?"

Brute snarled at me, showing his teeth at the doggie comment, but he gave a curt nod.

"Brute thinks an old church." I grinned and looked out the window, saying, "If we get close, just go *woof*."

Brute growled, a sound like a big generator coming on inside the car, before he turned his head away, effectively dismissing me. My people were getting good at that.

CHAPTER 15

Get Your Furry Ass to the Prison

By the time the sky was bright, we had checked out several damaged churches that might conceivably have statues standing in niches. All were in the vicinity of Angie Baby's pointing finger, but none looked anything like my visions, nor did any church make Brute go *woof.* In fact, he refused to even get out of the SUV. And the farther from HQ we drove, the wider grew our margin of error.

"Quint," Bruiser said, as we got back into the car after the last stop, "please drive." They switched places and Bruiser said, "Brute, If I show you the map, can you suggest a general vicinity where the angel might be?"

Brute, ignoring me as if I was a cat beneath his notice, pricked his ears at Bruiser and gave a regal nod, like, a better royal nod than I knew how to give.

My sweet-cheeks unfolded an honest-to-God paper map of New Orleans and nearby environs, and twisted over the seat and console to display it to Brute. "Some animals have a natural homing instinct."

Brute narrowed his eyes at Bruiser, and this time I wasn't on the receiving end of the werewolf's growls.

"Forgive me misspeaking," Bruiser said smoothly. "I wasn't calling you an animal. But Jane retains some of the traits of the creatures she shifts into. And I don't know what additional gifts you might naturally have as a were-creature. If you are tied to the angel, might you have an internal"—Bruiser rolled his free hand, as if searching for more appropriate phrasing—"indication of Hayyel's whereabouts?"

The growling stopped. The werewolf gave a dog chuff and tilted his head, his eyebrows wrinkling closer together in thought. He stood on the seat and turned around in a circle, tumbling the grindy into my lap.

"Easy with the steel claws," I said to the little killer. "I bleed."

Brute bopped the window with his snout and sniffed outside when it opened with a faint whirr. He shook his huge body, sending wolf hairs into the air, looked back to the map, and gave a dog frown. Turned around again, his nonretractable wolf claws denting the leather. He shook his head no, then yes.

"He doesn't know where Hayyel is, but he knows something," I said. "General direction?" I got the shake/nod again.

Bruiser held the map closer and said, "If I point at the map, can you give a better idea of the general direction?"

Brute stared at the map, the skin around his eyes tight, his mouth closed. I had a feeling he was going to fart as a joke, but I didn't say it. No point in giving him ideas. And kudos to me for keeping my big mouth shut.

"This is the direction Angie pointed." Bruiser indicated west and south.

Bruiser leaned in and studied the map, finally licking one area.

"Algiers," Bruiser said, circling the licked spot with a blue pen.

Brute nodded, but he didn't look particularly certain.

"Good an idea as any?" I asked.

Brute shook, nodded, and plopped back down. The vehicle rocked slightly.

"Okay," I said. "Quint, drive us across the river."

"Roger that," she said, pulling away as we buckled up.

Algiers. That the church was across the Mississippi never crossed my mind.

The traffic hit us before we crossed the river, slowing to a crawl as vehicles fought to get to someplace better than they were at now, creating long lines to take one of the bridges. Pain-in-the-butt traffic. More thumb twiddling.

On the far side of the river, Quint pulled through a mom-and-pop-style drive-through and handed over a huge bag of fried breakfast foods and paper plates, with plastic cutlery, including a family-sized bag of boudin balls fresh out of the fryer. They weren't as good as Deon's but they did relieve my twiddling. We shared the food on the disposable plates and ate as we rode into western NOLA, even Brute eating boudin from a greasy paper bag with the sides rolled down.

A few blocks into Algiers, the white werewolf perked up and looked out the window. He sniffed and snorted, licking grease off his jaw and pawing the window glass. Quint pulled over, I opened the door, and the werewolf, with the grindy again holding on to his ruff, jumped from the seat to the sidewalk. I oriented myself and cleaned my sticky hands with sanitizer before joining the others on the sidewalk. I smelled like fast-food boudin and bacon. I smelled heavenly. Best perfume ever.

Brute was ahead of us, standing in the parking area of a storefront church that had been damaged by vandals, the windows smashed. The area looked abandoned, though someone had made an unsuccessful attempt to clean the graffiti off the exterior walls, and the glass had been swept into a pile at the entrance. Brute stuck his nose into a broken section of glass and sniffed. He backed away, uncertainty wrinkling his forehead and the furry skin over his crystalline eyes.

Holding his huge head high, Brute sniffed the chilly air and took off at a brisk trot. Quint pointed at my door and we all got back in the SUV. She drove as we followed the white werewolf with the neon green grindy clinging to his head. Brute led us deeper into Algiers, winding around neighborhoods—which left me stunned at the number of residents who decorated for Thanksgiving, including one place that had an inflatable rainbow-hued turkey, a good twelve feet tall, that shook drumsticks at passersby when the wind fluffed it.

We passed storm-damaged areas where no hurricane repairs had been started, others that were nearly renovated, and we stopped at old churches. Some were tiny buildings tucked between larger ones, others were fancy places of brick and stained glass. A lot of them had been damaged by the recent storms and were undergoing repairs. Others had been abandoned, left to grow the dangerous black mold the Gulf states were known for.

The fourth Roman Catholic church was on Algiers Point, quiet, hidden behind scaffolding and a security fence to keep out troublemakers. There was rusted scaffolding up the sides, a ten-foot-tall Virgin Mary standing out front, and a statue of Jesus hanging on a cross in a small garden with concrete benches. There were signs of high water everywhere. Debris was piled here and there, and the foliage was saltwater-burned, brown and dead. A fog was rolling off the Mississippi and the air temps were dropping with a coming storm front, turning the landscape into a trope horror movie morning. All we needed was zombies.

We got out, standing protected by the SUV, while Brute sniffed wet, chilly air.

Spanish and English words rang in the air, and when the breeze pushed the fog off, two carpenters on the scaffolding crossed themselves at the sight of the three-hundred-pound werewolf. The grindy waved at them with its paw, which looked so cute, unless one knew about the steel claws hidden there, and the carpenters must have because the wave caused more shouting and general panic. Then they spotted me, and one guy almost fell off the high perch, shouting, *"Reina! Reina!"*

Brute sniffed, a disdainful sound, and trotted away. Quint thought it was all amusing. I didn't ask. I got back into the SUV and out of sight. After that I just stayed in the vehicle.

Two churches later, neither one of which were damaged, Brute came back to the SUV and stood on his hind legs to look in the window at me. His tongue was lolling comically, and when I opened the door, he stepped up and onto my thighs, which hurt more than I expected and probably left paw-shaped bruises on me, as he crossed to the empty seat. I asked, "No angels?"

Brute shook his head and lay down, panting. The grindy had braided his longer ruff hair into dozens of tiny braids. The small creature looked at me chittered, pointing at its handiwork.

"Pretty," I said. My cell signaled an incoming text. It was Molly telling me to "Get your royal butt back and take care of my babies."

"Okay," I said to my car mates. "We've wasted enough time. I'm hungry. Let's get back to HQ." Not every investigative lead panned out.

Angie was waiting at the back doors when I got out of my SUV. She was wearing jeans, sneakers, and a cable-knit sweater, her strawberry-blond hair in braids. "Ant Jane?" she called. "Why didn't you take me?"

I waggled my fingers at my lovebug. Bruiser blew me a kiss, which warmed me all over.

Angie looked far too interested and was far too precocious and observant for me to do anything else. I remembered that she had a crush on Edmund, my primo and the Emperor of Europe, who would be coming to NOLA for his coronation.

I took Angie's hand, leading her inside and toward the kitchens, explaining. "I didn't take you because bad people are after me and I can't keep you safe enough to satisfy your parents or anyone else."

"I can take care of myself. And now I can help hunt for my angel."

She probably could do all that, but I was not bringing that idea to Molly's attention nor was I encouraging Angie, not when her parents were busy at the null prison, and not now that I had discovered that Angie could put the security system on auto replay, knock out vamps with sleep spells, and generally take over the world. One of the texts I had received in the car informed me that the Everharts had plans at the null prison to look over the broken

wards today and keeping Angie and EJ safe was to be my
job until they returned. So much for being invited to
watch and help. Like Angie's, my talents were sorely under-
appreciated. Or maybe just dangerous.

"Yeah, I know." Even I heard my placating tone.

Angie speared me with a look that said she didn't appreciate being pacified.

Blue Voodoo fell in behind us and I said, "Tell Deon to
make a snack for the kids and me, and then send someone—
not Quint—to pick up little Evan and meet us in the
kitchen dining area." Quint was scary. "Cookies and sliced
apples and milk for the kids. A barbeque sandwich or
three for me."

"Yes, ma'am," he said, and repeated my orders into his
mic. The big man, who looked like a linebacker, but meaner
and tougher, handed me an earbud and a mini-mic, which
I hooked around my ear, leaving the mic dangling at my
jaw. "And just so you know," he said, "Cassy's with a half
dozen human blood-servants old enough to be grandpar-
ents, cooing all over her and changing diapers so the security teams don't have to mess with dirty diapers."

"Security was changing diapers?" I asked, trying not
to show *too* much shock.

Laughter in his tone, Voodoo said, "Your security
teams are trained to do most everything."

"True dat."

"I can *help*," Angie insisted. She was yanking on my
hand to keep my attention as we took the stairs to the
kitchens, "With my *finder*."

"What kind of finder?" I asked, adjusting the speaker
on the earbud to softer. We entered Deon's domain and
the newly created restaurant-like public-eating space.
Nothing like it had existed back in Leo's time, when the
kitchen help had transported food to the break room, to
individual suites, and to dormitory areas, and had generally run themselves ragged. This new space was much
more efficient. I bypassed the tables that sat four, six, and
twelve, picked Angie up, and placed her at the serving
bar on a tall stool.

Deon swished out of the door to the kitchen proper, a

tray held over his head like a waiter. With a flourish, he placed the tray on the bar and flapped his hand at the dark-haired blood-servant kitchen help. "I got this, suga'," he said. "Go help Antony with the prep and bring out the queenie's sandwiches when they come outta the oven. For you," he said to Angie, "your aunt Deon has Oreos and milk and the best apples I ever tasted. Try one." He popped a slice into Angie's mouth and she chewed experimentally.

"I like it. But don't expect EJ to like it. EJ's got a *peculiar* taster." She said it as if quoting someone else.

"There is nothing in the world wrong with being peculiar, honey child. I've been peculiar all my life. I'll find that boy an apple he likes to eat, I promise."

Angie dipped an Oreo into milk and counted to fifteen before removing it and sticking it into her mouth. By the time she finished the first Oreo, EJ had been carried into the food service area and deposited on my other side.

Watching everything in that still, silent way he had, he accepted an Oreo and a small glass of milk. Carefully, he copied his sister's method of cookie-prep (though he switched numbers seven and eight) and ate it. He nodded as he chewed and then grinned, showing a mouth full of cookie-blackened teeth. "Hey, Ant Jane."

"Hey, EJ."

Deon convinced EJ to try an apple slice, and the kid accepted it, holding it up and staring at it as if it might bite him.

"I got a finder now," Angie repeated.

"What kind of finder?"

"This one." She handed me a small gold statue. It was the temperature of living flesh and though I knew it was only warm from her pocket, it gave me the heebie-jeebies. The "finder" was the Christ, dead, a three-inch-tall gold figure of Jesus, arms outstretched, feet crossed and displayed as if still being crucified, but attached to no cross. On the back, tiny bars stuck out, as if for mounting the figure on a wall or bedpost or lintel. There were tiny rubies on his crown of thorns and at each palm and the upper ankle, and a much bigger ruby on his side. There was a strange shimmery stone above the head of the Christ. It was arcenciel blood.

Holy crap.

"When you get close to my angel, it will be hot," Angie said. "Don't get burned."

"Where did you get this, Angie? And when did you get it?" Because if it was a magical angel finder it would have been nice to have this morning.

Angie looked around, almost furtive, as if seeing who could hear. Deon was busy chattering with EJ about the different kinds of apples; otherwise we were alone in the eatery.

"Angie?" I asked, a faint warning tone in my voice.

She slid off her tall bar stool to the floor and took my hand, pulling me to the main elevator. "Deon?" I asked. "You got this?"

"Shoo," he said to me. "The girls and me got this." He pushed open the door to the kitchen and called out, "Bring more apples. And some cheese crackers and all the different kinds of apple butter." He turned back to EJ. "We have at least six varieties and they are luscious."

"L'shus," EJ repeated the new word.

I let Angie lead me and she took the elevator and hallways until we reached Leo's office. "You were in here?" I asked, with a sense of foreboding.

She nodded, still looking guilty. "Just a little while ago."

I tapped my tiny mic and said, "Send someone with a key to Leo's old office."

Two minutes later, a woman in my black security colors raced up and unlocked the door. "Thank you," I said, without looking at her. "Wait out here."

I stepped in front of Angie, pulled my side arm, opened the door, and walked inside. The office smelled and felt empty, that stillness that said no one had been breathing or moving in here for some time. But of course, a vamp could stand statue-still and not breathe . . . My gaze flew over the narrow hallway entrance and the walls of the office. Yeah. Empty. I was losing my touch. I should have let security clear the room.

"Here." Angie was pointing to the once-hidden entrance leading into the room next door. This time I called for the security woman to precede us and clear the room. When she returned, she gave me a small nod and stood to the side as we entered. The room hadn't been cleaned or decorated in ages, smelled musty, and was full of Leo's old office furniture. Leo's old desk was on its side, a C-clamp and two boards on the edge. Repairs, I guessed, from when I had demanded it be taken apart to find a magical doohickey. The tiny, private elevator was still there too.

"Angie, where and when did you find the statue?" I repeated.

Angie gave a long-suffering sigh and walked to the far corner of the room. She knelt and pushed at the floor molding in the middle of the wall. A small door flipped open. "It was in there. It called me in my between dreams but I couldn't find it until today. My angel is in danger."

The statue in my hand was still warm, warmer than my hand. It should have cooled off. "Well, crap." What was a gold crucified Jesus, magically attached to an angel, doing next door to Leo's office? Had Leo put it here? And if not Leo, then who left it in the hidden compartment? I dropped beside Angie and felt around in the small compartment. It was empty. And dusty. I ran a fingernail along the creases in the gold statue and scraped off grime. The dirt on it matched the dirt from the little hiding place. The statue had been hidden for a long time. I tapped my mic and said, "Who's on comms?"

"This is Wrassler. What can I do for you, Legs?"

I grinned. "That's way better than all that queen stuff. Who used the hidden-elevator-room next to Leo's office last? I'm talking officially, not for storage."

I could hear him tapping keys. "According to older records, Ming Zoya of Mearkanis kept an office there, back after they were first recognized as powerful Mithrans. Prior to that, when Amaury was MOC . . ." His voice trailed off. He started again. "Prior to that it was reserved, for a short time, for the Son of Darkness, Joses Santana."

"Ask Alex to get our research vamps to do a deep dig

in the histories and find out if there's a reason that either of the Ming twins might want to get involved in angel-trapping or demon-calling. And put video security monitoring on Long-Knife."

There was a slight pause as Wrassler either processed the demon part of the request or the Long-Knife part of the request, or he typed in something.

Long-Knife had come from one of the Ming twins; both women were masters of their own clans, and both put self before the cities and humans where they lived.

"I asked for Thema or Kojo to bleed and read him. Do we have an update?"

"According to Alex's report, Thema undertook that. Nothing to report. No secrets."

"Yeah? Crap. It would have been so easy if he had been the traitor." I remembered how little time it had taken Mainet to bind Leo even deeper. One forced bite. "Just in case, get Koun to do it again. I want a deep probe and if he ends up being bound—" I stopped. Koun was not the sort to take on blood-servants he didn't like. I rubbed my face, thinking, wishing I'd gotten more sleep. I dropped my hand and lowered my voice, speaking within my office, not my heart. "If Long-Knife has to be bound, we will come, and we will bind him to us." Everyone knew how much I hated that, but I couldn't ask my people to do something I wasn't willing to do myself.

"Yes, ma'am. Consider it done," he said quietly.

"Update on the *hedge of thorns* around HQ?"

"Ready to be activated. Currently, security receives a warning signal when someone crosses a boundary, and we're approving each time a signal sounds, but we can come and go as needed."

"Good."

"Anything else, My Queen?"

The Legs part didn't last long. Too much weirdness in my requests for simple friendship. "No," I said, feeling tired. "I'm good. Later, Wrassler." I ended the call to see an incoming call from Molly.

"Big Cat, we got problems. Get your furry ass to the prison."

*   *   *

The street in front of the null prison house was a circus, and not the fun kind with jugglers, trapeze artists, and clown cars. Instead, it was the kind with media vans, scooters, and walking lookie-loos taking pictures, trying to cross the crime scene tape, and no cops around to keep the public safe and away from an active witches' circle.

Bruiser and I watched as a young reporter leaned over the crime scene tape, trying to get a good shot of the inside of the witch circle with her cell phone. The cell phone started smoking and burst into flame. The reporter squealed, tossed the flaming cell away to the street. *Idiot.* She could have lost an arm.

Bruiser sighed softly, a concerned look on his face.

Quint, standing behind me, muttered, "Idiot," echoing my thought.

Things here were not going to get better on their own. There was no privacy for the Everhart witches to work in the street. And I had a heart growing under a too-small null circle in my closet, a heart that needed to be returned to the people best able to care for it. As soon as the null prison was actually working again.

I dialed Molly, who was standing on the null house's front porch. "Hey, BFF," I said when she answered. "You got a working that stinks like tear gas?"

Molly laughed. "I have one called a *skunky* working. It gets caught in clothes and hair. Only direct sunlight for a minimum of four hours will clear the stench away. No soap, no water, nothing else will touch it. And you will *not* want to be around if it goes off. But I don't have permission to release one."

"If you set it off, will it keep lookie-loos away?"

"For hours. Trust me on that."

"Hang on." I muted the call. To Bruiser, I said, "Thoughts?"

Bruiser called the chief of police. The chief's reply to a request for assistance was short and pointed. The chief had men out sick and if we wanted the street cleared, we would have to do it ourselves. Bruiser said, "I see. Of course the Dark Queen doesn't wish to demand too much of local law enforcement." There was faint undertone of sarcasm to his words and I grinned out at the street as Bruiser continued. "The media is out in force. I will be certain to let the reporters know that law enforcement was warned but couldn't be bothered to protect the public from a spell that might be about to go off."

The chief was silent. I could imagine the man rubbing his face in exhaustion. I wondered what kind of blood pressure meds he took. "What do you want, Mr. Dumas? Specifically."

"The bare minimum. Please send a single officer, in a marked car, with lights and sirens, to the null prison. With his loudspeaker please have said officer address bystanders to clear the street, and residents to close windows and doors. Have him inform them that the witches need to determine if the witch circle is safe. The working to determine its safety will be intensely and foully aromatic. And perhaps dangerous. People need to move back two blocks, minimum."

The chief said, "Fine. Ten minutes." He disconnected.

Beast thought, *Mate. Good strong mate.*

Yeah. He trips my trigger too.

Beast was not talking of white man's guns.

I smiled, and when Bruiser looked at me quizzically, I just shook my head. We were in one of the DQ's SUVs, one with heavily tinted windows so the photographers couldn't take pics, but I still wasn't gonna risk getting frisky here. We waited silently as the police unit arrived and the cop instructed the circus to move back two blocks. Using barricades that had been left on site the night of the attack, the officer then blocked off the streets and departed.

Bruiser sent two texts to the security detail and watched as they got out of the other vehicles and placed frames covered with cloth around the circle, outside of the crime scene tape. Then we all pulled farther out of range of the coming skunky working.

"Smart," I said.

"I can't stop photographs taken from second-story windows or roof gardens, but I can make it more difficult for the public to watch the Everharts."

Redheaded, curvy Liz Everhart walked into the street, upwind of the circle, her still-in-the-closet witch twin, Cia, half hiding behind dead foliage watching. Liz placed something on the pavement and backed away. Ten seconds later there was tiny flare of light and a huge puff of smoke. A long, high-pitched whistle split the air. The wind began to blow in and down. It was multidirectional and carried the smoke along the streets. I could hear screams and sounds of horror as the reporters and gawkers took off. I laughed. Then the smell leaked into the SUV.

"Holy crap in a bucket," I said at the skunky stench. "Get us out of here."

Bruiser was chuckling as he drove. "It's been some time since I smelled that working. The Richardson witch clan uses a slightly different odor but it's no less horrible."

My cell rang. "Hey, Alex," I answered. "What's up."

"Lachish Dutillett has been released from the hospital. She's meeting you at our place."

"To get the heart. No. She can't have it. But that should come from me. Okay. We'll be there soon?" I asked Bruiser.

"In this traffic it may take half an hour," he said. "Alex, please have whoever is on duty allow her in and make her a cup of coffee or tea. And check on the Trueblood kids. Make sure they have fully vetted people with them."

"Got it," Alex said, and ended the call.

"Lachish was injured in the prison attack," I said. "She's getting out of the hospital awfully fast."

"She was offered, and accepted, Mithran blood at the scene," Bruiser said with a slight smile.

"Right . . ." I remembered that. Thema had fed and healed Lachish after the vamp and witch attack. An important witch had accepted help from a fanghead and lived to tell the tale. That could go a long way to continue helping heal the rift between the two para groups.

Minutes later we were at the freebie house, my first and only real home, bartered in a fortuitous negotiation with its previous owner, Katie Fonteneau. Bruiser parked out front. We entered and joined Lachish and Alex at the kitchen table. There was still a chill in the air and Bruiser turned on the gas logs as soon as we entered. Lachish was pale and bandaged, and when she tried to stand up to greet me, her breath hitched in pain. She started, "Lachish Dutillett is pleased to greet—"

I held up a hand to stop her and then gestured to her chair. "Let's just dispense with the formal stuff. Sit down before you pass out."

"I'll get more tea," Bruiser said.

Lachish eased back to her chair, the smell of pain, hospital chemicals, traces of old blood, and sweat wafting from her. "The Englishman's answer to everything," Lachish said. "Tea."

"You should be home in bed," I said.

"I should be guarding the box."

"Where? The wards are still down at the null prison. I'm not even sure the windows are boarded over where the fangheads went through."

Bruiser placed a pot on the table, with a pink crocheted tea cozy on top, the one Quint had made for me. Quint had made a tea cozy that I could use to hide a recording device if I ever needed to, but I still thought the color was a jab, a bit of mockery, considering my detestation of the color pink. And then again, I was getting paranoid, looking for problems under every gift, like with the gift of Long-Knife. I was, maybe, turning into a Leo-version of myself, which I hated, but which was keeping my people alive.

"Our queen arranged to have the null prison building itself secured for the witches," Bruiser said. "The Everhearts are trying to get stronger wards up. Hopefully the reinforced *hedge of thorns* can be restored, but it won't be by tonight."

Lachish sipped her tea and sighed. "I do like a nice Earl Grey. Thank you, Consort." She cradled her cup and asked, "Why didn't you give the heartbox to Ailis, as I asked?"

"We had polite words. I had the better protected space."

Lachish raised her brows and sipped again. "Polite words. She was being difficult?"

"Young. Take-charge. Slightly rude. Unschooled." I

stopped short. I had been schooled by Leo. But I could do rude with the best of them. Or the worst of them. "I guess I was rude too."

"Guess?" she asked, with a slight smile. "May I see it? The heart?"

"Sure." I stood and went to my closet. The null ward and the small *hedge of thorns* were still in place. As I released the *hedge*, I caught sight of something from the corner of my eye. A flicker of light and smudge of shadow. I whipped around. Fear hit me, shocking through my system. But there was no one there.

Is not predator, Beast thought at me. *Is magic curse in vampire heart.*

Okay, I thought, staring at the box. Speaking to the heart, I said, "Last time I held you I was full of adrenaline, so I didn't feel it. But you put out a lot of fear and paranoia, don't you? That's another reason you need to be kept in a null room."

I wondered if the Heir could tell I had freed the heart from its restraints. To be on the safe side, I opened the laptop and checked the security system. No one. Nothing at all.

I picked up the box. The shaft of terror nearly had me dropping it, but I held on and my own magics pushed the fear back. It was still there, but not as strong. I returned to the kitchen with the heartbox, which felt a little heavier than when I had taken it from the witches. Bruiser cleared a space and I placed the box in front of Lachish. I managed to stand still and not step back from it. "If other emotions don't override it, it radiates fear," I said, making it a statement, as if I was informing her and not asking her.

"Yes." Lachish placed a small mouse-shaped carved wooden amulet on the table and pushed it until it touched the box. The fear receded and I took an unsteady breath.

The wood box opened easily, and the light fell on the heart. Except it wasn't just a heart. To both sides of the heart were pale pinkish tissue, stuff that might be pieces of lung. There were arteries and veins coming out the top of the heart and one that attached to the lungs. There was no blood. No heart pumping.

Then the heart quivered.

It was trying to beat. Even without a body to breathe for it or blood to pump through it, the flesh was still alive. Okay. That was creepy.

Lachish said, "It does that sometimes. Then it stops."

The pulsating of the bloodless muscle stopped.

Yeah. Creepy.

"It's grown," Lachish said. She looked up at me. "Unless it's your intent to let it grow into a full human-shaped body, it needs stronger null energies."

Strong heart. Good food, Beast thought.

I burst out laughing. "No," I said to both of them, waving away Lachish's stiff posture and insulted expression. "Sorry." I'd been warned not to let it be destroyed until after the Heir was true dead. I figured that also applied to not letting it grow bigger than it was now. "The moment the wards go up, you witches can have it. But not until then." I closed it and carried the heartbox back to my closet, setting it in place beside all the null objects. I opened the null ward and the fear disappeared.

This particular *hedge of thorns* was usually strong enough on its own, but it could be made stronger if I added a thin smear of my blood to activate it, something I did without thinking these days. I pricked my finger and triggered the *hedge* before wrapping my finger in a tissue. Then I stopped. Blood could be used in a spell or curse against me. In the bathroom, I found a box of small Band-Aids and put one over my fingertip. Just in case. Back in the kitchen, I tossed the tissue in the mostly new fireplace, and watched as it caught fire.

And then it hit me. Vamps burned in the daylight. The daylight had hit the heart just now. And it hadn't burned.

As the tissue flamed away, I said, "I know blood-witches can bind demons. What do you know about the possibility of binding an angel?" I looked from the flames to Lachish. She had stopped, the cup halfway to her mouth, her lips parted. "If someone had plans to bind an angel," I continued, "could they use the heart? And how much power would that kind of binding require?"

Lachish put her cup down and it rattled in the saucer. Her eyes narrowed, moving back and forth a little, as if scanning the tabletop, thinking. "I don't know." But it was clear she had a good educated guess she didn't want to share.

I said, "The heart is a vamp heart. We just exposed it to daylight, and it didn't go up in flames. The heart started out with Jodi Richoux, now Wrassler's wife. Then it got moved, and then moved again to you. It puts out fear. And it grows. Only a null working stops it from growing. It's always been under the effect of a *rejuvenation* working, hasn't it?"

Had Lachish not been weakened from trauma she wouldn't have reacted, but she did, just the barest flinch. Then she closed her eyes as if only the darkness allowed her to speak. "We think so. We don't know for certain. The fear started a few weeks ago, about the same time as the heart began to quiver, trying to beat. But if a demon has been summoned and bound to another's will, and if an angel has been bound . . ." She stopped as if she couldn't go on.

"If the original angel binding involved the blood of the Son of Darkness," I said, "then the Heart of Darkness might be pulling on the life force of the angel and the death force of a demon to rejuvenate itself. Especially if a lot of the power had been transferred to the Heir." Which we didn't know for sure, but what the heck. I'd take a shot and see what she might let go.

She opened her eyes to me. "There is little in the old tales or the few surviving grimoires about binding a demon. And nothing about binding an angel. I can only guess at the power such a practitioner would gain."

I started to say, "Should we—"

Lachish stood quickly, her chair legs scraping on the floor, her breath catching, as if the sudden movement sent pain through her. She leaned on the table and, unexpectedly, laughed. "Getting old sucks." More slowly, she stood and said, "Getting shot sucks too. My ride is here. Thank you for your hospitality, Jane Yellowrock. And the leader of the New Orleans coven thanks the Dark Queen for her assistance and help navigating these troubled waters."

Bruiser saw the witch to the door, while I contemplated the possibility of lunch and a long nap. However, Lachish was still in the street out front when Bruiser's cell buzzed. My honeybunch looked from his phone to me, saying, "One of the older Mithrans translating a journal you found in the library is awake and working in his room. He believes that we need to see what he's found in the journal." These were the journals that Leo had shown to me, when he was fighting the control of his master. I wondered if he was still fighting. Should I have staked him and left him at HQ, where he could be watched twenty-four-seven?

Every decision meant more danger, more problems, and unintended consequences.

I held in my sigh. A nap was off the table. But if Deon was up, at least the food would be good.

CHAPTER 16

My Last Master Had No Use for Symbolism

I glanced at Quint, who had accompanied me on this jaunt. She drew her weapons, entered, and cleared the vamp's personal quarters. The vamp with news was sitting at a table in the corner and didn't look up as Quint did her thing. From the doorway, I studied the room because rooms told a lot about a vamp's power, position, and aspirations.

This vamp's room at HQ was an inside room, windowless, with a Jack and Jill bathroom between it and the room beside it. It was tiny but well-appointed, with a four-poster rice bed and art deco–style furniture. There were trunks against one wall and the closet door was cracked open, revealing carefully folded clothes on shelves and suits on hangers. I had read his dossier on the way over. Santiago Molina had been one of the vamps displaced when Ming of Mearkanis went missing and her clan was disbanded. When she returned, many of her original vamps went back to her, but others, notably the less powerful or less aggressive ones who had suffered under her cruel rule, had chosen to remain clanless. He had gone from a moderately important vamp to someone who didn't socialize with other bloodsuckers, and who preferred solitude and the company of a rare human to feed from, instead of group blood feedings and forced orgy sex parties.

In his human life, back in the dark ages, Santiago had been Spanish, an ascetic monk, the kind who spent time in silent prayer and copied ancient manuscripts, and he still carried that mien of the scholar, unwillingly displaced into the twenty-first century. He spoke many languages and read more. The former monk was slight, delicate, and unremarkable, with brown hair and eyes. He was wearing a long tunic shirt with loose leggings and black velvet slippers. And in Alex's mind he must be utterly trustworthy, because in his room, the vamp had several of the journals Leo had pointed out in the library. There was a glass of white wine beside his elbow.

When Quint was done, she stepped back and I entered. Santiago stood and gave me a stiff bow, as if he wasn't sure of the niceties. "My Queen," he said.

"Santiago," I said. He stared at me, unmoving, that vamp stillness unaffected by heartbeat or breathing. "You have something for me?"

"Oh. Yes, My Queen." His fingers fluttered to the other chair. "Would you like to sit—" He stopped, flustered, uncertain of the protocol of a royal in his room.

"Yes, thank you," I said. Quint reached out, but I held up a hand, stopping her. I pulled out the extra chair and sat down. "I understand you have discovered something?"

"*Si*. Oh. Yes. Yes. I have found two maps inside a journal. One hand-drawn, annotated by several different hands. I would estimate it to be from the late seventeen hundreds." He carefully placed a piece of high-cloth-content paper on the table. It had been folded into quarters for a very long time, and was missing ink in the cross-shaped creases. "It appears to be from 1719, a map of the

Algiers Point, the swamp before the city was laid out and built."

Algiers again. I got a buzz of interest. "X marks the spot?" I asked.

"Exactly," Santiago said, his voice taking on a hint of excitement.

The old map showed the curve of land that still followed the shoreline of Algiers, on the far side of the river. In the general vicinity where we had searched with Brute and the grindylow was a big Celtic cross drawn in red ink. The cross covered the tongue of Algiers from the Mississippi back to the Mississippi along a U-shaped path. To one side of the tongue of land the map had an inked Celtic dragon and to the other side were three skulls, not with pirate crossbones, but just the skulls. The Gulf of Mexico was marked with a swirl like a hurricane and another dragon head rising from the waves.

This map was older than the city of Algiers. Maybe from the time of De Allyon, who had been in the states since the fifteen hundreds. It looked like a treasure map. The other map was newer, like something from an etching, maybe, and had the broken lines of a map that had been printed. It had originally been printed in black ink, though it was faded to grays now.

Santiago tapped the printed map. He was wearing white gloves, the fingertips slightly smudged. "Old Algiers was originally built in 1819, a rough-and-tumble place built up along the riverfront with shipbuilding and ship repair interests, dry docks, sawmills, and lumberyards. There was an iron foundry and ship building on the commercial corridor on the river." His finger traced the riverfront. "No real streets, no printed maps, mostly swamp and mud, shacks and saloons at that time. But the streets of the city, as it now stands, were planned much later, in 1841, consisting of Algiers Point, McDonogh, Whitney, Behrman, Gretna, and others, as you see here. The streets of Algiers were laid out and built later, according to this map, in 1864.

"This past dusk, your Consort let it be known that you were most interested in churches in Algiers. When I extrapolate from the two maps, the red X on the map from 1719 lies across these streets, from the 1864 map, but it does not indicate what buildings might have been churches in the past or which churches might have been torn down or destroyed by hurricane and are now something other than churches."

"That area is three or four times the size of the French Quarter," Quint said. "Nothing is to scale."

"*Si!*" Santiago said. He shifted yet another map out of a pile of papers, this one the touristy kind, and pointed. "It will be difficult to determine which church you may be searching for. At this time, there are eighteen churches in the area beneath the Celtic cross."

I leaned over the third map. His finger was close to several of the damaged churches that we had visited earlier. "Yes. I see. This may prove helpful," I said, with the formal politeness of my Christian children's home upbringing, but not the queen's formality. "Can you translate the words on the older map?"

"Indeed so, My Queen. This one says, 'Buried Bones.' This one says, 'Beware the Darkness.' This one says, 'Here lies evil.'"

"Three sayings, three skulls," I said.

"Yes!" His brown eyes lit with delight. "You comprehend the symbolism. My last master had no use for symbolism."

"I'm not sure what the dragons mean. Evil?"

"There are small faded lines here"—he pointed—"from the two dragons to the words 'Here lies evil.' So yes, it is possible."

"Thank you, Santiago. I am impressed. Whose journal is that?"

"It belonged to Immanuel Pellissier and one other."

Which made that question the one I should have led with. I blew out a breath. "Of course it did. Who else?"

"I'm not certain, but someone else took it over midway through the journal."

A cold shiver of certainty flashed through me. I said, "Show me."

Santiago opened the journal and showed me several

pages in the front half. "The penmanship is exquisite. It matches the penmanship on the old hand-drawn map, here and here." He pointed again. "A beautiful hand. But here"—he flipped a page—"there are two pages unused. Journals were expensive. No one wasted paper. And here"—he turned the second page—"the penmanship is vastly different. The ugly hand of an uneducated man."

His words weren't intended as an insult, simply a descriptive term. In Santiago's lingo, I had an "ugly hand," too, meaning that my writing was messy. I would have sympathized with the writer, but I had a feeling that Immanuel had been eaten by a liver-eater midway through the journal, and the liver-eater's handwriting was the ugly one—a *Tsalagi* skinwalker, turned *u'tlun'ta*, trying to write like a European educated vamp. Even with the memories obtained in the black magic ceremony, the muscle memory wasn't good enough to pass as equal. "May I?" I said, pointing at the journal.

"Of course, My Queen, of course." He swiveled the journal around to me.

I turned pages, studying the handwriting. "At the time this was written, few people were educated. It looks as if he was trying to learn from Immanuel's penmanship. Here at the end of the journal, his penmanship is much better." I flipped from the beginning to the end. "It looks similar to the original." He had learned from the journal and from the man he had eaten, body and memories, but I wasn't sure how the former priest would react to all that.

Santiago frowned. And then he crossed himself and whispered, "*Dios mío*. That is what I saw on the video." Santiago looked at me horror in his eyes. "The lion with the teeth, the creature you killed, he took the place of the Pellissier heir. He was not born the Pellissier heir but he became the heir. *Si?*"

"Yes, Santiago. I believe he was an evil, magical creature. He ate Immanuel and he took his place. It is the very worst of black magic." I jutted my chin at the other journals on his small table. "Whose else's journals?"

"Soledad Martinez and a very young Amaury Pellissier."

I tilted my head. Soledad was a vamp I had met. She was on an estate out in bayou country. She and her friend Malita and their few drug-dependent blood-servants had been kept isolated long enough to go bonkers, and when I discovered how bad it was, I'd had the blood-servants replaced. I should have checked on them before now. "You know Soledad?"

"She was my patron when I first became a scion." He smiled slightly. "My sire had died while I was in the devoveo, and I was alone. She was always kind to me when we were in Ming of Mearkanis's clan. It will be a joy to read her words."

"You didn't join Ming when she took her clan back over. Why?"

"Ming of Mearkanis was . . ." His eyes slid away, a very human reaction. ". . . not fully Naturaleza. But there was no kindness in her soul for the Mithran scions and humans in her clan."

"How many languages do you speak and read?"

"I am fluent in six spoken languages and read fluently twelve more. I am, as your people say today, *okay* in another dozen. I can understand and translate with a degree of certainty an additional five. I was a monk when human, of the Order of the Benedictines, in Northern Spain, and was charged with learning the languages of the pilgrims to better assist them." He smiled sadly. "I was changed against my will but the centuries after have shown me that I can be among the drinkers of blood and yet not of them."

How many languages was that? Would I run out of fingers and toes if I tried to count that high? Santiago's dossier had shown me a lot of his skills, but had concentrated on his abilities as a counselor, mediator between Blood Masters, and a translator. "Holy crap."

Santiago gave me his sad smile. "No."

"Oh. Right." Not holy crap. He'd been a priest. I'd have to watch my mouth around him. "Sorry. You want a job?" I asked.

"No, My Queen. I wish to join your clan."

I started to tell him no, that I had enough people in my

clan, but his eyes were sad. Or maybe *beseeching* was a better word.

He was an outsider, a misfit. He was asking to join a clan of other misfits. Santiago slipped from his chair to the floor, kneeling at my feet.

"Ahhh." I sighed, but tried to keep my dismay out of the breath sound. There were a lot of ways to be accepted into a clan, and not all involved sharing blood, but since the drawing of power from the fangheads loyal to me, it had occurred to me that I *should* share blood. At least a little, from time to time, with the vamps who swore to me, and definitely when they did the swearing thing. "Quint, I need a sharp throwing knife." I held a hand back over my shoulder. My lady-in-waiting placed one into my palm, hilt first.

I pulled my cell and dialed Alex. When he answered, I said, "I need a video witness to record the swearing-in of a scion."

"Yes, My Queen. You are on video record."

I handed the cell to Quint. "Record this."

"Yes, ma'am."

"Santiago, how many blood-servants do you bring?"

"Three, My Queen."

"I will be honored to accept your service," I said to the man at my feet. "How do you swear?"

"I, Eneko Jesus Santiago Molina, swear fealty to you as Blood Master of Clan Yellowrock, pledging my loyalty to you and to your many-creatured clan family. I swear to work for, to provide for, to protect and care for, to fight for—though I am no warrior, you must know this before you accept me—and to die true dead as you may need. I place my needs second to yours. I place my hunger second to yours and to your scions. I place all that I am and all that I own at your disposal, at your feet, into your hands. I am yours in life and undeath and in true-death."

As he talked, I figured out what I needed to say. He hadn't sworn loyalty to the Dark Queen, so that limited his service. "I, Jane Doe Yellowrock, Blood Master of Clan Yellowrock, Master of the City of New Orleans, will guard, protect, provide for, and care for Eneko Jesus Santiago Molina and three willing blood-servants, giving him solitude, family, safety, a place to work, and protection to the fullest extent of my abilities and power within those titles, accepting him as scion into Clan Yellowrock." I pricked my finger and offered it to Santiago. He took the tip into his mouth. It was cold, the same temperature as the furniture in his room, which always shocked me.

He took the knife and pricked his own finger. I leaned down and accepted the drop. Also cold on my tongue. *Yuck.* But his blood was . . . crisp? Maybe? It had a clean taste, like a delicate white tea made with glacier melt over an open fire.

Beast perked up. *Strong vampire blood. Jane must drink more.*

Nope, I thought at her.

I accepted the knife back and wiped the blade tip on the tissue Quint handed me, wrapping my finger into it, even though the vamp saliva had closed the wound.

"End recording but don't end call," I said to Alex.

"Recording ended," he said.

I took pics of the maps and sent them to Alex.

"How may I serve my mistress?" Santiago asked.

"Alex. Check your texts. Santiago found some old maps of Algiers. I'd like him to work with you on the maps and the journals." To my new scion, I said, "Copy Alex's number into your cell and you'll talk. We're looking for something of value, in some place of value, that we think could be a church, or maybe that was once a church but now is something else, or a site that used to be a church and is now long gone, with something else built over it, on Algiers Point." I was prevaricating. We knew very little. It was a lot of land and not-to-scale maps drawn over a hundred years apart. I needed help and maybe Santiago could provide that help. "Alex, Santiago is trying to align the streets and the buildings from old maps with current day."

"Copy. I think I have the shoreline resized and matched from your photos," Alex said, "but neither map is exactly to scale, and one doesn't even show streets. There are a number of churches that were wiped off the map in one hurricane or another, and several that have been more recently damaged. Repairs have been slow. Lots of buildings have been sealed shut."

"Alex Younger, I will call you on my cellular phone," Santiago said. "I will also take the original maps to you for scanning and computer adjustment, which might assist with the difficulties in scale."

I nodded, said all the polite things, ended the call, stood, and left Santiago's room. As I walked into the hallway, I felt the weight of all the people who had sworn to me, people I had to protect, people with long histories of abuse, possibly, *probably*, from each other.

And Leo . . . Leo had sent me to the journals. There was no way he had read them before I killed his son, which meant he'd found, read, and placed them in the library between then and now. Which also meant he had known the maps were there, in place to be given to me when needed, which also meant that Leo had seen this additional proof that his son wasn't really his son when he died at my hand, but an imposter. The change in the handwriting had been a dead giveaway. *Haha.* Dead giveaway. If I smiled it was a hard, unhappy smile. Leo and his blasted layered machinations.

"Quint," I said to my silent bodyguard / lady-in-waiting, "two things. Once Alex narrows locations down, schedule a trip to the area Santiago specified for whatever time the security team wants. Then write and send a letter to Wrassler. He's acting as something like an HR person, but we need HR protocols and methods to accept reports of abuse between humans and vamps, and vamps and vamps. Someone to investigate and deal with problems. And we need a mental health person available for counseling. I thought about that once before and never did anything about it. Get Wrassler to see if Santiago wants to be part of putting that together and, you know, counsel. And stuff."

Quint, who was walking just a little behind me, gave a delicate snort. "Forgive me, My Queen, but you want to start a human resources department and a counseling service for *vamps*? Abuse is their middle name."

"What two people do together, consensually, is their

business. But some vamps have a history of mesmerizing and coercion. They will stop, make reparations, and be good little bloodsuckers, or they can leave. And the counselor is for the abused."

"You will make more enemies on the inside, who may join the enemies on the outside."

"You're saying political considerations come before common decency?"

"No. But I agree with your brothers. They say you walk a tightrope between dangers."

My people had a point. But I had backup. I grinned as the thought occurred to me. "How's this? The Vampira Carta of the Americas will be the basis of the complaint system. And anyone who disagrees gets to deal with the Dark Queen and an *outclan priest. Personally.*" I glanced at her from the corner of my eye. "Leo was one of the vamps who put the new VC together. He'll want it followed to the letter. And the outclan have always been judges in issues with vamps."

I'm freaking brilliant, I thought.

Quint made a humming sound. "Good move." I heard her texting as we walked.

Jane is best hunter, Beast thought at me. *But Leo may die in Jane war.*

Okay. So it's not perfect, but it will do for now.

I turned a corner and came to a stop. Bruiser was leaning against the wall facing me, ankles crossed, arms crossed. I hadn't noticed what he was wearing earlier: white long-sleeved T, black jeans, his hair a little too long and hanging down over one eye. *Oh my. Sex on a stick.* There was something green held against the white tee.

Is good mate, Beast thought.

"Wait," I said to my escort.

I stepped forward but Beast shoved herself into the forefront of our brain and changed our walk. She stalked slowly to him. Eyes on his.

I could see the reflection of her golden eyes in Bruiser's brown ones. And when we got close my inner big-cat practically rolled over inside me and started purring. The green stuff was catnip and little violet flowers.

I slid a hand up the back of Bruiser's neck to his head. Brought his mouth down that few inches to mine. Even after all this time it was strange to kiss a man taller than me.

"Hey, Consort," I nearly growled. "You brought me a present."

"In my day it was called a posy," he said, his words vibrating against my lips. "Men brought them to their ladyloves."

"Uh-huh. Call it anything you want. I know seduction when I see it. Our rooms. Now."

His eyes kindled with heat and laughter. "Whatever my love desires."

"Now you're talking."

Later, I was loose and supple and feeling pretty spiffy. I was also happy the walls of the queen's quarters were soundproofed. Things had gotten loud. Then there was shower play, a massive dinner, a catnap, and then things got loud again. All in all, it was a *veeerrry* nice afternoon.

While I played, all my people worked: the Everharts on wards, my security teams on keeping us safe, city cops and ATF on explosive-filled trucks parked in the middle of town, the Roberes on legal and political stuff that I hated, and Alex and Santiago on the maps.

When I emerged from my room, it was to discover several problems had been dealt with, but as usual, there were new problems. PsyLED had finally shown up in New Orleans, liaising with ATF and Jodi Richoux, the head of the woo-woo department at cop central—not with the master of the city or the Dark Queen, which was an insult, if I chose to take it that way.

The guy who had shown up, and then displayed hideously bad manners, was a new special agent, at least to NOLA, named Roberto D. Jimenez. Besides being new to NOLA, and rude, Roberto was out of the Dallas office, not out of the southeast headquarters located in Knoxville. I found all of that peculiar and I wasn't alone. Alex was investigating why no one in PsyLED SE, who were also my allies in national law enforcement, had shown up here. He was also monitoring Jimenez's actions and whereabouts on law enforcement radio channels in case he was in league with Mainet.

In the good news department, Alex had found us a likely church to visit. The Blessed Virgin church in Algiers.

It was dark when we drove across the Mississippi.

I had been able to stay in human form for longer than expected and had shifted to half-form late in the day. To preserve muscle mass, I had eaten yet another massive dinner, and afterward dressed in fresh armor. I carried only a few weapons, though holy water was part of it this time, secured on a weapons harness, in plasticized glass to keep it from breaking and drenching me by accident. My hair was braided, tied off with an elastic, and tucked into the neckline of my armor and down my back.

We had a three-vehicle security detail, with Eli, Bruiser, Quint, and me in the middle one. Since we'd be going into a church, and vamps couldn't go into churches, and Alex, Bruiser, Eli, and I hadn't told anyone what church, Bruiser and Eli felt we were safer with a small motorcade than with an attention-getting large one. The relative safety, however, didn't mean anyone was taking chances. My crew was appropriately decked out for any unexpected war.

My honeybunch and I slouched in the back seat together on the drive, looking over floor plans and online pics of the damage sustained by the church. Armor was not comfortable slouching wear, but I got a good idea of the layout of the building, pre–hurricane damage. Getting into the Blessed Virgin church at night would be difficult. No electricity, no lights, structural and cosmetic damage, and everything probably still boarded up.

The church was on the west side of the river, on a corner near Algiers Point, farther south than we had searched before. It was once a beautiful old church but had been heavily damaged in several recent hurricanes. It was also only a hundred years or so old, younger than any of our maps. Since Mainet worked with witches, maybe the witches who marked the original spot had died off. Maybe something important had begun here, but the landscape had changed so much the vamps couldn't find the X-spot anymore. Maybe an original church had been destroyed.

Yeah. Could be. Or the site could have been a native holy site. Christian churches were often built on the sites of older, non-Christian holy places. All of those were likely possibilities.

Which meant Mainet and his pals could be hoping to use us to find his X-marked spot. Interesting possibility. And no way around them seeing us if they were already looking for us to find this place.

Our minds already synced, Eli said, "We should have split up and taken different routes."

"No," Koun said, over comms. "I stand by my original statement. We protect the queen."

Eli grunted. It was a sound that said he hadn't agreed originally, and didn't entirely agree now, but he could see the logic in Koun's preference.

The protection detail vehicles parked before us and behind us on a street with most of the streetlights out, the others with dull yellowish glows. It was a halfway decent neighborhood of homes and small business, many damaged by multiple storm surges and in various stages of repair.

I carried Angie's little gold Jesus in a right jacket pocket, and the Glob, wrapped in hankies, in the left, a specially designed and padded pocket. My crown hadn't been invited along but, as we parked, it showed up on the console. I figured that meant I might need it. *Crap.*

Eli ordered us to "Sit," as he and his units checked out the grounds before we were allowed out of the car. In this form, I had Beast's night vision, turning everything greens and silvers and almost nothing too shadowed to see.

The church was tall, constructed of reddish brick with lots of white woodwork, a huge wooden door in one of those pointed-arched openings, a clock and bell tower four stories tall, and stained glass windows, some beneath security glass and some with plywood protection over them. There were statues placed up high on the outside walls, maybe white marble, hard to tell much about them in the dark.

Eli jogged halfway to us in the night, silver-green in Beast's vision, wearing full night-combat gear. Over comms, he alerted us it was safe, and we opened our doors. I adjusted my earbuds to my oddly placed cat ears.

As we emerged into the chilly night, Leo appeared, walking out of the shadows.

As if he saw Leo the moment I did, Eli whipped around at his approach, a weapon that hadn't been in his hand only a moment before aimed at the vamp. It was reholstered instantly, the movements, the motions all slick and faster than I could focus. Quint mirrored Eli's actions, fast, but more on the human side of fast, while Eli was still hyped up on healing vamp blood. We were attuned to each other's reactions, and his own heart rate hadn't gone up, our bond steady and smooth as an ice-covered pond.

Leo stopped a few feet away. He was wearing black with the priest's collar, and once again a gold cross hung around his neck, the clothing between the holy icon and his undead flesh, but still close enough to cause a lot of pain and maybe even burns. "Eli Younger. My George." Leo looked at me, his voice a mesmerizing embrace, and, disregarding the others, said, "My Jane."

I frowned at him and ignored all the possessives. "How did you know we'd be here? We didn't know we'd be here until like an hour ago, and we didn't even tell our escort."

Leo smiled, the moonlight shining on his pale face like a lover's caress, chiseling his cheekbones, glinting from his dark eyes. "I have my ways." An elegant gesture to his side revealed the presence of a white werewolf trotting up the street, with a dark splotch on its back.

Brute and the Grindylow. Brute was working with the angel. And with Leo. I considered the werewolf, wondering how much humanity he still maintained after all the time in wolf form. How much autonomy did he have, working for the angel? How much did the werewolf contribute to the ongoing problems and solutions in the vamp world? The timewalking werewolf. Working with Leo. Brute was a player in the vamp political, multiple-dimensional chess game, and I had no way to plan for his potential moves on Leo's board.

"Brute," I said.

The werewolf snorted a greeting.

Quint glanced at Eli and nodded as if they had communicated something. She moved so she could cover the darkness across from the church, in the shadows of the buildings nearby. She flipped down a night vision ocular and looked ready to shoot anything that moved. So did all the team. Jittery. Tense. I hoped no one let their little yapper dog out to pee or it might end up blasted to pieces.

To Leo, I said, "Can you go inside the church?"

"It is unlikely. Sabina lived in a chapel, slept in a chapel, next to pieces of the Blood Cross, which would burn me to ashes. The priestess was ancient. Powerful. I am young for an outclan."

"Wait here," Bruiser said. "We'll try to remove the covering from a window so that you can see in."

Eli touched his earbud and adjusted an ocular, saying, "Copy that." To us, he said, "Koppa's human team members found a window with loose plywood over it, around the corner. There's also a broken window into the sanctuary at about a twelve-foot height, and four construction ladders were left in the grass by the last crew here. We can get in and Leo will have a place to watch."

We walked around the side of the building to see a small rectangular window, nails still in the frame where plywood had been pulled off. Eli placed the ladder, climbed up, directed a light inside. Setting a hook and a belaying rope in place, he crawled in.

I heard him landing, a soft, grinding slide of shoes on the wall. Small shafts of light from his penlight flashed over the broken window glass. A dark form in night combat gear, impossible to ID in the night, followed him. Human, since the vamps were all out at the perimeter, a safe distance from the holy ground.

We stood in the darkness, watching, until Eli appeared from around a corner. "Clear," he said softly to us, his voice floating over comms and on the quiet air. "Fawn, take your team to channel two. Guard the ladder at the sanctuary window. Set two guards to protect Leo, shooting and cover positions. Then join us inside."

"Copy." There was a faint click and a team of three guards moved to comply.

Fawn? Human is named after prey, Beast thought.

But the human named Fawn was brawny with muscle and looked like she could wrestle a vamp to the ground with one hand tied behind her back. *Not very prey-like,* I thought.

"Leo. You can see into the sanctuary through the window I entered," Eli said.

"Thank you, Eli Younger."

Leo followed the guard, Fawn, both of them vanishing into the shadows. The rest of the team dispersed into cover positions.

"I've opened a side door," Eli said. "Come."

Bruiser, Quint, and I followed Eli and entered through the open door, stepping past two-by-fours Eli had pulled off the doorjambs, bent nails sticking from the wood. We made our way through winding hallways, dim light entering from other broken windows, the church smelling of mold and dank water, old lino floor tiles squeaking and smushing beneath our boots. We reached a side or back entrance to the sanctuary and I spotted Leo outside, on the ladder, watching through the window.

Bruiser gave me my crown, which I hooked over an elbow, and a flashlight. I clicked on the flash, the sound sharp, bouncing off the walls. The bright light caught the white werewolf in its beam, the shining green grindy on his back. The wolf blinked against the glare and turned away. I hadn't seen them enter, which was a little strange, except that strange had become my norm.

That was a twisted bit of illogic I refused to follow.

I angled the light over the big open room. Stained glass windows reflected back the light, one broken, the others moldy. Black mold followed waterlines down the walls, long columns, like tears on the white plaster that reminded me vaguely of my dream-state visions. The wood trim everywhere was warped and bloated. The ancient wood floors were unsalvageable.

The sanctuary was in a state of utter chaos, odd-shaped offering tables and the pews had been removed and piled along one wall, stacked haphazardly, ten feet high. Equipment was everywhere: scaffolding, ladders, five-gallon buckets, hand tools, nail guns, a table saw, some kind of electric stirring machine, a disorganized mess.

I touched the Jesus amulet in my pocket. It was warmer than my fingers, warmer than the flesh on the other side of the layers of fabric. Angie's Jesus jewelry was telling me that something important was here, somewhere. Had Alex and Santiago sent us to the right church on the first try? That would be a record.

Flashing the light over the mold-streaked walls, I spotted regularly spaced niches up front, all empty. It was different from my visions, yet there were some similarities. "It's possible," I said, mostly to myself.

Eli moved around the room, weapons in hand, speaking softly into comms on the other channels. I needed to concentrate on the magical items in my pockets and had elected not to use a full comms headset but only earbuds this time, and though they gave me access to only Eli's channel and Alex's private channel, and not the vamp channel or Fawn's team channel, I could keep track of some things. Bruiser kept pace with me, always close, but not in my way. He walked with his weapon drawn, carried low, one-hand grip, flashlight in the other, his eyes taking in everything, including me.

I stopped and turned in a circle, the flashlights illuminating everything. There was no sign of Hayyel, and the room wasn't an exact match for the room in my vision. Brute seemed bored, not as if his angel was nearby. But as I walked toward the center of the large room, the gold Jesus began to grow warmer. I placed *le breloque* on my head and it snapped on, not as painfully tight as sometimes, thank goodness. I didn't need a headache.

In the far corner from where we entered, near the front doors that led outside, were blue tarps tied with string to keep the plastic sheets in place over something irregular in shape and height. Or maybe several things clumped together and covered for protection from the elements and construction dust. When I stepped closer, the Jesus grew hot enough for me to let it go.

"Okay," I said, shining my light on the tarps. "Under there."

Brute chuffed uncertainly.

Quint silently climbed a folding ladder near a wall, to cover us from above and the back of the sanctuary where we had entered. The other guard, Fawn, who had caught up with us, swung into scaffolding and took a firing position that covered the public street door and the . . . foyer, though Catholics might call it something else.

Bruiser and Eli cut the ties holding the tarps and Bruiser turned to look at me with warmth in his eyes. "You will love this, Jane." The guys lifted off the tarps, revealing people. People with wings and halos and long robes. White marble and painted plaster statues, some half naked, all with Greek and European faces. There were also stands, as if some of the statues had previously been mounted high, freestanding works of art.

I flashed my light around the front walls at the empty niches and felt stupid for associating the visions of Hayyel only with my soul home. I walked slowly to the statues and the Jesus amulet in my pocket flared bright with warmth. Not a burning heat, not yet. I walked around the statues and the heat decreased, like a kid's game of Hot and Cold, a game I'd played with magical stuff before.

Could Hayyel be bound to a statue, and not to a building? Or . . .

I wasn't going to say it aloud but maybe one of the statues was a real being, like frozen. All I could think of was Han Solo stuck in carbonite. Or like trapped by a curse in a statue. Could Hayyel himself be bound in one of these? Could it be so easy to find him?

I shined my light on the faces, and though none looked like Hayyel, the Jesus got hotter. "I think one of the statues is more than it seems." I removed the Jesus icon from my pocket and held it out over each statue in turn. There were a lot of them and as I moved through the angels and saints, I was able to narrow it down to three that were standing close to together. "Can you separate these three? It's one of them."

Bruiser was stronger than a normal human, but the

three statues were solid stone and incredibly heavy, so Eli holstered his weapon and the two men tilted and slid each of the interesting statues out a few feet. I walked around the perfect stone bodies, wondering suddenly if vamps had stood for the sculptor, able to remain unmoving for extended periods of time, unbreathing, their bodies perfect in undeath, and some as pale as the marble I was looking at. My flashlight glinted off the stained glass windows whenever I tilted it wrong and created strange glowing shadows, as if the statues were moving. The glints of red and blue matched my visions.

Could Hayyel be trapped inside a statue? I placed a fingertip on one cold-as-stone chest. The Jesus focal didn't react.

Playing the Hot and Cold game, I eliminated two of the statues, settling on one white marble angel statue that was now facing the pulpit, or whatever Catholics called it. Probably something fancy with a Latin origin. The angel had folded wings covering his lower body, and long curling hair with androgynous features. One beautifully carved, lifelike foot was exposed, partially covered with a carved robe. I looked up to see Leo watching through the open window.

Bending, I ran the Jesus up and down the statue, concentrating on the halo, the hands, the wings, but the icon stayed the current temp. I knelt and ran it along the base. At the feather-covered foot, the Jesus went scorching red. I dropped it with a few words for which I'd have gotten my mouth washed out had I said them as a kid. "Sorry," I mumbled to the angel statue. With one of the hankies I now carried around, I lifted the Jesus and slid it to the side to cool before I put it in my pocket. "The foot. Something about the foot."

Eli and Bruiser searched the statue with the lights and their fingers but found nothing. "Underneath," Eli said. He tilted the statue, taking the weight on his boot to protect the stone.

Bruiser, kneeling on the floor with me, ran his hands under the base. "Nothing," he said, "except a little irregular place here." His fingers moved in the shadows under the statue. "It feels as if the marble was damaged, roughly repaired, and wasn't smoothed properly." He shined his cell phone light beneath the statue and took a photo. He enlarged the pic, and when he spoke, his voice went sharp and animated. "The patch isn't marble. It's old, crumbling plaster."

CHAPTER 17

Undead Strippers and Tex in Love

I heard a scraping sound as Bruiser's fingers moved in the slanted light. Beside me, the cloth-wrapped Jesus was glowing, too hot to touch. A chill passed over me and I looked to Eli. His eyes were sweeping the room. High in the arches, a passing car's headlights made its way through a crack in the wood that covered a stained glass window. The reflection painted the ceiling in reds and blues and more dancing shadows.

In the odd light, for a moment, the sanctuary looked exactly like the vision of my soul home, as Hayyel's angel wings draped down the mold-stained walls, feathers bright in the reflected light. *Holy crap*. Hayyel was *here*. Here and somewhere else too. Here and not here. A between place? Pocket universe?

A breeze blew through, chilled and clammy, like dead flesh.

I drew in a breath. Pulled a weapon. If someone was going to attack, then with Eli's hands full and Bruiser on his knees now was the time.

Quint, Fawn, and I and scoured the space, weapons ready, searching for encom.

The only change was on the walls. An image of wings brightened there, as if the feathers brought their own light, becoming fully visible.

Bruiser took a sharp breath. Whipped his hand away from the statue as if it burned him.

Eli's heart rate sped. He jerked his boot out, as if the marble flared hot, yet I knew it hadn't. He set it flat, dropping it upright so quickly that the statue rocked. Pulled two weapons. This was no personal, spiritual vision. We could all see the wings.

But there was no physical threat. Just . . . angel wings on the walls. Into the shadows around us I asked, "How did you get trapped?"

Hayyel's wings glowed on the walls, shaped like a hawk's, now glowing with color in teal and charcoal and iridescent black. He didn't always look the same, yet I always knew him. Something flickered on the statue, close by Eli. Weapons still drawn, I turned my attention to it.

The marble statue seemed to darken. In seconds, the white stone grayed into the dark of a cloud-shrouded dawn. The statue rocked again, all by itself this time, a heavy grating sound. It went dark and then darker, not as if shadows were falling over it, but as if the white marble was . . . changing.

We stepped away.

Eli murmured into his mic, "Team Koppa. High alert. Maintain positions."

The statue deepened, dimmed until it was fully dark, lightless as black onyx, the same lightless shade as Hayyel's real skin in the visions I had of him. Hayyel's face reshaped the stone, bold features, unearthly beautiful. He blinked and his golden eyes roamed the church. The wings that were folded back from the black marble shifted from snowy white into golden tones with brown and red spots, streaks of teal, the feathers looking so real I almost reached out to them. In my pocket, the Glob grew warm, warning me not to touch. Something was off.

Except for his face and eyes, he still looked like a statue, and yet also like Hayyel, stone and angel-flesh all at once. Hayyel had both replaced the statue and become the statue. Around his waist hung a silver chain. I had seen that before, in the last vision at Aggie One Feather's sweathouse.

Hayyel's bright eyes alighted on me and he smiled. "How is your godchild, the one who is our . . . asset?"

Holy crap. There was a lot encapsulated in that question. Mostly that Hayyel had been listening in on my life. I was an asset. He had clearly heard that conversation. And Angie.

The angel had become Angelina Everhart Trueblood's guardian angel when I prayed for her, when I became her godmother. That made Hayyel and me, together, her guardians, and Angie *our asset.*

"She's good. Ummm. What's up?" *Crap.* Did I really just ask an angel of the Most High "What's up?"

His expression went from humanish to something other. Something that made my flesh want to crawl off my body and hide in a corner, mewling. Everyone shifted back and away from the statue that was no longer just a statue.

"Hear my words," he said. "Against the directives of the Most High, against mandates that bound my kind from interfering with *his humans*, I thought to intervene. I thought to stop the blasphemy of the darkest blood magic on the night of the creation of the drinkers of blood. I thought *my* actions were right and more holy than the instructions of the omnipotent, omnipresent, omniscient, omnibenevolent, *I AM*.

"I acted alone." The three words were filled with a bitter pathos.

"In my sin, I was trapped by the magic the magicians wielded. I was bound with the silver that had been paid for the redeemer's death. For my sin, I was left here and not here, neither heaven nor Earth, bound by the cursed silver. I have been attended from time to time, by the host, yet I am unable to join them. I am stuck in time, with the humans and their world. *I am alone.*

"Nearly two millennia later, I thought I had discovered a way to bring about the reversal of my sin. I thought to save a Mithran from destruction and end the reign of the Sons of Darkness," Hayyel said. "I nearly succeeded. He was ready to become outclan, a Mithran who would lead all of his kind into purity. But"—he met my eyes and I stepped back farther—"a creature who is the darkness of your kind took him and ate him."

That was a lot of information, but I latched on to the last part. "Immanuel?" I asked.

The silver chain flashed with black light and vanished. The ebony-toned statue glinted pure white, black, white, a stuttering change, like a lightbulb going off and on. Hayyel groaned as if in pain. His body froze into place again. The stone-hard white marble no longer wore the angel's face. In the arched ceilings I heard an echo of a faint, "Yes . . ."

"Are you trapped *here*, in this statue?" I asked.

The angel didn't answer.

Bruiser and Eli and I were sitting in the SUV, still parked at the curb, in silence, our eyes on the church. Quint and Fawn, both looking a little pale and a lot spooked, were at the front and back bumpers, the vamps in the team dispersed in the shadows, keeping watch.

"Should we steal the statue?" I asked. "Take it with us?"

"Was the angel actually *in* the statue or was it just angel-magic?" Eli asked. "A short-term way to communicate with us?"

"He said he was trapped by the silver, and he didn't mention the statue," Bruiser said. "How does one free a trapped angel?"

"How did it get trapped in the first place?" Eli asked.

"And what is this for?" Bruiser asked. He held up a small, shining-bright silver key, the ornate kind from the eighteen hundreds, with a fancy thumb hold and big teeth. It was large enough to be a gate key, about five inches long. "It was in a recess, a rough-carved slot in the marble of the statue's base, and was covered with very ancient plaster to seal it in place."

I had replaced the Jesus talisman in my pocket, wrapped in the hanky, before we left. It had returned to room temperature after Hayyel disappeared, and when I pulled it out, it didn't get hot again. I wasn't sure what that meant, except that maybe Hayyel wasn't tied to the key or the statue. Or maybe only to the key when it was *in* the statue?

I held out my hand. "May I?"

Bruiser placed it in my palm.

"It's silver," I said, turning the key over and over, "shiny, not tarnished." Not hot, not cold, just slightly warmer than ambient air from being in Bruiser's pocket and his hand.

"If the age of the plaster is an indication, it was in place a long time. But, plaster of Paris should have tarnished the silver badly," Bruiser said. "It shouldn't be bright, as if newly polished, even if it was only in the plaster for a little while." He studied the pic of the statue's base on his cell again. "But the plaster where it was hidden was clearly old. Very old."

"Could it be the key that secured the binding chain around Hayyel's waist?"

Bruiser stared at the key in my hand. "That makes sense. Though the chain on the statue appeared small, its true size may not be relative to what we saw." No one replied and he continued. "The chain appeared to be bright too. Perhaps Hayyel used the location of the key to manifest inside the statue when the crucifix-talisman was brought near."

"Like a witch working, hidden in place for a single event?" I asked. "Yeah, yeah, I can see that."

Eli, who had been watching the surroundings, glanced at me and asked, "More important from a timeline position, why would an angel try to protect Immanuel, a blood drinker, who, according to everything we know, was a lazy, selfish, woman-chasing fanghead?" He glanced at me and back outside. He was riding shotgun, sitting in the passenger front seat, a shotgun loaded with silver-shot flechette rounds across his lap, watching for attack around us.

"We've already figured out that Leo's kid was eaten earlier than we thought," I said, "and that means the *u'tlun'ta* skinwalker was in place longer than we thought. All of our conclusions about the timeline were off. Some of them by several millennia, if I understood what Hayyel said about the night he was chained."

Eli murmured something into his comms and then said, louder, "Maybe Immanuel, when he was born of Leo's body, in the human way and not the vamp way, was named after Christ because he was supposed to be special in some kind of spiritual way. And instead he was a lazy woman-chaser. Maybe when there was a complete personality change, it was so welcome that Leo didn't notice."

"That—"

Leo popped in from the shadows, standing next to the SUV.

We all flinched. Quint cursed quietly, her lips moving in the darkness. Fawn snorted with amusement at her and said something.

Leo stared inside, meeting first Eli's eyes, and then mine, despite the heavily darkened windows. He nodded, his head moving deliberately up and down, making certain that we knew he was agreeing with Eli. Leo pointed to his clerical collar.

I reached for the window button and slid the armored glass down, open to the chilly night air. Leo's vamp scent blew in, that odd scent he had developed, different top notes overlaying his natural vamp-scent undertones. Leo had changed scent when he changed. So yeah. Immanuel's scent change had been accepted. "Was Immanuel intended to become an outclan priest, like you?"

Leo stared hard at me and nodded again, but this time it was a jerky movement, as if it hurt him. His pupils went wide and black, the sclera bleeding scarlet, vamping out as he fought an internal battle. His hand gripped the pillar between the front window and mine. His claws extended and, despite the armor of the vehicle, pierced the metal. Something, that compulsion I had seen before, was stopping him from speaking, was causing him intense distress. He was losing control.

I had to ask this fast. I didn't have long before he broke or tried to kill something. Probably me. "You wanted Immanuel for something special, but he was a playboy vamp. Then something happened and he changed and told you he planned to become a Mithran outclan priest, didn't he?"

Leo nodded again, his black eyes widening as if encouraging me.

"But you never chose an heir, which is just weird in the vamp world," I said, watching his face. "And by not choosing, he became your default heir, the child of your body, the vamp closest to you, important but not protected. By not making him your heir, and not putting him to work, covered by a security detail, you set him free to see the world and roam, and to hopefully grow into the person you wanted him to become. That's where you screwed up and your enemies found him and got their hooks in him. Right?"

Leo lifted a shoulder as if saying I had a lot of it right and pointed to my pocket holding the hanky-wrapped key. Surprised, I pulled it out and placed it into his hand. Leo sniffed it and jerked back. He dropped the key into the grass. He disappeared, that faint vamp-popping sound of air displacement.

Eli slipped from the vehicle and searched for the key in the grass. Brute leaped over Eli's bent form and into the back seat, between Bruiser and me. Eli, who reacted faster than I could follow, aimed his shotgun away from the wolf and shook his head. He dropped the key into my palm. "Gonna get yourself shot, dog," he said.

"What just happened?" I asked. "Other than a stinky dog getting into the car." The werewolf stank as if he'd been rolling in something dead. "Holy moly. Opossum? Armadillo? Oh Crap. *Skunk?* Please say that isn't skunk." I would have shoved him farther away but I didn't want to touch him. "Is this the witches' skunk spell? Oh holy crap, I'm gonna die here."

Brute chuffed in amusement and rolled over against my leg.

Eli shut the driver's door, buckled in, and gave sotto voce orders and hand signals to the others. "Beats me," he said to us. "But let's get out of here. We've been too long in the open."

Brute chuffed again and made as if to crawl in my lap.

"I will shoot you dead," I threatened.

He panted at me. He had also tasted whatever he'd found.

Beast thought, *Good stinky smell. Would eat with Brute.*

Holy cow. No. Gack.

Quint got in the passenger seat and took up Eli's shotgun. We pulled away from the curb, as did our escort team. One block later, Bruiser lowered the windows, despite the security risk, and we headed toward the river and New Orleans with the night air doing its best to clear the stench from the SUV.

When we got to our freebie house, I said to the wolf, "You can take a bath in the backyard or go away."

The white wolf showed me teeth in what was clearly an insult, like being shot the finger, werewolf-style, but when I opened the SUV door, he trotted to the side gate and waited to be let in. Quint followed him into the dark and opened it.

Over her shoulder, she said, "I got him a kids' plastic pool for baths. I'll take care of it."

After we all changed out of battle gear, and Quint bathed the stinky wolf, we regathered in the kitchen and ate delivery pizza from Pizza Delicious. The vamps we had left guarding the Queen's Personal Residence in New Orleans, Koun and Tex, joined us, leaning against the wall, the far-less-stinky werewolf rolling on a beach blanket Quint had placed on the floor to dry himself off. He was still a little skunky but not as bad as before.

When we finished stuffing our faces, Quint poured coffee for the guys and tea for me, and Tex started on our few dishes. Not bad. Quint was a sociopath at best, a self-controlled psychopath at worst. Or maybe she just hid the bodies really well. But if she bathed the werewolf and kept me in tea, I really didn't care if she was a scary killer. And Tex was adorable in an apron and sudsy hands. Tex, who could have been NOLA's MOC, was washing dishes in my kitchen while one of his dogs joined Brute in his energetic rolling.

Eli said, "We got clarification on some things. Immanuel was eaten earlier than we first thought. Leo found us there, so he knows this church is important even if he isn't totally sure why. And we have the silver key and the crucifix but no idea how to use them or what they're for."

Bruiser said, "May I see the crucifix?"

"It's just a piece of Jesus jewelry. Not a— Holy crap." I unfolded the dead Jesus and held the back up to the light. There were three little knobs on back. "Leo recently, and tonight, was wearing a gold cross with three little holes in it."

"A vamp wearing a cross?" Alex asked, skeptical.

"Yeah, that was my impression too. It wasn't touching his skin, but he should still have been screaming in agony at the least or going up in flames at the worst. Anyway, there were holes in it. I don't remember how many, but the cross was about this size"—I held up the Jesus—"and Angie showed me where the Jesus jewelry was, in the office next to Leo's old office in HQ."

"Part of the same jewelry?" Bruiser asked, holding out his hand. He turned Jesus over and over.

"Brute." I snapped my fingers at the wet wolf. He snarled at me from his place on the floor, a fangy expression I ignored. "Is Hayyel trapped in the church?"

Brute's snarl disappeared. He nodded and then shook his head.

"So, maybe?"

Shake.

"Partially?"

Nod.

"And partially somewhere else too?"

Nod.

"So he's partially trapped here in the city, in our dimension. And partially trapped elsewhere. And the key and the crucifix are part of it all somehow."

Nod.

"Do you know where Hayyel is trapped?"

Head shake.

"Do we need the sound board?"

Shake. He sat down and sniffed the dog's backside. The dog jumped on him and began mock fighting, mouth and teeth and fake growls. The werewolf had nothing to add.

To my team, I said, "What about the journals? Were there any more maps in them?"

Alex called Santiago and asked, the cell on speaker phone.

The scholarly vamp said, "Yes, My Queen. There was a map of Dauphin Island, of the old fort when it was in use, Fort Gaines. That is all, thus far. And thank you, My Queen, for the rooms at the Yellowrock Clan Home. It is more than I ever expected."

I frowned at Bruiser, who smiled slightly at me, proving he had given Santiago rooms in the clan home, rooms that were obviously better than the one in HQ. Making the appropriate noises, I ended the call.

"Maps of Dauphin Island won't help us," I said, "despite the ancient history of a possible massacre there. We're wasting time. We know the angel is here, at least in some form. How do we set him free, or keep him safe?"

"We could bring the statue here," Alex said, "but if he's here and not here, and his wings were on the walls and he manifested within the statue, it could be that the statue and the place are both necessary for Hayyel to manifest. If so, bringing the statue here? I don't see how that would help."

"A *hedge of thorns*? Surrounding the church, to keep Mainet's witches out?" Eli asked.

"Can the witches handle two good wards at the same time?" Koun asked.

"That would be four. One at the null prison, HQ's, the clan home, and the church." I tapped the table as I counted, and finished my tea. "So I'd guess no."

"We're gonna need more witches," Alex said. "I'll contact Lachish and work with the Everharts."

"Speaking of witches," Bruiser said, "we are expected at HQ."

I looked at the wet-dog-stinking wolf. His crystal eyes turned from his playmate to me. "You coming with, or you doing that interdimensional timewalking thing you do?" The wolf stepped up to me and rubbed his damp coat across my jeans-covered thigh before walking out the doggie door. "And now I smell of wet werewolf."

Will use killing claws on stupid dog, Beast thought.

Don't hurt him too much. He has secrets we need to ferret out.

Beast has secrets. Beast will not tell stupid long furry rat creature.

It took a moment, but I put the long furry rat creature together with the secrets and ferret and thought back, *What secrets do I need to know?*

Beast went silent.

Dang cat.

I smelled like pizza with an undertang of wet dog and a hint of dead skunk when we pulled into the street at the back entrance of HQ, but I didn't really care how I smelled. I was tired and confused and worn and wanted to go back to bed, so the stink was more a background annoyance, even in my half-form. The vamps didn't have to breathe and the humans could avoid me. Or open a window. I was carrying some of my magical stuff with me, in pockets and wrapped in hankies, including the Glob, the key, and the gold Jesus. I'd left the crown at home, under the protective *hedge* in my closet.

The *hedge of thorns* around HQ was down, but a simpler warning ward was up and I felt it tingle across my pelt as we drove into the back entrance and over the closed tire-shredder mechanism. As we pulled to a stop under the porte cochere, Eli said, "The Everharts are refining the finished, beefed-up *hedge* wards at the null prison. Sarah Spieth and Wrassler sent a vamp security team to the prison grounds to protect them." His emotionless tone said the vamps better not miss anything and let his sweetie pie get hurt. His non-expression said he wanted to be there with Liz, but knew she had witch business to take care of and that he'd be in the way. Eli wasn't used to being the least important person on a security team. Or unnecessary to his significant other. I thought about patting his hand and saying, "There, there," but

I figured that might push him over the edge and he'd sock me.

There was no food in the security room and there was also nothing interesting happening anywhere on camera. However, I hadn't been in the security room more than five minutes when Deon pranced in. He was wearing black patent-faux-leather pants with feet, like Angie Baby's onesie but it stopped at the waist. He was also wearing a hot pink corset over a shimmery black top with spaghetti straps, a blond wig, and a huge pink feather boa flung around his neck.

My chef was pushing a food cart overloaded with chafing dishes full of grilled meat, shrimp, and veggies on skewers. The odor was fabulous and I may have drooled a little as Deon bent over the table putting the dishes in front of me. The position placed his butt at eye level. On it in silver glitter were the words "Cat Girl," with glittery whiskers out over each cheek.

Cat Girl?

Even for Deon it was a little over the top, so I asked, "What's all this?" and flashed my fingers up and down, indicating his wardrobe of the evening.

"This," he said, lifting a skewer of hot pepper shrimp and shoving it at my mouth. I opened it to avoid getting staked with the pointy end and he slid the shrimp off the skewer and into my mouth with his other fingers. "Is delicious. And this"—he did the finger flick up and down his body—"is because I needed a break from being babysitter and a reminder that I am finer than fine and my booty is just as delicious as my"—he did a quick hip snap—"skewers. Tonight's apparel is an homage to Lilly Christine, aka the Cat Girl, arguably the most famous and beloved burlesque exotic dancer of the nineteen forties and fifties. Tomorrow night I may be Blaze Starr, who became famous for her affair with Governor Earl Long. Such a disgusting man. But as long as I have to pull babysitter duty—though I do love the little ankle-biters—I will remind these heathen bloodsuckers"—he twirled his fingers at the vamps—"what real living is as soon as they have another babysitter in place."

He air-kissed both sides of my face and pranced out of the room, Cat Girl sparkling.

Tex had this dreamy look on his face, as if he had drunk deeply of his first drunk human and had a buzz on. "Lilly Christine, aka the Cat Girl, was the most beautiful woman I ever saw. She invited me up to her rooms after her last show on January 7, 1965. If you ever want to see her perform, let me know. I can arrange it."

"She died in 1965 at age forty-one, in Broward County, Florida, of peritonitis," Alex said, studying his screen, where he had pulled up her info.

Tex smiled. It was pure vamp, and not an expression I had ever seen on his face. "Or so they say."

Which was vamp for: Tex had turned her and she was undead and he was still smitten.

"I'll keep it in mind." *Not.* To Alex, I said, "Debrief. Now." But all I could think about was undead strippers and Tex in love. Both were scary.

"We went over the security tapes for HQ and found nothing. We went over the security tapes at the freebie house and then all the clan homes throughout the city—nada. Since the airport strike and Mainet trying to bomb HQ, no attacks have been directed at us. That doesn't mean our enemies died in their sleep and left us in the clear. It's much more likely they've been too busy planning something else." He didn't have to say it would be something nasty and deadly on a massive scale.

That was terror-inducing for all of my people, and a danger to the entire city, and was something I could not control or stop—yet. I couldn't go after the enemy because I had no idea where they were. I couldn't fight anything or kill anything. My pelt was itchy at the lack of action and I wasn't the only one upset. In the back of the room, I thought I saw Koun twitch trying to stay calm.

The security types started talking defensive strategy. Blah blah yada yada. I could listen to them or I could go for a walk. To keep from worrying like a wolf gnawing a leg bone, I inquired about EJ's, Cassy's, and Angie Baby's whereabouts, since Deon wasn't in charge of them. Informed of their location, I left the main security room and I wandered to the gym to see what my older godkids were up to.

I almost—not quite, but nearly—was able to ignore Quint's presence behind me in the hallways, and the presence of a vamp honor guard shadowing me ahead and far behind. Leaving the door open to the hallway at my back, I slipped into the gym, and into the shadows to watch.

The kids were in the care of Wrassler and Gee; the Mercy Blade was teaching them swordplay with small, appropriately sized, wooden sword sticks called staves, one short, one long. It was adorable, so freaking cute I thought I might up and die on the spot. From the expression on Koun's face, he agreed. But his face fell as we watched. Angie was clearly scary-quick to pick up the forms and mechanics of vamp blood-sport dueling, and that was not something the Dark Queen's Enforcer and Executioner had expected.

Dang. She was good. EJ was behind Angie in terms of speed and precision but that was the difference in ages. If his first lesson was an indication, EJ was going to be just as fast and powerful.

I tucked my hands into my pockets and wrapped my knobby fingers around the key amulet and the Jesus focal. Watching.

Angie lunged, lunged, lunged, and in between each lunge, she stabbed, stabbed, stabbed and cut, cut, cut. Ducked. Jumped over Gee's longsword. Darted in, beneath his short sword. On her knees, she stabbed Gee. Hard. Right in the groin.

Every male in the room flinched and gasped.

Gee grunted.

"Oops," I murmured, quietly stunned. That had to hurt, even for a glamoured bird. I had managed to strike Gee once or twice in sparring, but couldn't remember if I'd ever managed a kill strike. And I had tried.

Gee crumpled over and lay on the wood floor, stunned.

Angie saw me. She dropped her practice staves and raced over, shouting, "Ant Jane!" EJ copied her actions and raced over too, his high-pitched squeal echoing in the big gym.

I dropped to a knee and caught them, which nearly knocked me to my butt, but I found my balance and accepted dual hugs. When I was done being strangled, and my happy goofy expression had settled into something more queenly, I eased them back. But before I could say anything, I heard a whir from the door behind me.

Through the open door, the flying lizard flashed into the room, tail whipping, wings a blur. I had never seen it fly and it zipped across the high ceiling in acrobatic whirls. *Holy mackerel* it was fast.

From the far door, Pearl and Opal appeared. They hovered in the tall ceiling. Everything in the room stopped except the hovering scarlet lizard, the arcenciels, and Angie. The dragons, the lizard, and my godchild met gazes, back and forth. The flapping lizard wings sent Angie's lose red-gold hair back like a fan. The little girl tilted her head. The red lizard flipped energetically. Slowly, Angie held out her hand. The lizard back-winged away and in closer, but didn't land.

The rainbow dragons were watching Angie and the lizard. I maneuvered around the kids, which placed me in front of EJ, next to Angie. Quint and the security team eased up between the rainbow dragons and us all.

From the open gym door, Brute trotted in, taking a place next to Angie. A grindylow was on his back, and it stood up on Brute's shoulders. It growled at the dragons, clacking its claws, the razor-sharp steel glinting in the lights.

The lizard flew close to the werewolf and landed on Brute's back next to the grindy and promptly bopped his nose on the grindy's like a dog saying hello. The grindy mewled like a cat, sheathed its weapons, and wrapped its arms around the lizard in what was either the cutest hug on record or the beginning of a bloody battle.

The vamps in the room were riveted by the tableau, on the paranormal creatures interacting in their workout and challenge room.

The arcenciels shot rainbow lights into the gym, flipped end over end, and flew out the far door, tails snapping.

Several vamps exhaled as if in awe. Or maybe pain.

The werewolf and his burdens followed the dragons.

His riders were still hugging, which was freaking adorable. And there was no blood. Wins all around.

"Sooo. Okaaay." I was still on my knees and I hadn't drawn a weapon, my arms touching the children instead, ready to pull them away.

At my right and left, Quint and Blue Voodoo shifted, aiming from side to side. Angel Tit was in the hallway, covering our six.

"Ant Jane, was that a baby dragon?" Angie asked. She turned wide eyes to mine. "Is it yours?"

"I don't think it's a baby, Angie. I don't think it's really an arenciel. And I think it belongs to itself. Gee? What *is* that flying lizard?"

Gee, who was still on his knees after the groin strike, made it to his feet. "Originally, I believe it was a slightly reddish garden lizard from Mexico, perhaps from the anole family. But its former master allowed it to sip on his vampire blood for a number of years and it became brilliant red." Gee smiled. "And then it came to me. And it has sipped on my blood for some time now. It has grown larger and stronger and it grew wings. It understands three languages, and occasionally is willing to do tricks and small chores, though not with any dependability. In that respect it is very like yo— like a cat." He chuckled as if I had caught him out in a near insult.

But then, I wasn't willing to do *any* tricks.

Cats do not fetch like dogs, Beast thought. *Cats are vengeful and tricky . . .*

The lizard flew into the room again and sped from corner to corner, sniffing at light fixtures and HVAC ductwork. Longfellow's wings whizzed-flapped, like an electric fan slightly off balance. It dove at us like a hawk, pulled up short, and hovered in front of me, then in front of Angie, who again offered her arm as perch. He—it— ignored her arm.

Gee made a circle with his arms and said something fast in Spanish. The lizard hopped through, flapping its wings. "Good little Longfellow," Gee said, and gave the dragon a treat from his pocket like an animal trainer.

"But what is it to the arenciels?"

"They have not shared the answer to that question

with me. It is not the male of their species, as there is no male of their species. They seem to know what it is, and that it is not supposed to be. It is my impression that they have seen it in the timelines and that its appearance is portentous. So far as I know, this creature is a lovely new thing, Little Goddess, and such new things are rare and delightful. I am entranced to see where it shall take us all."

The lizard flipped its tail and somersaulted in midair, darted up, and landed on a light fixture overhead. Our entire group stepped back, loosening our defensive circle, relaxing from battle-ready to merely alert. The vamps and Quint replaced weapons into their various sheaths and holsters.

"Stupid lizard," Angie grumbled, dropping her arm. To me she said, "Show me what you found, Ant Jane."

The danger—if there had really been any—was over, so I unpocketed the two icons. I showed the little witch the Jesus focal and the key. "We used your little Jesus statue to find the key," I said.

"Ohhh. It's silver," Angie said, "like a necklace part."

EJ gave an uninterested frown and raced back to Gee. He leaped into the air and landed against the poor abused Mercy Blade's middle. Gee grunted again. I couldn't help my soft laugh. Poor little bird.

"I saw something when I was waking up this morning." Angie tapped the gold Jesus. "The one who owns this will help to save my angel, but you have to save her first." She twirled away, shouting for EJ to follow, and raced around the gym. They were intercepted by one of the human blood-servants watching over them while the Everharts worked.

I wasn't sure what to make of anything that had just happened, but I knew it was all probably important. Maybe vital. Maybe foretelling something deadly. How was I supposed to deal with stuff I didn't understand?

Bruiser, who had entered during the abuse of Gee Di-Mercy and the lizard antics, was standing nearby. He offered his hand to help me up, in that gentlemanly way of his, and though I didn't need the help, I did want his hand in mine. He tucked my fingers into the crook of his arm and tugged me to the door. "Let's step into the small sitting room across the hall."

The hallway outside the gym had two locker rooms and a small sitting room where I had taken tea and met with visitors from time to time. We sat, and Quint closed the door on us, leaving us in privacy.

"May I see the crucifix and the key again?" he asked, taking a seat beside me and pulling the small tea table over.

I placed the icons on the table. He pulled out a jeweler's loupe and lifted it to his eye, then tilted the crucified Jesus amulet so the overhead light caught the gold. "There is a maker's mark on the back, perhaps 'MD' and a tiny fleur-de-lis." He tilted it again. "And the numeral forty-two," he said. "Probably the year, so 1842." He tapped his earbud. "Alex, did you get that? Yes. Thank you."

To me said, "There were a number of goldsmiths plying their trade in New Orleans in the eighteen hundreds and fortunately, the city kept excellent records of addresses and occupations of every person in the city, including goldsmiths and silversmiths of any repute."

Placing the Jesus on the table, he tapped his cell and pulled up a directory. "Thank you, Alex. You are quite efficient at discovering such things."

A list of names appeared on the cell screen, not in alphabetical order, but easily searchable. Bruiser's fingers swiped up and down and back and forth. "MD." He made a soft hmmming sound. "The Delarues were a famous silversmithing family from the very early 1800s. M. Delarue was a well-known silversmith on Bourbon Street, and his brother or cousin, also M. Delarue, was a . . ." He shot me a quick grin, one that speared straight into my heart like Cupid's arrow.

I remembered the catnip sex and almost leaned in for a very quick kiss, but that was not something my cat lips could do easily. And also, it was . . . weird. To kiss with puma lips. "The other M. Delarue was what?"

"A goldsmith at the same address."

He applied his loupe to the silver key, turned it, angling

it, searching for something too small to see with eyesight alone. A small, satisfied smile curved his face. "MD. A similar maker's mark is on the key. The Delarue family made both of these." Bruiser studied the two dissimilar pieces. "Interesting."

"Would someone know who this was made for? And if they're still alive? Undead? Whatever?"

"Perhaps. May I take them and ask around at the local auction houses and the records departments? I have contacts at them all."

Of course he did. He had been the primo of NOLA's MOC. Now he was the Consort of the DQ. He knew how to make friends in all the right places, whereas I knew how to kill people. My skills were not the best way to make good contacts.

"Sure."

He kissed me on my furry temple and left the room.

I trailed close on his heels, into the hall, my stomach growling. I said to Quint, "Let Deon know I'm on the way in for some—"

The gym door burst open and Angie was just *there*. EJ beside her.

Quint with weapons.

I leaped in front of my godkids.

Quint scowled at me. "I wasn't going to shoot them."

"Right. Good." Her hands hadn't twitched to her weapons. I was the one still in protective mode.

"Ant Jane, Mama says we can have a bedtime snack. Come with us!" Angie said, grabbing one hand.

"Come wi' us," EJ repeated, grabbing my other hand.

Together they pulled me down the hall. "Deon is making real No'leens French toast," Angie said, trying to pronounce it like the locals. "He calls it pan purdy, but it's really French toast. And it is so good. You never ate anything so good!"

My stomach growled again. Deon's pain perdu, also known as Lost Bread, was delicious. And I was pretty sure I could get mine with a pound of bacon.

I didn't think about Deon's stripper wardrobe until we entered the kitchen. Fortunately, when he came through the kitchen doors, he was wearing a chef's coat over the corset. I'd had several good-versus-evil talks with Angie over the years, and just as many talks about my half-forms and my armor, and I had always told her that what I wore always had a purpose. I did not want to have the Deon-in-a-corset talk.

CHAPTER 18

Tea Is for Milksops and Sissies

My entourage—*crap*, I had an entourage—and I were all
back at the Queen's Personal Residence in New Orleans
with the children fed—even Cassy with Molly's breast
milk, which she had stored in the kitchen—and in bed upstairs by the time the Everhart adults returned. They had
upgraded, strengthened, and reset the wards at the null
prison, using the newest version of the *hedge of thorns*, the
protection ward developed by the family. With vamp
guards (a new dedicated team of twenty donated by the
city's clans) on the outside, and a coven of witches from
north Louisiana hired to police inside the null house, the
prisoners were finally safe from another rescue/escape
attempt.

The Everhart witches had also strengthened the wards
around the Yellowrock Clan Home, my personal home, and
had given Wrassler the trigger for the *hedge of thorns*
around HQ. The witches I called mine, Liz, Molly, and Big
Evan, gave me triggers to the updated wards at the freebie
house, the clan home, and HQ, before they dragged themselves inside and up to bed, all three so physically and

magically exhausted, they were almost incoherent. Eli followed Liz to his room and shut the door. The other two Everhart witches were either at the clan home or HQ. They had rooms in both places, wherever they needed to crash and felt safest.

Come morning, all I needed to do was to get the heartbox and its contents back to the witches and into protection, but that had to wait. For now, with all my people safe, sleep was more important, and I had time to sleep in my own bed. Maybe in the morning, I'd be human-shaped for a while. I hoped so. The pelt was itchy.

Bruiser and I sat at the kitchen table in our freebie house an hour before dawn, drinking caffeine with our vamp guards: Koun, his tattoos in whirled, geometric patterns over his visible flesh; Tex, his six-shooters slung low over his hips; Kojo; Thema; and Tex's dogs. I liked this team, especially now that Kojo and Thema were no longer so stingy with their blood. Just us with the vamps, while Quint, Eli, and Liz still slept.

It was chilly in the house, and when Tex's dogs curled up on my human-shaped feet, the warmth was deeply appreciated. I unbent enough to scratch a head I could reach and the dog licked my fingers.

Stupid dog, Beast thought. I ignored her.

All of us were drinking tea except Tex, who was drinking coffee. Coffee was an odd preference for a vamp. They usually only drank wine or tea in addition to the food meal of human blood, but when I asked why coffee, Tex said, "Begging your pardon, My Queen, and present company excepted, but tea is for milksops and sissies. I like coffee strong enough to char the silver off a spoon, and rye whiskey that's been aged a few decades, though not usually together. Ma'am."

I chuckled softly. "Them's killin' words, cowboy."

Tex grinned at me over the rim of his cup. "Anytime you wanna throw down, Queenie. But I'm more a boxer and not so much any a that mixed martial arts stuff. That's for sissies too."

Tex was picking at me like . . . like family. It felt good. He was sporting a slightly handlebar-ish moustache, and there was coffee in the hair over his lips. Made me wonder what it looked like after drinking blood. *Yuck*.

Those were the only words spoken in the quiet of the dark of morning, the sound of rain pattering against the windows, the flames flickering in the fireplace. We sat in silent companionship until the first cups—like manna from heaven—were done and we were all more or less alert.

Once the second cups were poured, Bruiser said, "Koun, Kojo, and Thema together bled and read Long-Knife. I listened in, but did not participate. They have news."

I met his eyes, understanding. He was an ethical, moral man, and he didn't believe in enslaving anyone who wasn't actively trying to kill him. He tilted his head in acknowledgment, as if he knew what I was thinking.

Bruiser glanced at Thema. "Report."

She twirled a silver earring through the hole in her lobe. "The human Long-Knife is an annoying little scrap of flesh. He thinks overmuch of himself. His mind is full of sex and power, but without the blood of one of us, he is unable to . . . I think the current term is 'get it up.' He enjoys dominating others and causing pain. He would swear to anyone who could provide a permanent cure to his *functional problem*." Thema almost snarled the last two words.

Kojo took over the report. "He is the one who lost the headset, and though it was by accident, he did not report the loss. He is neither loyal nor disloyal, at this time. Alex is keeping watch, following him through the halls of HQ via his wrist band locator, and elsewhere, by accessing his cell phone."

Kojo said, "We all agree he is not a danger to you at this time. But he is a *potential* danger."

"Good enough," I said. "I'm lucky to have anyone who's not disloyal at this point, since I can't force loyalty."

"No one can force loyalty, My Queen," Kojo said. "Obedience can be achieved by force. Should you wish."

"I'm not making slaves."

"One of many reasons we are still here. My Queen," Thema said.

Koun was smiling, that faint vamp smile they learn when they lose their humanity. "I agree, my Queen," he said. "Long-Knife is a pissant, potentially disloyal, but not currently dangerous. And should he become so, he might lead us to our enemies."

Our enemies. Not *your* enemies. Uncoerced loyalty and friendship were rare things in my life. "Thank you. We'll see what Alex finds out. Okeydokey. Bruiser?"

"We have a gold crucifix missing its cross. We have a silver key with no lock. They bear the maker's mark of M. Delarue, of 171 Bourbon Street, crafted in 1842. They were commissioned by a Mithran as a gift. Did any of you live here in New Orleans in 1842?"

"I resided here," Koun said. "But I had lost all of my close-at-hand wealth in the spate of recent wars and had not yet been to Ireland to my bankers there. I could not afford jewelry in 1842."

"We have all been short of funds from time to time," Kojo said, his dark warrior's hand holding a scarlet mug. "Involvement in human wars is often disadvantageous. But forgive us, Consort. You have news."

Bruiser picked up his narrative. "Overnight, I requested a trusted Mithran go to the City Archives and Special Collections, and then to a certain private collection of historical papers to search for the Delarue's records. According to a Delarue business journal, Joses Santana had the crucifix created as a gift for a female whom he fancied. Soledad Martinez."

Joses Santana was one of the Sons of Darkness, and I had heard Soledad's name from Santiago Molina. There was no such thing as coincidence.

Soledad and her friend Malita were ancient vamps who had been sent to an estate in bayou country by Leo's predecessor to be looked after by pot-smoking humans. The same small group of blood meal humans hadn't been changed out for way too long and, by the time Bruiser and I went to visit the vamps, they had been stoned to the gills for decades.

"Why would the SOD give a crucified Jesus to her? She might go up in flames," I said. "And when we saw her, she was not all there mentally. Like dementia or something."

"Yet he did. And yes, she was, though what she was like when the Son of Darkness arrived in New Orleans, I don't know. The crucifix was part of a necklace that came in a velvet-covered box. The silver key opened the jewelry box that contained the necklace." Bruiser let his eyes flicker to me and back to watching the vamps. I realized he was *examining* them. As if they might be dangerous.

"So . . . she had something he wanted. And he was going to get it by setting her on fire?"

"Some*thing* he wanted or some*one*."

Some*one*. A blood-servant he wanted? An introduction? I mused, "Joses wanted to possess the Ming twins way back when. They were turned by their master to keep them out of his hands. Then just before the Heir shows up here, Ming of Knoxville sends Long-Knife to me." I poured a third cup of tea and added sugar to the mug, stirring with a fancy silver spoon. "Any connection between the Mings and Soledad?"

"Not that anyone still undead has said," Bruiser said. "And Long-Knife was unlikely to have been alive back then."

Joses had been such a powerful vamp he could have taken anything he wanted, yet he made a lethal and valuable piece of jewelry—one crafted with timewalking arcenciel blood in place of one of the jewels—as some kind of enticement? Why?

I thought back to the night I met the old-lady vamps, suffering from drinking weed-laced blood or from the vamp version of dementia, living in a house that stank of marijuana. It would have been sad had they not been so content with their humans. And why hadn't Soledad kept her jewelry? Why had all the pieces been hidden away?

"Was Soledad a witch?" I asked.

"I'll check." Bruiser went to our room and returned with his laptop. He opened the file of dossiers and scanned through to Soledad's name. He frowned. "Yes. Low-level power, nothing significant. She was a sculptor. Her primary medium was stone. She carved the image of Katie in your fountain out back," he added to me.

Our eyes met, remembering the marble statues in the Blessed Virgin church. "Holy crap. That might be important," I said. "Why didn't we know that?"

"Why would we have searched for that information?" Bruiser asked. "We didn't need to know it until now. Mithrans live forever if they keep their heads. They try new things, new art, new music. They remake themselves often, because of boredom, war, ennui, or grief. None of us thought to consider Soledad as part of this."

"Could she have put a curse or a working on the crucifix?" Koun asked.

Bruiser placed the Jesus focal and the key on the table. "Perhaps. Perhaps we need the rest of the focal, the cross the figure of the Christ would have been mounted upon. Perhaps we need all of it, the cross, the gold chain, and the box as well."

The vamps turned to the stairs and after a moment I too heard the soft footsteps. Too soft and light to be Big Evan or Molly, the gait belonged to Angie.

My godchild peeked around the wall of the staircase, her green nightgown swinging forward, her strawberry-blond hair in a stiff braid to the middle of her back.

"Ant Jane? I had a dream."

"Come here," I said, holding out an arm. Angie walked sedately to me and into the crook of my arm.

"My feet are cold."

My goddaughter was getting too old to be held, yet she climbed to my lap and put her feet on Bruiser's thigh, as comfortable with us as she was with her parents. I melted into a gooey puddle inside at the trust in her actions, and from the look on his face, so did my honeybunch. Bruiser took her toes in his hand. "Very cold," he agreed.

"That feels good." Angie rested her head on my chest and looked at the gold Jesus and the silver key on the table. Sleepily, she said, "In my dream, you found him. You found my angel."

"I found something in an old church," I said hesitantly, "but Hayyel wasn't totally there, according to Brute."

Angie frowned hard. "He's in two places at one time? Or maybe in two times?"

I looked at the vamps. "Thank you for your service tonight. I need to speak privately with my godchild."

Koun and Tex went upstairs to the attic rooms and

Thema and Kojo went out the side door toward the new gate in the brick fence and their quarters in the former bordello that backed up to my home.

When the house was silent, I asked, "Angie, will you tell me what you see when you see futures? When you're in the between place?"

"All the maybes. All the ways to one thing happening and all the ways to this other thing happening and what it takes to get there. And what happens if someone changes stuff. And what happens if someone changes stuff. I don't remember them all. Just the really bad ones." She angled her head up to me and her braid fell over her shoulder. "Like when you die in between. Or my mama and daddy die. Or EJ. And I know I can't stop it from happening, but I can tell you and you can make things happen to fix it."

"How do I fix it?"

"You timewalk. You know. Like Brute."

All the blood felt as if it drained out of me and my heart fell out of my chest cavity, yet I managed to sound calm. Somehow. "You know about timewalking?"

"Yeah. I saw you doing it in some of the betweens. It's dangerous. I don't do it anymore. I'm afraid I'll step on butterflies." She cocked her head, her sleep-mussed strawberry-blond braid swinging, "In one of the betweens I heard Eli telling you to not step on any butterflies or you could die. And stepping on butterflies changes time. But you might have to timewalk again to save everything."

"I see. Yes, I'll be careful of all the butterflies." Which was weird, because Eli and I had had the butterfly talk about timewalking several times. "Can you tell me anything about the betweens coming up soon?"

"There was a dream about my angel. It was confusing and scary and I was watching you on a boat floating on the waves. A beach I've never been to. Underwater, there was a brick square, like what a house sits on."

"A foundation?"

"Yeah." She yawned hugely and stretched, her fists reaching out in front of her and crossing over before she took a normal breath and settled against me again. The complete trust was always my undoing. I kissed the top of her head and blinked away tears. She was eight, but when she sat in my lap, it was as if she were four again.

"There was some rusted cannons on the beach bottom. And the bottom part of a wooden boat, one with a broken stick up the middle like to hold a sail. It was way bigger than the house bottom. A really big boat. And there were three skulls. You know. Like people skulls in the boat bottom."

Holy crap. People skulls. Like the paper map.

"The land was shaped like this." She drew a long wiener-shaped island or isthmus.

"Barataria?" I asked.

Her eyes opened wide. "That was it. I thought they said Barktater."

I had been to Barataria, and with all the hurricanes it was easy to see how a large boat got swamped. A house foundation was a lot harder to figure, unless receding water sucked all the sand out from under the foundation and the house above it capsized in place, the building lot itself now underwater, washed away, and the land never reclaimed.

"Oh. And I saw a fire in a bucket and a naked lady and some witches, but it was really confused." She yawned again. "Mama wants to see the church where you found my angel."

"Ohhh." Hayyel might have been partially bound by Evangelina way back before I killed her and the demon she called. "I don't think that's a good idea."

"It's not, but the between place said she needed to make choices." Angie's shoulders shrugged. "And you have to give the Valentine box back to the witches. If you don't, me and EJ's dead."

Valentine box. Heartbox. *Dang.* I hugged her to my chest and held Bruiser's eyes as the sky outside brightened despite the rain clouds.

CHAPTER 19

Drooling on My Jeans

Just after dawn, against my better judgment, but knowing Angie's visions couldn't be ignored, Bruiser and I dropped the heartbox back off with Lachish in the newly repaired and properly *hedged* null prison. I had a bad feeling about letting it go, but the null ward in my closet wasn't enough to keep the heart from growing, so . . . I couldn't keep it any safer than the witches could. At least in the null prison it wouldn't grow bigger lungs and maybe a brain.

And having the Heart of Darkness out of my house felt very freeing as the low-level fear generated by the detached organ was instantly gone.

At ten a.m., after a narrow band of rain cleared the skies, and after protracted discussions and inventive witch-cursing, our crew headed back to the Blessed Virgin church. We had no vamp guards, no Leo, but with most of the Truebloods—Molly, Big Evan, and Angie—in the car behind us, Liz and Cia in the car in front of us, and Quint and Eli's handpicked human guards, their cars bracketing the rest of us, we were as safe as we could get. Brute was in the car with Bruiser, Eli, and me, the werewolf snoring, his head on my thigh, drooling on my jeans. *Yuck*. But at least he didn't still stink.

We'd be doing a B and E, in broad daylight, with two exhausted, sleep-deprived witches and a scary-powerful witch child who had convinced her parents that she had to be there. She had probably used her magic to get them to agree.

All this in broad *freaking* daylight.

What could go wrong?

It was a weekday and I fully expected there to be workers on site, but it was silent as the grave. With all the hurricanes and winter storms and the tornado that had torn through the state a few months past, every construction and roofing and electrical and heating-and-air crew in four states was booked solid, so nothing much was getting done except for rich people who paid a premium. The church was empty, no cars anywhere.

Into my earbuds, Alex said, "Security system is still not running, electricity is still out. Go in looking like workers. Bang around with hammers. Make it look good and get out fast."

"Copy," Eli said.

"Look like workers? With a kid?" I stepped out of the SUV. From the vehicle behind us, Angie broke away from her parents and skipped to me, happy and carefree and glowing with a nimbus of power Beast showed me with her vision. Angie was like a rainbow of energies today, purple at her head and sliding down to green at her feet. Thankfully only Beast could see the energies without opening a *seeing* working, or Angie would have been stolen by enemies or one government or another long ago.

There was no way we looked like workers, but no one stopped us or even passed us on the street as we entered the church through the same method as before—Eli on a ladder, through a different window, out of sight from the street, one security team hidden on the grounds, and the rest of us through the side door and along the moldy hallways. The sanctuary of the church was dim and shadowed, with an arc of red and blue lights bright in a ceiling arch. The rainbow of color came through a crack where the protective plywood had pulled away.

Angie raced through the place, Brute lumbering on her heels, the little witch shouting, "Oh! This is pretty!" her words echoing in the high ceilings as she admired the gilt objects and the doodads used in ritual worship. I'd been brought up in a Christian children's home. The worship taught there had been decidedly lacking in ritual, heavy on rules and sins, and rife with emotional enthusiasm. The gilt wasn't overly impressive to me.

Brute stopped and raised his head high, whuffing in and out, sniffing. I watched him, wondering if he smelled an angel. Wondered if this place smelled different in daylight from the way it did in the dark. He dropped his head and trotted after Angie.

Molly asked, "Angie? Is this the place from your dreams?"

"It could be!" She pointed high overhead. "But there was a hole right there in the last between dream."

Molly and Big Evan exchanged looks I couldn't decipher. The ceiling where she pointed was intact, so it was either the wrong church or a prophetic dream. A dream to worry about.

"Mama, there's gold everywhere!" Angie turned around and around, arms outstretched, staring at the stained glass and the gilt. "Ant Jane, this place is beautiful!"

The guys pulled the blue tarp off the white marble angels and plaster saints. Molly tapped her daughter on the head to get her attention and pointed to the statues. "Is the angel here?"

Angie raced over. Without a suggestion from any of us, Angie ran straight to the angel statue where we had found the key. She dropped to her backside and scooted around the base. At the rear of the statue, she rolled to her knees and crawled back around it, to the winged foot where the key had been hidden. Her jeans were dusted with plaster particles and construction filth, which only made her more adorable. I moved closer and she beamed up at me, patting the statue's foot. "He was here. Right here. In this one. But he's not here now."

"I—"

A boom sounded. The building shook like a minor earthquake. Gunfire erupted, close. Too close. I grabbed Angie from the statue and practically tossed her at her father.

"Get to cover," Eli said to the Trueblood witches. "Liz. You and Cia too."

Eli and I were holding weapons. Crouched.

Bruiser was standing near a support column, his eyes searching for something I didn't see. All Onorio, his posture that of the warrior, protector, lover, killer. All that, and more than that.

I wasn't watching, but I felt the prickle of a *hedge of thorns* opening over the small family. The *hedge* was a powerful one, but bloodless. No time for drawing a circle to set the energies properly.

A second boom sounded and for a heartbeat of time the walls of the church glowed with energy, letters or symbols painted on them. Greek? Hebrew? Gone before I could identify them.

The little grindy was suddenly *there*. Riding Brute. Its front paws holding on to his ears. Together, they galloped to the side door where we had entered. Bruiser was on comms to our backup on the outside. Weapon moving back and forth, Eli stepped to the back of the church; I went to the front entrance. We were mind-joined in this battle situation, but the attack didn't feel like the others we had seen and experienced. No rocket. Just the small arms fire and the sound, like a huge drum being hit.

Another boom sounded. The dome overhead shifted and shuddered. A shower of plaster dust and bigger particles of building material rained down. "Oh crap," I whispered. *Angie saw a hole in the ceiling.*

A fourth boom sounded. Heavy plaster fell in clumps. One of the statues toppled over. Shattered when it hit the floor. I glanced up to see a small hole in the ceiling far overhead. Like Angie's vision.

A fifth boom sounded, followed by a crack like a tree breaking in a storm. A huge wooden beam dropped from the dark hole and began a slow, tilting descent, one end still in place, the falling end splintered and broken. Sunlight gleamed in.

The Everharts' makeshift bloodless *hedge*, one that would allow the Everharts to make a run for it, would not be enough if the roof came down. Stay? Or run outside? That might be what our attackers wanted, where they could see us. Pick us off. Which was safest?

"Outer perimeter backup, close in," Eli said into his comms. He was holding a handgun, facing the back entrance on the other side of the altar. Bruiser had drawn a nine-mil handgun from a holster at the small of his back and gripped a .32 that had to have been strapped at his ankle. I stood with an H&K in a two-hand grip. We made a triangle of protection, each of us given some cover by a column.

Gunfire sounded again. The rat-a-tat of an automatic weapon. An abrupt silence. Likely jammed. Three bursts of gunfire followed. Our people, making the shots count.

Over comms I heard a woman say, "Two vehicles racing away. Got descriptions and plate numbers."

"Clear," a deep voice said.

Alex said, "One of the vehicles is carrying a tracker from when the null prison was attacked. There's a signal booster in the SUV you drove to the church, bro. Get out and follow. I'll give directions. Downloading its previous locations."

Angie under Big Evan's shoulder, Cia, Liz, Evan, and Molly huddled beneath the portable *hedge of thorns*. Eli took point and Bruiser and I followed at the Everharts' and Truebloods' six. In a tight group, we all sped through the door where we had entered.

We should have taken a different exit, except we hadn't opened a second escape route on the other side of the altar. Stupid all around. Not expecting this. Not expecting whatever this weapon was, not here, in daylight.

Eli covered us as we sped into the cloudy day. We tripped over bricks that hadn't been there when we entered. I got a glimpse of a circle of disturbed soil. Witch circle that hadn't been there before. Empty. But for how long?

Running to the cars—six of them, the Everharts piled into one and it raced away before they even slammed all the doors. *Safe*. I looked back to see the ground at the witch circle vibrate, grass and soil rippling. I followed Eli and Bruiser into the vehicle we had arrived in and our four-car motorcade took off. Alex's voice gave us directions.

Out the rear window, I examined the church. The clock and bell tower was missing an entire top corner down to about thirty feet, the brick all over the ground. The ceiling and roof of the sanctuary had not fallen in, but it looked precarious, as if an earthquake had shaken it from the top down instead of from the ground up.

That damage hadn't been made by mundane weapons. A rocket would have come straight in. Ruined the church. Killed us all. Which meant the attackers wanted something other than us dead. Something other than the church destroyed. I had no idea why I thought it, but I had a feeling Mainet's witches hadn't known we would be there.

Just before we turned a corner, three women appeared in the circle. Ursula, Fiona, and Endora trotted to the door we had left open. Behind them in the circle, three armed humans appeared and followed them.

I didn't believe in coincidence, but if they had known we would be at the church, they would have come through the circle they had opened sooner and killed us. And they hadn't. If they'd had access to the timelines, they had missed the opportunity to take us all out. So what had just happened?

The key? They wanted the key? They didn't know we took it earlier?

The booming was the sound of the circle opening? Too many questions, too few answers.

It looked as if whoever the Heir's seer was, they could see some timelines and not others. They were limited in what they could find out. Good to know. Other possibilities did jumping jacks in my brain, vying for attention.

Eli whipped the wheel and we took a corner too fast. I rammed against Bruiser. He put an arm around me and belted me in. Put a bottle of tepid water in my hand. I downed it. I needed to pee. We rocked to the other side as Eli zigged and zagged through Algiers.

Alex said, "The car with the tracker spent a lot of time at a vacation property in Barataria."

Barataria, again.

I knew Barataria. I'd had battles there. It was a good place to hide people, things.

"Did they know we'd be at the church?" Eli demanded of Alex. "If so, how? The comms set lost by Long-Knife was disconnected from the channels we use. Did they get around your block and track us via comms?"

"There is zero indication of that. The comms set has such a low charge I can't ping it at all now."

I wasn't satisfied, but the Kid knew his stuff. "Where's Quint?" I asked.

"She's behind you in the SUV. Why? You suspect her?" Alex asked.

"No. I want someone back at the church, watching to see when the witches leave, and then going inside to look for cameras. Specifically solar-powered cams with transmitters. Brute was acting weird when we got there, sniffing up high, as if he smelled something. Or someone. Maybe a random someone who had reconnoitered the church just before we arrived. If they were watching the sanctuary last night, they'd have shown up then but they didn't. They showed up today." I tilted my head side to side, weighing it all. "Maybe we triggered something and they sent magic bombs through to crush us, but the roof didn't fall in. I don't know. Something's off."

Alex said, "So, say they found out you went to the church last night, and after you left, they showed up and opened the transport witch circle, maybe set up cameras to monitor future visits. Waiting on you to show up again and lead them to the key, or maybe take it from you if you already had it. If it was cameras, they'd have had just enough time to open the witch circle in the yard, send through some magical bombs, and then attack. The timing is off but not by much. Or maybe there's another reason for them to show up at the church."

"Yeah, yeah. Okay. Like I said. Something's off."

Eli said, "There's enough ambient light to keep a battery charged for a few days to operate a motion-sensor camera."

"I'll send a team to check," Alex said. "Quint has other jobs. Head to Barataria, bro."

"The queen will not go," Bruiser said softly.

I swiveled my head to my honeybunch, my eyes narrowing. "What did you say? I thought that keep-Jane-safe thing was all settled."

"Angie arrived at the airport, and our queen was attacked. Angie was at HQ and our queen was attacked. Angie was here and our enemies attacked. Angie may be part of their plan, My Queen. Angie and you, taken together or killed together. Perhaps it doesn't matter to the Heir which way it all goes, kidnapping or death."

"Angie . . ." Angie and EJ had been kidnapped more than once by bad guys who recognized their power, without even knowing why they were so special. If Mainet had scryers, the Heir might have more information about them than I had thought.

Implacable, reasonable, Bruiser continued. "Barataria is where Angie saw a vision, my love. Barataria was Immanuel's hideout. Everything leads back to Immanuel and the distant past. And perhaps our enemies know that Angie has ties to the angel whom they have partially chained. That means Barataria might be a trap. We need to recon. You need to be safe. You and Angie."

Before I could respond Eli said, "It's only humans for this reconnaissance, on enemy territory, against enemy humans and witches. We're at a disadvantage. And our people's lives could suffer keeping you safe, when we only need to look around."

I said a bad word, like a really bad word, as Bruiser pulled over and braked hard. He got out and opened my door. Fuming, I got out too and walked—stomped is more like it—to the SUV being driven by Shemmy, Quint riding shotgun. I got in the back seat and Quint and Shemmy pulled into traffic, heading back to HQ. I thought that bad word all the way back to safety, remembering the time my mouth got washed out with soap back when I was being housed at the Christian children's home.

Using Alex's drones, the recon team located the tagged SUV abandoned in a parking lot behind a big-box home and garden store. The drone's cameras showed little cover and no sign of a circle of disturbed damp ground, churned and muddy—no witch transport circle.

Alex had gone in person with Eli to Barataria and sent up more drones to look for our enemies, then to look for a boat and a house foundation under the shallow waters of the Gulf. They had found two options but nothing definitive. The Gulf was churned up from a storm hanging off the coast, and visibility below the surface was low.

My team had talked through all the options and created a plan of action with lots of potential variables. I hadn't been included in that planning stage. I hadn't even been notified when they returned to their various stations for armor and weapons. Nor had I been notified when the team watching the church reported that the witches and their humans had departed through the circle in the yard. Nor that our people discovered two small solar-powered Wi-Fi cameras in the church.

Nope. I had been relegated to Auntie Jane duties, all safe and secure. Cassy was doing nothing but making cooing noises as she was passed from one older bloodservant to another for cuddles while her mother watched in amusement. I sicced the older kids on Gee in the gym and watched them for several hours as they abused his delicate sensibilities. Then I made Deon feed us homemade pizza and PB&J sandwiches. The entire time, I itched to be elsewhere and busy. But I was the queen, to be trotted out only for battles and ceremony.

At one point while Gee was adjusting Angie's arm and sword position, Beast thought at me, *Jane is acting like mewling kit after teat.*

Are you accusing me of whining?

Beast's tail flicked slightly as she considered my question and then turned away. *Jane is whining like kit after teat.*

I was insulted for the thirty seconds it took me to realize she was right. I was moderately ashamed of myself, so I picked a couple humans to spar with me, and got in a good sweaty workout without hurting them too much. After a little violent activity I felt better.

Some people gardened to feel better. I beat people up.

Now, after a meal and a nice shower, and with sunset an hour away, Eli and Alex had narrowed down the location of the missing headset by pinging the nearly dead device from the drones. Pretty nifty. The headset was in Barataria. Natch. They had triangulated the headset location with the two potential boat/foundation sites and narrowed it to one set of coordinates. A small house on the Gulf.

Alex was back running comms. The kids were safely in the gym with their parents, their witch aunts, and two guards who were helping them show off their new fighting skills, all of them surrounded by guards. I was watching the Everharts on a screen in the security room with Quint and my two-person honor guard. Deon was still bringing me food, still trying to fatten me up, successfully, as it turns out.

Accepting that I had no place in the mundane part of an investigation was hard. I kept having to push down the irritation and the jittery need to be doing something important. But being out in the streets for a purpose that literally any of my people could do created a danger to my people. So here I was. Sitting in the security room in HQ, I tried not to seethe but it was hard to be considered dispensable. Or so indispensable that I was all but wrapped in Bubble Wrap and kept in a vault. I was safe, watching as the Barataria teams made ready to go into the house where they had found a magical signature, their mundane weapons and time carefully determined to account for potential mundane and magical defenses. It would be our humans and one Onorio against witches and humans, with the enemy vamps asleep or at least weakened by daylight. Hopefully. And hopefully not expecting a daylight attack. Surprise was the lynchpin. It was the only thing going for us. No way was I missing this operation, even if only by camera. And I kept tucking my ire away someplace inside me and out of the way.

I wasn't a part of anything. But I wasn't getting anyone killed either, so I'd take it.

Quint and I sat at the nearly empty security room table, watching live vest cam footage, listening to comms. Alex's back was to the table, and a huge platter of roasted

whole pork boudin was in front of us, along with four
boxes of donuts from Krispy Kreme. Quint ate nothing,
watched everything, her weapons on the table, ready to
fire. Her not eating was unnerving, though it didn't prick
my predatory instincts, just a realization she was creepy-
intense focused. I mean. She turned down *Krispy Kreme*.

The team had been in Barataria for hours, armored
and weaponed up and wearing null sticks to protect them
against witches. I was watching the vest cams of a two-
man recon team, composed of Angel Tit and Blue Voodoo. The motion was jerky, offering bits and pieces to go
with the chatter on their dedicated comms channel.

"No external cams noted," Blue Voodoo said.

Angel Tit said, "No sign of heat sources inside. Walls
appear to be well insulated."

"No HVAC system to put a camera in through the
vents," Blue Voodoo said. "No open windows. Window
AC units offer no access. All window coverings are secure and unable to obtain view."

"Sound from inside," Angel Tit said. "Sounds like
news channel chatter. Some sounds of movement."

"House is old. Built on a slab instead of stilts, which
is crazy," Voodoo said. "No access through the floor
system."

*Beast should be with littermate and mate. Beast should
be at battle.*

*Yeah. We should. You figured out why we don't always
shift in mortal danger dying situations?*

Is many things. Hard to think like Jane does.

Try. The thought was snide.

Beast chuffed at my tone. *Was black magic when puma
and wesa fought and we became Beast. Black magic did
new things to Jane's human snake in center of all beings.
Beast magic made Jane able to shift to live when was
dying.*

She was talking about DNA. Right. All skinwalkers'
DNA was tangled. Mine had been a ball of knots, and
whatever had happened when the puma and the wesa/
human had merged had done that. *Go on.*

*Damour's witch-vampire spell put dark magic into
Jane, what was called motes of dark power. Angel Hayyel*

can see time back and forth. Angel gave Jane back and forth timewalking because snake in center of Jane was different and Jane had dark magic motes. Timewalking made Jane sick. Angel took back timewalking and healed snake in center of Jane. Jane is new skinwalker.

Crap. Why didn't you tell me this?

Beast gave the equivalent of a mental shrug—looking away and a tail twitch of unconcern. *Angel is trapped. Cage is smaller now. Angel cannot help now.*

That was a lot to process. I mulled it over. *Can I get back the shift-in-extremis ability without getting the time-walking gift? And the cancer?*

Beast gave another tail-shrug, bored with the conversation. *Beast does not know.*

So I'd have to be willing to die for it if I risk it. Gotcha.

Over comms, which Alex had set on the room's speakers, I heard a tortured scream. "They got somebody in there," Angel Tit said. "Sounds bad."

"Or that's what they want you to think," I said.

On screen and over comms, Eli said, "Copy that. Look lively. Go."

Fourteen vest cams quivered and shuddered with running. Six stopped behind the protection of parked vehicles, focusing on the house. Small arms with silencers were the weapons of choice. Tear gas. A battering ram. In nine seconds, the door had been shattered open and the teams were pouring inside, stepping over the base of the door.

The main room was empty, nothing but a TV playing the news and a small recorder sending out the sound of screams. The flooring had been torn up. The slab broken through, chunked and tossed as if it had been attacked with a pickax. The dirt and sand beneath the house were exposed. The house was empty.

Except for a stack of plastic explosives in the hole.

"Retreat!" Alex shouted into comms. "Get outta there!"

"MoveitMoveitMoveit," Eli shouted. His heart slammed. So did mine. My claws pierced the table.

The team scrambled back outside. Fast. Leaping over the remains of the door.

Cameras juddered with the motion.

My heart raised into my throat like the fist of death. Unmoving. Cold.

One camera looked back. Bruiser's camera as he dove through the door. Stumbled.

A massive boom sounded. Comms audio caught part of it. Went to static.

The place imploded.

Night had fallen. Three of our people had been sent to Tulane Medical Center with concussive injuries. Bruiser was one of the injured. And no one would tell me how bad, except that he was unconscious and bleeding. A trip wire had been at the base of the door, and Bruiser had triggered it on the way out. He'd caught the blast.

I was not allowed to go to Tulane, for fear my presence would call down an attack on the hospital. Instead, Florence had been escorted there to help them heal, the Infermieri under heavy guard.

Useless. I was *useless*. When Bruiser's cam went blank, I had unexpectedly shifted to a super-furry half-form. In utter agony.

I had just *shifted*. Out of control. Fast. Too freaking fast. That need to fight, to do something, *anything*, driving the shift. It was the kind of shift I had once done automatically when my body was dying. Maybe I was getting that gift back, not that it helped Bruiser. Even in half-form I could do nothing to help. I paced the floor around the big security room table, my claws out, damaging the floor. Ripping into it. Because I had to hurt something, damage something. I was angry, so angry that it leaked out of my pores, scented my breath. My eyes glowed a gold so bright that I could see the shine myself.

Bruiser . . .

Koun stood across the table from me, watching me pace, deeply focused on my every move. His face was kind. Which made me want to claw him. He was holding his cell phone, as if he had made a call. While Bruiser was dying, he had . . . *made a call*. I growled.

Gee appeared at Koun's side. Not coming through the door. He just appeared. Magic act.

"My Queen," Gee said, his tone slithery as a snake, mesmerizing, insulting. "You are weak. You are . . . what do the humans of today call it? A waste of air."

I stopped. My pulse pounded. My breath came in a low growl. "What did you say?"

Gee—delicate, diminutive Gee DiMercy—tossed me two staves. My wooden practice staves. I caught them from the air, my hands finding the shaped hilts by instinct. "You are weak," he said. "Wanting. Without use—"

I dove across the table and attacked. Wood staves raised. But he was gone in the same instant. I had no one to kill.

"I believe the Mercy Blade is in the gym," Koun said, his voice disconcertingly calm.

I moved. *Fastfastfast*. Out the door, along the hallways. *Le breloque* clamped itself onto my head. My crown. Useless piece of metal. I ripped the gym doors open with such force they dented the walls when they hit. I screamed. Puma cat challenge. Beast challenge. *"Kill!"* I screamed.

Gee DiMercy stood in the center of a fighting circle. The lights were on and bright. I took a breath, my nostrils fluttering. Smelling the Everharts. Angie, EJ, Molly. But they weren't here. They had left. Smelling vamps. Dozens of vamps. They stood along the walls. Watching. Waiting.

Gee tapped the mat at his feet. It was a slow tap, a single insolent gesture, as if he called me to him like a pet.

I screamed again. And I attacked.

Wood staves clicked and clacked, rose and fell. Gee defended. My long stave swept his staves up and away in a long circle. Again. Again. I stepped inside his guard. My short stave thrust, thrust, *thrust*. Advancing with each kill strike. Backing Gee off the mat. My thrusts and cuts perfect. Each one a killing strike. Each one dragging a grunt from Gee.

I stabbed him over and over. Blocked. Blocked. Blocked. Felt but ignored the return thrusts that made it through my defenses. Some of them kill strikes as well. Pain buried beneath the anger of being useless. *Useless*. Faster than I had ever moved.

I wanted him dead. Dead and rotting. He backed into

the gym wall. I stabbed him in the solar plexus with all my might. He dropped to the floor. I whirled and screamed. The rage echoed off the walls.

"Next," a calm voice said.

A vamp I knew stepped up to me. What was her name? I didn't care. With two strikes she was down. Bleeding across her forehead where I'd rattled her brains.

"Next," the voice said again.

A male vamp stepped up. Before he could raise his weapons, I ended him with a move that would have disemboweled him had I been holding steel.

"Next."

A third vamp. Lost his head. Or would have.

"Next."

Fourth. Dead. Then the fifth. Sixth.

"Next."

The vamp in front of me was Grégoire. Standing there. *Blondie*. With real swords.

Blondie was in France with Edmund.

Except he was here.

I attacked. Fast. Faster than I had ever moved in any form. Faster than time. Defensive strike. Thrust. Thrust. Thrust. Advancing. Retreating. The crown heated on my scalp. Grégoire caught each of my staves on his swords. He didn't bleed. I needed someone to bleed.

"Swords," I screamed.

"Here, My Queen," the calm voice said. Koun. My swords in his hands. I slung the staves against the wall. Noticed they knocked two vamps to the floor. Vamps who didn't move fast enough. I didn't care. Koun tossed the swords. I caught them and attacked Grégoire.

Blondie laughed. A happy, joyous sound. "Yes, My Queen. Finally, you fight."

Steel rang in the air, bright and clanging. Lights overhead glinted and flashed on killing blades. Advanced. Advanced. Backed away. Ducked. Leaped. Struck high. Low. Swords moving in the cage of death—the vampire version of La Destreza Verdadera. Backing my warlord against the wall. Lunge, block. Lunge. Lunge. Block. Whirling my longsword up and around. The cage of death.

I swept his steel away. With my short blade, I stabbed him in the heart. The blade pierced his chest.

A hand caught mine. Stopping the final sweep of my long blade across the throat. Beheading my enemy. "No, My Queen. Jane. George is alive. He is not dead. George is awake and will live."

I dropped my swords. Took two steps back. Blinked. Saw Grégoire. Bloody. My sword buried in his chest. "Oh shit. Oh shit shit shit."

Grégoire slid down the wall. Into a heap. Spraddle-legged. Blood smeared the gym wall in the path of his descent. He was covered in blood. Drenched. A hundred small cuts and dozens of deeper ones bled from all over him.

"Grégoire?" I whispered.

"This," the delicate vamp said, taking a breath in obvious pain. "This is what I have waited for. This is what I have fought for." He looked past me. "You were correct, my love. She is indeed My *Queen*."

He slumped. Unbreathing. Dead. I had killed him.

I had killed my friend.

Koun took my shoulders and drew me away, holding me, my back against his chest. Gently. Almost tenderly.

I sobbed, though the sound was more growl than tears.

I had killed my—

Four humans knelt near Grégoire. One cut her wrist and waved it under Grégoire's nose. His tongue came out and he licked the wrist. His eyes blinked. He vamped out, jaw opening like a snake. Fangs clicked down. Blondie looked like a wounded rabid beast, eyes bloody-red and black. But he didn't attack. Gently he raised an arm and cradled the woman's head. He bit into her throat. Sucked. They curled together on the floor. She moaned.

I backed away.

I didn't kill him.

Right. He was a vamp.

I couldn't kill him with a heart strike.

Koun had stepped in and prevented the killing, be-heading strike.

I swiveled around in his arms, caught them, pushing

his comfort away an arm's length. "Bruiser?" The word was a coarse whisper.

"Truly, My Queen. He is well. Deaf for a bit yet. But well. Two others are more damaged but will also be fine. And Eli is unharmed. Florence is a treasure."

I closed my eyes. My arms, which were holding him away, dropped slowly to my sides. I took a breath and my knees began to buckle. My forehead landed on his chest. I sobbed once more, letting Koun's clean crisp scent fill me, over the smell of the blood. So much blood.

Koun's hand stroked my head, down my hair, along my back. "All is well, My Queen. And you have now come into the fullness of the Dark Queen's power."

I tried to speak and had to clear my throat. "What?"

"Part of every Dark Queen's power is for war," Koun said. "You fought. You defeated your own warlord in battle."

I let the residual fear dissolve. "Well. That was . . . kinda sucky."

Koun laughed, his chest vibrating beneath my forehead.

Over the loudspeakers, Alex said, "And that, folks, has been recorded and at the proper time, this video can be sent to our enemies. The Dark Queen has come into her full powers of war."

I lifted my head and stepped back. To Koun's side, I saw Leo, standing quietly, watching Grégoire as his former lover fed and healed. The outclan priest took a step toward Grégoire. Another. Slowly, he crossed the floor, as the vamps in the gym went silent again. Blondie was turned away from me, away from Leo, and I heard the former MOC murmur something to the humans Grégoire cradled.

Grégoire's head canted up, then tilted to the side, that birdlike motion they have, and then twisted his head on his neck, too far for a human. He saw Leo.

If I hadn't known for certain that sunlight burned vamps to ashes, I'd have sworn the sun dawned on Grégoire's face. Faster than human, he stood. Bloody. Healed. He took a step that matched Leo's. Walked, in step with his former lover, until they met in the center of the gym. Standing, not speaking, eyes locked. There was the faintest smile on Grégoire's face.

Leo took Blondie's hand. They embraced. And then they just vanished. Popping away with the sound of displaced air. Faster than the eye could follow.

"Ummm," I said, thinking that my rooms had once been Leo's. Were they about to do the big nasty on what was now my bed?

Reading my mind, or my expression, Koun said, "The visiting Mithran guests have been given rooms at both HQ and the Yellowrock Clan Home, My Queen."

"Okay. Good."

I dropped to my backside on the gym floor. My body ached. I was bleeding from several lacerations. Maybe more than just several. I smelled my blood and sweat. My crown was hot, nearly burning.

Blood pooled beneath me. Spreading. "Oops," I whispered, suddenly feeling pain everywhere.

Koun knelt beside me. Ripped his wrist. Held it to me. Panic in his eyes. "Drink," he commanded, no longer calm.

"Nah," I said, feeling a familiar sensation in my chest. Heat and cold. Pain and pleasure. Skinwalker power. "I got a better idea." I pulled on my *between*. Gray and silver energies left me in a whoosh of power. Black motes spun up and into the air. Into my crown. Back into me.

Koun fell back, shock on his face as my magic brushed across him.

Pain cut across my spine. The crown grew more heated. My scalp scorched. I shifted.

CHAPTER 20

Could It Be the Tabitha?

When I came to myself, I was in a different half-form, sitting on the floor of the gym, my back against the wall. Someone was patting my face. Human skin to my human skin. Slapping it. Hard. I grabbed the hands.

Small hands.

"Wake up, Ant Jane. You got to save Miss Soledad and Miss Lachish. They're in danger. Wake up. Wake up. *Son of witch*, wake up!"

My eyes were glued shut, lids heavy, but I got them open. Angie Baby was kneeling in my lap, her hands on mine. She was wearing a peach-colored nightgown and her hair was in a mussed ponytail, strands sticking out everywhere. Her bony knees pressed into my very bloody lap, my blood all over her nightgown. Molly would kill me. And then her words penetrated. Angie had used witch cussing. "What?" I asked.

"I was in the betweens. Not like you and Beast, but *my* betweens. You have to save Miss Soledad and Miss Lachish. They're gonna be in danger."

The betweens . . . magical energy was—

"Ant Jane!" She pulled her hands free and slapped me again.

I jerked my head back, banging it on the gym wall. "Okay. Lachish and Soledad." Lachish was in the null prison, here in NOLA. Soledad was in the estate house and it was heck and gone from here. "How do you know Soledad?"

"We talk all the time. In the betweens. It's gonna happen soon." Angie wrapped her arms around my neck and hugged me tightly.

I looked at Koun, who had the weirdest look on his face. Soft and . . . sweet. It freaked me out. "Get Alex to warn Lachish and the new security team at the null prison and at the estate where Soledad stays. Full alert. No mercy. Then send them all reinforcements."

"Yes, My Queen."

I pushed up from the floor, taking Angie with me. There were vamps everywhere. Staring at me. The memory slammed back into my head. *Grégoire.* Holy crap. I had tried to kill Grégoire. And he had let me try. I looked back at the floor and the place where I had fallen. There was blood. Like, a lot of blood. It was smeared along the floor to the wall where I had been sitting, showing that someone had dragged their queen to the side. Grégoire had hurt me. Bad. Maybe mortally. On purpose. He had goaded me into . . . into fighting with all I had and all I was. And he had killed me. To make me use my combined powers to shift. I had shifted and healed. *Holy crap on crackers with toe jam.*

He knew I had already been drawing on my Dark Queen magic and my skinwalker magic when I was fighting. He had recognized that I was using the merged magics together, as one weapon, one tool. And he had killed me. On purpose?

No. I remembered the death strike. I had expected it to be from the left and it had come from the right. I had turned into the cut and it had sliced through my side, at the bottom of my rib cage, all the way to my midline. A death strike I should have blocked.

Using all my magics together, I had shifted like I used to.

I touched *le breloque*. It was still hot. My scalp and forehead were blistered.

My eyes swept the room, finding my warlord, Leo, and Edmund gone.

Carrying my goddaughter—who weighed a ton—I headed for the gym doors, Koun on my heels. The doors were opened by my security team, vamps moving fast, eyes lowered, deference in their stances.

Holy crap. They were scared of me. As if I really did beat Grégoire, the best swordsman on two continents. I thought back to the fight.

"Well. Dang," I muttered. I actually did.

I strode through the halls of HQ and to the rooms set aside for the witches in an increasingly crowded building. A very bloody Angie on my shoulder, I tapped on the door and Molly answered, still half asleep.

"She's not hurt," I said as Molly came awake fast.

"Son of a witch on a switch. How'd she get by me this time?"

"Beats me," I said, "but when she starts dating, you are screwed."

Molly took her daughter and glared at her. "I'll end up a gramma by the time she's fifteen and Big Evan will be in jail for killing the father."

"Angie, tell your mother what you told me."

Angie looked down, her lips pressed tight. Molly shook her, very slightly. "Angie?"

Angelina heaved a deep breath. "Fine. Miss Lachish and Miss Soledad are about to be in trouble and Ant Jane has to save them."

Molly closed her eyes and enfolded Angie against her. She met my gaze and murmured the word, "Seer?" She was asking if her daughter was growing into a prophet.

I said, "We are what we are, Molly. All of us. It's controlling the darkness and the light that makes us saints or devils. And, as to her warning, Alex already sent out teams and alerts."

Molly closed the door.

"My Master," a gentle voice said. I looked down and into the eyes of Edmund, the Emperor of Europe and my primo.

Crap. I threw my arms around him, half-form strong. He grunted.

The coronation was tomorrow night. Or the one after. My days were all mixed up. But now I knew why the halls were so crowded—visiting vamps were safer here than any place in the city. So my clan home, while fully prepped for company, was home to Santiago and not many others. My mouth formed the word *Ed*, but no sound emerged.

Edmund was here. And I hadn't killed Grégoire. And I had shifted when Blondie killed me. No one had died in Barataria. Bruiser was coming home to me. All was right with the world, or would be when Mainet was dead.

I squeezed him tighter. His breath wheezed out. A smile claimed my cat-faced features, though it probably looked alarming instead of happy.

Ed hugged me back.

I wasn't a hugger. I was pretty sure I had never hugged Ed. He was slight against my bigger mass. He was cold to the touch, so he hadn't fed. And he was still mine. I felt the bond I had accidently created. He was my primo for real. Hugging him was like magnets clicking together. I felt more whole than I had in a long time. And I didn't have time to think about that just now. I stepped slowly back and he mimicked my backward step until we were an arm's length apart. "I got you bloody. Sorry."

Behind me, the door to Molly's room was yanked open. Moll stuck her head out. "The null prison is being attacked right now. It's holding, but not for long. Can you escort us?"

"Yes," I said.

Chaos erupted.

Three blocks out from the null prison, the place where all this started, the SUVs—and a new, bigger transport-van-style vehicle—were parked. The vamp and human team, led by Eli, spread silently into the dead foliage, visible on the tactical map on the screens, audible over the SUV's speakers and earbuds. Twelve of our finest. And I was here, this time, because that was what a warrior shape-shifting queen did, show up to a battle looking like a blood-soaked monster.

In our oversized, parked vehicle sat Molly and Evan Trueblood, with Liz and Cia Everhart and Koun squished into a bench seat behind them. Quint was in the driver's seat, and I was riding shotgun, twisted in my seat so I could see the other passengers, my screens, and the street just by moving my head. The vehicle was totally tricked out and the screens were amazing.

We were staying out of the way as the crack teams in-fil'ed to do their jobs.

Quint eased our vehicle closer behind the one in front, giving us more protection from the scene several blocks down the street. We didn't have to be close. We had over-head drones, vest cams, and screens and speakers on every row of seats in the SUVs, allowing us to watch every-thing here and also at the house where Soledad and Mal-ita were being rescued. The plan was to bring everyone safely to HQ. But Eli couldn't run two ops at once, and the one at the estate was being handled by the leader on scene.

"Two attacks at one time," Koun said, his eyes watch-ing the street around us and keeping in contact with the two guards near our vehicle. "Everything we have seen before was stage-setting and emplacement of resources. Tonight, I wager, the Heir is starting the main thrust of his plan to take over the city and you. And he may think you were weakened by the explosion in Barataria."

"Yeah. I got that," I said. "Imma behead the lil' sucker."

Koun smiled placidly. "Of course you are, My Queen."

The Everharts and Truebloods leaned forward, heads together to get a clearer view of the screens. We all were also watching the action in the middle of the street. What-ever they saw on their screen had Molly sticking her head out the window for a more personal view, her red hair caught in a whipping breeze I had hardly noticed. "Son of a death witch," Molly whispered. Big Evan grabbed her hand in a warning gesture. That wasn't something they ever said. Not since Molly's death magics had appeared. But I could tell she and Evan had cast a working that let them see the energies being used in the street ahead, so there must be evidence of death magics.

The same three gramma witches—Ursula, Fiona, and Endora—were in the same circle, which the Everharts had hoped was closed, but they weren't alone long. As we watched, inside the circle with them appeared Butterfly Lily and Feather Storm and Sabina—which meant Grand-mother in her guise of the outclan priestess.

Koun swiveled his head and looked at me. My closest guards knew what had happened to the priestess, but we hadn't told everyone. Into my mic, I said, "Yellowrock here. The woman who looks like Sabina is not. That woman stole Sabina's flesh and wears it like a shape-changer. On my honor, that is not your priestess."

"Check your thermal imaging," Eli said. "She reads human. She isn't Mithran."

"Copy that," Kojo said from the null house's backyard.

"It's possible that she can change into others," Eli said. "Trust no shape."

Someone said something in a language I didn't know. Others of the guard muttered. A non-vamp had imper-sonated one of them, and I had a feeling they thought it was a witch, which could ignite the centuries long distrust between the races.

"She isn't a witch either," I said. "She's *other*."

The reaction among the vamps was odd, the sound of air as they breathed into their mics for no physical reason.

"What are they doing?" Thema asked, over comms. "It looks like magics."

"It is," I said. The witches were waving their arms in circles, twirling ugly green and orange energies tighter and tighter. I'd seen this before. The magics were tinged black at the edges, the black of a cave at midnight, the black of burned and smoking hell. This was death magic on steroids. Death magic tinged with demon power.

The Glob, forgotten in its padded pocket, heated through the padding. Hot. Too hot.

Molly leaned to me, her knuckles resting against my

pelted jaw, and steadied my mic with her hand, pulling it to her mouth, saying, "Molly Everhart Trueblood speaking. We cast a *seeing* working. It's death magics and a lot more than that. That's what death at the hands of a demon looks like. And since you vamps are dead, just the touch of that magic could destroy you."

"Fangheads, fall back," Eli said. "Cover the queen."

The witches threw the augmented death magics at the prison wards. A boom rocked the air. The dead trees and shrubs shook, brown desiccated leaves falling.

"Retreat, retreat, retreat," Koun said. "Fall back!"

The vamps on the monitor screens didn't move, not so much as a twitch. They were paralyzed. Or maybe more dead than undead. Couldn't think about that possibility just now. Koun reached for the door handle.

I practically leaped to the back of the Suburban and grabbed his shoulder, digging in with my claws. "No. You will stay with your queen." His shoulder twitched away but he remained in the car as I crawled back to my seat. "Eli, get our vamps to safety. The witch prison is on its own."

"Roger that, ma'am. On tactical screens." To his teams, Eli said, "Human units. Two-man teams, one to cover, one to stake the vamps. Do not—repeat—do *not* get close to their faces or fangs. Use all caution. Wood stake in the belly, grab, and drag them to cover. These are not sleeping beauties. Move, move, move."

On the tac screen, the vamps were dragged back as fast as our humans could run. On the overhead drone video screen, I studied the six witches in the circle. Butterfly Lily and Feather Storm were slumped in a tangled heap, looking far less perky than the last time I saw them. Sabina/Gramma was standing unmoving but not vampstill. She hadn't mastered the vamp ability to not breathe, and her human self still felt the fear of not drawing in air. Her long robes moved slightly with each breath and as she shifted her feet for better balance. I hadn't loved Sabina. But no one deserved to be eaten alive piece by piece.

Sabina is inside Jane's ancient family woman? Beast asked. *Same way Jane is inside Beast?*

Actually, Beast is inside Jane, but whatever.

I got a sensation of Beast turning away, cat insulted.

I glanced at the single screen dedicated to Soledad and Malita's house. The team was approaching the estate house, but they were there and I was here and they had no witch to help. The estate team would have to take care of things themselves. I swept that view to the top of the screen and out of the way.

On the center large screen, the three witches twirled up a second death magic ball, whirled demon energies into it, power I could see coming through the portal. Threw the ball of power. Another boom shook the air, rocked the armored van, and singed along my pelt.

Liz said, "Death magics and demon energy confirmed. They have a demon at least partially under their control. Evidence sent to the witch council of the U.S."

Big Evan's hand clenched on Molly's arm. "Moll?"

"Jane," Molly said. Her tone was full of warning. Her hand on my jaw had gone cold. In my Beast-vision, a mist of darkness puffed out of her mouth with her breath, slid along her body, a coat of smut across her energies. Whatever the witches were doing, it was doing more than just raising the hairs of my pelt. It was attracting Molly's own secret death magics, the energies that would get her killed if others knew about them.

"I've just received a notification signed by the entire witch council of the U.S. A death sentence has been issued for the three witches," Liz said softly, staring at her cell. "It was ready and waiting, apparently after the reports of the previous attack." She took a breath that sounded rough and painful. "Kill on sight." She opened her door. "I'm going in."

Cia opened the door on the other side of the vehicle and stepped into the street.

Molly lifted a hand as if to follow, but her energies were wrong. Very wrong.

"Evan?" I said, a warning. He wrapped his arms around his wife, holding her in place.

I covered my mic and said to Quint, "Get us out of here." Quint gunned the motor and whirled the wheel, circling the twins and putting on a burst of speed. Evan

started to sing, just the notes, no words, a soft and soothing melody.

"Evan, who takes point with the witches?" I asked.

"Liz," the big man sang in the midst of the song.

Into the mic I said, "Eli. Evan says Liz has witch-
point."

There was the faintest of hesitations as Eli processed
that he'd be working with his girlfriend fighting death
magic and demon power. She would be in danger. And
they did not have sufficient witch backup or any reliable
vamp backup. "Roger that."

I watched Molly's own death magics roil and shimmer
across her flesh as we zigzagged through traffic on St.
Charles Avenue, a sole oversized van with two witches, a
tattoed vamp, a skinwalker, and a sociopath driving like
a bat outta hell. And Evan sang, lots of minor notes.

If Molly released and used her death magic, she would
be sentenced the same way as the witches in the circle.
And possibly her children would be taken out too, in case
they carried a gene that allowed them to draw the life out
of living things. Death magics were considered dangerous
to the life of the very Earth itself. There would be no
quarter given.

On the vehicle's tac screen, back at the prison, the
vamps showed in low light from the RVAC cameras. They
had been stacked like cordwood between two SUVs. The
humans and witches had spread out, Liz near Eli, Cia to
the side, in the street, where the moonlight would hit her
full on, amplifying her moon magics. Carmen—when had
Carmen gotten there?—stood in the shadows of an alley
across the way.

"Sabina was the best of the outclan," Koun said quietly as Quint took a hard right. "She was the keeper of
many secrets. She was wise and full of the goodness of
the earth. She spent many years seeking redemption
for all of us, even such pagans as myself." A trace of a
smile softened his mouth as he spoke. "She searched for
our souls, for what happened to them when we died our
first death, and for what happens to us when we die true
dead."

I thought she also searched for and collected a lot of magical amulets that were still in my closet and in the weapons room at the freebie house. If Sabina was still conscious inside Gramma the way Beast was in me, then Sabina knew about the talismans. Most of them I had no idea how to use. Sabina had wanted them all and Gramma would have no shame in killing us all to take them from me.

Molly's cell rang and she took a cleansing breath before she lifted the phone. Her death magics, while still close to the surface, were under control, not trying to erupt like a volcano out of her flesh. Evan's voice trailed away. "Lachish," Moll said, instead of hello. "I'm sorry. We had to pull back. The death magics took out half of our team and were attacking us too. We left a human team and my sisters there, but I doubt they can stop the attacking witches throwing death magics and demon power. And once the death magics stop, enemy vamps will likely attack, moving too fast for the human team to provide much protection. You're on your own."

A massive boom sounded over comms. The neighborhoods behind us went dark, block after block losing power, spreading out and around. Electrical transformers exploded everywhere. Booms sounded and lightning shot into the sky here and there.

Molly relayed Lachish's words, "The wards are down." There was a burst of white noise on comms and on the cell. Moll stared at the screen, her fingers swiping once. "Call dropped."

On the RVAC and tac screens, we watched as Butterfly and Feather and Sabina disappeared through the transport circle in a flare of delicate magics like sparklers. The enemy humans rushed the prison. Enemy vamps came through the witch circle in groups of three. Our human team fired at the vamps as they appeared but were human-slow and didn't stop any of them. One shooter targeted Ursula, Fiona, and Endora, but their death magic wards held. At blurred vamp speed, the enemy vamps rushed the house.

The overhead drone moved lower and hard to the left

until we could see the prison on its cameras. Vamps on the lowlight screen disappeared inside the null prison. Enemy humans turned their weapons away from the null prison and our people, firing at the houses around them.

"They're shooting at the neighbors' homes," I said.

"Full retreat," Eli said. "Pull back. Pull back. Deliberate attacks on civilians. Pull back. Pull back."

Everything we had done and . . . this. Attacks on civilians. And my enemies get the Heart of Darkness after all because I'd brought it back to the prison. For freaking safekeeping.

If heart had been at Jane and Beast den, attack would have been there, Beast thought. *Would have been worse. Much deaths.*

I blew out a breath. She was right.

On the screen our people raced back to the SUVs and tossed staked vamps into the vehicles. They pulled back several blocks. Alex informed me that, from his hospital bed, Bruiser called the cops, the governor, and the mayor. SWAT was called out. Sirens split the air. Blue lights came from everywhere, passing us, heading to the blacked-out neighborhoods and death magics.

From a neighbor's house, return fire could be heard. Cop cars pulled up and the cops fired at Ursula, Fiona, and Endora in the street. The enemy attackers drew back from the null prison.

Over comms, Alex said, "EMS and police are on site. The new PsyLED guy, Special Agent Roberto Jimenez, is on site, taking reports, pissing off the local cops, and ignoring our people. He's a real piece of work. Meanwhile, there are injured humans in the neighborhood."

Bitterly, I said, "They knew we would keep fighting unless civilians were threatened or harmed. So they shot into homes in my city. Hoping to hit humans. On purpose."

The RVAC was maneuvered closer to the prison. On screen a vamp popped into sight. A woman with dark and gray hair was draped over his shoulder in a fireman's carry, limp. Lachish.

A vamp appeared beside him, a box under his arm. The heartbox.

They got what they came for.

And if the heartbox had been at the freebie house, we'd possibly be dead. Angie had seen . . . something horrible. Bad enough to make her tell me to give the box back. Something worse than what was happening here. I had to believe that. But the decision had been mine to make. I hadn't expected them to return here. I had expected the Everhart wards to hold and they hadn't. The results and the deaths were also on my shoulders.

Jane cannot stop enemies from taking heart. No matter what Jane does. When kit Angie Baby came to this place, all futures changed.

And how do you know that? I asked. She didn't answer.

The ward around the witch circle fell. The vamp carrying Lachish stepped in and disappeared. Then the vamp with the heartbox.

The cops were still firing. Endora threw a ball of scarlet energies at the cops and one dropped into the street. Out cold or dead. It wasn't death magics but . . .

The cops stopped firing. Dragging the injured cop, the others withdrew into better cover.

In rapid succession the enemy vamps and humans walked through the circle and disappeared. In seconds the witches vanished through the circle.

"Human members of Team Koppa, disarm," Eli said, battlefield-cold voice, "fast. Assist emergency services to triage the neighborhood. Team Delta, see if you can unstake the fangheads without getting your throats ripped out. Alex, we'll need blood donors."

"Copy that. On the way from Yellowrock Clan Home and Arceneau Clan Home."

Molly and Evan discussed something that was half whispered comments and half pointed looks.

"Jane," Alex said over the speakers. "We got action at Soledad and Malita's. And problems. Switching comms frequency and adding video."

The RVAC views of the prison disappeared. On the screen, I saw the estate house, the windows shattered, the front door hanging open, bright light spilling out in rectangles, forming obtuse angles on the lawn.

Over comms I heard, "Mithran team leader, Jaymie here. First on scene was a two-person team, Howard Cornith, vamp, and Emilie Showell, human. They had orders to not engage the enemy, but it appears that they did not follow orders. They did not activate their vest cams and we have no idea what happened. Both were discovered lying on the lawn, incapacitated, the human unconscious but unbloodied. The Mithran does not appear to be true dead. From inside, and from the lawn, I smell a butt-load of blood, both human and Mithran. There's also a rank stench of burned things, like the smell of burned flesh."

Jaymie was likely a female vamp, young enough to have a modern American accent, so no older than a hundred. Not someone I knew by voice alone.

"There are dead in the house," another vamp said. "I smell the dead. Our kind. Bloodied and burned. I have smelled this before, long ago."

"Jaymie, this is your queen. Do not approach," I said. "Maintain positions."

"Yes, ma'am, My Queen."

"Is there a witch circle in yard, the lawn turned up?" Molly asked.

"Affirmative," Jaymie said.

"Jaymie, keep your people clear of the circle," Big Evan said. "Give us video of the grounds and the house."

"Roger that," Jaymie said.

We watched as cameras and vest cams gave us access to the yard. There were bodies in the yard, hacked, bloodied, and dead. There were also two scorched places in the front yard without bodies.

"This is evidence of Mithran burnings," the older vamp said, his voice cold and hard.

Eli joined the discussion from back at the prison. "I placed security cameras in the house at the estate and also one in a tree. The one in the tree is solar-powered and can be downloaded. Someone can climb up and retrieve it, My Queen."

"Evan? Molly? Is it safe?"

"I think so," Moll said. "Yes."

"Move in. Get the memory card."

Jaymie's vest cam showed her trot into the yard, leap high, grab a branch, and pull herself up. Our team slowly jogged toward the house and their vest cameras gave us views of the inside of the house. Blood was everywhere. On the walls, on the floors, on the ceiling in a bright spray. The house had been ransacked.

Had I led the invading vamps to the old vamps when I visited? Had I killed them? I clenched my jaw against the rising guilt.

"No bodies inside," Jaymie said. "Will begin the process of gathering all papers and prepare the site for human law enforcement."

"I'll download and scan all the camera footage," Alex said, "and will prepare a downloadable file for the local law."

"We have to go back to the null prison," Molly said to me. "We thought all the circles had been successfully closed. Now we have two back open. We need to toss something into one and see if it disappears and reappears at this other circle."

"Or at the circle at the church, or the circle at the airport, or the estate," Alex said. "Or maybe the one in Barataria. They may all still be open. I can send three-man teams to each location."

Eli said, "This time, why don't we throw a few frags into them first. Maybe some C4 explosives. That'll shut them down."

Big Evan said, "If the circle at the Barataria house was shut down by the explosives there, then we know that works. Or, we might transport the explosives into a kids' school and blow it up. We don't how they work or how many there are."

Eli cursed.

Molly said. "We've been brainstorming ideas to test the circles. We can toss in leaves or something that might be nearby the circles. If the leaves appear at another circle, that might tell us something. We'll need a witch and communications with each team."

"Or the things we toss in might not appear anywhere," Evan said.

"In which case that might mean they have a hub somewhere," Alex said, over the speakers, "and they go back and forth through a central hub circle."

"Yeeees," Molly said, her eyes focused far away. "Six sites. Or if Barataria is really down, five sites. A central hub. Like a pentagram."

"Lemme check the GPS on a map," Alex said.

Quint's driving smoothed out. She slowed to the speed limit as she wove through the French Quarter's one-way streets. There was no festival this week, and there was less traffic than normal.

"It isn't perfect," Alex said, "but the locations we have so far do resemble a five-pointed star, with the null house falling vaguely in the center, but not absolutely in the center."

"It has to be in the center, exactly, or . . . Hmmm. Right. Of course," Moll murmured.

"Like a hub worm hole," Alex posited.

"Yes. That would fly," Molly said, her tone as distant as her gaze. "The physics alone would be incredible. The opposing team *has* to have a world-class physicist witch on board." She and Evan again exchanged a pointed look, followed by Molly's small head shake. It was a communication I couldn't decipher.

"If the circles are all active again," Evan said, "we need to find a way to close them down before someone ends up dead."

"Like dumping a truckload of cement into the holes at each site at the same time?" I asked.

Evan looked surprised. "That might work, actually. If they have a remote *deactivation* working in place, they still would have to initiate them, one by one, to stop the transport and with all of them transporting at one time, they could be overwhelmed. And concrete is unlikely to kill people if it went somewhere unexpected."

"Okay," I said. "We'll get out at the house and guards

will escort you where you need to go to test the circles. Alex, get small teams ready and to the other sites. We'll need a witch at each site if possible."

Molly asked her husband, "Could it be the Tabitha?"

"She's a myth," he said, his tone doubtful, as though he didn't quite believe his own words. To me he added, "Tabitha is a witch myth. A double-gened witch prodigy, with the power and the math ability to make most any working or curse fly."

"But Tabitha?" I asked. "Like the TV show witch?" Like Endora, whose name I had pulled out of a TV witch hat. Sorta.

"Tabitha was only a rumor. A falsehood. Like the misrepresentation of witches on TV," Evan said.

Except his own daughter had the raw power to, maybe, force a working as intricate and far-flung as the five- or six-pointed star, pentagram, circle transport working. His anxiety ratcheted up. I could smell it in his sweat.

"Alex. Get someone to check on Angie and the other kids at HQ," I said.

"She has eyes on her. The kids are all asleep and well-guarded. Oh, and if you're worried about their safety, there are two vamps and Deon in the suite with them, and Deon's armed with a filleting knife and a cast iron frying pan."

Molly laughed softly and closed her eyes. "That's an image I can appreciate." Evan put an arm around her shoulders and pulled her to him.

We stopped at the Queen's Personal Residence in New Orleans and Koun, Quint, and I got out. Guards took our places. The Truebloods pulled out back toward the prison. Back and forth. Back and forth. They needed a witch transport circle . . .

Could that be part of the reason for them to go back to the prison? To research? Stupid question. Of course it was. If I was a betting person, I'd bet the Everharts would have a transport circle of their own soon.

"Problem," Alex said into my comms. "Angie's awake and screaming for Aunt Jane."

"Have Deon call me," I said, "and give her the cell."

My cell buzzed, and on the screen was Angie's pic. "Angie? It's Aunt Jane."

"Ant Jane! Help!" We were on FaceTime and Angie was crying, terrified.

Every childhood horror film I had ever watched rushed back to the surface and my body clenched. "I'm here," I said.

"The vampire lady who owned the cross is in trouble."

The vampire lady who owned the cross was supposedly dead, burned at the estate house. Except that there hadn't even been a scorched piece of jewelry left at the burn sites. So the burned places could have been a distraction and a ruse for taking the old women and making us think they were dead instead. "Do you know where she is?"

"No. They took her. They hurt her." She was crying, huge broken sobs.

"How do you know—" A horrifying thought occurred to me. "Angie Baby? Were you inside the vampire's head when she was taken?"

"Yes. Yes." Angie broke down.

I turned to Koun. "Double the guards on the kids. Get us a new vehicle. I'm getting my doodads and then we're heading back to the prison house too."

"Doodads?"

I raced inside and yelled back, "My magical crap!" The door opened beneath my hand and I bumped hard into Bruiser. Threw my arms around him and kissed him soundly on the lips, holding him too tight, as fear I hadn't acknowledged dissipated. "You're home! They wouldn't let me visit you in the hospital because of stupid security rules. You okay?"

"I am now, my darling love." He kissed me back, softer.

When the kiss broke, I said, "We have trouble, sweetcheeks."

"When do we not?"

"Grab your armor and guns. You can change on the ride over."

Bruiser yanked armor out of the closet. I threw my bloody cloths into the corner, armored fast, and grabbed a bunch of my magical doodads, including the ones made with arcenciel blood, a couple amulets, a coyote earring I didn't remember getting but that always seemed to be with my magical stuff, and the broken stone I had taken off Gramma when she was first revealed as *u'tlun'ta*. I had no idea what to bring with me, so more was better.

CHAPTER 21

It's Not Fair and I Don't Care

Except for at the estate house—which was too far away to get to in time—at each of the circles was a witch and a security team to back up the witch. Each team included a trusted vamp and human. Each witch had a natural object ready to throw into the witch circle. In the mountains we might have used rocks, but rocks were not part of the landscape. Here, in Louisiana, shells were used for paving driveways and walkways, and sticks and blooming flowers could be found most any place, even in fall.

Liz was at the church with Eli, Tex with his dogs, and two other human team members.

Cia, Liz's twin, was in Barataria, inside the house where the witch circle was located, where the floor used to be and the bomb had gone off. Kojo and Lorraine, one of Grégoire's scions, and three human guards were with her. They had to step across the police tape from the ATF investigation, but as there was no police presence, they decided a little crime scene disturbance was acceptable under the circumstances.

Carmen was at the airport across Lake Ponchartrain. Thema and a team of four were with her.

There was no witch at the estate, but Jaymie seemed capable and willing to follow the witches' orders. Paranormal group cooperation was still happening, which gave me a sense of accomplishment even though I had no idea if the change was in response to my reign or a result of the witch-vamp attack against us. Probably both.

The Truebloods and my strongest team were standing in the street with me at the null house. The previous team of vamps had all recovered and were providing cover from farther back. The human team was still on-site and were wanting payback for losing to the enemy vamps earlier. So in addition to the extra guards posted up and down the street, our team consisted of Koun, Quint, Bruiser (who was mostly healed, though he moved slowly and with great care, as if he still hurt), two other vamp guards, six humans, and me, along with the unexpected addition of Grégoire and Edmund, now that peace had descended on Europe. My primo (the Emperor of Europe) and Blondie (my warlord) hadn't fought any duels or battles in weeks. Well, with the exception of me sorta nearly killing Grégoire. And that battle had seemed more like mild entertainment since it hadn't ended in a beheading. I thought they might be bored.

I was tripping over my protective detail. If we were attacked, I would as likely die from being trampled by my own people as from enemy weapons. Of course, I had magical weapons on me, so there was that.

Grégoire was downwind, thank goodness. He had elected to not clean his armor between battles, allowing the blood-stench to build up. It was an effective warning to vamps that he always killed his opponents, but the smell was awful to my cat-snout.

Edmund, standing upwind of him, at my side, was wearing a metallic silvery armor with sterling silver bits on it, to show his power and his more muscular physique. Building muscles was hard for the undead, especially Mithrans, and indicated he had drunk from the conquered and drunk well, without having to track down humans as prey. Ed was all glittery and drew the eyes. He'd also had his hair styled and his vamp-claws manicured and painted black. I hadn't noticed until now but my once ordinary-looking primo was pretty hot.

The night was chill, a stiff north breeze blowing rare early-season polar forces at us. Our armor did a surprisingly good job of cutting the wind, but it was still cold. Quint, her face pinched with chill, was sneaking glances at Koun in his black-and-blue-tattoo-painted armor. Koun was all vampy stoic. He did make quite the example of vamp-hood in all his Celtic glory. Of us all, only the witches were not wearing armor. Humans and witches were all wearing winter fleece, but even with winter clothes from the mountains, Molly was shivering.

Softly, Big Evan said, "I can whistle up some warmer air."

Molly frowned, glancing around, still afraid for her hubs to be outed for all the world to see as one of the rare male witches. "I'd rather shiver," she said.

The big man pulled her close, his red beard fluffing out on top of her red hair like a hairy hat. They looked like a totem. A thing of love and power and family identity.

Into my specially constructed earbuds, Eli said, "Team leaders, check in."

Each security team leader stated that they were ready. Koun gestured everyone back except the witches.

"Jane." Molly jerked her head to the right several times. "Brute and a grindy showed up."

"Okay," I said, my voice tight, following her eyes to see the werewolf at the edge of a dead lawn. That meant this location was likely to be the site of trouble. The presence of the grindy usually meant werewolf trouble, even Brute-type werewolf trouble.

"We have this well in hand, my Queen," Koun said. "Your friends and scions are safe with us. And unlike the other groups, we have backup." He gestured to the two cop cars parked down the street.

The police had moved the public and media back, probably the result of the last time we needed backup and the enemies of the city shot the place up.

"Members of local law enforcement are here for assistance," Koun said. "The media have, several times in the last few days, accused NOPD, New Orleans' duly elected mayor, and various new police chiefs and mayors in the surrounding cities, of refusing to provide police protection for the populace. However, your Koppa team is here for you, and only you, My Queen."

I chuffed softly and pulled the formal words to me. "I trust you with my life, my dear and trusted friend."

Gently, Koun said, "Thank you, my lady."

"The injured humans." I gestured to the surrounding houses, the ones shot up before. "Are the residents okay?"

"Your Mithrans provided healing and care to all, your humans will repair their homes, and your legal team is in negotiations with the most litigious for a settlement. We have moved the closest humans into a five-star hotel for tonight." The last was said with a trace of irony.

"This is costing a lot, then."

"Yes, My Queen. When you win against Mainet Pellissier, the Heir, his estate will be served with an accounting and it will be paid."

I looked over at Edmund in his fancy armor and Grégoire in his blood-coated duds. "They made a killing, didn't they? I mean besides the actual duels and beheadings. They got rich."

Koun chuckled softly. "Beyond their wildest dreams."

"I had a teacher in high school. She said that war was about one thing and one thing only. False pride and resources. People dolled it up all kinds of ways, with national identity, or being the genetically superior, or history with a whitewash, or even the claim to protect our allies. But false pride and resources are the sole answer for war even if the resources are only money into the hands of the military complex and the pockets of corporate military CEOs. Resources. Always have been. Always will be. We have to protect our resources from attack and the people of this city are the best resource we have. Price doesn't enter into it."

"My Queen is wise beyond her years." He bowed slightly, which was weird. Some of the humans nearby gave us a thumbs-up. The vamps all turned to me . . . and bowed.

"Oh crap." I reached up to my mic as I realized it had been live and everyone had heard me. *Oy* . . .

"Okay, people," Molly said into her mic. "Enough of all this yucky sweetness. Everharts and Jaymie, at your sites. Get up close to the circles. Remember to toss the object, and do not let your skin cross the circle in case it has an automatic defense system set into it. No one wants to lose an arm. On three, throw your shells or sticks into the circle and back up fast. One. Two . . . Three."

Molly tossed a Y-shaped stick into the circle and raced back to Big Evan. Into her mic she said, "Molly here. My stick went through the circle and is gone. Prison circle active."

Each of the others announced the disappearance of the tossed object, and the fact that their circle was active. Even the one that had been blown up in Barataria, so exploding them to hell and back wasn't going to work.

Koun waved us all farther away and took up a shooting stance, his back to the road, his weapon pointing at the circle and the prison beyond it in case he had to fire. And then we waited because we had no idea how long it might take for an object to transport to one of the other sites. Or the hub. If there was one.

But nothing happened.

Minutes ticked by.

Molly said, "Nothing has appeared. Has anyone had anything appear in their circle?"

"Negative," each team leader said.

Big Evan said, "I think that correlates with an irregular pentagram and a central hub. Could it be in downtown NOLA?"

"So their base would be right under our noses all this time," Eli said, disgusted.

"That's been their MO up until now," Alex said. "Maybe for good reason. Maybe a central hub of magic has always been here. I've made contact with every major hotel, B and B, even the RV lots for thirty miles around. Tex and his dogs took walks around the usual hotels, also the hotels in the central area between the five points of the pentagram, to sniff out unknown vamps. No one's spotted them or sniffed them."

"A house in the city?" Koun suggested. "They send their cattle—their humans; forgive me, My Queen—out for supplies and otherwise stay hidden? The Mithrans would have access to the transport system should they have to evacuate."

I gave Koun a closed-mouth cat smile and a slow blink of approval. I hadn't issued a command for the vamps to stop using offensive names for their dinners, but they were taking notice of my speech patterns and changing on their own. "Evacuate equals retreat? That makes sense."

"We have action," Molly said. The pavement in front of the prison house rippled. Big Evan pulled her farther back and she initiated a *hedge of thorns* around them. "Anyone else have rippling in their circles?"

"Negative," Eli said. The others echoed his comment.

A low-pitched hum started, felt under my skin as much as heard.

We all took several more steps away. I reached into my pocket and wrapped my hand around the Glob and its padding.

A flash of blackness shot up through the pavement and ripped across the night. I flew back. Vaguely, I recognized that I landed. Bounced. Then it all went black.

Later, I realized I was awake and staring at the night sky. Blinked into the darkness. Damage to my body made itself known in a wave of heaviness and pain. "Ohhh. That hurt." I had lost some time.

I was at the null prison. We had been attacked.

I curled up to sitting and nearly barfed as the world whirled around drunkenly. My ears were ringing. Over comms, I heard only what might be static. Locally I heard only distant sounds. I blinked debris out of my eyes and looked around. A boom of death magic had knocked me back, onto my butt.

Molly and Evan were okay behind their ward. Koun

was shaking his head, but was standing. Quint was down at my side. Somehow, she had ended up behind me. I was pretty sure I had landed on her. Our people seemed okay. Had we been standing a few feet closer that might not be the case.

There was a body in the circle.

An electric blast of shock zinged through me.

Koun sped to the circle as a human-shaped form rose to its knees and crawled across the pavement.

Female. Bloody. Throat torn out.

It was Soledad. I lurched to my feet. Quint rolled to her knees and tried to stand. Fell over onto her side, retching.

Koun tore his wrist and fed Soledad, even as he half carried her to the dead grass of the narrow prison yard.

"Check in," Eli said, his words tinny in my earbuds.

His voice just as muffled, Alex said, "Soledad came through the circle at the prison. She's hurt. Koun is feeding her. Jane landed on Quint. Both need healing."

The Emperor himself went to Quint, tearing his wrist, feeding her his powerful blood. That was a sign of status I'd have to consider when I had time. If I ever had time again. I looked around. Everyone else was okay. Grégoire stood in the center of the street, two swords drawn, his body language hopeful for a fight.

Except for Soledad and the vamps, there was no activity.

I worked my jaw, trying to pop my ears. Molly was still in their *hedge*, her husband's hands on her shoulders. He was humming a soft tune I could barely hear, similar to the working he had created to keep were-creatures calm when they couldn't shift in the full moon. Air magic. I moved closer. "Molly?"

"All safe, Janie," Evan said, though I read his lips as much as heard his voice. "She's good. Just got a shot of magic as Soledad came through."

Which might have affected her death magics. Within sight of the witches guarding the null prison. *Crap.* Still blinking to clear my eyes, I used Beast's sight and saw the death magics crawl across Moll's skin, the film of smut nearly transparent. "Drop the *hedge*," I said.

Evan, not really sure why I asked, did. *Trust* . . .

Pulling the Glob, holding it with its padded bag, I held it out toward Moll's waist, thinking about the death magics that needed to be taken away. And hoping it didn't damage her earth magics. Instantly the Glob swept up the dark energies, doing its thing, cleaning up excess and dangerous energies.

The Glob spun its own power into a tiny whirlwind of might that stung my skin and burned my eyes, plucking threads of death magic into a tiny storm of power. The Glob yanked all the death energies into a tiny pocket of blackness. A pocket universe that I . . . carried in my pocket. I wanted to laugh, but didn't. I might have sounded nervous or hysterical or something.

Molly heaved a relieved breath and nodded at me, her eyes wide. "Thank you. That worked." She shrugged her shoulders as if testing for a missing weight and smiled. "Much better."

"We're good," I said to Koun.

"My Queen is ready to move," he said into his mic.

"Each team, evac to your prearranged locations," Eli said. "Alex? Did you and Bruiser get it?"

"Affirmative, bro."

"Get what?" I asked.

Koun tapped his mic. Listening ears. Right.

"Never mind."

Molly touched my hand and pointed. "Leo just appeared. That poofy thing vamps do. Did you know he dresses like a priest and wears a gold cross?"

I had an instant image of Leo wearing his outclan priest suit with the gold cross dangling over the white band on his collar. The gold cross, with the three tiny holes.

That might possibly match the nubs on the back of the Jesus focal.

The dead Jesus that had arcenciel blood worked into the gold and had been hidden in the office next to his old one.

"Leo?" I touched the Jesus amulet in my pocket. Knowing he could hear me where he stood, I said, "We need to meet."

He looked at me across the dark and inclined his head.

"The Yellowrock Clan Home is closest," I said. Not the freebie house. The official clan home. "Koun?"

Koun snapped out orders, lifted Soledad over one shoulder, and carried her toward the waiting SUVs. In the rush, Quint and I moved together and somehow were separated from the others. I lost sight of Molly, Evan, Soledad, Koun, and Leo.

Quint tossed me the keys to the SUV she had claimed and said, "Drive." My lady-in-waiting pulled a shotgun and rearranged three semiautomatic handguns as she buckled in. "I'm not able. So I'll ride shotgun. Literally." She laughed. It sounded pained.

"You're still hurt."

"I got a sip from the new emperor. He's tasty. I'll do. You didn't take any blood. Drive."

Bruiser climbed in behind her, his weapons out. He met my eyes in the rearview and smiled. *That* smile. The one that warmed me all over.

The smile that told me whatever we currently faced, we faced together.

I drew up short when I entered the oversized dining room in Yellowrock Clan Home. The room was crowded. In a chair, facing me, was Soledad Martinez. Angie was sitting in her lap, her arms around the ancient vamp's very young-looking neck. How the heck had Angie gotten here from HQ?

Soledad's throat was healed. Her eyes were closed, pale pink tears sliding down her face. At her side, Florence licked her own wrist, closing her wounds where the Infermieri had provided healing blood.

Molly looked pissed. She and Big Evan were sitting to the side, holding hands so tightly Molly's fingertips were blue, as if she were dangling over a precipice and that grip was the only thing keeping her safe. Or the only thing keeping her from casting a death curse at Soledad. Watching her daughter in the lap of the crazy vamp. Or a once-upon-a-time crazy vamp.

Soledad was wearing fresh clothes, a rose-colored dress the old nun would probably never have worn had she been able to access her own things, which were still back at the estate. She looked far more sane than the last time I saw her. Calm. Peaceful. Unbloodied. Had drinking from humans who weren't stoned to the gills on weed over the last weeks possibly given her a clear mind?

Gee DiMercy was standing in the corner, the red flying lizard on his shoulder and a trace of blood on his sleeve. He hadn't been in a battle, so I figured he had helped in some way to heal the old vamp. Had he restored some of her mental stability?

Soledad's hand stroked Angie's hair down her back, a soothing gesture, and she said, "I heard you in my mind, little one. I never lost hope, even when my new humans..." Her voice trailed off and she looked at me. "They killed my people. The humans were sworn to feed and protect me, and I them." Her eyes bled to black as she slowly vamped out. "We will destroy the Heir of the Sons of Darkness and rescue the trapped one."

Trapped one. Hayyel? I stepped closer. The gold Jesus in my pocket heated. A warning? Or a recognition of its previous owner? Because, yeah. The SOD, Joses Santana, had the crucifix made for Soledad. A cross made for a vamp, with the blood of an extraterrestrial creature. It had never made sense.

I stepped around the table until I was standing with my back to the wall and beside Santiago Molina, the journals he had been working on spread before him. His eyes were on Soledad with what looked like joy. I remembered that Soledad had been his patron when they were part of the clan of Ming of Mearkanis. So much history to remember. So many people to protect.

The door opened. The room beyond was packed with humans and vamps. Eli and Liz elbowed their way through, Cia and Carmen on their heels. Leo Pellissier walked into the opening to the dining room, across from me. Brute and the grindylow were at his side. Leo's beautiful face was creased with pain. He seemed to be having problems walking, as if his legs and body pushed against a strong current. His desire to be here was stronger than his compulsion to stay away. The door shut, cutting out the murmur of voices and prying eyes.

Soledad stood, went to Leo, and they embraced, Angie

Baby between them. Angie twisted and transferred an arm to Leo's neck, hugging him into the pile. Molly's hand jerked out as if to grab her daughter away, but Evan cradled her in place. "Let's see what she says," he murmured. "We may learn something about her *betweens*."

"Good. You're together now," Angie said. She pushed Leo back a step and touched his cross. "I found it, just like you said, Uncle Leo. Ant Jane has it." Angie swiveled in Soledad's grip and she looked at me. She gave a four-fingered *come here* gesture.

Feeling Molly's and Evan's heavy scrutiny, I crossed the room again to Angie and the vamps. Leo unlatched the gold chain, removed it from around his neck, dropped the cross in my palm, and released the chain, leaving it dangling and swinging. "If you put it together," he said softly, "it will fortify the life and blood of the Mithran who wears it. It will strengthen his powers." He looked at Soledad. "Or hers, as was intended by Joses, the Son of Darkness, when he trapped and stole the blood of an arcenciel for its making. And the making of the other implements."

Implements made with arcenciel time-hopping blood. I put it together fast and a lance of worry pierced through me. Because there was some missing arcenciel blood—Storm's blood, collected when she was murdered—and I hadn't thought about that in too long.

We needed more privacy than we had. "Everyone out except Molly, Evan, Angie, Leo, Soledad, and Eli. Yes, Quint," I said, before she could object, "you too. Alex, private channel between Koun, Bruiser, and us, encrypted." Meaning only we four could listen in.

"Roger that." I heard a faint clicking in my earbuds as the ambient noise decreased.

"Alex, is anyone in the other room using their cell?" I murmured. "If so, who are they and who are they calling?"

"On it."

"Koun." He looked his question at me. "Don't let anyone leave. Talk to Alex. Anyone who called or texted, separate them, then bleed and read. Fast. Bruiser, we request your assistance," I said in my queenly vernacular.

"If you are willing, we need you to help find the traitor out there."

"Yes, My Queen." Bruiser and Koun left the room together, the Onorio who could bind vamps and my clan chief strategist who, I feared, had few morals except to protect me. The door closed behind them. "Alex, I'm going dark." Together they'd find and stop this traitor. They didn't need me.

"Okay." I glanced at our small group, gathered in the Yellowrock Clan Home. To Soledad, I said, "You had a natural ability to see the future, a sort of prescient gift." Like Angelina. But I didn't say that.

"Not a gift. A curse," Soledad said. "The Son of Darkness demanded the . . . use . . . of me from Amoury when he came on procession to New Orleans. He insisted that I wear the icon to bed at dawn so that it might make my visions stronger." Her face crumpled and Leo put a hand on her upper arm in comfort. "I always saw only dreadful things that might happen, and only for a few moments, but they were one horror layered upon another, like playing cards shuffled together at every sleeping and every waking. I called it the *betweens*, as it always happened between waking and sleeping."

Angie had always called it that too. *Crap.* I was guessing that Angie had been in mind-touch with Soledad for a long time.

"The cross made that ability stronger?" Eli asked.

"The curse of seeing all the futures. *Si*." She propped her chin on Angie's head. "And the terror and death and horror. Only that. With each rising, Joses drank from me, drank deeply, and shared the memories of the visions of the *betweens*. I was forced to relive them all, one by one, to study the horrors. Within a year of wearing the cross, it had burned my flesh into a scar that even blood will not heal." She pulled the collar of the rose dress to the side, revealing a cross-shaped scar. "Even now, the scar burns, every night when I wake, every moment until dawn, it burns as if the Holy Cross is still against my flesh. The scar will burn for all of my undead life."

She looked at me and then away, patting Angie's back

as if to soothe her. Across the room Molly looked like she might Hulk out at any moment, her eyes glaring, and her earth magic barely leashed. She wanted her daughter back. *Now.*

Soledad said, "The visions broke my mind. When Joses disappeared, I took the cross apart and placed one part in the Pellissier tomb and hid the other in Joses's office, where no one would think to look. The pain eased some then, and more when I moved into the estate."

"You hid it right under his nose," I said, amused at her cleverness.

Molly rose from her chair and started around the table. I shook my head at her. Held up one finger, begging silently for one more minute. Moll's eyes flashed but she stopped.

"Except," I said, "all the caskets in the mausoleum were banged around during the fire. And"—I looked at Leo—"Leo found the cross part, found it when they—Sabina?—pulled him from his coffin."

Leo turned away, shoulders hunching against pain. I decided I had been right.

Soledad smiled. "Yes. In the coffin of an unknown and seemingly unimportant true dead Mithran. Where no one would think to look. Later, after she came out of the devoveo and became a clan Blood Master, Ming wanted the icon. I told her Joses had taken it from me, and she believed my words as truth. Her treatment of her scions grew much worse after that. Bad enough that Amoury hid Malita and me away in the country with servants and drugs to give me peace, to keep me calm, the drugs to ease my pain." She touched the burn on her chest.

"That explains a lot," Eli said.

I turned the cross and the gold Jesus over in my hands. Yeah. They'd fit together perfectly. "If we put it back together—" I stopped. If I put it back together, I might be able to see the future again. Maybe time-jump safely. And maybe it would bring the cancer back. Or give me perfect control over my shifting. Or kill me. I stuck the pieces of the focal into different pockets.

The kitchen door opened and Deon entered, carrying

a tray of food, but even underneath the scent of fried meat and peppers, I smelled a lot of vamp blood on the air from the next room.

Bruiser stepped in behind him and said to me, "Your problem has been flushed from his hiding place and dealt with. It required Koun, with my assistance, to find him. Long-Knife has been restrained. What are your orders?"

That was interesting. "Long-Knife was sent to me by Ming of Knoxville. Did she send me a traitor?"

Bruiser's lips curled into a vicious smile. "According to Koun's bleed-and-read, and my own impressions as I read him, no. He was conscripted by Mainet only recently. The bleed-and-read by Mithrans did not discover this, and Thema is disturbed by her ineffectiveness." His lips quirked up on one side. "And that an Onorio was required for success."

Meaning her pride was pricked. *Gotcha.*

His words very British in the moment, Bruiser said, "Long-Knife's job was to slit your throat and behead Leo at the earliest opportunity, while you, quote, 'slept in Leo's bed.' Mainet assumed you were now sleeping with Leo. Our enemy has incorrect data, supplied to him by Leo in a forced read, and by—"

I interrupted, "Leo hid something from his master and gave false info? Go Leo."

Bruiser tilted his head in agreement and went on, "And by a man named Reach."

My head snapped up at that. "Reach?" Reach had been the researcher keeping all vamp data before he was attacked and tortured and disappeared. Alex had taken over Reach's database and improved upon it, but Reach had never been heard from again. "Reach gave someone bad info?"

Which explained Bruiser's vicious smile. "He is a prisoner of the Heir."

Which meant that Reach *deliberately* gave his captor bad info. He could be asking for help. Or leading us into a trap.

"Long-Knife was outside my rooms the night I knocked two vamps' heads together."

"Yes. It seems he was a very frustrated individual, unable to get to you, unable to follow his orders."

"Reach wants to be rescued," I guessed.

"That would be my interpretation of bad intel from that particular source. Or a trap."

I dropped my head in a tiny nod as Deon arranged the tray on the table and put a pot of tea at my elbow. The little man bowed at me and blew me a kiss, which made me grin.

Suddenly, I wasn't hungry. Just tired. Tired of fighting, of intrigue, of the constant conflicts and the layered machinations, tired of what I had become. However, there wasn't time to wallow in useless self-pity, and food was food. I popped a length of andouille sausage into my mouth, chewed, swallowed. To Soledad, I said, "A powerful vamp is invading. He's Leo's master, the maker of his bloodline. He's called the Heir. He wants the crucifix?"

"And the implements I hid when Joses disappeared. And me. And you. And if he discovers what she is, he will want this child." She hugged Angie gently and said, "Thank you, little one. I never gave up hope that your vision of the offerings through a witch circle would become truth. After they took me, I watched so carefully, and when it opened, I threw myself inside and got away, just as you said. You saved me."

"*De nada,*" Angie said. "That's right, isn't it?"

"*Si.* You are a smart little girl. You learn fast."

To me Angie said, "Can I have the cross?"

"No," we all said together.

"But I have a charm bracelet you may have," I said, "if your parents approve. I'll get it to you later."

Angie's eyes went wide. "I saw it in the *betweens.* It's pretty!"

"Cra—" I stopped. "It might be too grown-up for you yet. After you discuss *everything* you saw in the *betweens* with your parents and *only* if they approve."

Angie scowled. "That's not fair."

"You're right. It's not fair and I don't care." I stopped again. A short-term house mother used to say that to me when I was being punished for fighting at school. Her name was Carol Millhouse and she had been a short little thing, about five feet even, with black hair, and when she got mad her eyes squinched into narrow slits like a snake. I made her mad a lot. She wasn't the only house mother who had ever hit me, but Carol had slapped my face, saying, "You're right. It's not fair and I don't care."

CHAPTER 22

Short-Term Goal: Kill Mainet

The memories cascaded down on me, overlapping moments of clarity. First day of class. Standing in the heat, dripping sweat. A kid from the children's home being bullied by three older boys. I hadn't even known the poor kid's name yet, but somewhere deep inside I heard the word *Kit . . .* Moving with purpose, thinking what I could do, was going to do, and the dangerous consequences. And not thinking at all. I put my book bag on the ground. Pushed back my braid. Walked over. "Hey, dumbass," I said to the ringleader. *A white boy,* the thought surfaced. *White men are dangerous.* "You wanna push someone, you push me. Leave the kid alone."

Billy. His name had been Billy.

Billy was kit friend, Beast thought. *I/we protected kit often.*

Dumbass and his pals surrounded me. Gauging me, my skinny self, my golden, non-white skin. Dumbass shoved me, his hands landing on my boobs. He laughed. "I got a feel, guys. Small but firm."

A white man. Touching my mother.

The thought there in a flash and then gone.

I ducked and rammed his belly with my shoulder. Torqued my body. My other fist slammed into his crotch as we went down. With all the momentum of my lunge and every muscle in my body we hit the earth. The other boys piled on. Something inside me broke that day. And something else took over. The crazy voice said, *Roll. Up to paws. Kick. Hit. Roll onto knees. Claw face. Bite.*

A principal pulled me off. The bully with the busted balls was named Otis and he had been the center on the football team. Until the fight, which sent him to a specialist doctor for damage to his boy-parts. Otis and I were sent to the nurse along with Otis's pals, and then we were all sent home, suspended. In my case that meant back to the children's home. Back to Carol.

I hadn't gotten off easy in the fight, defending myself for protecting a kit. I had black eyes and really nasty bruises. Of it all, however, Carol's slap had stung the worst. She had left a few weeks later, after she slapped another girl, one who reported her. "Good riddance," the slapped girl said.

"Good riddance," I whispered.

"Jane?" Bruiser said. He slipped an arm around my waist. "Good riddance to what?"

"Huhn?" I blinked my way back from the past. Bruiser's body felt heated, as if I had been caught up in the winter chill. I leaned into him.

I had no idea what shadowed places inside me that memory had come from. Except for the fact that I was holding the cross and its matching gold Jesus, one in each hand. I placed them carefully on the table and stepped away, my eyes on the gold pieces as if they might bite. "I'm sorry, Angie. I didn't mean that."

"It's okay, Ant Jane. The futures are bad. You have to stop it." Angie looked at her mama. "You and me and Ant Jane need to talk about your bad magics."

Molly froze as still as a vamp on the hunt.

"Your bad magics are part of the sacrifice to take my angel and put him in a dark place full of shadows. I saw you, during one of the *betweens*." Tears gathered in Angie's eyes. "You were all bloody. And you were holding a silver knife." Angie's hand raised, as if holding a blade over her head. Her voice dropped lower. "It was bloody too. And Lachish was dead."

Soledad said softly, "The evil one whose name may not be spoken has not yet been fully bound."

I thought of the demon energies being pulled through the transport circle. The demon might not be bound but he had been called. He was partially here, on Earth.

"The evil one whose name may not be spoken is waiting," Soledad said, "watching, to see if Mainet fulfills his part of the bargain and binds the holy one."

Lachish, stolen by the vamps as a potential, what? Sacrifice? Part of Mainet's arcane bargain? "Soledad," I said. "Who is supposed to have the necklace?"

Leo convulsed and fell to the floor. "Attack," he grunted.

Evan shouted, "Everharts! Koppa! Defend!"

Using the fob, I raised the *hedge* around the clan home.

Bruiser grabbed the pieces of the icon off the table, slapped the crucifix pieces into my hand, and pushed me into the main room, the one where the blood duels with MacLaughlinn and his clan had taken place. He shoved some of the others in behind me. Quint slithered in through the closing door. I had a moment to realize that Long-Knife had gotten word off to my enemies before he had been caught.

The living room had no furniture, just a dueling mat, still set up for the Sangre Duello. The floor no longer stank of old blood and death, though there were still traces of bloodstains in the grain of the floor all around, a great deal of it Eli's. I had been so desperate to keep Eli alive. Keep him with me.

That night I had found and used my power. *Calling* Leo with my own will, my own need. Demanding that he save Eli, who was now bound to me in some previously unknown form of sharing of . . . bodies? Brains? Souls? And Leo, able to fight his master now, because of that night.

"Stay in here, safe," Bruiser ordered.

The memory eased. I could breathe. I shoved the cross and the Jesus focal into different pockets again.

I nodded and Bruiser left me there, staring at the bloodstains. My Consort closed the door, shutting out the sounds of preparations for battle. I realized I had my full hearing back. I adjusted the headgear and tapped the sound back on, so I could hear the commands and comments and know what was happening.

Soledad put Angie on her feet and said to her, "This is the third one."

"Third one what?" Quint asked.

Neither of them replied.

But I knew. Third attack tonight.

Angie moved to the far wall, where the elaborate carved staircase came down from the second story. She sat on the floor and touched it with her left index finger. She held out her right hand to Soledad, who took it and sat beside her. I caught two quick flashes of opposing visions. The crucifix was inside the circle with Angie and Soledad. They were both alive. The crucifix was in my hand and Angie was gone, taken, leaving behind bodies in a sea of blood. I dropped the gold cross and the Jesus into Angie's lap.

Soledad said to me, "It is always a child, or a young woman, with the greatest power. This is why men fear us so." She opened her mouth, unhinging her jaw. Huge fangs snapped down as her eyes bled slowly scarlet and black. "There are nights when even angels tremble with fear. On the new moon, when the world is dark and the spirits roam the night, if the proper sacrifices have been found, then both the called and the trapped will be bound. I do not think they have been found. Yet. Not where Joses hid them. But a bargain will be struck."

"What bargain?"

"There is always a bargain. An exchange. A contest. A life for a life. The dark one will provide to the summoner, the sacrificer, a power-for-power, in exchange for the angel."

"Sooo . . . the ultimate goal isn't to bind and use the angel, but to exchange him for something else?"

"Perhaps. There are layers upon layers of strategies and schemes. Plans that are called *contingencies*. You must act."

"What am I supposed to do?"

A boom hit the *hedge* around the house. I lurched, falling to one knee, catching myself on my palms. The outer *hedge* hadn't fallen, but it was taking a beating.

Around Soledad and herself, Angie closed a *hedge of thorns*. The ward was bright silver blue in my Beast vision, shining with power, raw energy shaped by Angie's hands and will. "Take care of my mama, Ant Jane. Please. Keep her safe."

I remembered Molly and Big Evan heading through the doors to meet the attack.

I smelled burned things. Smoke and rot like a garbage pile on fire. I drew my weapons. Quint raced up the stairs to the landing. She had excellent lines of fire from there, up the stairs and down, through the main rooms, and out the windows to the lawn. Her face was badly bruised and her left hand was purple from the attack of the demon death energies at the prison. Or me landing on her. But she moved well. Edmund had healed her.

The door opened and Quint nearly blew off Koun's head before she recognized him and pulled up the weapon. Koun, Grégoire, and Edmund entered, Koun dragging Leo's body by one arm, a longsword in the other hand.

Ed closed the door behind them and found me with his eyes. When he reached my side he said simply, "My Queen."

"Eddie the Great," I said back.

He laughed. I figured that was enough for the moment.

Koun propped Leo against the wall. The former master of the city had a stake in his belly to keep him from having to fight the compulsion that bound him.

A second boom sounded. This time the chandelier overhead tinkled with the vibration.

"You always plan such delightful entertainments, My Queen," Grégoire said, sweeping me a flourishing bow before presenting me with his back. His golden hair was swept into a tail with a complicated knot. He drew two longswords. The waistband of his bloody-crusted icy-toned armor bristled with smaller blades. I noted that there had been delicate lace at the neck and shoulders of his modern armor, and at the pockets and sleeves. It was all encrusted with filth now. He reeked of death.

My chief strategist and the Blood Master of Clan Arceneau and all of France scanned the room and adjusted his position based on Quint's high-ground. Their positions now allowed them to cover two entrances, which left Quint to cover the stairs and window. Grégoire gave her a serene nod. Even though unspoken, it was high praise from my official warlord, one of my highest-ranking vamps.

I glanced at my lady-in-waiting. Her eyes were bright as she took in Grégoire, Edmund, and Koun. It was clear the men were pure eye candy to her.

I searched back to the last words spoken and repeated, "Delightful entertainments?" It could have been a compliment. Or not. The reek of dried blood from Blondie's bloody armor filled the room, both gross and oddly attractive to Beast, who purred inside me. I fought a sneeze and said, "Thank you?"

Ed stood beside me, clasping his hands behind his back, looking deceptively meek and docile, unlike the master swordsman I knew him to be. He wore a sword on each hip, and like Blondie, several other blades. A third boom hit and Edmund scrutinized the room as if taking inventory and finding its lack of cover disappointing. Mildly he said, "My Queen. Grégoire hasn't had this much fun in weeks."

I snorted. "How about you? Has Eddie the Great gotten bored?"

"One could never become bored while serving you, my mistress. You stir up trouble like the queen of a killer hornet nest."

"You make that sound like a compliment."

"Oh, it is. It is indeed."

Over the closed channel I heard Alex say, "Got it. RVAC footage with Molly's spanking-new amulet seeing working on the main screens. Hey, Molly. It worked."

"Look fast," she said. "The amulet is only good for another two minutes."

I turned to the big screen on the wall to my right. On it appeared an overhead view of rooftops. It looked like the French Quarter, buildings chock-a-block, with tiny walled gardens hidden away all over. One such garden was near on Canal Street. This garden was glowing, not with fairy lanterns, landscape lights, or tiki lights, but with magic in a faint silver-black haze. The RVAC dropped lower, the cameras revealing a three-story house, one totally enclosed on four sides by commercial buildings, as if the buildings had been built around it, to hide and protect the house and its small, walled garden.

"Where is that?" I asked. "*What* is that?"

"Alex made a tracking device that looked like a shell," Eli said, sounding proud in my earbuds. "Lizzie dropped it into the witch circle during the test. Because it was a shell like a million other shells in the state, they didn't look it over when it popped into their circle. They just kicked it aside. The Kid was able to turn it on and find it. And Molly has this new working she wanted to try."

"Okay. And . . ."

"And *that*, babe," Eli said into my earbuds with satisfaction, "is your enemy's lair."

"Coolio. But why are they attacking us here instead of us attacking them there?"

"According to the mic included in the tracking device, they want Molly."

"They can't have my mama!" Angie wailed. "Ant Jane. Use your power!"

The clan home was hit with a boom that shook plaster off the ceiling and made the chandelier swing. "We can't hold this *hedge* for long," Molly said over comms. A crack opened in the tall wall over the doorway to the kitchen.

Somebody was messing with my clan home.

Another boom sounded. The walls shook. Death magics crawled across my skin like fire ants.

I yanked the Glob back out of its pocket. Added three null sticks.

The door opened.

Molly reeled through, coated with death energies.

Behind her walked a woman, her hands filled with glimmering black energies, magics darting with orange and green sparks and black-as-hell motes. She was a grandmotherly type, a late-middle-aged woman with steel gray hair, rounded at hips and butt, wearing a loose dress and sneakers. The witch I had named Ursula. Holding death in her hands.

The world slowed down. In overlapping energies, I felt/heard/saw everything.

Just like in my memory of protecting Billy, I lowered my shoulder. Turned the null sticks pointy end forward.

The witch reared back,

My paw-claws gouged into the floor. I shoved off with all my might.

She aimed at Molly.

She threw.

My body did a cat move, whipping around and forward.

The death magics shimmered. Just ahead. A sparkling death. Not Molly's.

My death. I curled into the path of the magics.

It hit my head. My neck.

Frozen pain. Darkness like the void of space.

The Glob sucked it all down.

Burning hot. The Glob's own black pockets of reality opened wide. In my bones, I felt its power open, revealing the tiny pockets where magic was safely stored. I felt the voids, like bubbles, like tiny black holes, full of energy. So much power. The icy electric death was sucked away. My mouth formed a small O. Those were pocket universes. The places where magic came from and went to.

My fist, holding the Glob, hit the witch. The null sticks in my other grip pierced her belly.

The witch screamed.

My momentum thrust us back. Down. My body above hers. Just like when I fought to protect Billy.

Except. She dropped a small stone as she fell. It tumbled in the air. Bounced. Landed. Our bodies landed on top of it. Skidded. The floor erupted. Fingernails raked my neck above my armor. Claws dug into my back. Tearing armor. Breaking skin. Tangling in my clothes.

A witch circle opened beneath us. Around us. And we were gone.

I couldn't breathe. Couldn't move. Blackness like the end of the world. Empty space.

A flash of light blinded me. An assault of vamp-smell hit me.

Screams.

My body slammed into something. Things inside me broke.

Claws raked my spine.

Then blackness again. Cold and empty, the way death must be to a vamp with no soul. Falling apart, bits of me sloughing away. Into nothingness.

I hadn't even gotten a breath.

Dark and cold. That aching lonely nothingness.

Pain like landing from a long fall, flat on my face. Brilliance burning my eyes. Exploding scarlet stars. I turned my head from the broken dead ground. Sucked in a breath. Groaned.

Slit open my eyes. Again, there was light in the dark. Streetlights. Headlights.

The smell of my blood.

And something licking it from my neck.

"Get offa me," I grumbled, flinging an arm back, expecting to find a vamp and hitting nothing.

Something else growled from beside me. *Wolf?*

The cold thing on my back shifted to my other side and I rolled over, facing the night sky. There was no witch with me. But just as bad, two guns were stuck into my face. Point-blank.

I was no longer in Oz, wherever that brief flash of light and stink of vamps had been, but guns were no better, and the snarling snouts complicated the lack of ambience. I was seeing double, managed a second breath, which hurt more than the first one. Was too tired to raise my arms. "I give up," I said, slurring, blinking up at the gun-toter, trying to focus past the barrels on their faces. Face. One face. My eyes had adjusted.

"I got Queenie," a laconic voice said. "Sit." The snarls moved back as the dogs sat. Tex holstered his weapons and touched his mic off. "Damn it, Janie, you scared ten years offa my unlife." One dog lifted a paw, whining an apology for growling at me. She leaned in and licked my face.

"Yeah, yeah," I said, trying to avoid that slobbering

tongue. "Fangheads don't lose years off their lives until they lose their heads."

"And if I'da shot you, Bruiser woulda taken my head." He offered me a hand up.

His was cold and hard as stone, still wearing the calluses of his human life. When he pulled me upright and out of the circle, I put way more weight on him than I expected to need. The earth tilted under my feet and Tex caught me under my arm.

"Easy there, my lady."

Looking back at the circle, I spotted the cold thing that had dug its claws into my neck for the ride through . . . wherever. It had been drinking my blood. It chirped, flapped its wings, and hopped from the ground to my shoulder. The earth shifted again and when I could, I turned my head to meet the up-close-and-personal gaze of Longfellow, Gee's flying lizard dragon. Its eyes were slitted like a snake's, but glowed like fire opals in the dim light, orange and reds and pinks. It leaned in and pecked me on the cheek. Like a kiss. I wrinkled my nose at it, holding its stare.

Snake thing with wings brought us here, from trap set by witch, Beast thought.

That scenario fit with what I had sensed and experienced. *Where's here?* I looked around, seeing brick on the dead lawn, a bell and clock tower, and caution tape everywhere. "We're at the church." I tried to look back at the ground where I had been and my body tilted sideways. I nearly fell. Tex caught me around the waist, lifted me like a baby, and carried me to a small, concrete bench.

"Who makes chairs out of concrete?" I complained. My last meal tried to come up and I made a horrible gagging noise.

"Janie?"

"Vertigo," I managed as I fought to not hurl.

Tex touched his mic again. "The queen is safe, though sick to her stomach."

I heard the ever-so-slight delay between his words near me and his words in the earbuds, which had survived the . . . transport circle. Yeah. I'd been through a transport circle. Again. This time was way worse than last time, in Natchez.

"She has the lizard. And we have visitors." Tex ignored his six-shooters and pulled a nine-millimeter handgun while I looked around for our visitors. In the distance, a rainbow coruscated, a prism of color that played havoc with the light spectrum. "Arcenciels," Tex said into his mic. "And they looked a mite pissed."

I waved a hand to Tex and pointed. "Look." The ground inside the witch's circle rippled. I pulled my mic back into place. "Something's coming through the circle."

His voice commanding, Tex said into his mic, "Guards. To me." A vamp popped in beside him. Two humans raced from cover and across the lawn to us. To them, Tex said, "I got iron rounds. Arcenciel killers if needed. Jermaine," he said to the vamp, "null sticks and steel blades. Take down attacking Mithrans and any Mithran coming through the circle. Fawn, you and Carmine hold crosses. Use the nonlethal rubber rounds and shoot to wound human unfriendlies who approach through the circle or across the grounds."

Fawn and Carmine pulled crosses out of their armor and left them hanging on the outside, where they already glowed in the presence of my vamps. Everyone checked their weapons. Carmine snugged a cannon-shaped weapon to her shoulder in a comfortable firing position.

While they worked, I put two and two together and came up with eighty-seven. A preposterous thought. But I couldn't see another explanation. I looked at Longfellow on my shoulder. "Did you jump on me at the clan home? When the circle opened? And then bring me here?"

Longfellow crooned softly and kissed my cheek again. Tightened its tail around my neck.

Alrighty, then. "But I'm not a vamp. I have to breathe."

The tail loosened. I stretched my shoulder and sharp pain shot down my back where Longfellow had ridden me through the circle. I decided that the damage from its claws was worth not being in the clutches of Mainet and Gramma and the three wicked witches. The wounds it had clawed would heal.

"Report," Bruiser demanded.

The ground rippled at the circle. "Circle's active. Incoming," I said.

"Get her back to the Council Chambers," Bruiser ordered.

"It's too late for me to go anywhere." I pulled an H&K and tried to steady my aim at the circle. Nearly fell off the bench.

Tex looked to the SUVs and back to me. He said, "My Queen. Reconsider."

"We run, they may kill the residents." I waved my weapon at the neighbors' homes across the street. "Nope. This is my war and these people are my responsibility."

Koun, back at Yellowrock Clan Home, cursed in a language I didn't know. Bruiser cursed, something about a goat. It made me laugh. Okay, a little drunkenly.

"You look like what women of my human-time used to call *peaked*. Can you shoot?" Tex demanded.

"I feel that way. And we'll see."

"Well. Try to miss your team, your queenship."

"Deal." My gut wasn't happy, but I half stood, one hand on the bench, and leaned in, using body weight to shove the concrete bench over. I dropped behind it and propped on it, swallowed the nausea away, changed out ammo, and injected a round into the chamber with a *schnick* that bounced off nearby walls like an audio ping-pong ball. My vision steadied. *Okay. That wasn't so bad.* I swallowed down the bitterness of bile and stomach acids. "As long as I'm propped steady, I can be backup."

A man dressed in a three-piece suit and wearing side-whiskers on his face appeared in the circle.

Instantly every weapon in the area aimed at him.

He disappeared a half second later. Reappeared, wearing longer hair and modern armor. Disappeared. Again. Over and over, each time in different garb and different hair. There was a break of several seconds. Then it started again. Once, he reappeared the instant he disappeared. Wherever he was coming from, he was cutting it close.

"Crap in a bucket," I said.

"Report," Eli demanded in my earbuds.

"Mainet," Koun said, his tone cold and bitter. "Appearing and disappearing in the circle."

"Backup is en route. ETA twenty. Fall back to cover," Eli said.

"Negative on that fall-back thing," I said. "Let's watch a minute."

"He's dressed differently each time," Jermaine said from a distance. "Look. Now he has short hair." Mainet rematerialized and vanished again and again. Each time wearing clothing from different time periods and sporting different hairstyles. Not coming from *where*ver but coming from *when*ever.

"I dig the sixties bell-bottoms and groovy fro," Carmine said. "My kinda guy. Oopsie. Not so much the wool frock coat from the mid eighteen hundreds." The petite African American woman positioned her body so she could defend the grounds near us, between us and the church, and also cover the circle. Fawn turned so she could cover the rest of the grounds. Both human guards were wearing low-light monocles with full tactical headgear, military armor, and weapons. So many weapons. Jermaine, vamp, wore steel blades. A *lot* of steel blades. My guards looked badass. But there weren't enough of them if Mainet's people came here too, through more mundane approaches.

I thought about standing, so I could help more, and tilted to the side. I nearly hurled. "Nope."

Without looking at me, Tex handed me a bottle of water. "Jermaine, take up position near the east corner of the church. Take out anyone who doesn't belong here."

I placed my weapon across my lap and added, "Try not to shoot any dog walkers or late-night joggers." I drank as Jermaine answered in the affirmative and trotted away, and the Heir came and went. My stomach settled some and I nodded my thanks to Koun, shoved the empty into a pocket, and picked up the weapon again. "I wonder what would happen if he landed inside himself," I said.

"An eight-limbed body or a lot of broken bones? Both maybe," Fawn said. The muscular woman moved into a better position across from me, providing protection from the side street.

"Hopefully really dead," Carmine said.

Koun said something else into my earbud, in that odd language. It sounded like agreement. I didn't ask.

I checked my load. "Next time he appears, Imma shoot him with silver-lead rounds."

No one else changed out ammo. I figured that was telling. In the distance I heard the screaming as crotch-rockets unwound, gathering speed. Drawing closer.

"What's happening?" Molly asked into my earbuds. "I see it on the screen from your guards' vest cams, but it's all fuzzy, and part tree."

"Best guess. Mainet's bouncing here, to this time and place, from different times," I said, checking Fawn's and Carmine's positions—against trees.

Mainet reappeared. My fingers didn't work. Three of the guards fired at the circle.

The air above the circle blazed in brilliant reds overlaying the orange green of a *death hedge* ward that hadn't shown until now. Mainet disappeared.

In Beast vision, the *death hedge* now looked like crazed glass. None of the rounds had penetrated it. But the ward looked familiar. Like the shattered remnants of a stone amulet Gramma had used once. I felt in my pockets for the remnants of the stone. They were in a plastic baggie somewhere, shoved into pockets as I geared up for this. Found it. I put down my weapon to tip open the plastic baggie. Yeah. Gramma had worn a stone amulet to keep her *u't'lun'ta* stink from getting free, and the stone was both crazed and broken.

"His oldest garb appears to be from the early to mid eighteen hundreds," Tex said. "I reckon this means this circle—and the other outlying pentagram circles—might have been placed in the city when—or even before—Algiers was first built."

Molly said, "That might mean that the hub circle, has been in NOLA just as long. Maybe much longer."

I thought about the image revealed by the drone camera, of the hidden lair of the vamps and their death magic witches, hidden in my city where no one would expect a lair to be. I poured the stone pieces of Hayalasti Sixmankiller's amulet into my palm. Bounced them a little. "And the one that opened up in the clan home and hauled me off?"

"A temporary circle," Molly said. "It closed instantly. We think it was opened by an amulet she dropped, possibly powered by a demon. There was demon smut on the walls in the room afterward, and the stench of brimstone. And we now think the circle at Soledad's estate was an amulet circle, not one put in place long ago, but a new, temporary one."

I grunted. I had seen something bounce as we fell and landed on it. The implications of transport circles that could be opened by an amulet and powered by a demon were scary.

The implication of old transport circles, especially the one here at the church, was that Mainet had known this night was coming and he had been trying to get to this place, this time, for nearly two hundred years, and so far he hadn't made it.

Why not just drive here? Jog over and walk in? Hubris? Ego? False pride? The old vamp hidebound mindset, the difficulty of learning new ways of thought, new tech, new lifestyles and political structures? Or maybe the location was lost because the church hadn't been here when they built the circle, way back whenever, and they lost the circle until they tried to use it, and then . . . Long-Knife told them about the church. And maybe at any moment, Mainet would figure out a better way to get here. All this because someone, sometime, trapped Hayyel here. Or the presence of the key buried in the statue forced the angel to manifest here. There were too many unknowns.

Had Immanuel set this all in motion? The skinwalker faking him? Mainet himself? Or Joses Santana when he came to NOLA and ended up pinned to the wall in HQ subbasement five, like a fangy butterfly?

Or had Mainet himself been to the city at some point and set it all up? Had he come to the city unbeknownst to the master of the city, working evil under Amaury's nose, from the hidden house? Crap.

Right now maybe the whys, whos, and whens didn't matter. They might never matter. We had enough for any grouping of paras to be part of a Rule of Three, for chaining an angel and a demon. And at any moment Mainet would get tired of trying to come through a circle and find a better way.

I had to end this war and kill Mainet Pellissier. *Right*. Short-term goal: kill Mainet.

CHAPTER 23

So Much for Cornbread

Stretching my shoulders, which were hurting and still bleeding beneath my armor, I searched the sky for the arcenciels. They had floated closer, fully visible to human eyes, Pearl glistening like the inside of a thousand sea-shells, Opal glowing like the stone for which she was called. Both arcenciels were staring at the circle, their eyes lustrous, their mouths snarling, with all those horrible fangs. Their frills were rippling with fury, tails lashing.

Mainet appeared again. Opal snapped at him. Yelped. Jerked back, as if she had been burned.

Her voice ringing like bells, Pearl said, "The circle is powered by the darkness of the realm of no return."

Demon smut coated the ward. Yeah. That was what I had seen when my team fired at Mainet. Demons . . . Maybe they had to use the transport circle to help a de-mon manifest? Or vice versa?

Opal said, "Behold, that drinker of blood is the one who ordered the death of our sister, Storm. In this time, he carries her blood upon him. As he appears from the past, he has not yet taken her blood. If you kill him from the past, she will not die."

Storm had been killed by Mainet's henchman, and her blood had been stolen, taken away in a cup. Back to Mainet. The Mainet who, if he came through from his younger time, into this time, if he was successful, would have different weapons from the ones used by this current Mainet. And crap. Would I be dealing with two Mainets? One from then and one from now? We needed to kill the old Mainet before he stopped trying to get through and went to Plan B. But if I killed him here, from another time, that would break the time cycle, and change the present, where I might then not be here to kill him. Time travel stuff made my head hurt. Was Mainet a butterfly in the pathway of time?

"We will kill him if we can," Pearl said. "We will fill him with our bites until he no longer exists."

Those words lingered on the night air. In some way, the arceneiels might be our allies tonight. Or perhaps our worst enemies who would just kill us all and be done with it.

Mainet appeared. I threw Hayalasti Sixmankiller's shattered stone at the *death hedge*. The stone bounced off. The Heir disappeared.

I asked into my mic, "Why tonight? What's so special about tonight, versus say, last night or tomorrow night?"

"Historically, nothing. Celestially, it's the new moon," Alex said.

Over a high-pitched engine in the background, screaming loud, Koun said, "Black magic is strongest on a new moon."

"But he could have taken a jet and walked in any night of any new moon."

"But you would not have been here, then, My Queen," Koun said. "This is likely to be the only new moon that you will spend here, in all of your life."

Okay. And if he had a seer, he might know I had the Glob and other stuff he might want. Right. My stomach did a gainer and I swallowed back more bile, wishing I had a Coke to settle me.

Mainet appeared again. Stabilized. He was dressed in

what looked like a modern black business suit. Every weapon focused on him. Jermaine and Koun moved closer, swords raised in case he dropped the *death hedge*.

Mainet lifted his hand, holding something in his fist. He started to step through the circle. And vanished. "What's stopping him?" I asked. And then it hit me. I reached up and touched where the null sticks had been threaded through my armor. There had been six. I had pulled three and stabbed a witch. I had no idea where they were. There were only two still threaded in my armor. "Somebody shine a flash into the circle. See if I dropped a null stick in it."

Tex gestured his dogs to sit and stay, then he moved closer. Fawn adjusted her aim to compensate for his position and to provide a wider arc of cover. Tex knelt well outside the circle and pulled a small penlight, which he shone across the well-turned ground.

I was still prone behind the bench and scooted across the dead grass to see better, but beneath the line of fire of my guards.

Tex chuckled softly. His Texas-voice a vamp-thrum, laced with delight, he said, "The Heir saw through time and space, Queenie, or his seers saw through time and space, to this time, this place, and you. He knew that you, the Dark Queen, would be here, tonight, and that the angel partially trapped here by his brother, or Immanuel, or who-dang-ever, could be made to manifest, tonight. But he didn't look close enough. Damn fool. He didn't see your blood and a null stick in his witch circle." Tex stood and backed away. "*That*, I declare, he did not see."

"Hey, everyone," I said into my mic, pushing myself back into safety and into a sitting position. I didn't feel quite as sick, so that was good. "Toss a null stick into the edge of your circles. It doesn't close them, but it makes them impassable."

I heard several replies. But not Molly's.

"Molly?" I asked.

"We're on the way to you," Big Evan said. "We're part of your backup." He didn't sound happy. And instantly, Mainet's appearances stopped, as abruptly as they began. There was silence.

I realized a hum I had felt in my bones more than heard stopped as well. Much closer, crotch-rockets screamed. Sirens wailed as if law enforcement followed them. Three gunshots sounded from a few blocks over. Possibly unrelated to supernatural conflicts. Robbery. Mugging. Gang fight.

"Alex," I said. "Who's heading this way on motorcycles? Moving fast."

"Eli and Koun."

"Okay. That's good."

Out of the darkness walked Leo Pellissier, his gait uneven. He was breathing hard, almost stumbling, as if he had run here from the Garden District. Or as if he struggled to be here at all. At his side walked Brute and the ever-present grindylow. Longfellow chittered in my ear. Leo crossed the grounds, heading straight for the witch's circle and our small group. In his left hand, he carried my crown. Smoke rose from where his hand touched it.

Tex backed away from the circle and changed out the ammo in one of his six shooters. Time consuming, except for his vamp speed. He whistled his dogs close.

Leo walked around the circle. When he got to me, he raised his arms and placed the laurel leaf crown on my head. I let him. *Le breloque* snapped into place. "It came to me," he said, sounding breathless. "I do not know why."

"And you didn't try to put it on?" I asked.

"I have been a fool many times in my life, my Jane, but I am aware that once the crown has chosen, it will not relinquish to another until its chosen is dead. I do not wish you to be dead." He laughed, the sound odd and strained. "Nor do I wish my head to be cleaved in two, though the stories suggest that such an occurrence is possible."

"It would cut your head in two?"

Leo gave a minuscule shoulder twitch. "Or so it has been said."

I looked at the circle, where nothing was happening, and back to Leo. "You're under compulsion to stay away from me, aren't you?"

"Yes. The pain is . . ." He managed a breath. Perspiration beaded on his forehead, faint bloody droplets. "Is extreme. I must go."

"Wait." I holstered my weapon and got to my knees. Fawn lifted the concrete bench upright and I dropped onto it, rolling up the sleeve of my armor. I pulled a small blade and pricked my inner arm, just above the wrist, in flesh I was pretty sure carried no major blood vessels. "Sip. See if it helps." Leo stared at me. "What?" I asked.

"You do not share your blood with me."

"Yeah. Well." I shrugged slightly. I didn't like people drinking my blood, but . . . I scowled at him. "You want to try this or not?"

Leo knelt at my side. He leaned forward and licked at the blood trailing across my wrist. His tongue was colder than the autumn night. At the first taste, his pupils went wider, but he didn't vamp out. His fangs stayed in the roof of his mouth where they belonged. He carefully licked my blood, not allowing his saliva to touch the cut, which would seal the wound.

Longfellow crawled down my arm, clutching my sleeve in its little clawed fingers, its body and tail rocking and snaking back and forth with each step. Again I had almost forgotten about the lizard. It stuck its snout close to where Leo was licking, as if sniffing my blood. It sat back and watched, unfurling its wings slightly.

I used to kill vamps for a living. Now I was wearing their crown, apparently had a pet flying lizard who clawed into my spine to propel me through a transport circle, and the former master of the city was on his knees drinking my blood, which I had willingly offered.

"My life is so freaking weird," I muttered.

Leo laughed softly and fell to his butt, sitting on the dead grass. His shoulders relaxed. "Ask your questions," he murmured. Though his voice was soft, he sounded less stressed, so I guessed the compulsion had weakened, at least for a while.

I already had one answer. Now I'd get the rest of the story. "Why now? Why here?"

"When I lay in my grave, I dreamed. I traveled through the air, knowing those of my line as they slept, seeing their own dreams. And when I was powerless, the power of my master called to me. I was in Mainet's dreams," Leo said. "I saw his mind. The Heir had no power until Joses, the elder Son of Darkness, died," he said, his words speeding as if he needed to say them fast. "Keeping that power bound was the reason Joses was kept alive, hanging in the subbasement of the Council Chambers. When you killed Joses, his power fell upon Mainet, but it was not the full power. It was only a—" His hand twirled in the air as he searched for a word. "Perhaps we can call it a partial power."

I should have offered blood sooner. This was more than I had learned in, like, ever. He licked again but the blood had slowed. His eyelids drooped and he started to sit back. I pricked my skin and held it to Leo. He looked at my blood but didn't move. His own blood began to flow from his nose, trails from both nostrils that twisted across his lips and down his chin. Thin blood. Watery.

The lizard shivered as if shaking raindrops from its hide. It inched closer and opened its mouth. It had tiny fangs. Above us, the arcenciels drew closer, their light throwing rainbows on the dead grass, their eyes watching the tableau. I looked back and forth between the lizard and the rainbow dragons. Other than general body shape, they had nothing in common and they didn't even seem to like each other. But neither was attacking.

I shoved my arm and its trail of blood against Leo's lips and he licked it away, taking in some of his own blood with mine. I knew that was the reason he smiled, just a touch lascivious.

Leo took a deep breath. "When you did not destroy the Son of Darkness utterly, when you kept his heart, the Heir did not receive his full power. From the moment the first Son of Darkness died true dead, Mainet coveted the full power of the Sons, and your crown, which even the fathers did not have. Whenever the year his scryer first saw you in their dreams, that is when he began to plan this night."

I looked back at the circle, which was still empty. No more reappearances of the evil villain. "Well, crap. I was born in the early-mid eighteen hundreds. So he's had nearly two centuries to plan for tonight. In some of his seers' visions and plans he succeeded, or he wouldn't still be trying to get here."

"If Soledad would speak about the old tales, she could tell you much." Leo leaned his forehead against my inner arm. I couldn't see his face, his hair falling forward like a silk veil across my skin. "I know little, but I can tell you this. When the sons of Judas Iscariot tried to raise their father from the dead, an angel appeared, attempting to stop them. The sons had stolen the cursed silver coins from the ground beneath their father's body. With them, they sought to bind the angel. For all of this time, the angel, who tried to stop the creation of my kind, has been partially bound with a chain of the cursed silver." Leo jerked back. His mouth moved as if he was trying to speak, but instead it unhinged and his fangs clicked down. His eyes bled black.

"Tex," I said, alerting my guard.

As I spoke, my protector staked the former master of the city. Leo slumped at my feet. "I was just forced to stake the former master of the city," Tex said into his mic. "Again. The queen's blood was controlling the Heir's compulsion over Leo until now." His tone changed, his body went fluid and liquid. He drew two swords. "Come to think of it. Something overrode her power. The Heir might be close. Maybe he decided on another tack."

Jermaine's swords came to ready. He moved between the street and Tex with his dogs.

White Kow-bikes screamed around the corner and up to us. It was Koun and Eli, no helmets, heavy armor, weapons bristling everywhere. The Chief Strategist and Enforcer of Clan Yellowrock leaped from his bike at full throttle, into a vamp spring, and popped into place at my side. Eli gunned a final whine from his engine, bopped the bike over the curb, into the air, and wheeled down on the church lawn. He laid the bike down on his good leg, shaving up a swathe of grass. And he was suddenly standing beside me.

I was still nauseated, but I didn't smell his blood, so that was good. I made it to my feet. Longfellow climbed up my arm and perched high on my shoulder. That little flying sucker was heavy.

Tex, Koun, and Eli exchanged looks. None of them

looked at me. Dang it. Though maybe I looked as if I was
gonna hurl or fall over, so there was that.

Koun demanded into his mic, "Alex. Backup. Local
LEOS. Where?"

Over the earbuds Alex said, "No local law enforcement presence will be forthcoming. You're on your own.
And our backup is two miles out, still trying to get there
from the Yellowrock Clan Home. Bro. Pull back from the
church. Pick Jane up and carry her if you have to."

No local law enforcement presence, not even to keep
the humans safe behind barricades. Again. Something
cold and hard formed in the back of my brain. A plan, a
decision, an idea.

"I'm staying." I pulled a stake and glared a threat at
Koun. "You can't carry me with a stake in your belly." I
looked at Eli. "Don't. I'll have to beat your ass in front of
the guys."

Eli chuckled. "Babe." Unspoken were the words, *You
could try.*

The high-pitched whine of more crotch-rocket bikes
shifting through gears sounded in the distance. The bikes
were moving closer.

"Ours?" I asked Koun.

"No, My Queen."

There were several, all coming from the same general
area. "Company?" I asked. "Advance troops? The kind
who figured out their stupid transport circle isn't working
and they decided to do it the hard way?"

There was a slight click and a change in the ambient
noise of comms. The general channel was off, and I was
on a personal channel. "Jane," Bruiser said into my earbuds. His voice softened into that special tone he saved
just for me. "My Queen. Listen."

Soledad's Spanish-accented voice was picked up by a
mic. "Mainet searched for the crown for many years. He
has claimed the heart and will claim the crown on the
same night. Angelina's visions began to grow the moment
she touched the crucifix. I have taken it away and given it
to her father. He brings it to you. But know this. Before I
put her into a deep sleep, she said many things. From her

words I have gleaned that the Heir will use the heart to kill the woman who killed the Son of Darkness, Angelina's Aunt Jane. The Heir will take the witch who cared for the Heart of Darkness and use her as the sacrifice. With those two deaths, he can force the crown to accept him. Then the Heir has all he needs to bargain with a demon and fully bind an angel. He can take the power of heaven. The old tales tell us that such a one will have the power of God."

"Rule of Three?" Bruiser asked.

Soledad whispered, but I heard her words. "He needs nine participants, any combination of three witches, three Skinwalkers, three Mithrans, or three Onorios."

Comms switched open again. Alex said, "I hate to interrupt but, update. Brandon and Brian Robere have been placed under heavy guard and are being escorted to HQ. Grégoire's personal guard is now at the null prison to protect it—human and vamp force. Heavily armed. We have Soledad and the kids with us at HQ, and secure."

"Angie is spelled asleep on the security room table with the strongest *hedge of thorns* they could make over her. Three Everhart witches are guarding her, arguing about where they're supposed to be. It's loud. They're pissed. The Truebloods are on their way to the queen's twenty."

Twenty. My location. Right.

Rule of Three. Ka, Gramma, me. Lachish as sacrifice. Mainet's own fangheads. His three witches, assuming Ursula survived my stakes. If I wasn't here, he wouldn't have enough for three groups of three anythings. Unless—"Crap. Has anyone checked on Aya's location?"

"Eli and I informed PsyLED Knoxville on the day of the first attack," Bruiser said, his tone neutral. "And they sent the new guy to NOLA. I haven't thought about FireWind since."

Because, yeah, my bio brother hadn't called me, and I was the queen, and so I was either supposed to think about family crap like that and I hadn't, or wasn't supposed to think about crap like that and someone else was. The role of being queen was along the lines of me flying by the seat of my pants, for my entire life. "Okay," I said. "That was my job." I punched his number. It went straight to voicemail and I left a message to call me. I even said *please*.

"PsyLED out of Knoxville was informed that Mainet Pellissier was here to wreak havoc in our city. I spoke to Soul herself," Eli said.

He was talking about the associate director of PsyLED, who happened to also be the head of the arceniels, insomuch as the rainbow dragons had a leader. Soul didn't like me much, but she cared about her people, her rainbow dragons, and her law enforcement crew. I had to assume she was keeping track of everything, though I'd never know which of her roles would come first, arceniel business or PsyLED business. Alex was murmuring into his comms, and I heard enough to know he was talking to someone in PsyLED Knoxville.

When he ended the call, Alex said, "There's a reason why they've shown so little interest in what's happening in NOLA. This time I got Nell Ingram on the line. She says FireWind and Rick LaFleur have been out on a case in a remote area near Sassafras Mountain, in South Carolina. She last spoke to him at five p.m., three days ago. She hasn't been able to get in touch since. They sent out a tracking party led by a wereleopard named Occam—no first name. Nell and her people think FireWind and LaFleur are out of cell range, but they should have been able to send up a drone and at least ping them."

"They're worried," I said.

"'Concerned' is how Nell put it."

My heart dropped slowly into my gut. My brother and I hadn't gotten along well at first. He did, after all, try to kill me when we first met. But lately we had gotten along better together, and he *was* my brother. And Rick was ... history, but an important part of my history. He might have been part of the reason I stayed on in NOLA, initially, back when we were seeing each other. And Aya and I were working on our non-relationship issues, when both of us found time away from our jobs. That weight in my gut solidified. "Ask Nell to keep trying and to keep us in the loop," I said.

"Copy that. She said they can send someone out of the Alabama office."

"No," I said. "But Sassafras Mountain falls within Linc's territory. As a courtesy, send a small team from the inn to help PsyLED in the search, a vamp and a couple of humans."

"Copy that," Alex said.

The bikes that had been heading this way cut off. They had to be at least a quarter mile away. So, they weren't coming here?

I huffed out a breath and stood. The lizard fluttered its wings to keep its balance. While I found my own equilibrium, I went back over our conversation and settled on the words, "Wreak havoc. That's what Mainet has been doing." I caught myself on the tree nearby. I was ready to fire, but the circle had gone still ages ago and nothing was happening. I holstered my weapon.

Koun removed an energy bar from his pocket and gave it to me. "Eat." I did. It wasn't enough but it took away the stomach pain, a hot burning sensation I hadn't even acknowledged. As I chewed, Brute and his neon green rider trotted down the middle of the street. The wolf came up to me and sniffed my energy bar, his curled lips telling me it was horrible.

"No kidding," I said to the werewolf.

Half an hour passed. Our backup was nearly here. My stomach grumbled with hunger. I'd be out of here soon, with the arrival of the second wave of defenders. Or maybe when Bruiser got here, he'd send me to safety and fish the stake from the circle, letting Mainet manifest fully. If that happened, I figured *If he comes back, shoot him, behead him, make him dead* might do.

My stomach grumbled as if the energy bar had waked it. I was in the mood for Deon's gumbo, rice, and hot pepper cornbread. Or even burgers and fries from a fast-food joint. I opened my mouth to ask our rescuers to pick up something.

Alex said into my earbuds, "The cameras inside the church pinged. There are three witches inside. Looks like Mainet's people showed up after all, from another access point. Better late than never?"

"How'd they get inside?" Tex asked. "Hell's bells, my dogs were just around back."

"The motorcycles seemed to stop a half mile out," I said. "They had time to get here by mundane means and enter elsewhere."

"Or they dropped a transport amulet in the church when they stuck their cameras in place and we didn't catch it because at the time we didn't even know that was a possibility," Tex said.

Koun added, "Nothing is as it appears."

Of course they had other ways to get around. The transport circle in the yard hadn't worked. Once they knew where the original one was opening, why not have a backup plan? "The circles all over town were useful, like a feint," I said, "but they also had other things in play. Like in swordplay, where a swordsman makes a fancy move with his longsword and stabs his opponent with a shorter, hidden sword." No one disagreed. I sighed. "So much for cornbread."

Tires squealed. I looked over and saw a string of SUVs round the block from the direction of the Highway 90 exit.

A boom rattled the stained-glass windows in the church. Bricks fell from the broken tower to the grass. Something cold and slimy shivered in the air and rushed over me. As if a ward had been opened. I had felt this. Recently. At the null prison, that first night.

"They just did something," I said. "Whatever it is, I think they tested it the first night at the null prison."

The arcenciels vanished in a sparkle of rainbow light. The flying lizard dashed after them, up high, into the dark, wings flapping.

"Get the queen to safety," Bruiser commanded through comms.

Koun picked me up in his arms. He hauled me toward the street, moving fast. Tex on his heels. Dogs spreading out, responsive to whistles and hand signals I couldn't even see.

SUVs roared up the street. Bruiser at the wheel, in the lead. The vehicles squealed to halts. Stopped in weird patterns that blocked the street.

A second boom followed. The ground shook.

"Son of a witch," Molly breathed into my earbuds.

"Someone opened a *death hedge of thorns* around the church."

I looked back at the church. Searching for the *death hedge*.

Koun stopped in the middle of his run. Recoiled as if we'd hit a wall. We fell and tumbled from the momentum, him bonelessly, me retching from vertigo. Koun spun in midair and landed on top of me. We bounced on the ground. I rolled out and re-landed on top of him. His chest expelled air and he didn't draw another breath, or close his eyes, or move again. "Koun?" I whispered. I looked for what had hit him and saw it. Koun had just run headfirst into a *death hedge of thorns* compounded by a *reverse death hedge of thorns*. On the sidewalk.

No one could get in or out.

I should have agreed to leave earlier.

We were trapped inside the *hedge*. With our enemies. And Koun might be true dead.

CHAPTER 24

A Body Bag

The SUVs were goners. They were outside the *hedge* but they had cut off and wouldn't restart. We were positioned just on the inside of the *hedge*. It was possible that Koun, lying beside me, was true dead, but I didn't let myself think about that. Leo, dragged over by Tex, was on my other side, undead face to the sky, still staked. Tex stood over us, watching our six at the church to the rear; Jermaine took up a spot midway between us and the transport circle. Neither man had enough cover against death magics. No one did.

Carmine and Fawn took up positions at either side of Tex, twenty feet apart, all three of my security unit between the church and me. Sitting ducks, all of us.

The tac teams Bruiser had brought were scouting everywhere, finding the perimeters of the *hedge* that covered the church and the grounds. Molly, Evan, and Eli were sitting in SUVs, only yards away, watching the tac team on comms monitors and my small group, filling my team and me in.

Quint and Bruiser sat down on the sidewalk in front of

me, weapons close to hand, holding up tablets for me to see the same screens our powerless rescuers were watching, two cams from inside the church. More of our teams were on the way, not that it was going to do any good. No one had ever seen or heard of a *death hedge no-way-out of thorns* of any size, let alone one this big. They were stuck on that side and I was stuck on this side with Tex, two dogs, a staked Leo, a dead Koun, Brute, and a three-person guard composed of one other awake vamp and two humans. And probably a lot of enemies. And a flying lizard, who tucked its wings, flew through the *hedge* without mishap, darted back in, and landed on the broken clock and bell tower.

Lizard, one. *Death hedge*, zero.

As far as I could tell, the bad guys, assuming there was an attack force with the witches inside the *hedge* with us—had no idea we were out here.

Or maybe they didn't care.

Or maybe they knew, and they planned on killing us at any moment and serving our roasted bodies up with fava beans and a bottle of Pellissier wine.

The feed from the cameras Alex had accessed from inside the damaged church showed the three witches in the sanctuary. The witch I had landed on in the clan home, and who had dragged me into the transport circle, had been healed. They all looked so sweet, dressed casual—jeans and tees with sneakers—as if they should be sliding trays of cookies out of the oven or pruning roses, not as if they would be duct-taping an unconscious, naked Lachish Dutillett to a six-foot-long altar table. Lachish was breathing, but not moving, not fighting. I didn't know if she was drugged or spelled, but she was totally vulnerable, and that alone was enough to make me hate the grandmotherly witches.

When Lachish was secure, they walked around the sanctuary, placing things on the floor at equal intervals. I couldn't tell what they were, but as each witch moved away, the wall near and above each item brightened with a symbol, a common three-tined rune, one even I was familiar with, called Yr. With the three tines upright, it looked a little like a trident and it stood for life or birth.

Upside down it stood for death, or it had since one of the World Wars. Yr reversed was also the Peace Symbol from the sixties, but no way did I take it for peace. This was death all the way.

Earlier, I had seen some symbols flash across the walls. Was that reality or in a vision? I wasn't sure anymore, but either way, I hadn't had time to recognize them then. Now? This church was being marked with life and death runes, being desecrated. My aching stomach roiled again.

On the screens held by my people on the other side of the death ward, I watched as the runes quickly surrounded the sanctuary. Several death runes appeared over one of the doorways near the altar of the church. There were candles lit in groups of three, here and there, beneath the domed ceiling, inside the damaged room, on ledges, flat surfaces. In the center of the room, a huge five-pointed star, a pentagram, was quickly painted on the floor with black spray paint. They worked fast. Or maybe there was a template beneath the floors, waiting. The long game . . . Build a black magic circle into the very building? I wasn't Roman Catholic, but the thought of building on top of such desecration made my bones ache.

Using a stick and a length of string, the three black magic practitioners spray-painted a scarlet circle, the outline touching the points of the star paint, a well-practiced circle, further desecrating the church recently used for worship. It was so easy to turn the holy to the profane, the light to the darker things. So easy. Humans did it all the time. I don't know why seeing this was so painful, when humans did so much worse to one another.

I knew many practicing witches. Real witches didn't desecrate the holy, even the holy of another religion, far different from their own. They just didn't.

Into my earbuds, Alex said, "Mainet."

On the screen, Mainet walked into the church through the death-runed entrance. A vamp. In a church. Without burning up in a fiery blaze of glory or screaming in pain. Vamps usually paid a big price for entering a church, but maybe the hurricane damage and the desecration taking place had made entering possible. Or maybe Mainet was just that powerful.

I remembered him standing inside HQ walls, on the circular driveway. Arms outspread. Formidable. Commanding. Showing us how powerful he was. This was less dramatic, but far more effective. *Holy crap.* How was I going to stop this? Stop him?

Ursula maneuvered the marble angel that had once housed the silver key over to the circle. Fiona lit a fire in a brazier in front of the stone angel. The flames flared high.

"Shadows," Alex said. "On the walls. Are those feathers?"

I studied the walls in the poor-quality video feeds, seeing patterns, shifting and fluttering shadows that deepened in the corners, merging with the mold that dripped down the plaster. "Yeah," I said. "I think so. Just like last time."

The shadows of massive wings feathered down the walls, darkening, becoming easier to see. At the front of the church, but far away from the altar, near the formal entrance doors, a shadow of a chained angel appeared, cast by the flickering light from the fire. "*Ah crap.* Hayyel is manifesting."

"And Lachish is to be the sacrifice that forces the Dark Queen to act," Molly said from the street side of the *death hedge*. Her voice was full of horror when she added, "Jane. He expects you to save her. He'll be waiting on you to try."

"Yeah. Looks like."

I yanked on my crown, hoping it would come free so that if someone planned to take it they didn't have to remove my head first. Nope. It wasn't coming off.

So here I was, stuck inside a *hedge of death*, with no way out, and limited magical weapons: the crown, the Glob, the ring Sabina had left for me to find before she was eaten (the one filled with arcenciel blood), a red lizard brooch (ditto on the arcenciel blood), and the two-piece crucifix (more arcenciel blood), a few amulets, and broken stone focals, none of which I was skilled in using. Skilled my ass. I had almost no idea how to control them and the few times I had managed to do something with the Glob and *le breloque* had been mostly by luck and willpower. I hadn't been able to reproduce most of the effects in test situations. I had no way to protect the people I was sworn to protect. Or myself. I was still a little woozy after being conveyed through two transport circles and then having a muscular Celtic vamp land on me, enough so that standing was difficult. I made it to my feet anyway, walking along the *hedge* a ways and back, working on my balance and studying the *hedge*.

"Jane," Bruiser said, a warning in his voice.

My sugarlips knew my life philosophy well: Have no skill in fixing something? Take a wild leap and see what happens. "Yeah, yeah. Don't do anything stupid," I groused. "I know. Queen and all that."

"Jane," Bruiser said, gentleness in his tone, as if he knew what I was thinking.

"I can't just sit out here and let them kill Lachish and chain an angel." I looked up to the arcenciels. They were flitting around and around above the dome of the *hedge*, as if testing its perimeters and trying to see how strong it was. Maybe they could—

Pearl stuck out a single pearly claw and almost touched the *hedge*. She jerked away and back-winged to a safer distance.

"Which they surely know," Bruiser said. "They are waiting on you to rush in."

"No. They're waiting on *us* to rush in."

I walked to my downed vamps, Leo and Koun, and pulled my magical weapons, laying them on the dead grass. I sat down in front of the amulets, facing the church, a vamp to each side, my body only feet from the *hedge*. I considered the ring, which in half-form only fit my pinky. I picked a finger and slid the ring with the oversized jeweled part over the knobby knuckle of my left pinky. I'd had the ring for a while. Still had no idea what it did. But the arcenciel had been brave, so why not me?

"Jane."

"Heard you the first time. I love you." Before I could chicken out, I stuck out my pinky finger. Touched the *hedge*. And yanked back my hand. "Holy crap." I shook my hand, which was now numb. "That didn't work."

Before I could think it through, I took up the lizard pin and tried again. The pain shot to my elbow. Numbness set in hard.

Without thinking of the what-ifs, I hooked gold Jesus

with its arcenciel blood jewels and the gold cross together, pressing them in place with three little metallic clicks. The magic inside the fully restored talisman shocked through me, frozen and cutting as a diamond blade dug from a glacier.

At the sound of the last snap, all around me globules appeared, hovering like droplets of mercury, silvery poison suspended from the sky. My gut wrenched. My muscles did something . . . odd. I fell back to the ground with a grunt of pain. It hurt like dying. I struggled to breathe.

Fawn stood over me, looking down. "You okay?"

"I'm freaking ducky," I lied. "Sit me up."

Fawn nodded to the others, holstered her weapons, and got an arm under my shoulders. Shoved me upright. Stood behind me and held me there, a knee between my shoulder blades.

Hands shaking, I lifted the gold chain over my head and settled the gold cross at the base of my neck, over my armor. More globules appeared. They were silvery. Reflective. All I could see was myself, kneeling on the grass.

"Y'all . . . y'all see those?" I gestured to the globules.

"Huhn?" Fawn said.

"See what, my love?" Bruiser asked.

"Okay," I gasped. "That answers that one." Pain began to seep away from my body. My breath came easier. But the globules were there, all around me, still reflective, showing me a Cherokee chick in black armor sitting on the ground with a party hat shaped like a crown on her head. Where I wasn't pelted, I was pale skinned from shock, and my eyes were hollowed holes in my puma skull. I looked like I was dying. Maybe already dead. I forced my knees to bend again so I could sit up by myself.

I twisted the ring upright and took the lizard amulet in my other hand. Additional globules appeared, but still they were reflective, showing me only myself.

I needed to see more. All this started when I put the cross together. That meant . . . *Crap.* Soledad had scars. So the icon had to go against my skin. Bet that was gonna be fun.

My heart rate sped. My breathing too, yet I couldn't get enough air. I tried to find calm, the way I used to, to change shapes. That didn't work either. Thinking one of the words I didn't use, ever, I pulled out my armor neckline, and let the crucifix fall against my chest at the base of my throat, above the other necklaces I habitually wore. The icy cross flattened itself against me as if an unseen hand shoved it tight. It was so cold it blistered my flesh. My blood froze. My skin pebbled and every hair of my pelt stood upright. My nerves twitched and burned as if fire ants had set up a nest inside my skin. I gasped in a painful breath. Not enough. Not enough air.

I dropped my fisted hands to the grass. My back bowed, then whipped into a hard arch. I thought I might have a seizure or I might hurl. Both. "Holy crap," I managed. And I looked around. There were a lot more globules now. Like a *lot* more.

Slowly the pain dulled except from the points of contact, the crucifix pressed against my skin, the ring around a pinky, the lizard amulet, each with arceneil blood in them. The Rule of Three. Around me, the globules, invisible to the people with me, became less reflective. My image of myself faded. Slowly the droplets of mercury became clear, crystalline, as if droplets of pure spring water now hung suspended in the air. Globules, some as large as softballs, were everywhere: front, between the church and me, up to the top of the damaged bell tower. Thousands upon thousands contained within the *hedge*.

In each globule close to me were visions of myself. Me, dead in any of a hundred ways; some of the visions were me dead inside the church. In one I saw how I would die if I used the Glob on the *hedge*. Badly. Good to know, as that had kinda been my next plan.

In another water bubble I saw what would happen if I went into the church alone. In others I saw what would happen if Leo wasn't with me, if Koun wasn't with me, if Bruiser *was* with me, if my small crew went in without me. Without backup. If, if, if. All of the dead Janes and dead friends and dead family and dead witches and dead lover. Every single one was a sign of utter defeat. And in every single one, I could see my actions that led to all that death. No matter what I did, we all died.

I reached out and flicked a droplet with a particularly

nasty dead me away. All of the dead-Jane droplets swept to the back, as if I had rearranged the columns in a database. "Holy crap," I said, shocked.

Closer to the front now were visions where I was alive inside the church. I sat straighter, tightened my knees in a guru position, waved Fawn away, and studied the futures as the cross scalded my flesh. Found one with me alive, walking out of the church, covered in blood. There were very few of those, *very* few, among all the possibilities. And in none did my people survive. Their bodies were in pieces on the church floor.

That . . . that would kill me quicker than dying at the hand of Mainet.

I flicked more negative potential futures away, analyzed timing more than weapons and tactics. The smell of burning synthetics and skin came to my nose from inside my armor. My gut did a somersault and wrenched in agony, the way it felt when I'd had cancer. My breathing sped even faster. My hands began to tingle. I was hyperventilating. I forced my breath to slow, studying the futures.

"Jane?" Bruiser asked. "Your finger and your other hand are burning."

"Mmmm." I held up an index finger, telling him to wait.

I was down to maybe twenty futures. In three of them Koun was beheaded. In three others, Tex was dead. I flicked those six out of the near present. I turned my head to the laptop screen Quint still held up for me. In it, in the church just yards away, Lachish had been painted in runes with what looked like lipstick, thick and scarlet. The witches were in place in their circle. Had too much time passed? I compared the scene on the screen to the remaining futures and calculated what would happen next. In every case, I had to wait. Wait. Or my people would die.

I sucked at waiting.

On the screen, Gramma and Ka entered from the door with the death runes. Three witches were present, and now two skinwalkers. Three vamps entered the sanctuary, carrying a long bag. A body bag.

The droplets told me that Soledad's prophecy had been true—Mainet needed nine participants, the Rule of Three, times three: any combination of three witches, three Skinwalkers, three Mithrans, or three Onorios. He didn't have Bruiser or the Roberes, he didn't have me, didn't seem to know I was on the grounds, or I figured he would have sent his people to get me and bring me in.

I looked at the droplets, flicking two more away.

On screen, the vamps unzipped a body bag. My heart plunged. A jaguar tumbled to the floor, bound hand and foot and seemingly unconscious. Aya. Had to be.

Alex cursed. I said nothing, comparing the scene to the futures.

Eli barked questions into his mic, and I learned that no one had been seen outside the church, so that meant that all of our enemies and Aya had been inside the church somewhere since at least a few minutes before the *death hedge* went up. Or the transports worked even through a warding. I tried to remember if the ward at Yellowrock Clan Home had still been up when I was pulled through one. Decided it didn't matter.

Around me, two of the images vanished by themselves and four more appeared, as the actions of the people in the church offered and created different possibilities. I flicked three more away.

"What's Jane doing?" Alex asked over the comms system.

"Hell if I know," Tex said, "but there's a ball of energy around and in front of her about twenty feet thick."

I didn't have time to deal with their concerns. The flesh over my breastbone was being burned away, my hands were blistered, and my gut was coiling like it was being tied in knots. I had a bad feeling I was out of time, which would have made me laugh except the pain was so bad, as I sat here, the futures changing.

I flicked away more droplets, until I was left with five possible futures in which all of us survived. In all of them, I was wearing the Mughal blade. Which, because it wasn't a magical weapon, was one of the few doodads I hadn't brought with me.

"How do I get the Mughal blade?" I whispered to myself.

I heard a cheep and a breath of wind brushed across my cheek. The too-heavy-to-fly lizard was back-winging in front of me like a hummingbird, its fire-opal eyes darting to each of the futures. Longfellow could see the futures like I did, which was interesting but useless. His fire-opal eyes turned to me and held my gaze as if waiting. I looked to the droplets and three more appeared, even as two others vanished.

It hit me. The lizard could cross over the *death hedge* energies with no ill effects. I'd seen that with my own eyes. So maybe the ability of Longfellow to see the futures wasn't useless. Gee had fed him blood, and Gee served the arcenciels in some capacity. And the arcenciels had a natural control over time. As I thought that, the arcenciels swooped closer to the *hedge*, hanging in the night sky, glowing with energy.

"Longfellow. Gee said you know several languages. Is one of them English?"

The lizard cheeped and then mewled like a kitten.

"The Mughal blade. You know what I'm talking about?" Another cheep.

"If you can cross a *death hedge*, then you can beat my portable *hedge* and the null stuff still in my closet. I need the blade brought here from my house." A new future option popped into the realm of the possible. Then three more. "Ahhh," I breathed. I was affecting the future, right now. *Okay. I can work with that.* Doing what I needed done would kill a human. Molly would slip over into death magics and kill everyone if she tried. Big Evan would have a heart attack and die. Eli . . . "Crap." Eli had metal parts in his legs. He'd die.

Bruiser or one of the Roberes, all Onorios, were my only choices. But the Roberes were too far away, and if Bruiser entered the sanctuary, he'd very likely die, or be horribly mangled.

Yet, only an Onorio could survive what needed to be done to the *hedge*. I'd have to find a way to make that work without Bruiser dying in the next step, an image that made no sense.

"Can you do that, Longfellow? Can you go get the blade? And give it to Bruiser?"

The lizard whipped its long tail and fluttered up high,

fast, before tucking its wings and diving up and through the *death hedge*. The energies didn't even flicker.

The futures altered again.

"Remember the prophecy of the blade," I said to Bruiser. "It might not be pure . . ." I chose a word he might use. ". . . balderdash. If the prophecy is right about the blade deflecting a death strike, then it might cut the *death hedge*. And be sure to cover your eyes. Protective lenses." I described what he had to do. Him. Only him. "If it works, see if you can get a team in here. I need . . ." I stopped. I knew he would never agree. "I need a team of humans and witches. Not you. You have to stay on that side. If you come inside the *hedge*, you'll die."

CHAPTER 25

Ow-Crap-Ow

His eyes went hard and cold, and when he spoke, that British lilt I heard so seldom came out. "If you think I'll leave you to face that alone, you are sadly mistaken, my love."

"Please don't follow me. You'll die. Totally dead. And I couldn't bear that."

He nodded thoughtfully, his gaze moving from mine to the *death hedge*. "You're seeing the futures, like Soledad did, like you used to."

I nodded slightly.

"If I go in, I die, but you live," he stated, as if he could see my futures just as I did. "If I stay out here, you win, I live, but you die. Right?"

"Not exactly. It's not so simple," I muttered.

Though maybe it was. In all the futures I could see right now, Bruiser and my team would live and I'd be carried out in pieces. I was breathing in them but in all of them, I'd lost a limb, or the top of my head, and *le breloque* was a warped crushed twisted knot of gold, tangled and dangling from my open skull and bloody hair.

Bruiser didn't promise. I hadn't really expected him to. His brown eyes softened on me. Warmth lit them. "You're my love. I'm your Consort. I go where you go. I promise to stay alive."

But he couldn't. No one could promise to stay alive.

I knew what to do next. I pulled my small blade, rolled up both sleeves and pricked both inner arms, then touched the blood with the fingers of both hands and wiped it on my crown. Dang thing went blazing-hot. I needed to pad the inside rim. Why hadn't I thought about doing that in all these months?

Leaning over, I tugged the stake from Leo's gut. It made a really awful sucking sound. Leo rose to sit upright, and I shoved my left arm against his mouth. He grabbed my wrist and latched on. Fortunately, his fangs were still tucked away in the roof of his mouth, so it was just human lips and teeth and dead-cold tongue. *Yuck.* "One vamp up."

Gently, careful of Leo's fangs, which were still too close to my flesh, I pulled us over closer to Koun. I maneuvered my right arm over Koun's face and down to his mouth. My blood dripped in. I thought about my crown, the power it gave me, and I *called* Koun. Willing him to wake, to come back to me. Nothing happened.

We held our positions for what felt like forever, but was likely less than a minute, before Koun stirred, licked his lips, and swallowed, taking in my blood. His eyes opened wide and he found me in the dark. He looked . . . Ecstatic was how he looked. *Crap.* I had bound him even closer to me. "Mistress. My Queen," he said. Smoothly, he lifted his head and sucked my blood away, healing the flesh as he did so.

"Two vamps up," I said. "Mainet is inside the church, which has been desecrated with death and life runes. I've seen potential futures and the only way we all live is if we get inside before Lachish is killed and if we all go in together. But the details are pretty murky and I don't know if I can take the potential futures with me, so I might lose something." I could lose everything.

"Yes, My Queen," Koun said. He stood and helped me peel Leo off of my arm.

The former master of the city was smiling in drunken bliss when he looked at me. "My Jane."

"Crap." Had I bound Leo to me too? I hadn't seen—

I stopped. The blood on the crown had been intended to allow me to make them safe. Instead they were kinda besotted, drunk, and happy. I could deal with binding them to me later. Right now, I had to keep us all alive.

"She's going in," Eli said calmly.

"Jane! No!" Bruiser said. "Don't risk yourself."

"If I don't go in, I die anyway. I love you."

Bruiser closed his eyes for the length of a single breath. "I love you too. Are you sure this is the only way?"

"Yeppers." I grinned at him in the dark, but when I spoke again it was to Eli. "Keep Molly away. Tie her ass up and shackle her feet."

"Son of a witch on a burning switch. You will *not* handcuff me." But Evan, standing behind her, nodded once. He'd keep her here long enough to prevent several of the worst futures.

I knew zip-tying her would only slow her down, but that was time I needed to get everything else done before she showed up. "When Longfellow comes back, give Bruiser the Mughal blade and protective lenses from the SUV. Moll has to be secured before that happens, you hear? Then Bruiser cuts the *hedge*—" I stopped as pain scorched and pierced my chest like shark's teeth made of molten iron. "Eli, you and a team meet me inside," I managed. The stench of my burned flesh was acrid. The burn went to bone. My knees wobbled where I stood. I gave him the names of the humans and vamps who needed to be there.

"You left out me," Quint said.

"You aren't going in," I said calmly. I had seen two possible futures for Quint. Dead, bisected by a closing *hedge*, and alive, in the SUV. "I need you positioned to take out anyone leaving the church who isn't one of ours. It needs to be silver-lead rounds. Clean head shot. The distance and lack of light means it has to be Eli or you. Eli will be with me."

Quint cursed.

"Too many will die if you don't do what I say. I've seen

it in the futures." It was a partial truth, but close enough. I flicked three futures away and more appeared in the air around me. All of them were bad. Like, really bad. I had to fight to stop my tears. My breath shuddered when I drew it. Eli moved closer to the *hedge*. His calm spread around me, coating the air I breathed like fog. "And even with everything I'm doing"—I found another breath and flashed a tight smile at Eli as I pinned the flying lizard to the leather flap on my armor where the null sticks hung—"I still might fail."

I dropped the ring in a pocket and sealed it shut. Drawing on the crown and the Glob, I forced healing into my hands. I wasn't good at it yet, but I had seen myself in a future healing my hands, and remembered using their magic once for healing. Sorta. The pain did decrease. If I didn't do this just right, Bruiser or Eli or Leo or Aya, and some not even on site yet, would die. Or any combination of them. I needed my hands. I flexed my fists. "Good enough."

Tex said, "Jermaine, when we get inside, you stay at the entrance and take down anyone who gets by us. You're first line of defense. Quint, per Jane's orders, when she can access the *death hedge*, you are our last line of defense."

"Will do," Jermaine said.

The blade was supposed to be back by now. It wasn't. My team was supposed to be inside with me by now. They weren't. The awful possibilities shifted around again. I had to move now.

"Get Molly secure. Fawn, Carmine. Flank me. If you get inside with me, assume shooting positions and attempt to take out the witches first, then these two." I pointed at the screen, indicating Gramma and Ka. "Note their positions in the circle. They may look like other people when you get to them in person but their positions in the circle should stay the same. Don't hesitate, no matter who they look like." I knew what the *u'tlun'tas* were going to do in the middle of the ceremony to bind an angel. There was no way we would survive if the skinwalkers got to that point in the binding.

"This one, on the ground." I pointed to the bound jaguar, Aya. "Do *not* fire at him. He's my brother. Once you get the three witches, and the two others, the ceremony will be disrupted. Then take out the vamps if you can get good shots. Others of us may still be fighting them."

I looked at Bruiser. "When Longfellow gets back, use the blade. You'll know what to—"

Alex interrupted into my earbuds, "Better move fast, Jane. They just opened the circle and Hayalasti Six-mankiller just shifted to look like Sabina."

I took in the screen with a single glance. On it, Sabina, the outclan priestess eaten by Gramma, stood at an angle to Lachish's body. She held an athame in her right hand. Across from her stood Mainet. On the altar, Lachish's chest continued to rise and fall slowly, faintly. Mainet and Sabina leaned over the unconscious witch.

To save Lachish, I needed Eli with me. Which meant I needed the Mughal blade. But if Lachish died before I got in the sanctuary . . . "No!" I pulled on Beast strength and speed, dashing to the side door of the church. The three vamps kept up with me, but the humans were left behind. Just as in the last few futures I had seen.

I reached the side door we had entered earlier and grabbed the door handle. Yanked away, "Ow-crap-ow," shaking my hand. It had stung my palm at the webbing of my fingers, but it hadn't damaged it. Much. I held my un-injured hand to the wood and felt the ward sealing it shut. I hadn't seen this in the futures, so how—

To the side, a window was open to the night air. I gestured to the open window and Koun dropped to one knee, lacing his fingers together into a cup. I pulled my nice new H&K, double-checked the load for silver-lead rounds, and racked the slide. Stepped back and ran forward, one foot landing in Koun's hand. He boosted me up and I grabbed the upper jamb, using momentum to lift my legs and slide in. As I fell, I fired two shots. Killed the vamp waiting there, keeping guard.

He fell. I landed, bright energies inches from my face. Shoved back on my heels hard and whispered into my mic, "Stop!" *Crap.* I breathed fast, pushing through the fear. The vamp I had just shot was now in two pieces.

I muttered, "There's a second, inner *death hedge* inside

the church, and the vamp I just shot is half in, half out, and
now we know what happens if someone falls across the
hedge." If the vamps came through and landed on top,
they'd be halfsies like the guy at my feet; if they landed
against it, they'd be asleep, like Koun had been. The humans would be dead. I backed away from the two-part
vamp in the bloody suit, until my spine was against the
wall beneath the window. The room was like a big meeting area, with movable dividers that could be used to create smaller rooms. It stank of mold and disuse. And the
doors we had used to get in last time were on the other
side of the room, on the other side of the inner ward.

I looked from the dead vamp, up. Koun and Tex were
leaning side-by-side in the window, holding, one-armed,
to the window jamb.

"Careful. You have about eighteen inches."

"So I see, My Queen," Koun said as he maneuvered in,
braced on his two arms, maneuvering his legs and feet
inside. It was a spider-lizard-monkey motion, nothing a
human, even an Olympic athlete, could manage, but one
of those inhuman moves that made vamps so creepy to
watch sometimes. Using his arms, he angled his body inside over the window ledge, like a tripod on its side, and
inspected the body that had been cut in half when it fell
through the *death hedge*. He curled and landed below the
window, turned, and worked his way to me.

"Nice shooting," Tex said. He looked back and said
something like, "Patrullan," and I heard a dog woof. Tex
lowered himself inside and down to the floor one-handed.
As feats of strength went, the two maneuvers were pretty
amazing. "Ain't been in a church since I was human. It
feels unnatural." He shrugged his shoulders as if they
carried a heavy weight.

"I told Jermaine to keep watch at the circle with orders
to kill anything that manages to walk out of it," Tex said
to me. Into his mic, he said, "Fawn and Carmine, come
on in." The two human guards, standing on a ladder, for
sure, followed, and Tex caught them, lowering them to
the floor, saying, "We need y'all to keep our six open and
guarded for the second and his team. Y'all shoot anyone

who ain't ours, ya hear? Keep each other safe. Follow us inside when you can."

I heard a voice but couldn't make out the words. Tex replied, "Ain't no buts. Them's the orders."

Leo dropped in behind Carmine. Silent, shaking as if he was being hit with a cattle prod. Vamps in a church without going up in flames. Dang.

I edged around the small open area as he talked, looking for a way through, over, or around the *hedge*. There was a black curtain I hadn't noticed and I pulled it back to reveal a closet inset with shelving loaded with kids' toys and puzzles. I turned back to my guards and pointed at the death energies. "This *hedge* wasn't in any of the futures I saw." I pointed the way we had come and we worked back, past the window, and stepped over the vamp's legs. "Two-piece suit," I said. "Get it?"

Tex looked to heaven as if he was conferring with God. Koun gave a beautiful smile. Blood-bound for sure.

There was a click in my earbuds, and I heard Alex say, "Janie, private to you. Your flying dinosaur is back. The Consort is cutting the hedge and cursing you like . . . I don't know what like. Except he likes barn animals. Expect assistance from your Consort and a team."

I closed my eyes as if to block out all the horrible futures of Bruiser dying. *Stupid man.* "Copy that," I said instead. Ten minutes later, Alex said, "The Consort, your second, and a small team are inside the outer *hedge*."

"Right. Put me back on the general channel." The Mughal blade had done its work and my backup was on site, which the visions had said I needed. But so was my Consort. I didn't have the futures to flick around now, but I had the memories of them. "Bruiser, Eli, slowly. No flying leaps."

Fawn said, "Careful."

Eli was silhouetted in the night sky as he crawled through the window. Hanging on with both hands, he stared into the darkness. Our heart rates synced, his battle readiness like a calm, cold, underground lake. "That inner ward's strong enough to see even with human eyes."

I made a sound of half agreement as he dropped down. Eli no longer had fully human eyes, but I wasn't saying that. Bruiser followed him, the smell of Onorio blood a faint tinge on the moldy air. I looked him over, seeing the oozing puncture on his cheek. In my visions he had lost an eye, which is why I'd asked for protective lenses. Quiet relief settled on me as I understood that there were still ways to alter the worst of the possibilities. I touched his beautiful face with the pad of my thumb. A vamp had licked the wound to stop the worst of the bleeding, but to heal it would take more time. "What condition is the Mughal blade in?" I asked.

Bruiser unsheathed it from its velvet-covered scabbard. In the pale orange and green glow of the *hedge*, the curved damascene blade was blackened and chipped, its tip missing, leaving it cracked and jagged. Ruined forever. But the remnant of the blade was long enough to get us through this one too. I hoped.

Then I saw Bruiser's hands. Blistered. Blackened flesh hanging off where heated metal had burned him. His clothes were pierced and singed where bits of metal had burned through as they flew by. If he made another cut, he might not heal right, his hands were so damaged. It hadda hurt like a son of a gun. I held out my hand. Bruiser hesitated just a moment and then placed the hilt in my palm, and his goggles around my head to protect my eyes.

"The tip is gone," he said.

"Yeah. And in none of my future possibilities did I see this inner *hedge*, so either it will be easy peasy to get through or just cutting the exterior one changed all the futures." Kneeling, I turned the blade so I could cut into the *death hedge* at my head height. "Protect yourselves."

"Cut fast," Bruiser advised. "An oval worked for us. If you cut straight lines, when you turn it, you have to start over. And"—his voice hardened—"it is like cutting lightning."

That sounded painful. With my free hand I pulled the Glob out of my pocket and held it near the energy patterns. I touched the broken tip of the blade to the *hedge* and a sizzle shot up my arm. A shower of energies spat at me and I jerked back. "Okay. Trying this again." I held the Glob at the hilt so both hands were in front of me, wrists one atop the other. I touched the blade again to the hedge, and the Glob sucked in all the spitting energies. The blade heated, smoking on the humid air. I pressed down on it and cut into the *hedge*. The Glob grew hotter and hotter in my already-burned, mostly healed hand. The blade blackened even more, and slivers of steel broke off and fell to the floor.

From the corner of my eye, I saw a flashlight beam. Fawn and Carmine were covering us, other people behind them, armed, ready to fight my war. I couldn't concentrate on them, not when the hole I was cutting was trying to electrocute me.

Sweat slid down my spine, through my pelt, beneath my quivering arms as I made a large oval cut with the blade that carried its own prophecy about death. When I reached my starting point, the energies in the middle sizzled away. Holding the blade carefully, I backed to the side, remembering other glimpses into the future that had made no sense. "Koun. Prick my wrist. Sip. Hurry. Hold my blood in your mouth. Step through."

"Yes, my Queen."

He started to slice my skin and I added, "If I'm wrong, you could die crossing over death energies."

Koun smiled placidly and rested his pale eyes on me. "I'll not die breaking into a *bloody* Christian church with a skinwalker queen. I'll die in battle or live forever." He cut me and I flinched, just enough to notice that the crucifix was no longer burning. I'd put the other two amulets away, and the connection was broken. New info. Good.

Koun lapped up my blood and stepped through the oval hole to stand, weapons out and ready, on the other side. Tex, then Leo, came through, each sipping my blood, and all three slithering like lizards. Carmine and Fawn entered, no blood needed.

Eli went after them, touching my shoulder. His dark calm flowed into me, his nearness spreading that cold pool of tranquility. His eyes met mine and I tried to let him know what I was about to do. His pupils, already large, widened more. In the vision that had made no sense. I was next in line.

Bruiser took the hilt and gestured me inside the *hedge*. I hesitated. I had hoped the team behind Bruiser would be next, but the lack of space meant there would be no breaking in line or cheating the timeline. Our numbers would be lower than I had hoped.

I duckwalked through the opening and reached back to take the hilt so Bruiser could get inside. He lifted a leg to insert it and I shoved off, backward, into the room behind me. The oval hole in the energies closed. I landed in Eli's arms and he stood me upright.

Bruiser's eyes were shocked. "Jane?" he whispered. Then fury flashed into them. "Jane!"

I shook my head. "You being in here with me means you die. You being out there means you live and you can take care of Leo, Koun, and Eli after. I . . . I *need* you alive. Do you understand? Alive, not crisped like bacon or"—I took a breath and said—"or dead by my hand. And if you come in here, Mainet will have Leo and you. And I'll have to shoot you."

"In one of your futures? You saw me betray you?"

"I saw us blending our magics to fight Mainet. We were winning. And then you were pulled in, under Leo's blood bond. If you are inside, Mainet gets you, Leo, and me. Everyone dies."

Bruiser stood and walked away. As if my words had betrayed him.

"Whimper later," Alex said. "Weird shit's happening inside."

Eli and I met eyes and said together, "Language."

We moved silently through the dark, the vamps clearing the space in front of us, me holding the Mughal blade, what was left of it. I was sandwiched between them and Eli. The door ahead was open and the sound of a drum beating came through. The tempo was like a heartbeat layered over more heartbeats, the reverberation due to the size of the sanctuary creating echoes. The overlaid rhythm had an odd effect on my own heart rate, making it speed. I was certain the outcome was intentional.

Eli touched my shoulder. He shared that dark, calm pool of his battle readiness. I inhaled deeply and let the breath go. Right. Breathe. He dropped his hand and led the way through the dark, closer to the doorway. The people at the front had to know we were here but they didn't know we had gotten through the inner ward. I hoped. The vamps with me stopped as if they had been transformed to stone midstep. As one, they all stepped back. Another. They stopped again and turned to me. Their movements were measured, in cadence to the drumbeats.

Koun took a breath himself and said, "This is as far as we can go, My Queen. My flesh was burning, even in a desecrated church for a God I do not worship."

I leaned and caught a whiff of burned vamp. Softly I asked, "Mainet's vamps got inside. Was it because of the runes over the other door?"

"We will seek that path. But you will be alone until we can find a way to enter the place that was once holy."

"Not alone. I've got Eli."

The three vamps moved along the hallway, Koun and Tex, holding Leo by an arm. Carmine and Fawn covered Eli and me. I slipped to the open doorway and eased my head around.

In the sanctuary, the circle had been activated. There were three witches, three vamps, and Aya, sitting, or in my brother's case, lying, at the outer ring. In the center of it, Mainet and Sabina/Gramma stood together. Lachish was on the altar, and from this angle, I could see she had been cut from breastbone to groin. The cut wasn't deep, more like a scoring, a pattern for a future, deeper cut. It also didn't look as if it was a single line, but rather something more complex. Maybe the rune for death. She was still alive.

The heart rate, drummed by Endora, increased in speed slightly. It was air magic, and it resonated in my chest cavity, making my breath shudder. A slight tremor caught at my fingers and climbed up my wrists. Eli touched my shoulder again. Our heartbeats synced. So did our breathing. *Calm. Calm.*

The smell of smoke rose on the air. Woodsmoke and rosemary. *Gramma . . .*

The doorway was wreathed in shadow. I slid my head farther into the room to get a better view and saw a red-headed vamp standing to the side of Sabina. I had seen her before. Ka had taken her form. But why? Why here now as a vamp? I had thought she was here to be a sacrifice, but—

And then it hit me. Gramma and Ka were helping Mainet bind an angel and take its power at the same time as Mainet did whatever he was going to do with the heart to take the final power of the Sons of Darkness, and negotiate with or bind a demon that had already been summoned. I pulled back in to the dark so I could think.

What if—in Granny's mind—Ka, as a vamp, was intended to be the designated new Heir? If so, when Mainet became the Master, Ka would gain some power as Heir. And then Gramma would kill Mainet and the full power would fall onto Ka with a demon and an angel bound to her. A skinwalker would have all the power of the vamps, the creatures who had killed off so many skinwalkers. So of course, then, Gramma would become the next Heir.

In almost all vamp clans, there was an heir to accept the power and the curse. Leo had broken that rule until he was ready to name Immanuel his heir. Why? Because of this? Because Mainet was next in line, and Leo had Mainet's big bro chained in his basement.

Ka as a vamp was probably more insane than all other fangheads put together. She had been bitten by an arcenciel. She was expendable to Gramma. Of course . . .

The whole concept made me dizzy. Dizzier. The heartbeat echo was disorienting. I tried to find my last train of thought and ended up with Mainet.

Did Mainet expect Gramma's betrayal? Not even a megalomaniac would allow his greatest enemy into such a ceremony. He had to have a way around possible betrayal just as he'd found a way into the church without burning to a crisp. The long game. One of the SODs had desecrated the church and had begun the summoning of a demon and the angel Hayyel when the church was being built.

The heartbeat drum sped again, increasing incrementally. The tremor returned to my fingers. Eli placed a hand on my shoulder and I felt the same tremor in him. It was affecting both of us now. I managed a slow breath. The heartbeat was a kind of magic, like Big Evan's musical air magic. The hand holding the Glob wasn't shaking. I lifted the Glob to my chest, just below the burned place on my breastbone, and the heated cross. Relief spread through me and into Eli like a balm. My brain started working again.

Ka. Gramma. The Heir. In one place with a bound angel. So, where was the demon? In the futures, there had been a demon. Mainet needed both, angel and demon.

The final pieces fell into place in my mind. Starting with Immanuel. That had been Gramma's plan. To give all the power in heaven and hell to someone in her bloodline. *U'tlun'tas* had selfish goals, warped morals, and less compassion even than the monster De Allyon, who had killed so many of our kind. So after the SODs were dead, Immanuel would have been Mainet's heir? Yeah. But. Gramma would have killed Immanuel and taken his place. Now she would kill Ka and take her place. It's what *u'tlun'tas* did.

I glanced in. Across from me, I saw Tex, standing at the other door, the one marked with death runes, waiting for me to see him. I gave a faint nod, just as Alex said into the earbuds, "Eli. Vamps are in position."

Eli said, "Carmine, Fawn, see if you can move to a firing position in the balcony."

"Your initial targets are the witches. Stop the drumming," I said. "Once it stops, we can take out the primaries."

"Copy," Fawn said softly, the humans sliding into darkness.

Balcony? I looked at the sanctuary again and spotted the narrow second floor. I had thought it was just a decorative shelf. My visions made more sense now. After what felt like forever, I spotted Fawn moving to the front of the balcony near the side wall and laying her upper body across the divider. She aimed a handgun down with a braced two-hand grip, acquiring a target. Not a rifle. A freaking nine-millimeter semiautomatic. Carmine took the other side of the balcony, and at least she had a long-rifle. We now had people but few decent weapons against witches with death bombs. Fawn considered her targets. And waited for the order to fire.

To me, Eli asked, "What's our 'Go' point?"

"We have to wait until the demon and the angel are physically manifested before we act. No matter how bad it gets."

"Roger that." His voice was grim and toneless.

Endora's heartbeat drum increased in volume, suddenly shaking the walls, rattling the stained glass. The magic within it began to pound, and on its heels flashed fear, acrid and tart as death. Only the connection between Eli and me kept me still. The Glob was so hot I could feel it through the padded cloth and wondered when I had put it away. I didn't remember. I wondered if my clothes would catch fire. If the Glob itself could. Could it get so hot it sucked my own magic down with the other stuff it was protecting me from?

Carmine chose her target. Mainet. Not the witches, as I had ordered. The futures had showed me that possibility. Dang it.

Mainet lifted his hands over Lachish's body and placed a cup beside her, handleless white stoneware. Beside me, Eli aimed to the left of my shoulder, keeping contact with me, but Mainet's location, so close to Lachish, made it an impossible shot. In the balcony, Fawn and Carmine exchanged hand signals and changed targets again. I caught sight of Fawn's face, which was badly burned, blistered, sloughing. It looked as if she had brushed by the *death hedge*. She was shaking just a little, the tiniest of tremors, and she was aimed at Mainet. The death beat and the pain were affecting her. If she fired, she might kill Lachish.

I gestured the tiniest bit and shook my head at her. I pointed to the witch standing beside the altar. That would take out two witches, Carmine's target and Fawn's. Fawn steadied her aim and gave a single nod. "On three," I said, ready to begin the raid.

"Our vamps are down," Alex said.

I looked back at our vamps. The doorway was empty. I looked at Mainet's vamps; they were all fine, but they were sitting inside the circle.

Eli leaned out and back in. "Four of us left. Concentrate fire on drummer and witches. Fire on command." He looked at me. "We're in at first shot."

I nodded. "Fire."

Fawn fired. The drumming stopped. Endora slid to the floor of the church. Dead. Head shot. Ursula, the witch to the left of north, threw something into the balcony. A death bomb exploded. Fawn crumpled. Carmine was no

CHAPTER 26

Like a Fire Burning in Reverse

In my earbuds, Alex said, "Leo's moving."

I didn't know what to do. Eli's hand held me in place. His cold, dark calm filled me. "Hold," he whispered. "There's nothing we can do right now but die. If your vamps are waking that will make the difference. We'll know when to move."

Eli had more faith in us than I did. I had seen a lot in the droplet visions, but so much was different now, so much was missing. And every one of my wrong moves meant disaster.

The I/we of Beast and Eli are joined. Are now best hunter. We are one.

Holy crap. She was right. With this strange connection, we were one. The Rule of Three. That fact slammed into me. We three were the Rule of Three.

Sabina/Gramma was holding the crystal athame. Gently, she cut Lachish, tracing the rune made by Mainet, but only deep enough to bleed, not deep enough to do damage to the muscle and organs beneath her blade. That didn't make it hurt any less, however. Lachish twitched. Tears ran down her face. Her breathing sped. I wanted to dart in and save her, but if I did, we would all die and Lachish wouldn't survive either. The witch gasped. Her pain meant nothing to a skinwalker who had gone into the darkness of her own desires. Suffering meant nothing to *u'tlun'ta*, who began that part of the life cycle by eating a living human. I would jump off a cliff before I went that route.

I/we would shed mass and become bird, Beast thought, *and fly away, losing self in flight. Or shift to ugly dog, good nose, and become lost in scent. Would not become* u'tlun'ta. *Jane should not fear. We will kill Mainet. The angel will be free.*

Mainet lowered his hands over Lachish. Placed something on her cleaved belly. The vamp heart.

Eli muttered a curse that disappeared beneath the drumming.

Kill Mainet! Beast demanded.

But I didn't know how. In the visions, if I tried to stop Mainet now, before the demon and Hayyel manifested in the flesh, before Mainet was fully occupied by the ceremony, we all died, and the ceremony went on as Mainet planned. In the same images of the possibilities, I had seen the probability of Molly dying and Bruiser dead, which was why I'd made sure they were both safe, outside the *death hedge*.

But I'd had to study the futures fast, and I had searched only for outcomes where the people I loved survived, and where Eli walked out under his own power, and where I *might* have survived. I hadn't noticed, hadn't studied, what Mainet was doing in between, only the steps I needed to take. I should have studied the potential futures better. Lachish was suffering unbearably. And the demon and the angel were not flesh yet.

Mainet leaned away from Lachish. The heart was larger than it had been. It was now heart and part of both lungs and aorta and pulmonary vessels . . . It had grown. It twitched with its own regenerative power, power it had stolen from its bloodline. From Leo . . . Right. But also from Mainet. I had to remember that the Heir was only the Heir for as long as the Heart of Darkness survived. He wasn't full of power. Not yet.

In an eyeblink, the vessels lengthened and pressed into Lachish's sliced body. Everything I was, everything I had ever been, pushed me to step in now, to save Lachish. But if I moved too soon, she would die even more horribly, and so would all of my people, and the ceremony would be fulfilled. And the world would belong to the Heir. I had to wait until just the right moment.

My lips pulled back from my fangs in a silent snarl as Lachish struggled, awful sounds coming from her throat. The vessels expanded and filled with her blood. And the heart began to beat.

Lachish struggled, her body arching and bowing against the altar table. Her throat gurgled in pain. That sound of agony was too much.

I pushed off with my toes, stepping through the doorway and the concealing shadows, into the light.

Eli yanked me back. Wrapped one arm around my waist to hold me in place. When I struggled, he whispered, "Look at the walls."

Draped down one wall, his form flickering in the light from the brazier, the image of an angel writhed in the reflection of the flames. "Help me, Lord of the Most High," Hayyel sang, his voice like bells and woodwinds and a distant harp. "Do not abandon me to the Dark of the Pit. Do not, I pray Thee, leave me as prey to the Darkness."

Hayyel was manifesting here. In the flesh.

On the opposite wall, a shadow grew, murky, malevolent, vibrating in time with the fast-beating drum and the fast-beating heart. Even though I couldn't bring its unsteady outlines into focus, there was something inherently wrong about the form, something that repelled, repulsed. Something that should not be. I tried to look away and the attempt sent arrows of pain through my head.

The demon shadow took on dimension and mass, growing from trails of smoke. I forced my eyes to follow the smoke and found my gaze on the fire in the brazier. My eyes were dry and I blinked to clear them. The fire wasn't all one thing like fire usually was: composed of a source or sustenance, flame, and smoke. This fire was burning cedar kindling and rosemary but the rest of it was in two parts, the smoke drifting toward the demon, the flames leaning to Hayyel.

I remembered the odd thought about the fire of ceremony, back in Aggie's sweathouse. That image, that metaphor, fit here too: the different potentials of mass and energy—versions of the same thing in the same place, here to bring beings from two different dimensions into this one.

The fire was bringing both entities closer to this realm. Both were growing more solid, like a fire burning in reverse. Hayyel was winged and feathered, his skin black as a moonless night, shining with pinpricks of light. Around his waist was a silver chain, delicate as the chain on a baby's first necklace. This part. This I had seen.

And Lachish was still alive. I could save her yet.

"When the time comes," Eli whispered, "I have holy water. Six vials."

I looked at the demon, lampblack smoke, wisps of brimstone stink. We knew holy water harmed fire demons encased in mud. Would they work on this thing? This monstrously powerful demon? Unknown.

The demon spoke in a language I didn't understand, and as he breathed in, the smoke coalesced into his chest. His body grew more dense. His left hand and shoulder separated from the shadows and extended out of the wall, into the room. He held out that hand to Sabina and pricked his finger on her athame. "Take. Eat," he said.

"Holy crap," I tried to say, but there was no breath in my lungs. My lips moved, like sandpaper against each other. I hadn't seen this. Not in any of the droplets.

Sabina/Gramma lifted the demon's finger to her mouth. She sucked. Bit down. Began to chew. Smoke billowed out between her lips and out her nose with each exhalation. The stink of brimstone rose in the room. *U'tlun'ta*, eating demon flesh.

I looked from the blasphemous feast to Hayyel. Tears like rainbows of sunlight ran down his ebony face, lids closing over golden eyes. His shoulders curled forward and his feathers rustled with fear. The thin silver chain tightened on his waist, cutting into him, the links growing thicker, stronger, catching all the light in the room, gleaming like moonbeams.

The drum beat, beat, beat, a fast heartbeat of rhythm overlaid with the echoes.

Mainet took the bloody athame and sliced open his own belly, a strong, deep cut. His blood splattered the vampires in the circle and they snapped up their heads. Their jaws unhinged and they licked their skin where his blood landed. I had seen some of this, but not enough. Not nearly enough. And I had changed so much with each and every action.

I looked back at Gramma. She now looked like the grandmother I remembered, not the outclan priestess she had eaten. She chewed into the fingers of the demon. She chewed and her body began to writhe.

The demon laughed. The sound sent ice through my blood.

Mainet lay across Lachish's body, the heart and lungs pumping between his sliced belly and hers. The witch struggled, grunting and gasping. Mainet unhinged his jaw, bit into her neck, gently, and began to suck.

Molly and Big Evan ran onto the balcony. They had gotten through the ward. Fury rode into my soul like one of the horses of the apocalypse, taking me over. I had told them to keep her safe. I had also kept Bruiser out, but if Moll was in, then so was he. And they would both be dead. Unless . . . My eyes met Evan's. He nodded, hard. He had something.

Against my breastbone, the gold crucifix heated and froze, burning my flesh again. *Le breloque* flashed with scalding heat, singeing my hair and skin.

Now, Beast said.

"Now," I whispered.

Eli's battlefield awareness took me over.

The world slowed. Everything went crystalline and clear, sharp-edged. The entire room came into focus.

Eli and I sprinted forward.

Evan whirled something over his head. Released it at Ursula, the witch with the drum.

We pushed off with our toes. Stretching into our run.

Evan's magical snare spun through the air. Wrapped around Ursula's neck. Tightened.

Instead of the next witch in line catching the drum and continuing the rhythm, Fiona missed her grab. Her hand batted across the bottom of the heartbeat drum. She dropped it. The drum landed. A clanging, discordant, twanging rattle. The death circle wavered.

We were eight strides into the echoing room.

The cord strangled Ursula. She stepped out of her position in the circle and began to fall. Clawing at her throat. The circle flickered. Losing power.

Leo stepped into the sanctuary, his arm on fire.

Lachish wailed, the sound muffled by her gag. The sound my memories had been waiting for.

Except Molly was here. Too many futures had collided. Ten strides.

The demon on the wall turned to Molly. With his free hand, he reached to her. Molly froze. The demon latched on to her death magics, his claws gripping the air in front of her.

I leaped. Stretched out in midair. Eli running at my side. Together we broke through the faltering circle. I fell forward as Eli fired three shots. Ka dropped. Dead, if she didn't shift fast enough.

Three shots. Sabina/Grandmother staggered.

Horizontal in the air, I cut into Mainet with the broken Mughal blade. Waist high, deep. At his kidney. The broken blade ripped deep into him and up, caught on ribs. Pulling my arm back.

Gramma began to fall. Still with the demon's fingers in her mouth as she toppled.

She pulled the shadow-flesh off the wall and down.

In front of me.

I fell across the smoky arm of the dark one. Against his chest.

My world lit up with electric pain. Frozen agony. No breath. A roar like an earthquake. Gunshots in the far distance. Wind whipping my face. Frigid cold freezing my pelt. *I/we did not see this possibility,* Beast thought.

A shaft of ice into my brain. Words.

Mine mine mine, the demon thought.

My arm was behind me now, stretching me out between Mainet and the demon.

The blade ripped from Mainet.

I slashed the shadow-flesh with the Mughal blade. There was little resistance. He was here and not here. Even steel created to withstand death and coated with the blood of the Heir couldn't cut through demonic smoke. It parted and reformed around the cut. He clasped me against him. I caught a glimpse of Molly. She was free. *Ahhh.* Free because the demon had let go of her death magics, taking me as his sacrifice.

He had shaken his finger free of Gramma when she was shot. As she fell.

Jane. Jane is your name, his thoughts sang into my brain, ringing like broken bells. *Jane Doe Yellowrock. Ahhh. Dalonige'i Digadoli. Yeeesss. I choose you.* He pulled on my skinwalker energies, the silver mist with dark motes exploding out of me.

No. Is not Jane. Is I/we. Is Beast*! Is Eli! Is three!*

Beast wrenched our magic back inside of us. I/we shoved the Glob into the smoky shadowed cavern of the demon's chest. I/we slashed with the Mughal blade. Together, Beast and I pulled on the power of *le breloque.* The crown sizzled against the horrible cold and scalding heat.

The building rocked.

The angel statue fell and shattered, white stone shards, sharp as knives, shooting out.

Something splashed onto my face. Eli. Holy water. The demon roared. Shook my body.

Visions of war exploded through my brain. Men fighting with wood and stone spears and rock hammers. Blood spraying across fields in a blood sacrifice to the Earth. Then metal blades. Spears pierced. Swords cleaved. Axes cut. Blood everywhere. War with guns. Explosions. Fire and rockets. And always blood drenching the land. Land that sucked it up. Land that devoured hate and dark purpose and the blackness of deeds along with the blood.

The Glob burst into black flames. I cut the smoke with the brittle, broken blade. I struck again. Again. The slashing of the blackened steel separated the shadows for an instant, like a sharp wind tears fog. Holy water splattered through the opening. The Glob heated. Sucked up the damaged shadow. A whirlwind of smoky energies tore around us three. Through us.

My scalp scalded. My hand seared. Eli screamed a war cry pierced with pain.

It wasn't enough.

I wasn't enough.

The demon cursed in words that sliced like knives. Words that *were* knives. The specific stench of my blood mixed with the smell of Lachish's blood. Ka's. Grandmother's. The rotten meat scent of *u'tlun'ta* blood. A different kind of Rule of Three, but enough were dead or damaged beyond participating.

The smell of feces and urine and vomit. The clean smell of holy water.

Nitrocellulose from fired weapons.

The taste of dark magic like rotten lemons and maggoty meat on my tongue. The stench of demon, the reek of hell and brimstone.

The desecrated church was permeated by the darkness and the might of the demon. Death and demon energies rolled out like shock waves into the building. The earth rocked and quaked.

Everything slowed until I could see it all. Time almost standing still.

I looked down to see my left hand holding the Glob. A dark pocket of night opened from it. A thing so foreign to our universe it had no name, a thing of no matter. No energy. The nothingness grew wider and longer, the center empty, a void of no-time, no-space, so dark I couldn't see it clearly. The nothingness intensified, forming a spear of power so black it appeared to blink here and then away. *Le breloque* wrapped might and power around the Glob's void. Gave it form and shape and mass/no mass, a thing I understood, yet didn't, all at once.

With the hand holding the Glob, I threw the spear.

It flew into the demon's smoky flesh.

The pointed end of the spear opened like a clawed

hand, like my own clawed hand in the strongest of my half-form shapes. It gripped the smoke.

With a scream that shattered the night, the will of my spirit and the power of the Glob yanked on the demon energies. A whirlwind of churning power, a tornado of blackness, and the smoke of demon flesh. Coiled it into a knot and began to shove it into the pocket world of the Glob. The demon raised me over his head and slapped me down.

I landed hard across the broken angel statue near the altar where Lachish was tied.

My ribs shattered.

Pain held off for a moment, but my breath was gone.

I hadn't dropped the Glob. The demon darkness was still being sucked into its pocket universe. The demon screamed. From the altar, Mainet reached for me. With one taloned hand, he picked me up. Pulled me close to his vamped-out face, fangs and eyes the black of hell. He laughed. "You thought to steal the dark one from me. He is mine. I am the true Heir. The Heir of Darkness."

His power was a tornado of energies tearing through the room. The Glob was not going to be enough. Not enough to bind and capture the demon and destroy the Heir and free the angel.

But. He was still lying across Lachish. There was still time.

Even as I thought that, Mainet threw me up into the ceiling. I hit the broken beam. My clavicle broke, my ribs displacing even more. The pain hit now. Time slowed almost to a stop. From above, I could see all the strands of power, each different, unique, but each just energy, despite how it manifested.

Dying, I pulled it all in, all into the Glob. *Le breloque* added its might, its purpose.

Gravity began to drop me to the floor.

As I fell, I held on to the Glob. Somehow. The crucifix burned into me. Power of a different kind. I wove it all together. It still wasn't too late.

To the demon, on my last breath, I whispered, "Be gone."

Wailing, the last of the demon vanished into the Glob.

Mainet caught me and threw me back up. High. I slapped against the dome above.

Fell. The floor of the church rushing toward me as time sped back to normal.

I tried to maneuver my broken body to land feet downward.

Landed badly. My lower leg snapped. Body whiplashed headfirst into the floor.

Everything went black.

In the night of near unconsciousness, gunfire sounded.

The stink of death magics hung on the air. Eli's heart drummed steady, hard.

I opened my eyes. Cheek to the floor in a puddle of blood. The pain was . . . the pain was everything. I vomited on the floor as the agony took over.

Beast shoved her strength into me, her ability to ignore pain for a moment or two.

When I could focus my eyes, I saw Grandmother. She was dead, her body eaten away by death energies, burned by the taste of demon flesh she had tried to steal, her skinwalker energies taken with the demon into the Glob. There was nothing left of her but a blackened shell, her bones carbonized.

Ka was breathing, her eyes open, staring at the ceiling overhead. One round had entered her skull, two rounds in her chest. And still she breathed.

The pain spiked through Beast's ability to hold it at bay, the pain of broken bones, all-encompassing pain.

Beast thought, *Bone pain. Taste of dandelion flowers and rotten skunk meat. Is the color of smoke and the flesh of starved prey.*

Yeah. That. I looked down at my body. My right leg was bent at a nasty angle a few inches above the ankle.

I gagged, the motion juddering my chest and the broken ribs. The taste bitter. I was bleeding across my chest and belly as if I'd been scored by giant claws. Oh. Right. The demon's claws had cut through my armor. And Longfellow's claws. I was bleeding inside the clothes. Probably pretty badly. I managed one breath, my ribs not moving properly, multiple breaks on each side, and the muscles that stretched between my ruined ribs were torn. *Flail chest*. The term came back from my EMT studies. Fat lot of good it did me.

I was dying. I couldn't fight. I hadn't shifted.

But Mainet had discarded me. For now, I was alive.

The storm of the remaining death magics blew and spun around the room, the Glob still drinking them in. Lightning cracked outside, visible through the broken dome overhead. Rain slashed in and pelted the statues off to the side.

The prophecy of the blade had saved me. So far. I had seen parts of this.

Without moving my head, I looked up and back at the balcony.

Molly was standing atop the short wall marking the edge of the upper level, her dress blown tight against her body by the wind of death magic, the cloth rotting and tearing, wrapped around her legs. Her red curls were swept back. Her eyes were blazing with magic, with power. She held a small rosemary plant in one hand. It still had leaves. *Earth magic*. Molly was using her earth magic to fight the witches' darkness. To fight the death magics of the enemy that were still active.

In the circle, the last living witch, Fiona, threw a death bomb. Molly flicked it to the side with a *wyrd* working. *"Anam."*

The death bomb stopped midair. Hovered.

"Anam." The Irish Gaelic of her family language.

Evan was standing on the floor of the balcony, at Molly's side, one arm around her hips, giving her stability, holding her in place. He sang out a single note, steady and pure. His air magic was gifted to his wife, letting her lead the charge against the death magic of the witch still alive in the circle.

Drawing on his magic, Molly said, *"Bri!"*

The death bomb reversed course. Toward Fiona. The witch sat down. Hard. She landed on the body of a beheaded vamp. A hand out, throwing up a ward in midair.

Molly finished, *"Bua an tsaoil."*

Fiona's ward tore into tatters. Her own death magic hit her. She curled into a tight ball. Relaxed. Died.

In the desecrated, ruined sanctuary, nothing moved but the last threads of a dying breeze.

Eli's heart beat with ours, with Beast's and mine.

Holding to that connection, I pulled healing out of my crown and tried to repair the worst of my bleeding. When that didn't seem to be working, I twisted the energies that were mine to call into a balm that eased enough of my pain to allow me to shove myself over with my good arm. To see the rest of the room.

The enemy vamps had been beheaded. Koun and Tex sat beside them, bleeding, still undead. My vamps were outside the circle, alive, despite their swords having crossed the death magic circle to behead the vamps inside it.

Aya had shifted into human, naked, spattered with gore and filth. His fingers jerked. He breathed out in a soft groan. At some point he had freed his hands and was holding a blade, bloodied.

Hayyel was still present, a black, twinkling glow on the wall, watching us. Still bound by the silver chain, his physical body writhing as if to pull free of the wall.

The Heir lifted himself from Lachish a few inches. The blackness between them sparked with black motes and crackled with power.

Sitting, Tex raised a six-shooter at Mainet.

Mainet cut his own arm and aimed his pulsing blood at the circle. It splattered with a sizzle onto the arcane energies and across the symbols on the wall where the angel rippled. A drop of the vamp blood landed on the chain around the angel.

Hayyel shrieked, a discordant sound of cracked bells and broken wood instruments.

The chain tightened on Hayyel's ebony flesh, glistening like sterling on black velvet. It cut into the angel. Angel blood dripped, a long, glowing trail, light shimmering from the blood itself.

The demon was gone, but Mainet had layers upon layers of potential plans, like a chess game played over eons. He wasn't done. Not yet. And Lachish still lived, resting beneath the weight of his body.

I pulled again on my power and felt it undulate inside

me, to my ribs. I caught a breath that hurt like the frozen fires of hell.

The Heir picked up a cup from beside Lachish's body and threw it at the angel.

The contents splashed on his image. An iridescent arc, a rainbow of light.

The white stoneware cup followed and cracked into pieces against the wall.

Ka lifted her head. She whirled her finger. Green and orange energies reeled around her hand. She threw a death bomb at Tex. The foul energies enveloped him. Tex crumpled, one hand out to catch himself. The gun butt hit the floor with a steel-on-wood thump. Ka sang a note of triumph. Tex bounced. Raised his head. Forced his gun hand up. Fired. Head shot. Through the eye.

It blew out the back of her head.

Big-assed round, silver and lead.

Ka fell back again. Tex went limp.

Aya leaned over Ka and, with the blade he had found somewhere, began to saw off Ka's head. She was dead, so it wasn't bloody. But it was necessary.

Mainet shoved himself away from the body of Lachish. With the crystal athame, he cut into her, separating the bloody heart, lungs, and, now, other organs. From somewhere, Eli began to fire into Mainet. Blood splattered out, healed over instantly. Mainet paused and flicked his fingers at a sooty column. Power wrapped around the column and hit behind. A form fell back.

Eli dropped, landed in the dark. The Heir's flick of power like a battering ram. Eli's pain was a mass of broken flesh, matching mine. Reflecting mine.

I called on the crown for more healing. I was getting a feel for it now and directed some of the Dark Queen's power to my brother through the bonding of our souls. I felt him stabilize and, together, we both sat upright, breathing.

I started to twitch the power back to myself. Saw. Saw *him*.

Behind Ka was the slumped body of Bruiser. Not breathing. Blood everywhere.

Fear shocked through me, an electrified pain.

I reached for my healing power again. Shoved it at Bruiser. Thrust it with all my might. But there was no soul bond. No way to reach him. Just like in the visions. My soul screamed.

Mainet returned to his work. As he cut, I called on Beast's strength. Wrenched on my crown, hauled up everything I had left. If I could touch Bruiser, I could, possibly, transfer the healing. Brute was suddenly standing at my side, legs braced. I placed a bloody hand on his back at his shoulders and began to drag myself up, taking my weight on my one good leg, trying to take in air with tiny breaths, knowing it wasn't enough. Pain sliced all through me like knives coated with lightning, so that I couldn't tell where the pain actually came from. It was everywhere.

Brute edged closer until I was between him and the wall, leaning on the wall near Yr upright, the sign of life, a parody in this awful place.

Molly and her husband still sang a harmony of strident notes, *"Anam! Bri! Bua an tsaoil!"* like a call to war and a claiming of life all at once. Notes rising. *"Anam! Bri! Bua an tsaoil! Anam! Bri! Bua an tsaoil! Anam! Bri! Bua an tsaoil!"*

Hayyel sang with them, his voice rising above theirs. Drawing on their magic, sharing his with them and with their working. An earth witch, an air witch, and a chained angel.

Their magics seemed to separate and fray as they reached Mainet, dissipating into nothing.

Lachish gurgled, trying to draw breath. Mainet cut the last of the organs free from her.

Now. Now. I had to move now. I hopped a step.

I felt Eli, sharing his energy with me. Taking my pain. The air in his lungs pressed out of my brother. Leaving him breathless. Unable to inhale. *Stupid man.* Stupid to share his life force with me. *Stupid.*

But his heart still beat, and I'd not let his gift go to waste.

My one good leg took my weight.

Ka's head rolled away. Dead at last. Aya moved upright, clearly in pain, and held his only weapon by the pointed tip. He flipped the hilt against his lower arm. And threw.

The Heir didn't even notice. The blade stopped inches from him and tumbled to the floor.

Mainet stuffed the severed organs of Joses Santana into his own chest.

As if with a will of their own, they shoved their veins and arteries into him. His body still a gaping wound, he roared with power. He turned to the vision of Hayyel.

Lachish managed a breath. She might have only two more in her.

Now, I thought. *This moment.*

Holding the Mughal blade in an awkward three-fingered half grip, I dropped the Glob into my armor at my neck. With the same hand, I tore the crucifix away from my flesh, leaving a bleeding cross-shaped wound where it had adhered to me. Grown into me.

Pushing off with my one good leg, I scooted my foot back and forth, moving forward. Brute walked with me, taking my weight. Toward Mainet. Toward the brazier still flickering with flames. Toward the dying body of Lachish. Hoping I could save her. Hoping I wasn't too late.

Stretching out one hand, I collapsed forward.

Released the crucifix, watching it fall into Lachish's open body cavity. As it dropped, I noted that it was covered in my blood and bits of pelt. My blood splattered from my fingers. Some landed into the cavity of her chest. Onto the floor. Into the flame on the brazier. The flame that had been feeding the image of Hayyel licked high, as if I had thrown gasoline onto it.

With my other hand, I flipped the blade into a proper grip, still falling. Extending my arms, I wrapped myself around him.

I/we landed beside the brazier. Hard. The Heir's body beneath mine. My broken leg twisted. My ribs giving out. The pain splintering, fragmenting, crushing.

The dark of death began to gather at the edges of my vision.

My crown heated, healing as best it could, blistering, a backdrop to the accumulated injuries. But my heart rate

was too fast. Breathing was impossible. I was dying. Eli
tried to send me more of his power, but I shut the connection between us down. Not Eli. Not him too.

Screw it. I'd finish this.

I still held the blade. It was shattered. Not much of it
left. The broken edge pierced Mainet at the juncture of
his shoulder and neck, torquing down and in, curving.

Eli battered through my defenses. His hand in my
mind. Guiding the blade into a perfect killing strike.
Down. Into the Heir's own heart. Through it. Out the
other side of the Heart of Darkness.

Mainet roared again, this time with fury and pain. He
rose up.

I ripped out the blade.

Heard a gunshot. Three more. Eli had fired vamp-
killer rounds into Mainet's head.

But despite being cut in half, the Heart of Darkness
was still beating.

I caught myself on the altar. Lachish breathed out a
final breath. The futures were colliding.

Molly's song echoed high in the sanctuary, fierce. The
angelic tones followed her call. Evan's harmony dropped
low. *"Anam! Bri! Bua an tsaoil!"*

Using the Mughal Blade like a sickle, I stabbed the
point into Mainet's chest. Curved my hand down. Shoving the blade into the new heart again, three times. Its
rhythm shuddered and the tissues quivered. I stabbed it
again, cutting it apart. Again. It stopped beating. I cut the
heart out of his chest.

Eli was suddenly beside me. With his bare hands he
lifted the chunked-up heart and lungs that did not belong
out of Mainet's chest cavity. Held them up and away so I
could see what I was doing.

With the Mughal Blade I cut the veins and arteries attaching the heart and lungs of the Son of Darkness out of
the vamp. The last time I had done this, Brute ate all the
other parts of Joses Santana. Now, the werewolf backed
away, growling low, so loud I felt it in my own chest.

I understood. This was demon smut and all the power
of the two Sons of Darkness gathered in one body.

With the dripping blade, I pointed at the fire.

Eli threw the bloody mass on the brazier. It flamed high. A bonfire. Roaring. This time there would be nothing left to regenerate.

Walking on broken feet bones, one arm held tight to his side, Eli dragged me back. Away.

In the brazier, fire spit in a fountain of sparks. Everywhere the droplets of fire landed, new fires grew. In a heartbeat, the flames reached toward the damaged roof.

With the last sharp metal of the Mughal blade steel, I leaned in and began to cut off Mainet's head.

Even with his brain scrambled, his body fought. Clawed into me. His fangs slashed and tore me as I sawed. But Eli's hands on my shoulders steadied me. His heart beat with mine. Somehow the pain receded.

From the corner of my eye, I saw Aya crawl to my injured vamps and begin pulling them away from the fires. Others raced in and began to assist. There were people, my people, everywhere. Fire extinguishers sprayed. I gestured to the brazier and shook my head.

"Don't put out the brazier," Eli said.

I went back to the head. Cut and cut. The lace of jagged steel severed Mainet's spine. The last threads of flesh. I cut through and shoved the head from the body.

When I was done, the final sliver of damaged blade shattered and fell. I dropped the beautiful hilt to the bloody floor. Looked at my other hand. At some point I had retrieved the Glob from my chest. My palm and fingers were scorched as if I'd put my hand on a hot grill. My flesh was once again seared into place around the Glob, palm and fingers blistered and weeping serous fluid. I picked up Mainet's head and set it on the brazier. The flames licked high again. Searing.

As soon as the body was ashes as well, the rule of the Sons of Darkness and their Heir would finally be over. The pain hit. My breath fled and the room dimmed as I nearly passed out. "Burn it," I whispered. But I knew no one heard me.

Molly's and Evan's singing earth and air magic and the angel song ended with long, plaintive notes, the witch and angelic tones slightly out of harmony, a faint difference in key. Hayyel sounded lost. Grieving. I looked up at the wall where he had manifested and the angel met my gaze. Waiting.

Leo picked me up in his arms. I gasped with breathless pain as he handed me to Bruiser. Bruiser, who was not dead. *Not dead. Not dead.* The words matching the last notes of angel song.

"Feed her," Leo directed.

CHAPTER 27

You'll Stop Bleeding Eventually, One Way or Another

I smelled Onorio blood and caught a glimpse of Bruiser's hands. They were burned, his fingers broken. He had hurt himself trying to get to me. Trying to get through the *death hedge*. Broken while fighting to keep me safe even as I had schemed to keep him alive.

Stupid wonderful man.

He turned toward the door, took a step to carry me to safety.

"Wait," I whispered when I could find the breath to speak.

Bruiser stopped and bowed his head to touch mine, the crown between our flesh, which had to say something about our lives right now. "Jane. Please. I don't want to lose you. And you are bleeding to death." Flames danced around us, up toward the ceiling. The smoke was choking.

"No. We have to . . ." My breath gave out. I took in air that came in shallow gasps. "I can shift in a minute." Well, I was *fairly* certain that Beast and I could change to puma. "Mainet has to burn. And Hayyel isn't free yet. I think Mainet threw *arenciel* blood on him. I think he's fully bound."

From somewhere in the church, Molly's cell rang. Over Bruiser's shoulder, I saw Molly, Evan, Fawn, and Carmine enter the sanctuary from an access beneath the balcony. Evan hummed a soft note and the smoke blew away from them as they walked, like some cinematic effect in a film. The big man, the air sorcerer, said, *"Ventus,"* and whistled a sharp note, like calling a horse on a ranch somewhere. The smoke all around us whipped away, up through the broken ceiling.

Molly had her cell phone to her ear.

"Please," I whispered, not sure what I was asking, or praying, the room swirling around me. My heart was beating too fast and my breathing was too shallow and rapid. I had lost a lot of blood. Too much. Eli was at my side. Wounded. Bleeding. Broken, but breathing. Trying to give me his calm. It wasn't working. I had again shut down the connection between us.

Bruiser turned back into the room, holding me close, as if he feared I'd be plucked away.

"Jane's bleeding to death," Eli said. "We need the Infermieri."

"Florence isn't on site," Alex said into my one earbud that was still in place.

Evan stepped across bodies to us and pulled four feathers from his pockets. "You do know George is drenched in your blood, right?"

"Ummm. No?"

Whistling "Pop Goes the Weasel," he inserted the feathers into the cuts of my clothing.

I jerked, "Owww!"

"Stop being such a whiny baby," Evan said, adding more feathers, knowing that an insult would work better than kindness to keep me going. "You'll stop bleeding eventually, one way or another."

I may have laughed. It was hard to be sure.

The feathers snapped and stank like burned feathers, but they stopped my blood loss. It freaking hurt. It burned like firecrackers going off against my flesh, like styptic powder liberally dumped on me. "Oww," I said, louder. But when the sharp pain faded, the underlying pain was less. I felt better, more alert.

He stuck more feathers into various rents in my armor. It didn't fix the shattered misplaced ribs or my leg bones, but it did ease the pain.

"Thanks. I think." I scowled at Evan and he chuckled, his red beard moving with amusement at my discomfort.

Evan patted the top of my head like he might pat Angie's. To distract myself from saying something snarky to the guy who was probably stabilizing me if not saving my life, I croaked out, "Molly? What did Angie say?" Because it had to be Angie calling.

"Whistle the smoke away from him," she said to her husband.

"From who?"

Moll pointed at the wall where the flames from the brazier had been drawn when the demon disappeared. The smoke from the brazier, which stank of filth and horror, had gathered there. A pall of smoke hung on the wall, like a black cloud pressed tight to the angel. Demon smut and brimstone cradling the angelic. Big Evan frowned. Pursing his lips, he gave long trilling notes, high-pitched, like a yodel. The smoke furled back, dissipating.

I took in the angel. *Holy crap.*

A deep hush fell on the group.

Everyone, even those of us who had seen the angel manifest from the stone statue, was silent and maybe awed. Even me. Because I had seen Hayyel in visions before, but never physical form. And here he . . .

Here he was.

Leo fell to his knees and bowed his head.

Moll's whole being was focused on the angel sticking from the wall. Her face went through this series of changes, from shock to fury, back to shock. Tears welled in her eyes and ran down, cleaning trails in her smoke-stained face.

Molly had admitted once that she had lost her faith in anything divine. Someone had said something to Moll about how she had to find her faith to survive and to protect the ones she loved, faith to control the death magics. I was pretty sure it had been her daughter. Now there was this massive angelic being hanging out of the church wall.

Bruiser's heart rate sped beneath my fingertips.

Eli's heart pounded steady but hard, as if it would

burst. He moved closer to me. I felt his position change through our bond. His shoulder touched mine. There was no calm in him now. No dark pools of battle readiness. Just . . . wonder. Maybe reverence.

The other vamps stared but stepped back and away, breathing as humans. I felt their reactions through the bond of the Dark Queen.

Hayyel was fully formed, twelve feet tall, his right leg and his body partially out of the wall, his left leg, hip, and up to his armpit still trapped in the plaster and red brick on the other side of . . . elsewhere. His head hung, his beautiful hair loose and catching the light of the candles. His hawklike wings were both free, but the flight feathers were gone, the pinions burned away to the metacarpals, the flesh blistered and leaking.

Where he was still attached to the wall, cracks radiated out into the plaster from his black skin. He was as unmoving as the marble statue he had spoken through the first time I came to this sanctuary. As unmoving as the vampire kneeling at the tip of his scorched wings.

Leo reached out, slowly. With one finger he touched the blackened feathers. They crumbled into dust. But his finger wasn't burned and his body didn't go up in flames. Leo. In a church with his vamps, touching an angel. Not on fire.

"Yes. That was Angie," Molly said, answering my question. "Angie said to give Leo the key that was found here. She said he would use the key to open the silver chain." Her voice was carefully neutral. Because her double-gened witch daughter had called with a solution to a problem she should not know about. And she should be asleep. And guarded by her aunts.

With my one good hand I opened the flap in my armor that held the key we had removed from the marble angel statue. It was covered with my blood, but so was everything else.

Eli took it from me and knelt at Leo's side. "Leo," he said gently. "Leo?"

The former master of the city raised his human-looking eyes to his friend, his former primo. "My George," he said softly, the look of wonder lighting his face. "The angel . . ."

To Leo, I said, "The key is silver, made from the thirty silver coins paid to Judas Iscariot. The chain is silver from the coins too. Ordinary silver is toxic to vamps. This will . . . This *may* be worse."

Leo turned his head to me in the curiously birdlike way vamps have when they aren't aping humans. "I know this."

Molly said, "The shackling is a powerful death magic working. If you unlock the chain, you and the other vamps may go up in flames. The chain might be only thing keeping you all from burning to ash."

Leo smiled sadly. "The black magic that made my kind took our souls. *You* know *this*. The chain made from the silver bartered for the redeemer's death, and the black magic that made my kind, gave us eternal life, stole our souls, and partially bound the angel. With the chain unlocked we may all die, yes. Or"—he shrugged slightly, like a raven fluttering its wings—"we may find our souls. Those who have gone before may finally rest rather than continue to wander the place of the dead."

"I don't understand," I said.

"He," Leo said, again touching a burned feather, "was first bound in Jerusalem over two thousand years ago bound with that silver of Judas Iscariot's betrayal. A second binding was attempted soon after, and the result was Krakatoa. Other attempts were made during the Crusades. There was a fire the night of one such black magic ceremony and Constantinople burned. The key was lost in the battle, or so it is said."

As Leo was speaking freely, I assumed Mainet's bindings were undone. Hayyel stared at the vampire as the outclan priest told his story.

"The next attempt to bind the Angel of the Most High, so far as I know, was here, on this land, long ago, before the church was built on this spot, when Immanuel was still my son. It is said that ceremony required the sacrifice of three human virgins."

Three, I thought. *Like the three skulls on the map and the three skulls in Angie's dream.*

"Perhaps the black magic ceremony that created Immanuel the False, the night he lost his life to the *u'tlun'ta*, was that same night." Leo shrugged again. "There were certainly other attempts to bind and use the holy messenger.

"We did not know where the key was located, only that Joses brought it to this city when he visited. The Son of Darkness placed the key to our creation somewhere in New Orleans, hidden during the time that Soledad dreamed, and also created her beautiful statues. But when Joses was bitten by the arcenciel, he lost his sanity and the key was lost to us as well. In return, his blood gave to those who drank it, visions of potential futures and glimpses of the past.

"Once, when I drank of him, I saw Joses Santana, in the past, placing the key in a groove of marble, and covering the damage with plaster. I did not know it was in a statue of an angel, created by Soledad." Leo made a soft sound of amusement. "He would have found that amusing, ironic, macabre, to place it in an angel.

"And there the key resided, there rested the angel, but . . . Hayyel was lost to us. I knew from my own visions that a war woman was coming, but not that you, Jane Yellowrock, were she. Not until you appeared as the half-form lion warrior. When I first laid eyes on that form of you, I knew that our end or our redemption was at hand."

Okay, I thought. *Leo's timeline worked.*

Leo held out his hand for the key. Eli placed it into his palm.

Leo tilted his head forward a fraction of an inch. *"Je comprends,"* he said to the angel on the wall, as if Hayyel had spoken to him. And maybe he had.

Leo reached out and stroked the angel's burned wings. He shuddered and nodded as if in agreement with more unspoken words. The former master of the city stood from where he knelt and looked around.

"Mithrans. Depart." His power pushed out at us, as strong as when he was master of the city, but Koun and Tex didn't run. They were feeding Eli and watching me. Bound to my orders now, not Leo's.

I nodded in agreement and glanced at the door. The two left the church.

Bruiser held me closer. The shattered ends of my ribs ground together, stealing my breath.

Leo pointed and Eli, who was better after the blood, seemed to know what was needed. He motioned for Big Evan to help move a long altar-type table close. While they worked, Leo went to Lachish's body, still bound to the altar. "Such a sacrifice on the credence table has desecrated it for the Host. This place will again be holy. I will see to it that it is cleansed and restored to its beauty for the faithful."

Leo tilted his head to me, birdlike again.

"I require two knives. One can be any blade. One must never have been bloodied."

Unbloodied kinda left out all of mine.

Fawn extended two knives, lifting the one in her left, saying, "Bloodied." She lifted her right. "Unbloodied."

With the bloodied blade, Leo cut through the ropes holding Lachish. He whispered something over her body and made the sign of the cross in the air over her. As he spoke, the crucifix I had dropped into the cavern of her belly gushed up through her cooling blood and viscera. Leo wiped it clean on a cloth and placed it in the same palm as the key. His body shuddered when they made contact and smoke rose from his hand. The stench of searing vamp was discernable beneath the burning reek of Mainet's head and the cursed organs. Leo didn't react to the pain, but it had to hurt.

Leo returned the bloodied blade to Fawn and lifted Lachish in his arms. He carried her out of the profane circle, placing her on a cloth-covered bench. Blood splashed from her wound over the cloth to the floor. Leo drew the edges of the cloth across her body, covering her. He closed her eyes and said softly, "Rest now, sweet witch. You served well."

Which made no sense. Unless . . . Lachish protecting the heart had been some powerful position, like the witch version of the outclan.

And I had given the heart to Jodi, not even a witch. Somehow it had been passed up the witch food chain to Lachish. *Dang.* Had Leo made sure the heart got to her? Yeah. Of course.

Leo walked to the table that Eli and Evan had moved beneath the angel. He made a tiny jump, landing on top, perfectly balanced. He opened his burning hand and pulled the key and the crucifix out of his flesh. I could hear the ripping sounds from where I was held in Bruiser's arms.

I could breathe with less pain, though I now felt as if I was being attacked by fire ants inside and out. My body was healing and that hurt. I leaned into my honeybunch and he cradled me closer. Onorio strength, to hold my weight so long.

Leo's hand, where the cross and the key had rested, was healed. He put the cross around his neck on its tiny gold chain. He reached up with the key to unlatch the silver chain, but the angel spoke. "You are now the Heir."

Bruiser jerked, just a tiny bit. Leo was from the line of the Heir. Sooo. Yeah. He was now the Heir. *Crap.*

"If you free me, my son, the power you could have claimed will be lost."

"If we will finally be free as well, our souls returned, it is a bargain well struck, messenger."

"I can promise your souls, but I cannot say if you and your kind will live or all die when that happens."

"I no longer care. I am tired of collusions and intrigues and the power wars of Mithran life. I am tired of watching the Naturaleza hunt and bind and destroy humans. I am tired of killing. Tired of war. If we die to free you, you who have been chained for two millennia, so be it."

The angel lifted a hand and placed it on Leo's head. Again, Leo didn't burst into flame. "You have answered well, my son. For your wisdom, I grace you with life. I grace you with power. I grace you with healing. But there are costs. Every drinker of blood will now have a soul. For many, having a soul will be a great burden."

Leo laughed, the sound joyous, echoing in the church that had heard only screams and gunfire all night. "A blessing from an angel of the Most High could be nothing else." He unlocked the chain and placed the key into the angel's hand.

But the chain didn't fall.

"Unbloodied blade," Leo said, holding out his hand. Fawn stepped close and lifted the knife, placing the hilt into his palm. Leo sliced his palm and wiped his blood on the chain. His bloody handprints marred the black skin and blue robe the angel wore. "There was no ceremony in the visions I had of this night," Leo said. "There were only three things: the death of the Heir, the demon returned into darkness, freedom of the angel through blood freely given." He touched his chest. "I had hoped for my soul, but I never saw it in the myriad futures."

The blood on the silver chain bubbled. The chain fell and landed with a metallic clang on the table at Leo's feet. "You are free, Hayyel."

"As you and your kind," Hayyel said, "will now be free."

Leo's head snapped back. He gusted in a deep breath. He screamed, that piercing ululation of death. Dropped to his knees. Leo fell to the floor, screaming, curled like a baby. My vamps, out on the lawn, screamed.

The sound was a sonic weapon, drilling into every nerve ending in my whole body.

My crown went hot, blistering hot.

Outside, my people fell to the ground.

Bruiser turned us both away. I pressed one ear against Bruiser's chest and covered the other. A headache lanced through me from *le breloque*. It was the pain of my vamps. My vamps, everywhere. In my soul there was an opening, and through it a light pierced, the light where there had been only darkness.

My brain burned. My forehead blistered.

I was screaming. Tears and snot ran down my face.

Bruiser was screaming, bending his body away from the crown, trying to distance himself while holding me safe.

From away, beyond the church grounds, other vamps joined in Leo's scream. From across the city. Across the world. I felt them through the crown. Heat shot through my brain and out to them like lightning, like a storm of magic and spirit and immense power. After long minutes, the electric energies softened into waves, healing.

The spear of lightning in my brain flashed a last time. Disappeared. It left me in a red haze of darkness, like blood on a moonless night.

I was gasping. Bruiser was weeping.

We were sitting on the floor in a pile of aching limbs and shattered statuary.

The heat of *le breloque* began to fade, the temperature dropping to warm.

The crown expanded; I caught it, holding it in place with the hand over my ear.

As the pain eased, Bruiser turned toward the angel, and I managed to get my eyes open. Wiped the tears and mucous and blood from my face. Dropped the crown over my arm.

The angel looked at me, his face kind. "The evil of the heart of the Sons of Darkness is ended. The fallen one has been bound into utter darkness. You must place the body and the ashes of the former Heir outside, on the grounds, so the dawn sunlight burns it completely, and then scatter the ashes to the winds."

I managed, "Finally something easy."

Bruiser chuckled silently, his chest moving against me.

"The words I speak are from the Most High, a prophecy of truth." Hayyel raised his arm as if gesturing to the broken ceiling. His tone altered, sang out, ringing as if bells pealed, resonating into the night, "'The power of the Dark Queen will remain within Jane Yellowrock, and *le breloque* shall be hers, but her purpose for warfare among the undead is no more.'"

My skin pebbled in chills and the hair stood up all over me. There was power, raw, universe-shaking power in the words. The tones made my bones ache.

Hayyel's face, black as the night sky, glowed with power that was both dark and light, his words sang with both sound and utter silence. His eyes were golden and shining as the sun, and they burned my skin when he looked our way. Bruiser lurched to his feet, took a dozen steps back, and I had to fight not to cringe with him. Hayyel was terrible and beautiful to look upon. I didn't think it was God himself talking, but the visage of Hayyel when he was restored to the Host. And I was glad of that. I knew I didn't want to lay eyes on anything with more power than the angel. I might not survive the experience.

"'The drinkers of blood have been transformed,'" he

continued, speaking the words of God. "'The trapped souls of the true dead are freed, to go where I, the Most High, will send them. The souls of those still undead have been restored. The drinkers of blood have choice and free will and redemption, should they choose. The Heir is Mine, thus speaks the Most High. The Heir is and ever shall be an outclan priest, to serve Me and to serve the souls of the undead, to counsel, to judge. The curses of the past are broken.'"

The words and the horrible ringing settled, and the deep, bone-deep pain receded enough that I didn't have to vomit. My throat was dry, my eyes raw, as if I had been sitting in a desert wind. I could feel my own heartbeat, hard against my chest, mine and Eli's both too fast where Eli still leaned against me.

His voice went back to purely angel tones, and Hayyel said, "Come to me, Jane Yellowrock."

Bruiser carried me to the wall.

Hayyel put a hand on my head, like a wordless blessing. Warmth flowed through me, sweet as honey, rich as cream, soft as velvet, all the colors of the rainbow, the scent of vanilla and caramel—the sensory equivalent of a parent's loving blessing. I didn't really remember my parents, but thought I must have been loved. This, this wonder, this safety, was what it must have felt like.

Bruiser let me slide to my feet. Gingerly, I tested my leg. The bones weren't brand-spanking new but my leg could bear weight. The angel of my visions, of my soul home, had healed me. Again. That healing flowed into Bruiser. Into Eli. Into my Mithrans out on the lawn.

"It is as I had always hoped," Hayyel said, "as I have worked toward for so many human lifetimes. The curse laid upon the scions of the sons of Ioudas Issachar for their evil is broken. In the same way, the curse of the soulless is lifted from the drinkers of blood and from the servants and slaves they made their own. The curse laid upon the werewolves is broken. You are free as well, *Dalonige'i Digadoli.* No longer bound by the past and the blood of others, and no longer able to bind others with your blood, but only by the love they have for you. The

curse of *u'tlun'ta* that Beast made of you when she took
your soul is removed from you."

Jane is no longer killer only, Beast thought. *I/we are
Beast! Best ambush hunter.*

As I watched, the angel began to fade like mist over
the Mississippi at dawn, his hand growing lighter, ephemeral,
until I could see through it. Hayyel was less than a
mist, a dream half remembered upon waking. If he was
speaking truth, he had changed our world, forever. I wondered
if his actions and words had really been sanctioned
by the Almighty and what the Host would think about his
actions.

Before I could ask the outclan priest all that, Leo
popped away.

My vamps drove off in various SUVs back to safety
from the rising sun. I felt them go, not through the crown,
not through blood spent, taken, or given, but through the
touch of the angel on Leo's head.

As the sun grayed the skies, Hayyel faded into nothing.
He was gone, leaving behind only the chain of his
imprisonment stained with Leo's bloody handprints,
freely given.

Aya rose to his feet, uncoiling his legs. "My sister. You
are Beloved Woman. War Woman." He bowed from the
waist and stood upright, naked as a jaybird. "I honor
you."

At his feet, Mainet's true-dead fingers twitched. Aya
stepped back fast.

Before I could give the order, Fawn and Carmine
dragged Mainet's headless body outside into the dawn.
Then they found a few two-by-fours and used them to lift
the red-hot brazier and Mainet's still-burning skull and
carried it out as well. A human handed Ayatas a pair of
pants and a shirt and he dressed swiftly as Bruiser and I
walked outside.

Together our small group of humans watched the sun
rise, pale peach sky and soft rosy clouds, as the remains
of the Heir flamed up and burned into ash.

The river breeze kicked up as the tide changed and the
sun's heat began to warm the earth. Big Evan whistled up
a small whirlwind and the ashes twisted into the sky and

away, out over the water of the Mississippi toward the Gulf of Mexico.

Using the two-by-fours, I stirred the ashes of evil and scattered them into the river wind. We watched them float away.

I knew up front I'd be in the way. I didn't even ask to go along. Instead, Longfellow and I watched the action on the screen of the large tablet Alex positioned for us on the back porch of my freebie house, rocked, and sipped tea. The little flying dragon liked tea with honey, so he got his own cup, which he could reach from his perch on the arm of my rocking chair. Molly, Big Evan, and the kids were with us, the kids playing on my broken rock garden, all of us under heavy guard. As we watched the screens, a soft rain blew in, a muggy front across the landscape from the Gulf, slow patters of rain and no lightning, a warm soaking, perfect for the kids to play in and keep them out of our hair.

On the screens, Eli and Bruiser led the human and witch teams as they stormed Mainet's HQ for the cleanup. They cleared the house hidden in the middle of the French Quarter, mostly buried by the hotels and businesses that had been built up around it. Room by room, hidden lair by lair, half underground, the vamps were found, staked, and piled like cordwood until they could be transported to my scion room for judgment by the outclan priest. Based on information gathered from the humans there, they tracked down the sleeping quarters of other vamps and humans, set free prisoners, and acquired vast amounts of intel.

In one weather-beaten house on the edge of Petit Lac Des Allemands, they also discovered a hoard of gold a dragon would have lusted over. Did lust over, I presumed, because Longfellow popped away from my rocking chair and appeared at the gold, hovering and squeaking what sounded like, "Mine! Mine! Mine!" Fortunately the little dragon couldn't actually breathe fire and he was satisfied with a gold coin, which he held like prey in his back feet as he popped back for more tea. I had no idea what I was going to do with the little dragon.

Over the course of the daylight, my people staked seventy-two sleeping vamps scattered across the area and—from sunset to midnight—transported them to the scion room in HQ. They were stacked wall to wall and the small-ish room reeked of vamp and blood, enough to make me sneeze when I did the queenly thing and inspected my enemies.

There would be a trial. Heads would roll.

The humans who had served the staked vamps numbered three hundred forty-two, and were given care and food, the edibles ordered in from local restaurants. The humans who wanted to stay in vamp service, despite the binding no longer working as it used to, would be dispersed across the nation to all the MOCs who owed me fealty. Even with the sharing out among my national clans, I'd have to create new vamp clans in NOLA to house some. Life in NOLA would change again, and hopefully, someone would step up and become master of the city. Eventually. So far, all my own vamps had been too smart to want that job.

To address the transport circle problem, the Everharts and local witches paired with local concrete companies and local law enforcement as well as a company out in the boonies at the estate, and, in a well-timed release, dumped multiple loads of concrete into the open witch circles at the distant points of the star.

The concrete spewed out of the circle in the central small garden of the hidden house in NOLA, the walled-in witch circle from which Mainet had carried out his attacks. There was a lesser eruption in the smaller, amulet-created circle in a bathroom of the church, through which the witches had transported Mainet and his vamps.

Safely from my squeaky metal rocker, I sat and let my well-trained and enthusiastic teams do what they did best—protect my city and each other. For once I didn't care that I wasn't in the midst of things. I was bone tired, so exhausted that even a platter full of bacon and an entire pot of tea did little to keep me awake as the human and witch teams tracked, trapped, and transported our enemies.

Midafternoon, the skies opened up as the first late fall storm blew in, necessitating a venue change for the press conference Bruiser had agreed to. The governor, the local officials, two senators, and the media wanted the conference at HQ, claiming the location was based on the rain (but it was likely because the ratings would be higher if it took place there). The mayor, who was suddenly my new BFF, was all about keeping me and my tax money in NOLA, and had a long phone chat with my Consort to consolidate the vamp relationship with his city. He too wanted the press conference in vamp HQ, in the HQ ballroom. I even had interview requests from national media. *Gag.*

The media and political interest was the result of the release of camera feed from inside the desecrated church, timed with the statement about me moving to Asheville, leaked by two reporters, one who gained access to the Dark Queen's winter court inn. At the same time, a documentary video about the horrors of the vamp war in Europe had been released on YouTube. Coincidence? Nope. That timing had my honeybunch's fingerprints all over it.

Deon had offered to create a spread for the event, but he was exhausted from ordering in enough food for all the new humans. Like the rest of us, he'd been running himself ragged for days. So I put my paw down and insisted on coffee only. Just because I had to open HQ to the media and political types didn't mean I had to make them feel welcome, especially after the way some of them had treated my people.

The press and the VIPs started to gather half an hour before start time, at which point I unexpectedly shifted to human form. The shift then was marginally better than during the press conference, but it did necessitate a wardrobe change. Fortunately I didn't feel any lump in my gut (meaning I was likely cancer free) and I had plenty of clothes in my HQ bedroom suite. Quint helped me into black business trousers with a gold tunic and a black jacket with a tiny gold pinstripe the color of my eyes and the color of my crown, which I stuck back on me after the shift. (The miserably uncomfortable crown was good for politics. And I was now, for better or worse, a political symbol.) Dancing shoes and my amulets completed my ensemble. That's what Quint called it. "My Queen's ensemble." I carried a few weapons—fully hidden—just in case someone decided to bring the dregs of the war here and shoot me dead on live TV. It could happen.

Eli and Bruiser, state senators and members of the House, the governor of Louisiana, the mayor of NOLA, the city council, the bigwigs and dignitaries in state, parish, and city politics and law enforcement were all gathered at the dais when I walked in the doors. The mayor lifted his wrist and checked the time on a fancy wrist piece to let me know that I had cut it close. I smiled at him and touched my crown as I walked down the aisle. I had home court advantage. I had a crown. He had . . . votes. My expression said, *I win*.

The place fell silent as I made my way down the middle of the room, on the same carpet that had been used at Wrassler and Jodi's wedding. Quint followed me. Cameras followed us both. Lots and lots of cameras. People shouted questions, dumb questions, as we walked the carpet and I took my place, not answering. I stopped and faced the room, standing slightly in front of the mayor. I was taller than New Orleans's new mayor. He had to move to the side to be seen by the reporters.

Yeah, it was petty. And catlike. Vengeful Cat. I had been called that once and it kinda fit. I stood silent, my face expressionless, and let all the local law talk, then all the politicians. I let my mind wander, thinking about maybe putting a pool in at the DQ's Winter Court. Not an Olympic thing, but a family thing, something the kids would like. And then I heard Bruiser say, "The Dark Queen has a short statement. She will not be taking questions." My Consort stepped to the side and I took his place at the podium, a narrow plexiglass thing I had noticed subconsciously, but not fully.

The stupid questions started again. I let them shout. After a bit I said softly, "I have allotted two minutes to speak to this room. You have one minute left." A few beats later I said, "Fifty seconds. Forty-five." The racket continued. "I detest public speaking. Make my day. Thirty seconds."

The room quieted.

I decided on the royal "we." Narrowed my eyes at the crowd.

"The Dark Queen and the clan masters of this city, our Mithrans, our blood-servants, our Onorios, the New Orleans's witches, a werewolf, and our humans have defeated every incursion made by domestic and foreign terrorists and invaders intent on turning our citizens into cattle, bleeding you and leaving you to die. We have done this, most often without parish, local, or state law enforcement backup, and lately, without political assistance. We have done this not for money, but for love of New Orleans, for love of Louisiana, for love of her people. No more. The Dark Queen will be moving to Asheville as of Monday next, taking that city as our year-round permanent residence and our permanent headquarters."

The mayor blanched. Probably due to all the videos of the vamp war in Europe.

The room broke into pure pandemonium with a side order of fury.

My voice just as calm, I continued as the room returned to quiet. "Yellowrock Clan Home will remain here. We will maintain a personal, part-time residence here. But it will be up to those other clan Blood Masters if they stay or leave. Hopefully, one of the clan masters will accept the position as master of the city, but so far, due to the lack of respect shown to the protectors of this populace, no one is willing." I looked at Bruiser and nodded toward the door behind us. "Consort?"

Together, my honeybunch and I left the room, Quint covering our six.

As the door closed behind us, Bruiser said, casually, "Moving?"

"The Dark Queen likes the mountains. We'll have homes here as often as we want. I should have asked you first, but the mayor . . ."

"I saw his expression. He hates you."

"Hates all paras. I should have discussed it with you."

"Negative on that, my love." He took my hand and kissed my knuckles. "My home is not coordinates on a map. Home is wherever you are."

"This way we can come and go. Christmas in the mountains? Maybe we'll get lucky and have snow."

"That sounds lovely," Bruiser said. "For now, however, you are dead on your feet. Let's get some sleep."

CHAPTER 28

A Good Ol' Boy Who Ain't Gotten Laid

A space was open before me. Inside me. It was wide and long, tall and deep, dark as night, yet warmed by crackling firelight and the scent of hickory and oak smoke. Stalagmites and stalactites rose and hung from the floor and rock ceiling. Water dripped, an irregular echo that filled the chamber.

I was sitting by the fire, yellow and gold flames, a column of smoke rising to the domed ceiling. My soul home. After all this time, still my place of spiritual refuge. Beast lay beside me, on her side, against my thigh, her big head on my knee. She was asleep, or nearly so, purring. My hand was around her chest, my fingers over her heart.

Across the fire from us sat people, my people. Bruiser. Eli and Alex. Edmund. Koun. Tex. Molly, with all the Truebloods and Everharts, even Shiloh and her primo. Aya, wearing his traditional garb. Jodi and Wrassler. Rick, which was a surprise. All of my people. So many of them.

All of them were free.

Dozens and dozens of them, human, vampire, witch. All of the people who were once bound to me, who had sworn to me in one way or another. Among them, oddly, was Leo.

They were no longer bound, no longer mine by ceremony or blood, but only mine by choice, should they wish it so. And there was, somehow, in my soul home, room for them all. Safe at my fire. Sheltering in peace.

I was dreaming. I knew that. But I could still, in my dream, feel Hayyel's hand on my head in blessing. And I remembered his words after the battle. "You are free as well, *Dalonige'i Digadoli*. No longer bound by the past and the blood of others, and no longer able to bind others with your blood, but only by the love they have for you. The curse of *u'tlun'ta* that Beast made of you when she took your soul is removed from you."

As his hand lifted away, I woke.

Inside me, Beast rolled over and yawned. *I/we hunger. Want to hunt and eat boar.*

Is he gone? Hayyel?

Angel is gone and not gone. Not in cage of silver chain and dark magics. Can still see Jane and Beast. And kits. Angie. EJ. Cassy. Beast gave the equivalent of a mental shrug—a tail smack up my head. *Is angel. Is with other angels. Is happy.*

I opened my eyes. I was in bed in the freebie house— our house—on the wrong side, facing away from the door, lying on my side, with Bruiser spooned up behind me. I vaguely remembered we had ended up in some uncomfortable position, so tired we had stripped, showered off the blood, and fallen into bed in a heap, asleep before we hit the sheets. Apparently we had never repositioned and now his arm was warm and strong around my waist. We were skin to skin. He snored softly, moved his leg, and fell silent, tightening his arm around me. Pulling me closer.

Mate, Beast thought at me. *Is good safe den with mate. Is not puma way, but is Jane/Beast/I/we way. Is good. Is safe.*

I was human-shaped. I was warm. I was out of pain. I was content. Beast was right. I/we were safe.

And so were all the people I was responsible for, the people across from the fire in my soul home dream. Safe.

For the first time in years. Wondering if that connection was broken too, I reached out to Eli, and found his heart beating in deep sleep. Pain-free. We had all been healed by Florence. I withdrew and closed the shielding between us, wishing I could do that permanently, for his sake.

Once I finished the coronation, I would be . . . done.

Tears gathered in my eyes, great big juicy tears, and because I was lying on my side, when I blinked, they rolled down my face and gathered in the hollow at my nose and eye, and into my ear on the other side.

We were safe. My godchildren, Angie Baby and EJ and Cassy, were *safe*. The witches. Even the vamps were safe.

My life had changed. Utterly. Completely.

We are safe.

I caught the sob before it could shudder across me and wake Bruiser. Breathed through the emotion that welled through me like a spring, flooding.

We are safe.

I no longer had to fight to keep people alive. Once Edmund was crowned and once someone took over as NOLA MOC, I no longer had to play politics in New Orleans. I no longer had to stay anywhere, not even at the Dark Queen's Winter Court in Asheville. I could take time off. Travel. I'd probably still have Dark Queen responsibilities, but if Hayyel was to be believed, I would no longer have to fight to win loyalty and demand peace.

No Dark Queen had ever lived past the war they started. All the others had tried to bind vamps and force them to obey, like marionettes dancing on strings, and had died young. I had no idea what my job description would actually be. So maybe I could wing it and do what I wanted?

I was, for the first time since I rode into NOLA on my bastard Harley, Bitsa, free.

Shoving my hair out of the way, I rolled over slowly and slid closer into Bruiser's arms, letting my thoughts seek some form of coherency, letting them mesh and solidify. Bruiser murmured but didn't wake. I had no more battles to fight.

My people were safe.

I was free. When people have an epiphany, they often have to study it and then find a place for it inside themselves. I decided it was a little like moving things around in a house when you buy a new piece of furniture. Like—"Okay. This once went here, and that once went there, but I no longer need that ratty sofa, or that rocking chair with its uneven rocker that thumps, or that emotional baggage that's been torturing me since I was twelve, or whatever. So I'll toss away that stuff that is no longer a part of me." And suddenly there was room inside for this new thing.

This new thing that was freedom.

I slid my hand up Bruiser's back, along the bumps of his spine, and I felt him wake. I cupped his face and pressed a kiss to either corner of his mouth, and then lips to lips.

Whispering, "Morning, my love," he opened to me, and our tongues explored.

Is Consort, Beast thought. *Is best mate.*

Bruiser pulled me close. Loving him was the best way to start a day.

A shifting of leather against wood yanked me out of a deep sleep. My hand went to my weapon. My palm slapped on the empty bedside tabletop then dove into the drawer as I shook the muzziness of sleep away.

The door didn't open. Didn't crash in. Didn't do anything at all.

Outside, through the window, I heard the patter of rainfall. The squish of a guard's footsteps making rounds.

I was holding the Beretta I kept in the drawer, not on top, not when the kids were in residence. I was breathing hard. Ready to fire. It had taken a second and a half too long had I needed to defend us.

I didn't.

I was in bed with Bruiser, twisted in linens that smelled of love and tenderness and hot sweaty sex. It was sunset outside. Quiet inside the house.

"Jane?" Bruiser mumbled, concern in his tone.

"I thought I heard . . . something." I couldn't remember what had waked me as I blinked and kicked to untangle my legs from the sheets.

Sitting naked on the side of the bed, holding the weapon, I caught a scent.

Is cooked pig, Beast thought, salivating. *Is good smell.*

"Smoked meat. And, *oh God,* bacon." My mouth started watering too.

Bruiser eased gracefully out of bed, and I caught a glimpse of my Consort's ass as he pulled on his robe, covering up that splendid butt.

"Best ass ever."

Which I did not mean to say aloud, but which made him chuckle, that knowing, pleased sound a man makes when he's satisfied his lover.

Beast rolled over inside me, purring at the sound of his laughter.

Bruiser tossed me my robe. His voice had a liquid British sound I seldom heard. "When was the last time we woke together, love? And made love as the sun set?"

"You mean without someone attacking the house or trying to kill us just at the juicy parts? Been a while. Your ass is still spectacular."

When had we ever had the time and the freedom to laugh together? Never.

Still sitting, I pulled on my robe too.

When we were both decent, Bruiser opened the door. "I'm bloody well starv—" He leaped back.

A man stood in the opening. I took him in a heartbeat. *Stranger. Jeans. Tight T-shirt.* Weapon in hand, I came to my feet. Two-hand stance, evaluating as I moved.

White hair. High-topped sneakers. No weapon.

Brute, Beast thought.

"Brute?" I lowered the weapon and straightened my finger from the trigger. "Holy crap on a cracker, you nearly got dead," I said. *"Brute?"*

"I thought you wouldn't recognize me," he said, his voice a low rumble. "You only saw me maybe twice in human form and I was busy trying to kill you."

Brute was standing there. Human-shaped Brute.

Had Beast not known the scent, I'd have shot him. I

had no memory of the human form of the werewolf biker Brute had once been, except he'd been big as a firetruck. Redheaded? Maybe? Firetruck was the moniker I had put on him when I first saw him. Firetruck. Then Brute the werewolf. Now . . . a human?

Bruiser turned on a bedside lamp, revealing the man who had been in wolf form for years. This new Brute had no tats. No biker kutte. No weapons. No beard. He looked nothing like a werewolf biker dude with attitude. He didn't even look human now.

Angel-touched, I thought.

His skin was a glistening golden, neither Caucasian nor a person of color, but gold-colored skin, as if he'd been dusted with gold dust. His hair was a shaggy white that rested on his shoulders. His face was all angles and planes, with cheekbones that looked sharp enough to cut. He hooked his thumbs into his skintight five-button jeans and let me look. His pale blue wolf eyes contrasted oddly with the gold skin but fit the white hair perfectly. Strong muscles and still as big as a brick shithouse. He looked kinda hot.

I remembered the angel's words. Or God's. Not sure about which, and either one still gave me the willies. "The curses are gone," I said, paraphrasing the angel. "Hayyel said that, but I didn't know it meant you too. You used to be redheaded. He left you with white hair, blue eyes," I said, "and golden skin."

"Yeah. I look nothin' like I used to. It's gonna be a bitch gettin' ID but I figure the Montana pack can help me there." He sounded southern. Maybe an Alabama boy.

"So what now?" I asked.

"Hell if I know. You're the one who put all this shit into motion. I'm jist a big dumb biker until the full moon, then I'm jist a big dumb dog. Woof." He laughed. "Best get dressed. There's a big hoedown at Fanghead HQ tonight."

"Hoedown?"

"Trying for the casual vernacular that makes me seem less menacing. Maybe keep people from shitting their pants when they meet me."

"Not working. What happens at this hoedown?"

"The Dark Queen gets all gussied up and gives some speeches, crowns the new king, and then parties till dawn. Lots a liquor. Lots a food. And a good ol' boy who ain't gotten laid in too long to remember might get lucky.

"From what I hear, people are gettin' lucky already over there. Rules have changed, the power has shifted, and vamps aren't sure what to do about it. But the upshot is that humans are in charge of the feeding times now. I hear it's interesting." He chuckled and the vibration shook through my chest just the way Brute's growls once had.

"Interesting how?" I asked.

"Interesting enough for the witches to move out, including Butterfly Lily and Feather Storm, and congregate at the Yellowrock Clan Home with the Everharts and the Truebloods. You don't mind, Imma head over to HQ now and get nekkid too. Werewolves can't give the taint to Fangheads, and I've been outta action for too damn long."

"Ooookay. How about you tell them the Dark Queen will be there at ten p.m. and expects to see people dressed for the ceremony part of the *hoedown*."

"Will do. Oh. Nearly forgot. Dude came by a couple hours ago. Said he was among the rescued from Mainet's guards. His name is Reach and he owes you a boon."

Brute closed the door and I heard him go out the front and into the rain. A moment later a motorbike throbbed into life, the distinctive note of a Harley. Not mine, so either he had his bike locked down all this time or he . . . bought one. Not stole. He'd been under Hayyel's thumb long enough for the goodness to keep him honest. I hoped.

And Reach was free. That was good. I guess.

I tilted my head to my Consort as he sat down beside me. "I gotta get prettied up, which means I need a shower. You wanna . . ." I jerked my head at the queen's bathroom.

A slow smile spread across Bruiser's face and he stood, dropping the robe. He turned and walked to the open door, letting me look my fill.

When the water came on, I followed him.

We were arguing about my hair, me sitting in the small chair and Quint standing behind me in the bathroom. She had put makeup on my face. Not a lot. Mostly shimmery golds and bronzes on my cheeks, my eyes, and across my upper chest. Mascara, which made my eyelids feel heavy. I was wearing my usual scarlet lipstick and the navy robe, my hair down in a long drape to my butt. My clothes for the coronation were hanging on a hook on the door. "I don't want my hair *fixed*."

"No. That is not strictly true, My Queen. You don't want *me* to braid your hair."

"True."

"Why?"

I smiled slightly, watching her eyes over my shoulder as she stood behind me at the long bathroom mirror. There were a lot of answers. Only one really mattered, and that one I wouldn't share. "Your loyalty's temporary, bought and paid for, via contract." True enough, though mostly it was a Cherokee thing. The ones who braid hair must be calm of spirit, peaceful, and trusted, because the ritual of braiding was the pathway to the spirit. Quint was cold of spirit, steady, and useful, which were all good qualities, but not ones I wanted in my hair or treading the pathway to my spirit. I added, "You aren't *mine*."

"I am yours." Edmund stood at my bathroom door.

I pulled my lapels closer, in some kind of uncomfortable modesty, which was stupid. He'd seen the full monty when he'd healed me in the past. Yeah, he'd seen me naked multiple times over the course of my ascent to my reign, and after. But it seemed different now and I didn't know why, except Edmund was wearing a tux and he looked . . . amazing. And I was robed but naked otherwise. And he wasn't bound to me.

As if she understood what I didn't, Quint left the room with a simple, "Excuse me, my Queen. I'll be back when you wish to dress." The bedroom door closed behind her.

My primo leaned against the doorjamb. Alone together, we studied each other.

"It's been a long time," I said. "You look good. You know. Tuxedo and all."

"Every man looks good in a tuxedo." Edmund smiled, showing me the reason he had been turned in the first place. That glorious smile, transforming him from ordinary to spectacular. And now, after all his success in Europe, he fairly sizzled with vamp power, more than Leo had ever displayed. His magic danced across his skin and through his words. That and the smile made him breathtaking. "You look rested," he said, his smile softening. "Do you need more blood?"

"No. I'm good. I hear things are different at HQ."

Edmund laughed, a low, slow chuckle that slid under my skin.

If things had been different, if I'd never met Bruiser, Ed and I might have been something other than master and primo. We'd never have had what Bruiser and I did, but it might have been something more than just friends. Leo had surely known of that possibility when he sent Edmund to me as primo.

"*Things*, as you say, are very different. Many bloodslaves and the witches moved out before we woke, which is well. It seems our souls have changed us. Our blood is very"—his hand lifted as if trying to draw an acceptable word out of the air—"*zesty* to humans, but not binding." He tucked his hand into a pocket, lounging, and shook his head, still smiling. "I have no idea what it all means yet, to have a soul again, but the changes are beginning. We laugh easily. We cry easily. We are enamored of the humans we drink from. We are changed in fundamental ways, I think."

"So your coronation is going to be . . ."

"Lively. Different. Not quite so formal and boring as such events in the past. In fact, I shall usher in a new thing. A new way of accepting power."

"You already have the power."

"Yes, My Queen, my lady, I do. But you, the Dark Queen—not my friend and my clan master," he clarified, "will cement that power. When you as the Dark Queen place that crown upon my head, the entire world will see who and what I am, who and what you made me, and will see your power as it is now, without war."

"Yeah. I get that. I'm going to crown you tonight. And everything will change again."

"And so I come, now, while we are simply master and primo, to braid your hair. One last time."

He stepped behind me, taking Quint's place, and took the comb that always rested on the narrow shelf. With long slow strokes, he combed out my hair, working out the few tangles, leaving it straight and smooth. "You have beautiful hair." He parted out a small strip in a long angle from my temple to my ear and smoothed the rest out of the way. "It feels rich and heavy, and the black catches the light, reflecting like a halo."

Uncomfortable, embarrassed, I joked, "My one good feature."

Ed laughed again, sadly this time. "Ah, Jane. I wish you could see yourself as others see you. Even if your features were not striking, and your eyes not such an amazing shade of amber. Even if your hair did not flow like the night beneath a full moon, and your skin did not gleam like gold, your powers and gifts would still make you beautiful. And I speak not of the Dark Queen."

He began to braid the small strip, a tight, perfect plait that left the ends loose, and twisted an elastic over the end of the braided part. "I speak of the *person you are*. Your honor. Your strength of spirit. Your compassion, kindness, dedication to people instead of cause. Willingness to bend, to give of yourself even unto death. These are your personal powers, and are what give you indescribable beauty. These qualities are what make others bow to you, far more than does a crown."

I had to look away from his face in the mirror as he spoke. I wasn't bad-looking. I even had days when I liked the way I looked. But what he described was . . . not me. *Holy cow.*

With deft fingers, he matched the plait on the other side and curled it out of the way too. Then he parted the hair over my forehead and worked that section. And three to either side. When he paused again, I had a lot of partial braids, all pinned out of the way. "I never thought, when I was a slave and working in a brothel, that I would enjoy the skills I learned as a ladies' maid quite so much. But working with your hair is a joy."

I couldn't have described the exact feeling that swept

through me, except a sense of being ridiculously honored and loved. Since I had no idea what to say, I said nothing.

Ed studied my face in the mirror, his lips pursed as if making a judgment. Pulling the plaits on the left together, he wrapped them around my head and then braided the ends into one. He repeated the process with the ones on the right. He pulled up the partial braids in front, then twisted them around and braided the ends together until I had a crown of braids all around my head.

"Yes. Sophisticated. Elegant. This will do for now," he muttered. "I'll have Quint call me when you are dressed and ready for your crown."

He pursed his lips again, his eyes making sure each braid was perfect. Adjusted a pin here and a pin there. "Are you wearing weapons tonight?"

"I hadn't decided. It was supposed to be the Mughal blade, but I kind of ruined it."

"Hmmm. I have something that might do." Without another word he left the room, speaking to Quint on the way past my bodyguard.

My cell rang and I answered a video call from my sweet-cheeks, who was wearing black tie and tails. He looked old-fashioned and what people used to call *debonair.* Scrumptious, elegant, sex on a stick. His brown eyes appeared darker against the black tux, his hair darker too, slicked back with some hair product. His slightly Roman nose appeared sharper, giving him a commanding look. Bruiser had never risen to his full potential under Leo. Now he was coming into his own as a Consort to the Queen, and in reality, the hand behind the throne I didn't want but couldn't give away.

Bruiser's face softened as his eyes met mine. He took my breath away.

"You look beautiful," he said to me by way of greeting.

"You look edible," I said back.

His eyes took on that glow again and he said, "Done and done, though seconds and thirds would be lovely."

I was pretty sure I blushed, but I pretended I didn't. "How are things?"

"Everything is in place. Your honor guard is ready.

You will arrive just before ten p.m. with Edmund, in the same limo—though not *our* limo."

I blushed again.

Bruiser grinned. "You two will proceed up the front stairs." He continued on in the same vein, telling me what was going to happen, who would be where and when. And I mostly ignored his words, watching his face, and eyes, and knowing that he was mine, that I was his. And we suddenly, finally, might have a future together.

When the call ended, Eli and Alex entered my bedroom. I pulled my lapels closer, muttering, "This is not Grand Central Station. Don't you ever knock? And shouldn't you be at HQ already, all tuxed up and prettified? Because if you get to wear jeans to the coronation, I should be able to wear jeans."

Eli, a faint lift to one corner of his mouth, said, "We're backing up Koun and making sure that the sexcapades at HQ are over so the children aren't scarred for life when they walk in the door. Then we'll dress and pick up the Everharts and the outliers, making sure they get to HQ safely."

"So not fair," Alex said, shaking his head, his expression woebegone, his dark curls swinging over his brown-skinned face. "All that sex. And me having to cover security."

"Don't pretend you didn't watch it all through the security cameras," I said. The Kid was legally old enough to participate in vampire games, but . . . *ick.*

"Watching ain't doing," Alex said, sounding all grown-up, and maybe a little droll. "Anyway, everything is good to go, Janie, no hitches, no problems that haven't been handled."

Eli said, "You got this, Janie." He leaned in and kissed me on the cheek.

Through that soft kiss, I felt Eli's connection all through me, like light in the darkness. "No," I said. "*We* got this. Because I have you guys." The last few words were whispered, and blast it if I didn't start to tear up.

Alex rolled his eyes and handed me a tissue. "Girls."

Eli shook his head and said, "Babe." He socked my

shoulder, which felt much more normal. "I'll make sure all the body fluids are cleaned up at HQ. Don't be late."

By nine, Quint had painted my nails with a scarlet that matched my lipstick and helped me into my clothes, as if I couldn't do all that by myself.

I was wearing a silky body smoother beneath a long shimmering slinky dress of heavy black fabric, split to my right midthigh, with long sleeves that came to points on my wrists. The neckline plunged in front, low enough to be interesting, exposing my gold nugget necklace, held in place on the smoother with tiny clasps. The dress was low enough in back to be dangerous, also held in place.

I had ended the *hedge of thorns* in my closet and was wearing all the magical jewelry I had: The ring Sabina—the real Sabina—had left for me in the muck below her burned chapel weighted down my left index finger. The red flying lizard amulet was pinned over my heart and matched my lips like a splotch of blood. The locket was looped around my left wrist like a bracelet. *Le breloque* rested on the foot of the bed. I looked good. But not finished. And it wasn't just the crown that was missing. I looked . . . safe.

I was staring at myself in the mirror when Edmund knocked again and reentered as Quint left again. "I look boring."

Edmund stood to the side. "You do not look boring. But you do look like a queen who was granted her title rather than claiming it herself, and being claimed by her crown. You should look what you are—a warrior queen. It's the edge of danger that you are missing."

"War woman. Yeah. Think I should splash some blood over me?"

"I think I have just the thing." He gestured to the chair I had occupied when he braided my hair, and I lifted the gown enough to sit without stretching and pulling at all the tiny snaps and clips holding it in place. When he met my eyes in the mirror, Edmund placed a small, flat folded bag on the shelf that held the pins and combs and elastics and gewgaws. He opened it and pulled out a feather. It was a dark gray feather that caught the light, flashing like steel. The next feather was shorter and black, and when it caught the light it glistened like a moonbow.

I frowned as he pinned both in place among the braids. "You want me to wear buzzard feathers?"

Edmund pulled out another one and pinned it as well, his lips turned up in the faintest of smiles. Then more feathers, black and gray until twelve feathers dangled to my shoulders, complementing the black dress, making me look grave, forbidding, and a lot dangerous. Pretty amazing, actually.

But. "Again. *Buzzard feathers*?"

"Not *buzzard*. Such a coarse word for such a powerful creature. Vulture flight feathers: turkey vultures and black vultures." His small smile spread. "They dispose of the dead."

I burst out laughing and was still laughing when he placed *le breloque* into my hands.

"Try to place it just here"—he indicated on my forehead—"and tilted back to here, to hold the braids and give the feathers stability."

It had come off easily. *It might not grab my head anymore,* I thought.

I lifted the gold laurel-leaf circlet into place and the crown of the Dark Queen snapped on tight—too tight, of course, but what else was new.

He took small hairpins with citrines, or maybe yellow diamonds, on the ends, and placed them here and there in my braids, followed by twelve more pins graced with smaller red stones. I hoped they weren't rubies, but feared they were. I'd lose them for sure, but I didn't argue. They made a statement.

"And now your silver weapons." Edmund pulled thin gloves onto his fingers to protect them from the metal, and took a stake into his hands.

"You don't need the gloves," I said.

"No. But if Quint returns, she needn't be made aware of that."

"You still keep secrets, even though you're the Emperor of Europe."

"Mmmm. More so now, actually. As do you."

I looked closer at the stakes as he slid them into my braids, gold and silver, engraved and patterned, each different and ornate and gorgeous. "Those aren't mine."

"They are my gift to you, My Queen. I had them made by a Mithran goldsmith and his human silversmith partner. The Mithran has been a master at his craft since Medieval times. The stakes are not purely decorative. Should you have to fight again someday—despite the angel's prediction—all will know who you staked."

He turned the chair and stepped back, assessing. "Yes. That will do." He held out a hand and, as if I needed help to stand, I placed my left hand into his and rose to my feet. "And then there is this." Edmund stepped into the bedroom and returned with a sheathed knife.

"Unlike the Mughal blade, this lion head kukri does not have a prophecy attached, however it is rich in history. It is said it that this blade is the original, upon which all the others are based, from the military kukri to the trinkets sold in the marketplaces. This blade is damascene, the hilt steel and gold with amber and ruby ornamentation. The eyes of the lion are golden diamonds and quite lovely. I had them valued. George added them to the insurance policy of the Dark Queen."

"I have an insurance policy?"

He smiled slightly. "The sheath is constructed of hand-carved ebony with black silk overlay, and crisscrossed in pure hammered gold."

He inspected my dress with its thigh-high split and said, "Pull your skirt aside."

I'd been dressed many times by other people, but it still felt weird. I gathered the skirt and pulled it between my legs, up and away, revealing my entire leg from hip to ankle.

Edmund knelt and buckled the sheath into place, attaching its antique metal teeth, tugging the bands until it all clung in the right position. "It will likely slip if you dance, so I suggest you remove it if you—when you—dance after the coronation." He gestured, and I dropped the skirt. He smiled and though I knew Ed would never hurt me, that smile was scary, the smile of a conqueror. "Yes. Look," he commanded, pointing at the mirror.

I went to the tall mirror in the corner and pulled the two sidepieces out, giving me a three-angled view. "I look badass."

"A warrior queen. Now," he said, more to himself than to me. "Boots or dancing shoes?" He frowned. "I think the boots will snag on the fabric no matter what we do. So dancing shoes it is." He placed a pair by my feet and undid the buckles. I stepped in and he buckled them for me, his hands sure and certain.

"And now your primary weapon, a weapon such as the world has never seen before. I understand that Madame Melisende provided a well-secured, padded pocket at your left side. I also understand she still grouches quite dreadfully at being forced to design *pockets* in all your creations."

I took the Glob and dropped it in. It was fairly heavy, but the dress continued to hang properly, not pulled lopsided, thanks to all the clips and snaps and stuff. I looked at myself again, Edmund behind me, both of us wearing black and expressions that were similar—considering, evaluating, assessing. I was taller, of course. Neither one of us was beautiful in any strict sense of the word. Striking, yes. Powerful, yes.

We looked good together. Standing together we could have been real royalty or maybe lovers.

"Ed? Did Leo expect us to . . . you know."

Edmund lifted his brows and the smile he turned on me now was totally different. A smile meant to cajole and seduce. "What do you think, my mistress?"

"I think Leo was a blackhearted devil who threw men at me until I picked one, and then he was pissed because I picked the wrong one. And now that he's among the thrice born, he may be more dangerous than ever. Especially as a priest."

Edmund chuckled. "My Queen is wise."

I stepped from the limo and took Edmund's arm. My honor guard and his, all wearing black military armor and fully armed, stepped to the side, separated, and took

up their prearranged positions. Together, escorted before
and after, we walked up the steps to the Mithran Council
Chambers as media helicopters buzzed overhead getting
live news footage.

There was no formula to follow for the ceremony because no Dark Queen had ever crowned an emperor. And
despite Edmund's promise of a new kind of ceremony, I figured it would be tedious, wordy, full of flowery speeches
and long titles, and descriptions of conquest and killing
other vamps.

At least I'd be sitting once I called the fangheads to
gather and finished my part.

We passed through to the back of HQ and were escorted to the ballroom, to stop in the entrance so the
gathered could see us. To either side of a long carpet, people were standing, silent, staring.

The people in the ballroom were looking pretty spiffy,
all the black tails and ball gowns and fancy hair and
enough jewels to fund a small country for a year. Humans,
witches, a cadre of arcenciels, a werewolf in human form
who, though he had been a wolf for years, had somehow
been fitted for a fancy tux in the last few hours. A red-
striped flying lizard was perched on his shoulder, its long
tail wrapped around Brute's neck. There was no grindylow. Which was interesting.

The honor guard separated, half going to stand up
front like at Wrassler and Jodi's wedding, half along the
walls. *Good line of fire.*

Ed and I started down the carpet—an honest-to-God
red carpet—that stretched from the doorway to a raised
dais. On the dais was what looked, at first glance, like a
freaking throne love seat. Turned out it was just two oversized chairs, both draped in black cloth, and one sitting a
little lower than the other.

As we walked down the aisle, Leo stepped to the dais
and waited, hands clasped in front. He wore a black suit
with a white priest collar and the gold crucifix dangling
on his chest. His hair was longer, below his shoulders, his
face pale. He hadn't fed. The outclan didn't drink much
as a rule.

Photographers with shoulder cameras stepped around

the room, filming everything and sending it out live to vamp masters of the cities all over the world. Crap. I had forgotten that part.

Ed released my hand and I climbed the steps to the top of the dais. I turned to stare out over my people and my friends and my family. Bruiser stepped up and stood beside me, though down a step and a little to the side. Eli took his place on the ground level, all doodied up in a tux.

I spotted Ayatas FireWind, a little off to the side of the crowd, his golden eyes on me. To his side stood Rick La-Fleur, which gave me the faintest jolt. Rick, white-haired, looked older than a were-creature should. But he too was safe. Maybe later I'd get the story out of them of where they had been and what had happened near Sassafras Mountain.

Leo nodded to me and faced the congregants. He said simply, "The Dark Queen of the Mithrans. Her Consort. Her second."

I reached for my power and pulled it from both inside me and from my crown. It appeared all around me, my skinwalker magic, silver with dark motes, and the power of *le breloque*, glittering like sunlight through cut crystal.

From the crowd a voice shouted, "Hey, Angie. Looky. Ant Jane is all glowy!"

"EJ. Shush!" Molly said, going as bright as her red hair.

A titter ran through the crowd, uncertain and embarrassed.

I laughed. "Yes, EJ. I'm the Dark Queen." Following Leo's lead, I said, "We are . . . *gathered*." And I shot my power into the crowd. Every vamp bowed.

The rest of the *gather* was just as boring as I predicted, speeches, lots of jibber jabber, but at least I got to sit for all the boring orations and sermons. Until we got to the good part and I stood.

Edmund knelt at my feet.

There was no blood bond between us now, but when

his eyes met mine, the contact was strong, so intense, it tingled from my crown all the way through me to my toes. "My Queen," he whispered. "I will serve you forever. My word is my binding. I give myself to you."

I felt the sworn binding zing between us. "My friend," I said back. "I will love you forever, and through love, we are bound."

Tears, human and watery, gathered in his eyes. That's what the angel had said. No one will serve me except through love. So, love it is.

"The first emperor of Europe since Charles the Fifth," I said, letting my voice ring out. Without looking away from him, I took the crown off the pillow Eli offered me. The crown wasn't magic. It didn't have a will of its own. But it was freaking heavy, which surprised me. "Eddie the Great," I whispered.

He laughed, even as our gazes broke so he could lower his head. I placed his heavy crown on his head.

Our powers meshed and blazed, a light show seen even by the humans in the room, as if we were surrounded by an internal aurora borealis. My hands still on his crown, Edmund raised his head again and met my eyes, his brown and awed, mine reflecting in his, the golden glow of my cat. Our powers shifted, changed. Balanced. Without fully understanding how, without our former bond, I knew Edmund could *call* me, just as I could call him. That was pretty spectacular.

Edmund stood. He turned, a step below me, and faced the crowd.

I said, "Behold. The Mithran Emperor of Europe. Edmund the First."

The party after was radical.

It started when the dance floor had been cleared and Edmund and I were standing—him with a lighter-weight crown, because honestly he'd have fallen over trying to dance in the heavy one—as a string quartet played the first notes of a waltz. Angie, who hadn't visited with *her vampire*, due to protocol issues and people dying, raced up, stepped between us, and held up her hands. She said,

"I know you can't be my fiancé, but you can be my bestest vampire friend. BVFFs forever."

"Angelina," Molly gasped, horrified, as her daughter claimed the first dance with the new Emperor.

The plan had been for that first dance to be between the Emperor and the Dark Queen, but what good was having power if you couldn't change things on the fly?

Edmund laughed, I shrugged, and Ed took her hands. Her feet followed the steps of his shiny boots as the waltz began. I took Bruiser's hand and was led into the dance as well. Beside me, Eli led Liz onto the dance floor, while the vamps, humans, and witches watched.

Loud enough to be heard over the music, Koun said, "And so begins a new era of peace and cooperation between Mithrans, witches, Onorios, humans, and our queen."

Ohhh. Perfect. Yeah. It was a good start to a great party.

When the first waltz ended, Ed led Angie to her father and handed her off. "I do not envy you the next decade or two," he said mildly.

"Me neither," Evan said gruffly.

Then the Emperor of Europe turned, walked to me, and lifted his arms. "My Queen. This is our dance." The floor cleared, and Jane Yellowrock, the Dark Queen, and Eddie the Great, Emperor of Europe, danced across the ballroom floor.

The dancing and drinking lasted till dawn, which is when Bruiser and I fell into bed in the small quarters that used to be Leo's. We did take the time to strip off our finery, let down our hair—in my case, literally—and rinse off the dancing sweat and the odors of food, and make love under the pulsating showers. Priorities and all that.

After amazing sex we fell into the bed and snuggled in together, face-to-face, arms resting on hips and waist. Exhausted. Happy.

Our eyes met and held, sharing love and promise. Our breathing evened out.

"I'm glad the crown came off so easily," I said.

"Making love in it sounds painful."

"Hmmm. We should be tired," I said.

"Sometimes a good party and even better sex is energizing."

"Sometimes."

Bruiser raised his hand and stroked a strand of my hair behind my ear. His smile was soft. His eyes were full of emotion, of need, so intense it brought tears to my eyes. "I wasn't supposed to love you. He wanted you for himself or for Edmund."

"It wasn't love at first sight for either of us."

"I think I loved you from the first time I danced with you. Perhaps before that. Just a little. I never thought I would have you, though. I always thought you would end up where Leo wanted you."

"I'm ornery. I tend to go where I want."

"You are a cat, thank all that's holy." He slid a hand up and down my side, over the curve of my hip. "What's next for us, my love and My Queen?"

"We have to deal with Mainet's vamps in the scion room."

"Ummm. That could be bloody work."

"Isn't it always? And then I have to have a meeting with the Blood Masters here and force them to pick a Master of the City of New Orleans."

"That should be entertaining." His tone was droll and it made me grin.

I stroked back the little curl at his forehead. "I'm guessing we can give it a few days here to push things through. It's nearly winter. The day after Thanksgiving—because I am not missing Deon's spread—let's load up everything and head into the mountains. Stay for Christmas in our house. Maybe take the bikes out. Camp by an open fire, maybe one night in a snowfall. Make love by moonlight. Dance in cheap dives and drink cheap beer. Stay in B and Bs and eat breakfast in bed. Think we can slip away from the guards?"

"I am quite certain you can do anything you want, my love. You are the wild card. You always have been."

"Oh," I said. "In that case . . . Let's get married before we leave NOLA. Some little roadside church. Just us and a preacher and some strangers to witness. That is if the proposal is still open?"

The look on Bruiser's face was . . . I had no words for that look. Except he loved me. *Me*. Not the Dark Queen. Just me. And that was enough, forever.

"Our first Christmas in our new home as man and wife." His expression said he was almost tasting the words on his tongue as he said them. "Yes. Yes, let's."

Is best mate, Beast thought. *I/we are happy.*

Yeah. I/we are happy.

ACKNOWLEDGMENTS

My thanks to:

Teri Lee Akar, Timeline and Continuity Editor Extraordinaire. Your help and care of the timelines and databases and your attention to detail is deeply missed. I grieve for you, my friend, and will miss you cracking a whip over me.

Mindy "Mud" Mymudes, Beta Reader and PR.

Let's Talk Promotions, at ltpromos.com, for managing my blog tours and the Beast Claws fan club.

Beast Claws! Best Street Team Evah!

Mike Pruette at celticleatherworks.com for all the fabo merch!

David B. Coe for vulture info.

Lucienne Diver of the Knight Agency, as always, for guiding my career, being a font of wisdom and career guidance, and being the woman who pulls me down to Earth when I get riled and mouthy.

My thanks to editor Miranda Hill of Penguin Random House for all the myriad tasks involved in editing, keeping everything on track, and handling all the many problems that arise in the production of a book.

To Courtney Vincento, who did a bang-up job on the copyedits!

As always, a huge thank-you to senior editor Jessica Wade of Penguin Random House. Without you there would be no book at all!

Ready to find
your next great read?

Let us help.

Visit prh.com/nextread

Penguin
Random
House